Simon Williams

The Endless Shore

BOOK III OF THE AONA SERIES

The Aona Series by Simon Williams

Oblivion's Forge
Secret Roads
The Endless Shore
The Spiral Heart
Salvation's Door

APHENHAST

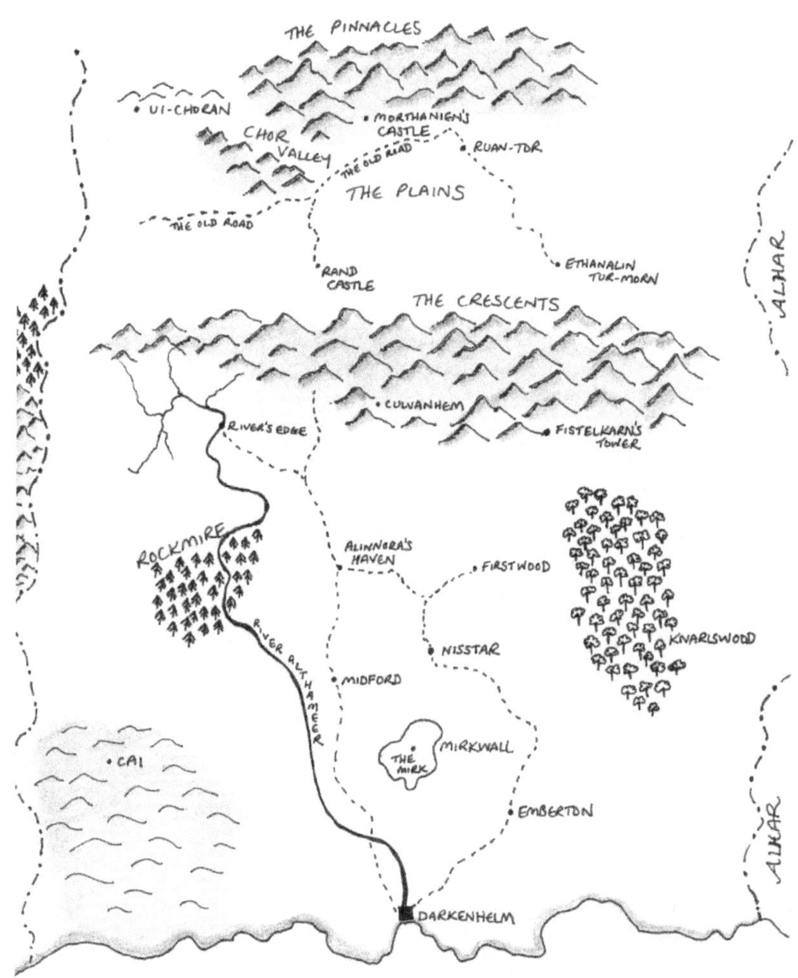

THE PINNACLES
UI-CHORAN
MORTHANIEN'S CASTLE
CHOR VALLEY
THE OLD ROAD
RUAN-TOR
THE PLAINS
THE OLD ROAD
RAND CASTLE
ETHANALIN TUR-MORN
ALHAR
THE CRESCENTS
CULVANHEM
FISTELKARN'S TOWER
RIVER'S EDGE
ROCKMIRE
ALINNORA'S HAVEN
FIRSTWOOD
KIVARISWOOD
RIVER AVTHAMEER
NISSTAR
MIDFORD
CAI
THE MIRK
MIRKWALL
EMBERTON
ALHAR
DARKENHELM
THE SOUTH OCEAN

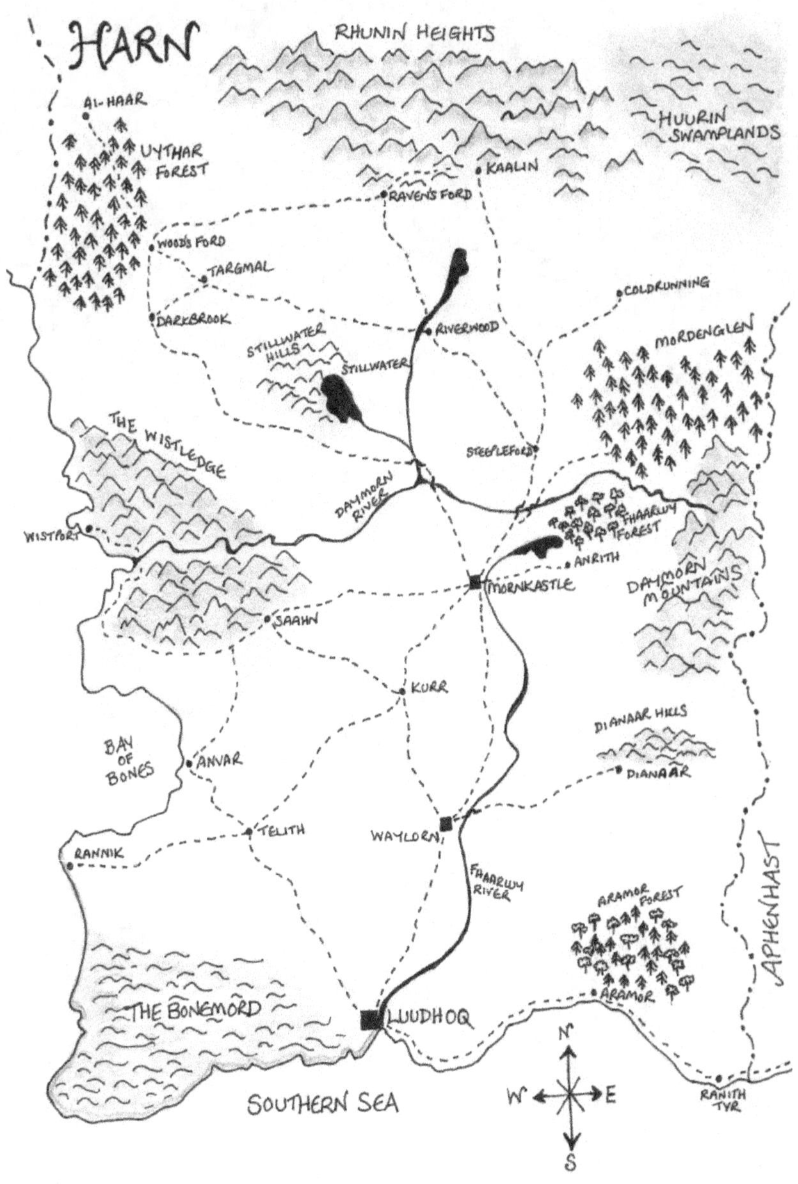

HARN
RHUNIN HEIGHTS
HUURIN SWAMPLANDS
AL-HAAR
UYTHAR FOREST
KAALIN
RAVEN'S FORD
WOOD'S FORD
TARGMAL
COLDRUNNING
DARKBROOK
RIVERWOOD
MORDENGLEN
STILLWATER HILLS
STILLWATER
STEEPLEFORD
THE WISTLEDGE
DAYMORN RIVER
FHAARWY FOREST
WISTPORT
ANRITH
DAYMORN MOUNTAINS
MORNKASTLE
SAAHN
KURR
DIANAAR HILLS
BAY OF BONES
ANVAR
DIANAAR
TELITH
WAYLORN
RANNIK
FHAARWY RIVER
ARAMOR FOREST
APHENHAST
ARAMOR
THE BONEMORD
LUUDHOQ
N
W E
S
SOUTHERN SEA
RANITH TYR

I – Immortal Errors

In a high grey-walled chamber within one of the Sanctum's vast stone towers, a door opened and a woman who no one had set eyes upon for five years walked into the room.

Her name was Phaedra, and she was one of the Seven.

As usual, Anya was the first of the other six to recover her composure. "Phaedra," she said evenly, as if they might have crossed paths only yesterday. "How unusual for you to join us. Tell me, what stirred you from your self-imposed exile?"

Phaedra regarded each of them in turn, a flicker of a smile upon her lips. Her eyes- small, hard and grey like chips of stone- stared out of a face largely untouched by age. She had been twenty-five years old when they arrived in Harn, and she still appeared no older. She could have been a porcelain snapshot of cold, resentful youth.

"What stirred me?" Her amusement became more evident. "Why Anya, the stench of panic- what else? Did you think in your conceit that they would never find this world? After all, *eternity* stretches ahead- for them as well as for us." She paused and tilted her head to one side, considering something. "We should welcome this war. It brings with it the possibility of mortality, don't you think?"

Ignoring the hostility that stirred at the table, Phaedra ceased her pacing for a moment and looked around as if something that she alone could sense had started to materialise. "Ah! So many choices."

"Please enlighten us, Phaedra," Omir prompted her. "What do *you* see as our options?"

"You could flee. You could prepare to fight. You could bow your heads and wait for them to destroy you." Phaedra laughed suddenly. "Wait! All three roads lead to the same place!"

"Matters are not that simple," Issele spoke up, and glanced around the table as gazes turned in her direction. "Remember that when we came to this world, we were not as we are now. We look much the same, yes, but in many aspects this place has changed us and we have seldom paused to consider *why*. We became caught up in the mechanics of empire-building."

"Why, my dear, you make it sound almost like a crime," Garret said from the other end of the table.

Issele's eyes met his. "We are caught in time; immortal and sterile. There can be no future generation. We have been remade this way for a reason, surely- to defend this place against the *marandaal*. A fitting task, one might say- given that we are in part responsible for their proliferation. And if we destroy them"- she sat back, arms folded- "then we may persist forever."

"I find it very touching that you still hold a certain passion for life, Issele," Garret remarked, "even after the passing of centuries."

"A passion for my own life, yes," she retorted. "I seem to recall your desperate urge to produce *new* life, Garret. A vain hope indeed, sending that urgent seed into the desert of my womb."

They stared hatefully at each other until Daniel broke the oppressive silence. "I say we prepare to destroy them; they'll come to us regardless sooner or later. But what about the north?"

"Let those creatures tend to their own affairs," Omir declared. "Issele makes a point. And as we helped to create the *marandaal*, we can be the ones to hasten their ruin."

"And the rebellious Watchers?" Daniel persisted.

"They will meet their end in the north," Garret said. "The powers in that region will crush those who are seen to commit treachery against them, and they will crush the Watchers who have joined with those people."

"But haven't you all forgotten something?" Phaedra favoured them with a secretive smile. "What if there are *other* Watchers who plot and conspire against you?"

A pensive silence fell around the table. They had all considered that possibility but maintained a reluctance to speak of it. "There can be no easy way of knowing," Phaedra continued, and although none of them replied, they could not help but silently agree with her. By the very nature of the powers instilled in them, Watchers were highly skilled not only in discerning the truth of a given situation but also in hiding it if necessary. The truth could be delved from them eventually, of course, but the process was lengthy and its outcome never certain.

"We can talk about that later," Garret said finally, and turned his attention to Omir. "Assuming that we *are* going to stand and fight, we have something far more important to discuss. The matter of the child. Tell me, Omir- how much did you and Stephan discover before you let her escape?"

Omir ignored the jibe. "At first, we prised a few of the visions from her, even though she refused to describe them. They came to us in detail- even their coordinates. But the procedure became more and more difficult. She would not be coaxed." He scowled, the lines on his tanned face deepening at the recollection. "We tried promising her things- anything she wanted. Still she refused- and somehow, she weaved a kind of defensive web about herself. Oh, we could hurt her body, but her mind retreated further each time. What we *do* know, however, is that the visions are of places and even *times* when Gates will appear."

"We must know how she escaped," Anya stated, "because we have to find her, and when we do we must ensure two things- that we do everything necessary to discover the locations and times of all these openings, and that she *never* escapes again."

"I quite agree with you." Omir smiled grimly. "Unfortunately, we have no idea…"

"We *will* find her," Anya interrupted. "Every High Watcher we can spare should be engaged in the search. And when the girl is secured, we ensure that she is being watched by one of us at all times. There can be no exceptions."

"Her father also escaped, or rather, he was let out of prison," Garret noted. "In all likelihood, they will be together. Certainly she had a hand in his release. It could not have happened otherwise."

"Not unless another treacherous Watcher or jailer lurks near the cells," Phaedra remarked, and laughed when they turned their icy stares on her.

"When we find them," Garret continued after a moment, "we will start to take him apart in front of her, piece by screaming piece, each time she refuses to share her visions."

None of them could disagree with the logic of that course of action; all of them reflected that perhaps they ought to have adopted it in the first place.

"Speaking of escapes," Issele said after a while, "do we know exactly what happened to that prison guard? The one who was…" She favoured Garret with a suggestive smile. "Injured in quite an interesting way."

Garret shrugged. He had heard the news but attached little importance to it. "As far as I know, the prisoner who escaped was a young woman who worked for one of the traitors."

"Her name was Nia," Omir spoke up. "She was a spy for Kelandra, one of the treacherous Watchers. She somehow found her way into one of the tunnels that date back to the old city, and managed to get as far as the Bonemord. Stephan and I followed her. We didn't catch her before she threw herself to her death, but no matter…"

"Wait," Issele said sharply. "How could you not catch her?"

"She was watching us as we worked in the transformation chamber..."

"What?! She saw *that*?"

Omir gave Issele a scathing look. "It hardly matters now, Issele. We pursued her through the tunnel, as far as where it emerges into the swampland. She would have been ripped apart."

Anya shook her head. "I don't like this. What if she somehow survived?"

"That's impossible," Omir said angrily.

"It is *not* impossible," Anya pointed out, "and I say we scan that entire area to determine whether or not she still lives. It *is* extremely unlikely, but if by some incredible luck she persists, and if she comprehended what she saw... well, she must die and that knowledge must die with her."

"That will take some time and effort," Stephan said, "and we must direct all our efforts towards our preparation for the *marandaal* when they come..."

"Yes- they will come for you!" Phaedra laughed, as if to imply that they would somehow leave her untouched in so doing, but this time they ignored her.

"I agree with Stephan." Garret shook his head. "The *marandaal* will not wait for us to be ready. This child who can apparently walk through walls..."

"Or fly," Daniel commented dryly.

"Or create a Gate and flee through it, never to be seen again," Phaedra added with a grin.

"...must be caught. And our so-called High Watchers must be instructed to watch over their underlings with utter, absolute vigilance. I suspect these matters are more than enough to occupy our time."

"Then we put it to the vote," Anya said.

Six of the Seven voted. Phaedra left before anyone had cast their vote; she had little time for the reluctant democracy that her comrades played out suspiciously as they sat around the table. In her absence Anya and Daniel voted that the Bonemord be searched; however the other four voted that the escapee be left to float through the mists in one piece or a thousand- alive, dead or mad.

Sometime later as the skies darkened outside and sleet lashed against the windows, Daniel made his way down the corridor that led towards his quarters, suspicious thoughts skittering around in his mind like whispers that never faded. He felt frustrated that the others- except for Anya, who he had always thought the most sensible and practical of them all- had thought it a waste of time to scan the marshes for the remains of Kelandra's former spy. Surely it would not have taken *that* amount of time and effort with two or perhaps three of them working together- and it would have solved one loose end even if many others remained.

But that was not the matter that mostly preoccupied him.

The music, he thought for perhaps the hundredth time, and he stopped suddenly, leaning against the cold wall. Every shimmering nuance of those sounds returned, pristine and exact, almost as if he could hear it inside his head even now. He had memorised it without knowing.

I must have the music.

But Garret was older and wiser than him, he told himself as he continued on along the passageway. Older, wiser and perhaps stronger, although they all they had their relative strengths and weaknesses. Not only would he find it impossible to break into Garret's little antechamber, where he felt certain the music had been played, but he remained equally sure that even the attempt itself would trigger a reaction from that environment, something that, even though it could not kill him, could hurt him immensely.

I can beg him to let me listen, Daniel told himself, but that would never happen. Garret's response would be one of disgust, nothing more than that. Or perhaps he would continue to deny that he even had it in his possession.

If I told Issele, he thought, *she might find a way to force it from him, somehow. Oh, he loathes her and has done for centuries, and her hatred is equally bright- but that might be what it takes to goad her into action.*

But then I would have to share...

"A bright silver penny for your thoughts," a voice invited him from to his left, and Daniel spun round to see Phaedra standing in an alcove, leaning against the wall and cast half in shadow. She grinned and stepped forward, reaching out to brush back a lock of wavy, dark hair before he slapped her hand away. "Little Daniel!" she exclaimed. "So lost and pensive!"

"Place your hand on me again and I'll crush your fingers into meat and dust," he hissed.

Phaedra opened her mouth in mock outrage. "Such venom! Spare me your energies, Daniel- you know these beautiful digits of mine will grow back and heal in moments. I wanted to talk with you. I expect you were outvoted- but no matter. I will help you scan the great marshes. It takes two, after all. I'd expect to find nothing, but that's our preferred result, is it not?"

"Why would you do that?" he demanded. "Why would you help me? What do you want from me?"

"I'm lonely," she said, and smiled suddenly. "I enjoyed the solitude for years, Daniel. I thought intensely, sometimes for days on end, without sleep, without even food and water occasionally. Did you know, I even wrote theories about the Existence itself..."

"And does it end in utter darkness and cold or does the light of creation burst forth again?" he asked scornfully, then shook his head, irritated that he had even entered into conversation with her. "I'll ask you again, Phaedra. What do you want from me?"

"I already told you I was lonely," she said. "Now, are you going to crush my errant hand?"

She reached out to caress his cheek. Daniel closed his eyes and wished by all the world's powers that fate had brought him a different ally.

II – A Reluctant Awakening

I

The girl pressed herself to the soft ground, hardly daring to take a breath. Her lungs cried out for air. Blood pounded in her ears like the boom of a drum, a constant measure of the panic that coursed through her body.

Somewhere to the south she heard the measured footfall of those who had pursued her. She had evaded them for the moment, but they drew closer. She was certain that they were looking for her; she had even heard her name mentioned but her knowledge had not needed that proof.

If she ran now, they might see her- certainly they would hear her frightened trampling through the undergrowth- and although she was fast and agile and knew this part of the forest blindfolded, it was entirely possible that they knew the area as well as she did.

No, she thought suddenly. *Something else guides them. It isn't local knowledge.*

It's me.

She had no idea what they wanted from her, only that they would kill her if she allowed them a chance. She had no idea if they were even human, although she had caught a glimpse of them and saw that whatever they might really be, they nevertheless wore the shapes of human men.

She lay in the dirt, hidden by thick bushes on one side and a rocky cliff on the other. Thorns ripped the flesh of her arms as her cheek pressed against the soft mulch of the ground, but the tears she silently wept were of fear; she barely felt the pain.

What will they do if they fail to find me? What if they go to my home, to my parents? Who are they? These questions and others chased one another through her thoughts. One of her hands involuntarily grasped at a thick tendril of bramble, wickedly barbed and coiled, and the thorns cut into her hand. Somehow she stopped herself from crying out.

They came nearer, perhaps to within forty paces or so. She could not see them, but she could hear their voices. They seemed to be arguing about something.

"She'll have fled east. Further in," one of the men said after what seemed an age. He spat slowly and methodically upon the ground. "Far from here by now."

Why would he suddenly speak so much more loudly, the girl asked herself, *if not to trick me out of hiding after they pretend to leave?*

So she remained where she was, and she knew also that they also had decided to stay where they were. Despair sank into her as the light began to fail and her arms and legs grew numb. *How long will they remain there?* she wondered desperately.

But as dusk came they left, and it seemed to their quarry that they departed in a great hurry, as if they had seen something in the gathering shadows that frightened them more than returning to their masters without her.

Finally she moved from her hiding place, and breathed a long, tremulous sigh of relief.

Her name was Anlerran. She knew the vast forest of Mordenglen about as well as anyone, or so she believed. She had been born here, to parents who had themselves spent much of their lives in this place. She was *of* the forest and knew it intimately. The idea that malevolent creatures from some other place, whether they looked like men or not, could follow her into her heartland to hunt her down filled Anlerran with a sense of terror that felt entirely alien.

I belong here, she thought fiercely as she brushed mud from her cheek. *This is my home. They should not have been able to pass through without something happening to them. A tendril here, a fallen boulder there; Mordenglen itself should have torn them to the ground and made them a part of it, to be taken into the earth and crushed.*

But evidently that had not happened, and instead it had taken the onset of evening- which in this place would have cast fear into anyone less than welcome- to harry them back to the fringes of the great forest and then on to whichever stone city or other such unnatural place they had crept from to find her.

Anlerran let out a little sob, hating herself for the fear she still felt and for what had happened, because she could not explain it. *They may come back for me,* she thought. *They may bring others.*

A moment later she found herself on her feet, and a short while after that, she ran, heading along the path that would lead her home, a startled creature of the woodland hurtling heedlessly through the gloom.

Even in the near-full darkness, Anlerran would probably have evaded the tree root that spread across the path, had she not been so concerned with her near-encounter. She tripped and fell forwards, and a sudden searing pain leapt through her right leg.

Anlerran cursed and cried out, then pushed herself up into a sitting position. A moment later, she heard the sedate, unhurried approach of someone from out of the undergrowth. Exhausted, she could only let out a feeble cry as the old woman knelt near her, dark eyes seeming to bore into her as she surveyed the girl.

Unkempt and wrapped in a shawl, she also had a sack slung over her back from which a number of long plants protruded. In the dark, Anlerran could not tell what they were.

The old woman laughed suddenly, placed her sack on the ground and clapped her hands. "Well, well!" she cried. "Old Essyl's got herself a plump meal here!"

Then she pressed a finger to her lips at the sight of Anlerran's look of dawning horror. "I'm jesting with you, girl." She folded her arms and looked Anlerran up and down. "You're in a bit of a mess. Think you may need some help from an old lady?"

Thoughts whirled through the girl's head, but she could come to only one bitter conclusion- that she was in no condition to decline this mysterious old woman's aid. *If she means me ill then I'm helpless,* Anlerran thought darkly to herself as she lay prone in the gloom. *Besides which, if I decline the offer it may anger her.*

Shakily she tried to smile up at her unlikely benefactor. "I've hurt my leg," she admitted. "My father always says that fear makes a good servant but a bad master. I shouldn't have run so quickly. I'm surprised I didn't fall on my foolish face before now."

Essyl bent down and squinted at her leg in the failing light. "Well, it's not broken," she said after a moment. "I see that much."

"You can?" Anlerran frowned.

"Of course. I'll warrant it hurts mightily, though."

Anlerran could only nod wearily. The sudden appearance of the old woman had made her almost forget about it for a short while, but now the sharp pain in her leg grew worse.

"You're Joran and Emelle's daughter," Essyl said suddenly. "I thought you looked familiar." She helped Anlerran to her feet. "I know them. Not well, but well enough."

"You don't look familiar to me," Anlerran commented as she limped along the path and winced at the worsening pain, but Essyl ignored the remark. *I can hardly walk like this all the way home,* Anlerran thought. *But I need to get home. I need to warn Mother and Father about the men who hunted me today. Maybe they know something about them, maybe not, but even though those men may be gone now I'm certain that they'll return, or that others will come in their place. I have to warn my parents about them.*

Such thoughts and others darker still, came and went through her exhausted mind.

Eventually they reached an area where the trees thinned out a little. Before them stood a grey stone cliff that rose above the level of the trees and continued laterally for some distance; craggy and possibly only just climbable, it was marked with loose overhangs and withered, spindly trees, little more than bushes. Ildar had now risen, and by the moon's light Anlerran espied intricate nests in the upper reaches, and a large buzzard perched upon an overhang, watching events below with a beady, savage eye. Ivy and other creepers grew thickly upon the stony surface. At the base of the cliff, the same trails of vegetation formed a hanging curtain over a sturdy wooden cottage.

The colour of the sky above rapidly deepened now. As she looked up, Anlerran saw the brightest of the stars already emerging.

Essyl paused and looked her up and down. "You can stay here tonight and I will tend to your leg," she said simply. "Are you hungry?"

"Oh, well, I..." Anlerran tried to smile, but the expression turned into a grimace as she took a cautious step forward. "I ought to get back..."

"You can't walk unaided," the old woman told her, "and I am certainly not going to take you all the way to your parents' house under full darkness."

"But they'll be worried!"

"You shouldn't have tripped," Essyl pointed out, "should you now?"

"I was..." Anlerran bit her lip as she reminded herself that she did not know this woman, no matter that she claimed to be an acquaintance of her parents. Essyl stared at her, shrugged and took her arm. The two of them walked slowly up to the cottage and Essyl fumbled with a key briefly before unlocking the door and pushing it open.

"You didn't tell me if you were hungry or not," Essyl remarked.

"A little," Anlerran admitted.

Essyl nodded. "Good. Now let's be inside. Even I prefer not to wander Mordenglen in the full-dark these days."

"Why?" Anlerran asked as she limped into the cottage after the old woman and eased herself painfully into an old rocking chair that the woman waved her towards. She watched as Essyl lit the fire in the hearth.

"Things are not as they were. And now it seems matters have caught up with you as well." She glanced solemnly in Anlerran's direction for a moment, and then resumed her building of the fire as Anlerran stared wordlessly at her.

"Yes, I saw them," she said as the flames began to lick around the wood and old parchment. "Or I *sensed* them, which is much the same thing to me. Odd how they failed to track you, as you lay hiding, don't you think?"

"You watched me..."

"No, although I still knew where you were, roughly. Perhaps I confused them a little. I could do no more from that distance."

"And you made them leave?"

Essyl shrugged, rubbing her hands in front of the fire. "In a manner of speaking. It only needs a suggestion, which then takes root. The darkness itself does the rest. It's always been that way, but you know that already, don't you? You've always known. You grew up here; how could you not know?"

Anlerran fell silent, thinking quickly to herself. *She's some kind of witch,* she decided, and although the realisation made her uneasy, she did not feel unduly afraid. Her parents had occasionally mentioned witches, but only to remind her to be polite and respectful of them. *Did she save my life? I think she might have done.*

"Thank you," she said awkwardly.

Essyl glanced at her and said nothing. She sat at a wooden table near the back of the room, and the two of them watched as the flames cast wild shadows upon the walls. "They were *choragh-kin*," Essyl said finally. "Creatures who had given themselves over to the dark part of the Old Powers. They were no longer men. Not so long ago the *kin* were little more than myth in the eyes of most folk, thought vanished from the world along with their masters."

Anlerran could think of nothing to say to that, but she felt mightily troubled. Although the name should have meant nothing to her, somehow it *did* mean something, as if a long-forgotten dream tried to force its way back into her conscious mind. She was about to ask what such beings might want with her when another bolt of pain ran through her leg. "I will tend to you," Essyl said as she rummaged around in her sack and belt-pouch, presumably for ingredients with which to do just that.

The old woman was deeply engaged in her ministrations when a shuffling sound came from outside, and Essyl swiftly turned to face the door, suddenly intent. *Like a wild animal,* Anlerran thought, and wondered fearfully if her enemies had plucked up the courage not only to come back for her but also to walk all the way to the door of a forest witch.

"My son," Essyl murmured with a smile, even before the newcomer knocked upon the door. She called for him to come in, and Anlerran watched as the door opened and a tall, sturdy-looking man walked in, having to stoop at the entrance. He was the sort of man, Anlerran reckoned, who her mother would have called *all sinew and sword.* He also wore a couple of scars, one of them especially pronounced, and his hair had started to grey. He smiled briefly as Essyl rose to embrace him, but his expression became grim a moment later as he glanced towards Anlerran.

"Is this her?" he demanded.

"Undoubtedly." Essyl frowned. "You remember Falvor's instructions, Ruhal. You can have nothing to do with her until..."

"Until the time comes. I know, Mother. Well, the time has come." He took something small from his pocket and showed it to her in his palm. Anlerran could not see what the object was, but its effect on Essyl was instant. "This is the sign?" she whispered, eyes wide.

Ruhal nodded, then glanced towards her. The odd, pained expression in his eyes caused a chill to stir within her. "Tomorrow, once you can move a little more freely, you must leave Mordenglen," he said quietly.

Anlerran stared from Ruhal to Essyl, then back to Ruhal again, utterly confounded. "Why by all the Powers would I go anywhere with you?" she finally demanded. "As soon as my leg is better, I'll make my own way back to my parents' house. They'll be wondering where I am..."

"No, they won't," Ruhal said quietly, and looked away. "Your parents are dead, Anlerran."

II

For a while afterwards, Anlerran felt adrift from everything that happened around her. She jumped, startled when Essyl gently grasped her leg to ease her pain and help her heal more swiftly. She became vaguely aware of an odd tingling in that leg, the result, no doubt, of some mysterious healing ability that the old woman had brought to bear. But for what could have been an age she simply stared at the fire and felt none of its warmth.

They're not dead. He's lying.
Why would he lie?
Why wouldn't he?

22

Such thoughts clamoured for attention in her mind until she could barely think at all. Ruhal came to stand nearby and then knelt. Eventually she glanced at him, but looked swiftly away, unable to bear that grim expression.

"He speaks the truth," Essyl said gently, and removed her hands from Anlerran's leg. The girl blinked in surprise, for the pain was all but gone. Cautiously she moved her ankle back and forth, and gaining in confidence she moved her foot in a semicircular motion several times. Still she could feel no pain.

"It's... it's much better," she murmured, but Essyl had wandered away to a back room, leaving Anlerran with Ruhal.

"Take me back to my home," Anlerran whispered fiercely.

Ruhal shook his head. "I can't do that. Certainly not in the night. There are..."

"You expect me to abandon them?!" Anlerran leapt to her feet and stalked over to the door that led outside.

The handle would not turn.

"It's locked," Ruhal said, "and will remain so until the morning." With a sigh he sank down into a chair at the table, drumming his fingers on the wooden surface, a deep frown upon his face.

Anlerran returned to her chair, frustrated. She was about to ask him something- she could never remember what it might have been later- but instead, a tumult of emotion and sudden realisation overwhelmed her, and she began to sob quietly to herself.

Ruhal glanced at her and then rested his head in his hands as if in defeat. He said nothing at all, perhaps because he had no idea what to say, or thought silence might be a better option than saying anything. After a while he took out what looked like a small, marked pebble from his pocket, and rotated it on the table, over and over, as lost in thought as she was lost in grief.

She did not recall eventually falling into a light, fitful sleep.

Anlerran woke with a start, hearing the noise of the door opening. Ruhal stepped through from outside, carrying some firewood which he placed to the side of the hearth. The light of a grey, misty morning poured through the open doorway.

The memory of what had been said the previous night came back to her in a rush. She stood up and said to him as he turned to look at her: "I'm going home. If what you said is true, I have to see them for myself."

Ruhal said nothing.

"It may well be of the utmost importance to you that I leave the only world I know in the morning," she continued, recalling his words from earlier. "But I can't leave until..." She drew a deep breath as tears pricked her eyes again. "I owe them a decent burial."

Anlerran sat and watched as Ruhal moved a little nearer to the fire to warm his hands. He remained like that for a while, kneeling near the flames, bent slightly forwards, and somehow looking older than his years, as if the weight of some terrible knowledge bore down upon him, crippling even his will to persist.

"They will need more than a decent burial," he said finally.

Anlerran's stomach crawled at those words. "Why?" she demanded.

Ruhal glanced at Essyl, who had just walked in from her little bedroom at the rear of the cottage. She gazed back at him for a moment before giving a grudging nod. Ruhal turned slightly to face her and continued softly, "The *choragh* choose sometimes to fight their enemies by using the cadavers of those who return to the earth. It takes a warding to stop such desecration, but that is what we shall have to do. And then, immediately after the rites are done, we leave. You will come south with me, and when there's time for me to tell you everything you need to know, I will tell you.”

“Why?” Anlerran whispered. “I don’t understand! I don’t even know that word *choragh*...” And although it *was* foreign to her- before Essyl had uttered it yesterday evening she had never even heard it before, and it left a strange, bitter taste in her mouth- something told her that she ought somehow to know it.

“You will,” Ruhal said. “I can allow you only a moment to grieve, when we return to your home...”

“A *moment* to grieve.” Anlerran was aghast.

“That’s all I can allow.” Ruhal’s words sounded harsh. Then he appeared to relent a little. “I don’t say such things out of cruelty, Anlerran, nor out of dispassion, but simply out of necessity. I won’t willingly fail in my duty to you. Do you understand?”

“No. I don’t understand,” she said. “I want to see their bodies.” She did not, of course- the thought frightened her- but at the same time Anlerran knew that only then could she fully believe anything that this man said.

She watched as Ruhal and his mother talked quietly for a moment. She heard a little of what they said, and it troubled her.

“...will be a treacherous journey,” Essyl murmured.

“I’ll return... take you from...” Ruhal’s voice was like brittle iron.

The old woman shook her head. “No... this is where... remain in Mordenglen...”

They embraced, both of them visibly upset, and then Ruhal turned to leave, motioning abruptly to Anlerran for her to go outside. “Thank you for healing my leg,” she said to Essyl on her way out, but the old woman merely nodded distractedly as if she barely heard the words.

Anlerran and Ruhal turned and made their way through the forest, heading in the direction of her parents’ house. After a while she began to recognise most of the paths they followed, and Anlerran strode on with trepidation, fearful of what she would find. Rage and grief mingled within her as they came nearer to her home, until at last they stood upon the threshold and gazed upon the beaten-down door, and then at the bodies of her parents, throats slit, still and pale upon the kitchen floor, stiffened and cold in their dried blood. Whoever or whatever had attacked them had left them no time at all to defend themselves, which they certainly would have done had they been able.

Anlerran stood silently by the doorway as the fog drifted in. Her gaze took in the place she had called home. Much of it still stood intact, but it could never be her home again. She wept, and then, cold and empty, she made herself a vow of vengeance- bloody, terrible vengeance- upon those that had committed this act. *I don't know who you are,* she thought. *I don't even know what you are. But I will find you, and I will destroy you.*

Ruhal had remained silent the whole while, and stood a respectful distance away, but now he spoke. "I will help you dig," he offered, "if you permit it."

Anlerran turned and nodded wearily. They took spades from the outhouse at the rear, and began to dig through the soft earth in the back garden. "One grave?" Ruhal asked her uncertainly.

"Of course," she retorted without looking at him. "They lived as one, they should..." She shook her head angrily, wiping away fresh tears.

By the time the grave was sufficiently deep and they had placed the bodies of her parents gently within it, Anlerran felt numb; grief had abated for a time, the void filled by a curious detachment, at the centre of which a hard, violent core of rage still nestled.

"One day," she whispered to herself as she touched their lips, and then began the task of covering them forever in the dirt.

The rain had cleared and the sun shone as Anlerran issued the rites of passing upon the graves, then placed a traditional bundle of brambles and crossed twigs at the head and foot of the grave.

"It must be warded," Ruhal reminded her, and he raised a hand towards the resting place. Anlerran stepped back and watched as he knelt on the ground. For a moment she thought that perhaps the knot of twigs and brambles she had made moved and became tighter, harder. Finally Ruhal lowered his hand and uttered a faint sigh. His head dropped slightly. "It's done," he said, "in so much as I'm able."

"What are you?" Anlerran asked him on an impulse.

He smiled thinly. "What I am is not important. What *you* are *is*." He stood up and brushed wet earth from his knees. "Anlerran, you cannot return here- not for a long time, anyway. Perhaps you can never enter Mordenglen again." He glanced back at the cottage. "Do you have any belongings you wish to take?"

Anlerran blinked and thought for a moment. The door creaked slightly in the breeze as if asking her the same question. "No," she said eventually. "They would serve as reminders. I have my memories. I need nothing else."

She had no idea if she even meant these words, but Ruhal nodded as if that was exactly what he had expected her to say.

A faint, low groaning sound issued from some distance away in the direction they had come from. To Anlerran it sounded almost like wood breaking under immense pressure. Her unease intensified when she saw Ruhal pale noticeably and glance quickly around. "How fast can you run, Anlerran?"

Anlerran saw in that moment the fear in Ruhal's eyes. Only days ago the great forest had seemed such a familiar, even comfortable place, but now it was a tangle of darkness and secrets, filled with terrors she preferred not to imagine- and one such *thing* was hurtling its way towards them.

"Fast enough," she said, wondering at the same time how her ankle would bear up to the task. What if she tripped and fell again? She would slow them both down.

"Good," he answered, oblivious to her worries. "Follow me."

He turned and began sprinting away along one of the narrow, twisting paths, heading roughly south-west. Anlerran followed, keeping him in sight, her heart thumping painfully. She could sense that life or death, for her and for this stranger who had helped her and come against his better judgement to bury and ward her parents, might be decided by the beat of mere moments.

She rushed on through the forest in the wake of Ruhal's dull blur. Remembering her fall from yesterday, she focussed and concentrated on running and looking, trying to keep to the furious pace Ruhal had set, casting aside all the questions that could distract her from this grim flight. Occasionally, if the path opened out a little he would glance swiftly behind to ensure that she had kept up. She wondered how it was that such a sturdy-looking man could also run so quickly.

As they ran the dreadful sound of snapping, bending, groaning wood, an entire swathe of woodland yielding in pain before some transformation, came clearly through the cold air. Anlerran slipped twice on a still-damp root bulging above the hardened ground, but scrambled to her feet unhurt and in good time on both occasions, thankful that Essyl's good work on her limb had not been undone by her haste.

Finally, at the edge of a great clearing, through which a small river meandered, Ruhal came to a stop. Anlerran knelt almost doubled over by the edge of the water, then raised her head. "Is it... still... after us?" she gasped. Ruhal said nothing; he walked some way down the side of the river bank and pulled from beneath the overhanging turf of the bank a small rowing boat that Anlerran had not noticed until now. He beckoned her over and helped her into the vessel, then stepped into the rear. Holding an oar in each hand, he began to row away- not especially well, Anlerran noticed, but at least they were moving. "For the time being, we're safe- at least, from *that*," he said after a while.

"Will it not chase us anyway?" Anlerran asked, worried at the sedate pace being set by her companion.

He shook his head. "It can't cross water. Water is not its dominion."

"Then what *is* its dominion?" She turned to face Ruhal, who glanced only briefly at her.

"It is one of the dark things of the earth," he told her eventually, and would say no more.

III

"I have enough silver for horses," Ruhal said abruptly a little later. "You *can* ride?"

"Of course." Anlerran had been dragging her hand in the water, absent-mindedly watching the disturbance of her reflection, but thought quickly to herself after her utterance. She *could* ride well enough, although she had seldom needed to in her close forest home. The paths she had followed most of her life were for the most part more easily travelled by foot if one trod carefully. *And if one did not fall and twist one's ankle,* she added ruefully, then thinking, *I wonder what would have happened if I hadn't tripped and fallen? What if I'd hurtled on and on through the darkness? Where would I be now? Would I be* anywhere *now?*

Or would Essyl and Ruhal have found me anyway? Essyl said that she knew more or less where I was, and something of the danger I was in. Would she have found me? And would Ruhal have come for me later regardless? Perhaps my fall changed nothing.

29

She shuddered at the thought of entities that caused Essyl- surely a witch of some kind, and therefore to be feared by any who crossed her- to think twice about walking Mordenglen at night. *Things that frighten Ruhal as well,* she thought, glancing at her companion. He had slackened the pace of his rowing, taking the opportunity to recover a little. His expression remained as grim as ever.

"Were you and Essyl *both* looking for me?" she asked suddenly- as soon as the question occurred to her. The next moment, as his eyes turned to hers, she wondered briefly if she ought to have asked the question.

"Yes," he said simply, and then, "I didn't know for certain that it was *you* in danger, but I suspected it might be." He lay down the oars for a moment, took the marked pebble from his pocket and showed it to her as if that might somehow explain his actions. "It was a matter of who found you first."

As morning became afternoon the trees gradually thinned out until finally they left the shadows of ancient Mordenglen behind. Anlerran gave the forest a cursory backward glance. It no longer seemed like a home to her. It felt oppressive, dark and seeping with the worst kind of nightmares, even if she had yet to look any of them squarely in the eye.

I don't expect I shall be back, she thought suddenly, *but then again, I don't think I could ever bring myself to go back.*

She wondered briefly what would happen to the house that had been her home. Would it fall into neglect and ruin as the years wore on? Would some visitor to Mordenglen come across it and perhaps even choose to stay awhile, desperate for shelter? Or would he or she study the abandoned building, notice the faded stains and perhaps the grave behind the house and hurry away, suddenly seeing the scene of the atrocity for what it was?

With an effort Anlerran pushed those thoughts to one side.

The pace of the river increased as several tributary streams joined the flow at various points along the way, and they headed into rough, open scrubland. As mid-afternoon approached, Ruhal paddled the boat over to the south-facing bank and helped her out. Anlerran's legs already ached after their exertion in the morning; she winced as they set off on foot, eventually reaching a wide dirt track that took them roughly south-west. Later, with the failing of the light, Ruhal opted to stop for the night a short distance away from the track, in the shadow of a lone, tall tree. He unrolled two blankets from his pack and gave one to her.

Anlerran slept fitfully that night, troubled by dreams that made her relive the worst parts of the last few days. She woke at least half a dozen times, sometimes as soon as she looked through the doorway of her home in her dream, staring numbly at the bodies of her mother and father. Each time she woke, she found Ruhal already awake- unless he was able to sleep sitting cross-legged with his arms folded and his head unbowed. She said nothing to him, and he in turn gave no indication that he knew she'd woken up, though one time Anlerran felt sure that she had shouted something as she opened her eyes- perhaps a response to some fragment from her dream that she feared had followed her into the waking world.

Ruhal simply waited for the dawn light, and when it arrived he prepared to set off. Anlerran was relieved to be on the move again despite the gnawing hunger in her stomach. They made a silent and miserable pair that morning, their environment oppressive and their footsteps leaden as they followed the track towards a horizon that seemed no closer by the time they stopped briefly to lunch on some dry bread and cured pork that Ruhal brought from his pack.

"Where are we headed?" Anlerran asked tiredly, grimacing at the intense saltiness of the meat. She peered up at the sun and then the path ahead, trying to figure whereabouts they might be by now. "Southbridge? Somewhere near there?"

Ruhal nodded, taking a swig from the water flask he had filled before they left the river behind the previous day. "Southbridge is less than a half league from here," he said, passing her the flask, "so we'll press on and reach the town by sundown with any luck. We can buy horses there, and be on our way the next morning."

Anlerran had visited only a few settlements in her life, and the small town of Southbridge had not been amongst them. She had heard occasional mentions of it during conversations between her parents, and she had been shown its location on one of their old parchment maps, but she knew almost nothing about the place.

She had therefore not known what to expect, but as they drew close to the town's edge she saw that the place had a certain ghostly beauty in the twilight, as if it hid secret memories from a long-gone age. Southbridge was evidently an old settlement; twisting little streets were bordered by mainly timber buildings, lit only sporadically by oil lanterns that sputtered in the failing light.

Ruhal stopped at a tavern named *The Warlock and Watchtower* in the middle of the main town square, from which the cacophony of mass revelry fled out through the opened windows.

Nothing could have prepared Anlerran for the reception they received as they stepped into the lights, odours and warmth of the inn. Even before the door had creaked and swung shut behind them, the place went deadly silent. All eyes turned their way as if drawn by some unseen power. Anlerran stared fearfully back at the motley assortment of ruffians and never-do-wells gathered here, and was about to take a step back when Ruhal's hand grabbed her wrist as if to prevent her from turning and fleeing into the dusk.

"My lord," one of the men said finally. "My lord Ruhal! You've returned! And you bring a witchling to summon in the passing to the new season!" His eyes darted between Ruhal and Anlerran, and swiftly back to Ruhal again, as if Anlerran might indeed have the power to bewitch him.

Ruhal quickly raised a hand as others began to make similar pronouncements, perhaps emboldened by the first speaker. "Listen to me- and *listen well*. She is not for your festival. She travels under my protection. Therefore, you will leave her be. You will not cast so much as a quick glance in her direction."

With everyone around them hovering between fawning and fearful, Anlerran and Ruhal were led by the innkeeper to a large table up on the higher floor, overlooking the main tap room. "We'll need two rooms prepared for tonight, if you have them, and baths to be poured," Ruhal said, pressing a silver crescent into the man's hand. The innkeeper bobbed his head in understanding and then hurried away. Ruhal leaned forward and said quietly, "I am known well here, as you have gathered."

Anlerran remained troubled, even more so when she glanced down and saw a dozen or more fevered, almost worshipful eyes looking up at her through the blue haze of *kyush* smoke despite Ruhal's warning. "They called me a *witchling*," she whispered. "Why would they do that? I'm nothing of the sort. And what did they mean by the passing to the new season?"

Ruhal shook his head as if to dismiss the questions out of hand. "Don't heed their words. They'll not dare to even approach you. Old beliefs are held strongly here, but the drink brings out the worst of them." He paused and looked down at the table, seeming uncomfortable. "Aside from that, you're pretty. Exceptionally pretty."

"Am I?" Anlerran blinked. "I've never thought about it."

Ruhal frowned and looked one way and another, any direction except at her. Anlerran found his behaviour perplexing. "Thank you for saying so," she said finally.

"Ruhal!" came a call from the tap-room below. Worriedly, Anlerran peered over the parapet to see one of the men remove his shirt and proceed to carve deeply into his arms with a longknife. "My blood as a gift to your woman!" he exclaimed, eyes wide and fervent. "By the coming of the season, the blood of the earth and of my veins!"

Anlerran could only stare down in horror at this wilful mutilation, as her eyes met those of the man standing below in a quickening pool of his own making. Ruhal cursed to himself and stood up.

"Let the earth keep your gift," he called out, amidst the hush that had descended in the tap-room. "A time will soon come when you'll not be so keen to spill your own blood."

The man's longknife clattered to the floor; he swayed forward and then back. Finally he sank to his knees and fell forwards.

"If anyone else is enough of a fool," Ruhal warned them all, "then take your implements out into the fields and ruin yourselves there, unseen."

No one, Anlerran noted with relief, appeared to be enough of a fool. The man who had mutilated himself was carried out of the tavern either unconscious or dead. Eventually the matter was put aside and a murmur of conversation rose once again, occasionally punctuated by a bellow of raucous laughter or indignation, as the locals returned to their drinking and their table games. The innkeeper directed an unfortunate serving-girl to scrub clean the floor that had seen blood upon it.

Anlerran took a deep breath and sat back. Although she had not eaten properly for a long while her appetite had shrivelled away to nothing, and the sight of the girl downstairs wringing red-hued water into her cleaning bucket did not help.

"Where are we headed tomorrow?" she asked quietly, eager to break the silence between them.

"Into Fhaarluy a little way," Ruhal told her. "I'll buy the horses and we should get there by the afternoon. It was quicker to travel here than to walk directly south- there are no well-trodden paths that way- and in any case we need to visit the guild library tomorrow as we leave." He paused as if considering something. "We will meet three friends of mine when we arrive in Mordenglen later. But before we leave Southbridge tomorrow morning, there is something I need to tell you, or show you. That's why we need to stop at the guild library."

They lapsed into silence again. Soon Anlerran found her eyelids dropping and her head starting to slump forwards; quietly, Ruhal ushered her up the second flight of stairs to where their bedchambers waited. At the landing, as he opened her chamber door for her he said quietly, "Make the most of tonight- we won't be sleeping in beds for a while I expect." He looked her up and down, looking as if he had suddenly forgotten whatever else he had been about to say. "Good night," he said eventually. Abruptly he turned and made his way into his own room.

Anlerran found the room uncomfortably grand. The bed had been made for two people, and looked soft and inviting, with four plump pillows. Across on the other side of the chamber steam rose from a great porcelain bath that had been prepared. Carefully she tested the water with her hand; judging it to be neither too hot nor too cool she removed her clothes and slowly sank into the water with a sigh of pleasure.

She luxuriated perhaps longer than she ought in her bath, enjoying the sensation of the warm water, before emerging, her aching muscles feeling somewhat better.

Standing naked for a few moments before the full-length mirror in her room, Anlerran saw how haggard and sunken-eyed she looked. *Pretty?* She frowned. *Why would he think I'm pretty? Why would dull brown hair and dark eyes be pretty? I remember I always wanted to have blue eyes when I was younger. And maybe lighter hair, maybe even hair you could almost see through, like the* luyan *people have.*

The room was comfortably warm, so after barring the door she lay down to sleep without clothing herself. She slept deeply without waking once during the night, and it seemed that only moments had passed before Ruhal was knocking upon the door, telling her to dress and be ready to leave.

When Anlerran went downstairs she found him in the tap-room purchasing some items for breakfast which he then put into a small pack. She could smell freshly-baked bread, cheese and meat amongst some other, herbal aromas, and her stomach growled loudly in anticipation.

"Time to ride. I've purchased a couple of horses," he said to her as they made their way into the stables adjacent to the tavern. The morning had dawned bright and cold, and a coating of frost still lingered in the shadier areas. Their breath and that of the horses rose visibly into the air as they prepared to ride.

"The light will last well today," Ruhal commented, "so we should make good progress. But as I mentioned, we'll stop at the guild library on the edge of the town. I'll tell you everything that you need to know. As much as I can, that is." His expression darkened, as if a shadow passed over them both, even in the cloudless sky. "It may well be far more than you want to know."

Anlerran stared at him. "You talk in riddles. Why do we need to stop at this... *guild* place? Can you not just tell me whatever is so important?"

Ruhal shook his head. "The guild is the right place. Because there are things I need to *show* you, Anlerran. It's all very well for me to tell you things, but the written word must back up the spoken word, should you fail to believe me. It's also one of the few places where we may talk without others listening, if we have the library room to ourselves. And one more reason- I don't want an untold secret left hanging over me still when we ride out to Fhaarluy."

"I can read and write well enough," she told him. "My parents taught me, but..." She bit her lip, trying not to recall such times.

"They did well in all regards, from what I heard," he said quietly.

Anlerran and Ruhal rode out to the southern edge of Southbridge, and tethered the horses at a post outside a large, plain building with a great domed roof of stone. After they had been granted entrance by the lone guardsman, Ruhal led Anlerran to a great room filled with vast high shelves of books. It was here, at a long wooden table, that he finally stopped and bade her be seated. They were alone, she noticed.

"I'm a poor wordsmith at the best of times," he said quietly, "and what I'm about to tell you may seem overly harsh. But it has to be said." He took something from his pocket and placed it on the table; Anlerran recognised the object as the mysterious stone she remembered seeing him with in Essyl's cottage. "Is that stone important?" she asked him. "You keep showing it to me."

"The stone is simply a call to action. *You* are important, Anlerran."

She frowned. "I've had enough of this, Ruhal. How about you explain to me *why* you think I'm so important? Isn't that why we're sitting here?"

He stared at the symbol on the stone for a short while as if it might help him find the right words. Finally he said, "There is no easy way to tell you this. The man and woman you knew as your parents- well, in truth they were *not* your parents. Not by birth. They were instructed to raise you as if you were their own child, and they did that very well as I mentioned..."

Anlerran blinked, utterly dumbfounded. "Then... I don't understand..." Suddenly an idea came to her. "Oh! Are *you* my father? Is that why you..."

"No, no." Ruhal sighed. "Anlerran, seventeen years ago I was one of a group of men who brought an infant child from the distant north- from the Rhunin Heights- to Mordenglen. You were that child."

Anlerran shook her head. "This makes no sense. Why would you do that? Why would you take me away from my real parents, all that distance?"

"Who *are* my real parents?" she asked him bluntly when he failed to answer.

"Their names are Larn and Elluron," Ruhal said quietly. "Larn, your mother, was from a small village not far from the Wistledge. Your father... I don't know where he was from, but I know..."

"Are they still alive?"

"I have no idea, Anlerran. I know only what I was told by my teacher, Falvor, some years ago. I never met either of them. The child- I mean *you*- was passed to us by someone else- someone they trusted absolutely. You were handed over to us and we returned south with you, to Mordenglen. I remember only a little of that journey. Enough to tell you, perhaps, and no more."

Anlerran fell silent, not sure what to make of all this, nor how to feel about this revelation. Other questions about her parents would come, she felt sure of it. "I still don't understand. Why would they willingly give me away?"

"They had no choice," he said quietly. "They were being hunted by *choragh* and their agents."

"By what?" But no sooner had she heard him utter that word than she recalled him mentioning it before. Essyl had mentioned the word too. "Oh. I remember."

"There have been certain movements and activities within Mordenglen for a while," Ruhal said. "Stirrings made by the dark, wild part of the Old Powers. More in recent times than I can ever recall previously. Then this"- he rolled the pebble around in a circle upon the slate table- "*this* arrived."

"What does it mean?"

"It was the clearest possible sign that I had to take you from Mordenglen, take you from your guardians and all you knew, and keep you safe."

"Safe from what? From the men who were hunting me? The men who killed my parents?! Or from the *choragh?!*" she retorted bitterly. And then: "My *guardians*, you called them."

"The two that hunted you- they were not men," he said quietly.

"I know," Anlerran said after a moment. "But what were they?"

"Minions of the *choragh*. They call themselves *kin*. Creatures through which an untamed darkness flows; the wild side of the Old Powers."

Anlerran nodded tiredly. "Yes. Your mother mentioned them."

"It was clear that they intended your death. Tell me, Anlerran- this may sound a strange question, but have you ever felt as if you were... something *other* than what you know yourself to be?"

I think I'm in the company of a madman, Anlerran thought to herself, but at the same time his words resonated with her in a way she could barely comprehend.

"Sometimes," she admitted finally, and in that exact moment she remembered an occasion perhaps two or three Ildarian months ago, when she had felt exactly that way, as she sat and watched the sun set from a remote clearing somewhere to the south of her home. Nothing had happened to make her feel different, or so she had supposed, and the sensation had been a subtle one. Only later, as she lay awake that night, had she even considered that something far beyond her understanding might have happened.

It was as if I could have become something else, she remembered thinking that night, restless and unable to sleep. *Something was awakened inside me, just for a short while.*

Ruhal sat back in his chair. "Let me now tell you a little about the *marandaal.* I could spend a while telling you about them- but we haven't the time. They are an ancient race of beings- immensely powerful and intelligent in a way we cannot properly comprehend - whose purpose throughout the history of the Existence has been to find new worlds to destroy. According to the few stories about them, they came originally from the first human world, millions of years ago. They were created by some immensely powerful magic wielded by the humans of that time. Over decades, perhaps centuries, they gathered power themselves, overthrew their creators, and eventually found ways of reaching other worlds, through gaps into the void that we now know simply as Gates. Still they continued to spread through the Existence. And eventually they found Aona. Already they have emerged into the land of Aphenhast to the east. Whatever places they find, they destroy. That, it seems, is their one purpose above and beyond any other. They will aim to do to Harn what they are doing already to Aphenhast. In time, they will bring ruin and darkness to the entire world unless they can be defeated."

Anlerran had not heard anything of what such beings might have done to that eastern land, yet she shuddered at the thought.

"The power of the *marandaal* is such that unless old enmities are put aside and new alliances forged, however distasteful they may be, then Harn shall fall into darkness- a darkness worse than that wrought by the worst of the *choragh* more than two thousand years ago when the earth lay soaked with the blood of sacrifice. And if Harn falls, Aona falls." He stared intently at her. "You may wonder why I speak of such ancient times- but the *choragh* never went away entirely. Still they linger, in the strange places of the land, and in the hot fervour and mad bloodlust and depravity of their unknowing worshippers..."

"Like that man in Steepleford," Anlerran whispered, even though she could barely understand what Ruhal was saying. She felt as if all the blood had drained from her face. The dreadful sound of splitting timber as she and Ruhal fled her parents' warded grave flitted through her mind again.

"In the wilds, and the places where superstition holds," Ruhal said, "some people can sense the calling of the lost world their ancestors knew, almost as if their blood runs differently when they are near to one such as you- one close to the Old Powers. Some of the good people of Steepleford would happily disembowel themselves and eat their own innards if you told them to."

Anlerran swallowed and looked away, nauseous.

"There is a reason," Ruhal continued quietly, "why you have sensed that you might be something more than you appear to be- that there's another, hidden life inside the one you know. The *choragh* are one part of an ancient family of beings, Anlerran. The others- their cousins, if you will- were known as the *illeagh*. The reason..." He lowered his voice even further, although no one else had entered the room. "The reason I have to protect you, keep you with me, is that you are part-*illeagh*. A quarter, to be exact. Your father was half-*illeagh*, your mother was human, and so..."

Anlerran could do nothing but stare back at him, barely aware of anything now except for her companion, the dim lamplight of the library, and the table, cold and unyielding under her shaking hands.

"It's true, Anlerran," he whispered.

She looked for the hint of a lie, for something that could be seized upon as proof that he was making it up or simply delusional, but she could find no trace of deceit. Instead his intense gaze melted as she saw fear in his eyes; fear, perhaps, that she would scream her disbelief at him, or laugh without control, or run shrieking through the Guild passageways and out into the town streets, deriding him as a lunatic who had kidnapped her.

"You're mad," Anlerran said flatly, willing herself to be calm, and wondered if she might make it out of the library and even outside onto the street before he could grab her. She reckoned she might be as fast as him; could she ride better than him? Probably not. Could she seek help from some of the townsfolk? That was even less likely; from what she had seen, Ruhal was a figure of some authority here, whereas she had no idea what they might make of her- particularly if she pointed the finger of accusation at him. *A pyre,* she thought darkly.

Before she could act, his hand had grasped her wrist, not painfully but with enough force to show he would let her go only when he had finished what he had to say. Anlerran's other hand stole instinctively towards her belt-knife, but Ruhal shook his head. "Listen now to me. I must tell you from where you came and how you came to be, and why your enemies and my enemies are the one and same."

"I don't want to know," she said miserably, but her confused protest ended there as Ruhal began to speak. Whether or not some spell suffused his words she could not tell, but somehow she felt compelled to listen to him, in abject silence. It seemed that around where they sat the light grew brighter, and the rest of the library darker, and also that the distant sounds of footfall in corridors around the building could no longer be heard.

"Thousands of years ago," Ruhal said, "the *choragh* and the *illeagh* were a single race- of wild and powerful beings, both spiritual and physical, and they wielded what we now call the Old Powers- the forces of Aona itself. The humans and other humanlike races of that time worshipped them. In return, some demanded nothing whereas some demanded sacrifices, and sought to control and subvert the younger races. A few even created enmities between humans to fuel their power. This is the magic of life and death, Anlerran- the most potent of all- the most wonderful and the vilest.

"At some point in this distant age, differences arose between those who wished simply to exist away from and apart from the human races, for which they had no regard, and those who wished to gather more power about them through sacrifice, through ritual, through utter worship and devotion from their subjects. Some humans had begun to learn of the Old Powers, and shape them- and those who sought power from the bloodletting and destruction of their subjects sought also to capture and change those humans- or other races- that had reached such a level of revelation and knowledge.

"These were savage times, and a war ensued in which that ancient race was split forever. At the same time, those who sought to empower themselves- now what we call the *choragh*- fashioned into being the creatures known as *diafagh*- shambolic but dangerous creatures that were once human, slain and made to rise again, condemned to walk the land as soulless vessels of the *choragh*.

"Those that avoided humanity all but disappeared, eventually retreating to the far depths of the Rhunin Heights in the distant north. There they named themselves the *illeagh*, which means Alone. It is said that in time, without worship, without contact- for nothing except such beings could exist so far within the Rhunin- they faded from existence.

"Over many centuries, humans, *luyan* and others learned more of the Old Powers. There is only a certain amount of power, of energy in this world and all other worlds- that is a basic of principle of the Powers, Anlerran- and as the power of humans- be they circles of witches, or lone warlocks- grew, the power of the *choragh* became less. And so they faded in time, retreating to distant places, weaving wards about themselves so that they could exist, and not be found, but do little else."

"Now they have come back," Anlerran whispered.

"They never went away entirely. But the chains around their prisons are falling apart. The reason for this is that their ancient enemies the *marandaal* have come again to Aona."

"Then we stand between two evils," Anlerran said.

Ruhal sat back. "As I said, your father was half-*illeagh*..."

"You also said that they faded from existence!"

"That's what is commonly believed. But I have spent time amongst the people of the Rhunin foothills, enough time to hear of movements, of sightings- and more. Both the *illeagh* and the *choragh* are present- in different places- deep within the Rhunin, and the people nearest those mountains are affected most."

"How could he possibly be half... half-*illeagh*?" Anlerran demanded. "How would such union be possible, between a human and *illeagh*, for him to even be created?"

Ruhal smiled faintly. "Now *that* I have no idea about. Perhaps only the *illeagh* themselves hold the answer." He sighed. "You cannot imagine the power of the Old Magic until you feel it, Anlerran, or until you see it unfold before you. It is a terrible, wonderful thing. The heartbeat of the world itself."

Anlerran glanced around them. Were the shadows a little blacker, deeper than she had thought, or were Ruhal's words stirring her imagination in some terrible way?

"So it falls to you to *protect* me," she said, as he finally relinquished his grip upon her wrist. "Why you, and not all these others you travelled with to steal me, all those years ago?"

A darkness gathered in his expression. "Falvor told me something of their fate. The others are all dead by one means or another, and perhaps the only reason I did not meet the same fate is that both Falvor and my mother wielded the Old Powers. It could be that they protected me somehow, or perhaps I was simply fortunate. But Falvor is dead now, and I have had to take you from Mordenglen." He tapped the pebble with his finger. "I had no choice in the matter. If something comes for me..." He smiled grimly. "Well, you'll see soon enough that we have many enemies to contend with..."

In an instant, Anlerran decided to flee; but perhaps some subtle change in her expression had given her away, for he ran after her across the tiled floor of the library, catching her halfway to the door, whereupon he wrestled the brandished knife from her hand with ease. "You need to trust me," he hissed angrily. "There is *no one else.* If you try anything like that again..."

But Anlerran could not make out the words that followed. She collapsed to the floor, to be lifted gently a moment later. As she struggled against unconsciousness, Anlerran felt as weak as an infant in Ruhal's arms, and a strange thought occurred to her: *Here I am again, helpless as he carries me away.* When had she thought that before?

He gathered her up, and the last things Anlerran remembered before a black sleep came for her were the sound of his footsteps and then, for a lucid moment a while later, the cold air rushing to greet them as they stepped out of the building.

It must be night, Anlerran remembered thinking, though she could not open her eyes. Somehow, despite this, she could see the stars of the sky. And then those points of distant light, and Ruhal murmuring something that soothed her as he bore her away to some other place, became a dream into which she willingly sank.

III – A Place Without Stars

I

The long, ramshackle rowing boat emerged slowly from the bank of mist, taking a languid route through the waters. The wretched-looking creature paddling the oars rowed slowly, although anyone looking at the thick, knotted muscles of his arms would have seen that he could row much faster should he have needed to. On either side of the boat, towards the rear, nets dragged through the murky water, the catch from which- if luck gave him any at all- would form his daily meal later as day melted into night.

Pad's existence was dreary and devoid of much excitement, but he nevertheless was reminded almost daily by his mother how lucky he was to have survived to adulthood. He hardly needed to be told, having seen more than enough stillbirths, or even worse, infants that were spat from the womb as true monsters, snapping and screeching from their first breath until their skulls were flattened with a hammer. That he had been born with such looks was a gift from the Gods, according to his mother, although she could not say which Gods. "He moves gracefully," she had noted proudly but incorrectly as soon as Pad could walk. "And he's quiet. He will be a hunter." And so he was given his name. Certainly his mother felt a certain relief that he was not especially deformed or disabled in some terrible way; she herself sometimes reminded him that the infants she had given birth to previously had either been pushed out of her already dead, or had breathed their last shuddering gasps of the damp air mere days after breathing their first.

Pad was dimly aware that his mother, like a few others of his people, had been born somewhere else, but on the few occasions he had asked her about that place, she had

46

grown fearful and angry. "We *never* speak of it," she always said, "because we may never return. To even attempt to do so would mean death."

For many of their people, death came hurrying regardless. *I am lucky,* Pad had dutifully reminded himself on countless occasions. Believing the mantra was more difficult than saying it, particularly as sometimes he dreamed or daydreamed of places he had never seen and would never see, whose bright colours and extreme contours made a beguiling puzzle he returned helplessly to again and again. *Either I am lucky to be alive here,* he often thought, *or I am held in a prison.*

He barely reacted at first when he saw the body lying half in and half out of the water, draped on the edge of one of the many small grassy islands nearby. Then, with a flicker of interest lightening his expression, he paddled the boat over to the still form, stepped onto the island and with one of his oars, cautiously turned the body over.

Pad took a couple of uneasy steps backwards, confused. *Not one of us,* he thought blankly.

The girl's features were smooth, and even under the mud and reeds adorning her, he could tell that her skin was relatively unblemished. Pad removed more of the marsh decoration from her face and stared helplessly at her. He had never seen anyone so beautiful, so *different,* in his life. Where had she come from? Had she fallen from the sky?

Is she dead? Pad was not sure how to tell. Cautiously he prodded her with the oar, then took several further steps back as the woman suddenly twitched, coughed, then rolled on her side. Her body gave a violent spasm and she coughed up some water. When she was done, she finally noticed Pad looming nearby.

They stared at each other for a long while. Finally Pad thought: *I must take her back. I must show her to everyone. Maybe someone will know how she got here.*

He picked up her slight frame easily enough and placed her in the boat, encountering only feeble resistance. Once the woman lay in the boat her struggles increased, but he held her firmly for a short while and she then slumped back, exhausted. Pad waited until the boat had steadied itself, and then began carefully rowing back the way he had come, a faint spark of purpose in his eyes.

How did she survive being in the water? he wondered; it was a question the survivor herself would ponder later on.

II

Even before she opened her eyes, Nia struggled not to retch at the damp and overpowering stench.

When she did finally look around her she saw three people, all of them older than the man who had found her. They each had about them a grey, dispassionate look, and were clad in rags and blankets. They stood in a semicircle and watched her. The walls of what appeared to be a half-built, roofless hut of mud and wood surrounded them. One wall had already cracked badly and started to crumble away. The ground underneath her was soft and slippery; short damp grass mingled with the underlying mud.

At first, Nia's bewilderment only deepened. How could she have swam for so long through the waters of the Bonemord and yet remained untouched by the creatures that patrolled those deeps? Who were these people- decidedly ugly, misshapen people- that loomed over her? Had they saved her? Or had she been plucked from the waters for some worse fate? She remembered reaching an islet, numb with exhaustion and ready to give up entirely, before passing out.

Although she had no compulsion to stare at the revolting visages of the three marsh people, Nia nevertheless found herself doing just that. She wondered how they had come to be here. Who would possibly choose to eke out a sorry existence in this dismal place? Nia had always thought the Bonemord to be uninhabited by people, nothing more than an abandoned watery maze of murk and monsters, shunned and never even talked about except in stories spun by songsters who had never been within a league of the place.

Were these hideous people examples of such monsters? Or were they somehow a race that had kept its own existence a secret from the outside world? Nia reflected that if a place existed where that might be achieved, then this was surely it.

One of the creatures, whose mouth was lined with giant misshapen teeth, stretched out one of its long, mostly bare legs and prodded sharply at her. Dull fury flared behind Nia's confusion. She struggled to a sitting position, wincing as pain stabbed through a dozen different parts of her body. The three commenced a conversation, turning partly away from her but glancing back frequently as if to ensure that she had not moved. *Fear not,* she thought wearily. *I'm in no condition for fighting or fleeing. And I doubt you'll find much meat on my bones if I'm destined for your cooking pot.*

To pass the time she listened to their urgent, jabbering speech. Some of their words she could understand; others remained entirely unintelligible. That all three of them suffered from various deformities of the mouth did not help. Fearful though these marsh people might be, Nia decided that anything- being pulled apart by these ogres, or thrown to the creatures in the watery murk that she had previously eluded- would be preferable to her fate in the hands of the Seven.

The conversation around her grew more animated, and as a consequence the number of words she could recognise became fewer and fewer until it seemed that the three creatures communicated only in violent gestures and harsh, guttural roars.

Nia's brief thought of the Seven led inevitably back to her discovery in that horrific chamber beneath the Sanctum, and as the memory of it rushed back she forgot her surroundings entirely for a moment, lost in the awful, numbing truth that she had stumbled upon.

Could it be that none of the Watchers except the High Ones knew *anything* of that truth? Nia found the idea that she could know something of this magnitude, something that Watchers did not, almost impossible to believe.

Then does this mean that Kelandra was herself the product of the same terrible procedure I witnessed? And not only her of course, but all the others? Luudhoq's feared army built upon a lie? People taken from their lives in the city, and then changed and shaped to become something else?

Nia's thoughts raced. What would happen if this became common knowledge amongst the Watchers? She imagined a bloody civil war within the Sanctum, spreading out and consuming even the entire citadel. And what then? Luudhoq would doubtless fall into decay and lawlessness, perhaps to a time that mirrored the era before the coming of the Watchers and the Seven many centuries ago.

Nia had no love of Watchers, but she had no wish for the order of Luudhoq to disintegrate, however brutal it might be. *If chaos ever took the south,* Kelandra had often liked to say, *then the tribal factions and crazed sorcerors we keep at bay and out of civilised lands, all these and worse will smell the mayhem and come charging from out of their miserable territories.*

One of the marsh folk reached down and lifted up her chin with a bony finger, rousing Nia suddenly from her thoughts. *Of course,* she realised dully. *None of that will happen, for the telling of the secret that would spark all this will stay with me here forever.*

The smallest of the three knelt nearby, a glint of hungry intent in his eyes. Nia recognised the nature of that look straight away and tried to wriggle away, but he grabbed her arm, pawing at her with his other hand. Somehow she managed to writhe her way free, and as he came slowly after her again, grunting, a sudden idea came to her. *A last throw of the dice,* she thought. *If this doesn't work, then I am done for. They can pull me apart and throw me to the fish, and I'll rest at long last.*

The very thought gave her strength, and she staggered to her feet, fixing them each with a cold stare. "I am a powerful sorceror," she intoned calmly, smiling to herself as at first they stared back at her with their yellow muddy eyes before they then looked at each other, rows of bent and broken teeth looming from their mouths.

Nia took a deep breath and began removing her clothing. Their laughter ceased and they watched in attentive silence. The one who had taken a liking to her drank in the sight of her nakedness with his mouth open and drool dripping from one side.

The *shifting* had always been easier with her clothes removed, and regardless of that fact the change would look far more impressive in full view. She reflected, as her undergarments fell to the muddy ground, that this had been the first time she had ever willingly revealed the *shifting* to anyone. *And it may well be the last,* she thought.

Nia stood before them, and slowly she willed the transformation to begin. As ever she stilled her body and retreated into herself, concentrating both on the very core of her being and on the movement around it, imagining and visualising the changes to her appearance. At first, for one frightening moment, she feared that she might be unable to *shift*, that her hopes would drown in the laughter of her captors.

Then the *shifting* rippled through her in earnest, and when Nia opened her eyes and lifted her head a moment later, she beheld very different expressions in the faces of the three marsh-folk.

Now for the final part of the gamble, she thought swiftly, *where all will be won or lost.* Yet even in this pivotal moment she felt nothing but a serene calmness. Perhaps that cold confidence seeped into her expression, for the marsh folk shrank back visibly as she fixed them with an icy smile. "Unless you wish for *your* forms to be changed, even pulled apart," she said, "you will take me..."- she paused, though if they even noticed then they gave no hint of having done so- "to the northern edge of this place. To the edge of the mist. The *northern edge.*"

Nia figured that north would be by far her best bet; anywhere east would be too close to Luudhoq, surely now a place where she could never set foot again- and south and west would lead her eventually to the land's edge. No settlements existed in those directions; the marshland met the ocean at the great cliffs, and that was it.

Two of the marsh folk reacted with horrified bewilderment to her demand, but the third nodded quickly. "Yes, yes. North."

"Make ready a boat," Nia told him. He bowed frantically, turned and scuttled away.

Nia bent to pick up her clothes and put them on, shivering in the damp chilly air. Her heart hammered furiously. *So close,* she thought. *So close to freedom. Keep your wits about you. Find yourself a way out of this place and then some existence elsewhere- any existence- and you can rightfully call yourself the luckiest girl alive.*

It was only then that she heard the sound of someone approaching behind her, slapping purposefully through the mud. Before she could turn around, a sharp blow struck her on the side of the head and she went reeling into unconsciousness.

III

"Why is it, do you think, that this place is called the Bonemord?"

I know the answer, Nia thought, even as she pulled herself from the black murk of slumber. *The soft ground under the waters is made from the bones of many thousands who ventured here to explore these lands, centuries ago.*

But she could not speak, and at first, even when someone or something roughly grabbed her arm and hauled her up into a sitting position, tilting her head back and forth, she could barely open her eyes.

"Eventually, someone would survive," the same voice spoke up. Nia opened her eyes and gradually took in the detail of her surroundings- the inside of a simple dwelling whose walls were fashioned from mud and wood. Stark wooden furniture stood positioned around the small, cramped room. She was lying in some sort of low-slung hammock tied between two wooden poles. The structure creaked as she sat up, her effort helped by the strong pull of the hand that had grabbed her.

The man sitting nearby was thick-set, muscular and squash-nosed, with close-set eyes that stared appraisingly at her as she struggled to maintain her sitting position. "Shapechanger," he said quietly, as if to himself, and Nia's heart sank. *They know me for what I am,* she thought. *What now? How do I bargain my way out of this place? Or am I here forever?*

The events of the last few days- or might it be tennights now?- flooded suddenly back to her with such an unbearable intensity that she leaned forward, curled up and wept. *The truth of the Watchers dies here with me,* she thought. *I should have fled Luudhoq when I had the chance. I should never even have returned.*

Her miserable remonstrations with herself reached even further back. *I should never have taken the task*

*Kelandra set me. No, I should never have even sought
employment with her. I should...*

"It could be," the man said thoughtfully, "that your
taint repelled the same creatures that have eaten countless
thousands. Certainly I know of no other possible
explanation, other than pure luck of course. Are you a lucky
woman?"

That caught Nia's attention; she sat up, and he
nodded. "They are not natural creatures, you see. Like us,
they were put here."

As Nia considered those words he added, "My name
is Barrik. I am..." He shrugged. "I am influential here."
Suddenly he laughed out loud. "So much more handsome
than the others, you see. And your name is?"

"Nia," she whispered, staring at him. In Luudhoq he
would be considered an ugly and misshapen man; but she
had seen what some of the other denizens of the Bonemord
looked like, and if they were typical then in comparison to
them he *was* handsome. "You were brought here to me as a
gift," he said with a smile. "It seems that they thought a
young woman as beautiful as you could *only* be fit for me. If I
had a heart, surely it would warm to such kindness." He
looked her up and down, and suddenly asked, "Would you be
considered beautiful where you are from?"

"I..." Nia frowned and shrugged. "Not especially. I
would be considered plain and ordinary, I think. I've never
been called pretty."

"Ordinary." Barrik gave a brief laugh. "*Ordinary.* I
would like that." He moved to a makeshift table where a
flagon of water stood, together with some weed-like plant
and fish, all of which he handed to her. "I expect you are
hungry?"

Nia glanced uncertainly at the offerings and then
remembered how long it had been since she had last eaten
properly. Tentatively she began to eat, and then, once she
found that the taste was nothing like as bad as the

appearance of the food, she ate more and more quickly until Barrik cautioned her to slow down. "It will only come back up, and food is precious here," he warned.

Once she had finished, Nia washed her meal down with some of the water and sat back in the hammock a little, trying to collect her thoughts together. As she did, Barrik managed to answer some of her questions without being asked. "The folk from the lower slopes brought you here to be my wife, I think. I expect at some point they will want some favour in return…" He flashed a toothy smile. "We're all the one and the same in most ways. I'll honour the favour they demand, whatever it might be. We all live under the leaden sky after all. We have agreements- we do not encroach upon each others' territories, and they hunt the waters whilst we hunt the land. We have the better of it, but then we're stronger, fitter than them. This is how the centuries have carved us."

Nia's gaze turned briefly to the doorway, beyond which she could see only a grassy slope with a muddy path leading to and from the doorway. A light breeze, cold and damp, rustled through the grass. "What will you do with me?" she asked, fearing the answer.

Barrik leaned forward intently. "I have no need of a wife," he said, "but I did not tell them that. I think they fear you- it took two dozen of them to bear you here- and they say that you shapechanged in front of them." He shook his head. "A bad idea. Many of them are ignorant and frightened of everything they cannot immediately understand, as well they would be. It's just as well that they brought you to me. They would otherwise argue for days about whether to worship you or kill you."

"What will you do with me?" Nia repeated.

"I will hear your story," he said simply. The stark intelligence in his eyes unnerved her. "Clearly you are not from anywhere in the Bonemord, and if you were brought here, then you were brought here for a unique reason."

"Only luck has taken me this far," Nia said.

Barrik gave a shrug of his broad shoulders. "Be that as it may, I will hear everything from you - how you came to be here, who you are, *why* you are here."

He sat back, and the wooden chair creaked alarmingly. Nia took a deep breath, and began the retelling of her tale.

Full darkness had fallen by the time Nia had finished. She had moved from the hammock to the sawdust floor; somehow it seemed more appropriate. There she had sat for hours, and the whole nightmare had poured forth. At first her natural hesitancy to relive her last few tennights had stifled her story. She remained unwilling to dwell on her escape from her cell, but from that point on, she found that the details of her journey out of the Sanctum and eventually into the Bonemord came back to her with a fearsome clarity. *It still feels like a dream from which I've just awoken,* she realised at one point as she paused and took a gulp of water. *Will it always remain that way? Will I ever be rid of it, or perhaps just forget it a little?*

Nia drew a long, ragged breath. *That's it,* she was about to say. *I swam to shore, and knew no more after that until one of your people found me.* Then, suddenly, she remembered that her retelling had included not only her description of the events in the room where the man was being tortured, but everything that his captors had said. She remembered every detail, and had described every detail as she spoke. *Powers, I've told the secret,* she thought, stealing a glance at Barrik. *Does that matter, here? Are all these marsh folk trapped in this place? They must be, or else why would they be here eking out such a miserable existence? If they could leave, then the outside world would know of them. But I had never even heard of these people and I doubt anyone else has.*

Except the Seven and their High Watchers, I don't doubt.

"Were this story any less extraordinary," Barrik said, "I would name you a liar, and there would be meat to feast upon tonight on the higher slopes."

Nia laughed weakly. "I've told many lies," she said. "I am as dishonourable a creature as you can imagine. I only wish everything that happened never had. That it *was* a dream, nothing but a dream." She grew morose again. "To wake up from all this!"

Barrik pondered the matter in silence, a frown upon his great ugly countenance. *He's like a creature-tale,* Nia thought. *The giant who lives on the hill and craves meat to feast upon.*

Eventually she felt compelled to say something, for the silence was becoming as close and dank as their environment. "Will you allow me to leave?" she dared to ask.

Barrik looked her up and down. "Have you forgotten where you are?" he asked softly.

"I..." Nia's voice trailed away. *Of course,* she reminded herself disconsolately. *If it were possible to leave, many of these people would have done so, or attempted to. But some sorcery holds this place together as if it's a world in itself. Generations upon generations of these people would have been born here, lived here, died here and sunk into the soft ground, since...*

Since when? she echoed, and she turned to Barrik. "How long have your people lived here? I mean, have *you* always lived here? Where did you come from originally?"

He regarded her with an odd, unreadable expression. Finally he said, "It seems I have a tale of my own to tell you- although by now you are clearly used to remarkable stories. The truth is that we are *brought* here, or at least, brought to the edge of the Bonemord and compelled to walk westwards into the mists and the marshlands. This has been the way for many centuries. As you can imagine, many people perish here. But the Bonemord is always replenished. Perhaps over time the authorities of Luudhoq have figured how many of their own people to pluck from the city, work their evil on, and if the crafting does not work, send into the Bonemord to be forgotten forever. Most are criminals or accused of being criminals; the people of the city will shrug their shoulders at their disappearance, if they even know of it. But that said, very few have arrived here in recent years. Perhaps the Seven have given up replenishing this place.

"I have thought about what you saw in the Sanctum, Nia. You saw two men of the Seven desperately working to create something- to create a Watcher. But that is not all they've sought to create. For many centuries they have taken people- just ordinary people- and *worked on them* down in the Sanctum."

"For what purpose?" Nia breathed, horrified.

Barrik shrugged. "To create new creatures, new beings, for their own purposes. Perhaps they succeed sometimes. But I think most of the time they must fail."

"Why?"

"Because so many are sent into the Bonemord. I am one of them." He stared directly ahead. "I cannot remember how many years ago I was brought here. I cannot remember anything of my family, or even if I had a family. Nor can I remember much of my time in the Sanctum, except in dreams."

"What did they do to you?" Nia asked.

Barrik shrugged. "Who knows? I certainly cannot recall. Yet apart from that I'm missing the mental and physical deformities that afflict most of my people. Whatever they did, I assume their sorcery failed to work as expected, and so I was brought here."

"Why did they not simply kill all the people who... could not be turned into whatever they were trying to create?"

"In honesty I don't know. Perhaps they have a way of *seeing* us somehow, and they observe over time, to see what we do, how we survive. Much of what you've seen here- boats, materials for building huts, weapons for hunting- was brought to this place over decades, perhaps centuries. Tools and devices to help their abandoned subjects build their own sorry race. Who knows how the Seven and their cohorts think?"

Powers, is that possible? Nia felt a pang of sudden alarm. *Could they perhaps see* me *somehow?*

That they might be powerful enough was certainly possible, even likely. *I had hoped beyond hope that they think me dead, ripped to shreds by the creatures of the Bonemord swamps,* Nia thought swiftly, *but what if they somehow found that I was still alive? What then? Surely they would send someone to dispose of me for good?*

"There is a reason why we cannot simply leave," Barrik said, watching her. He unbuttoned the front of his robe, and bared his chest. Nia stared at the symbol that had been burned into the skin, leaving charred-black flesh that even now had failed to heal properly.

"So they brand everyone they send here," she persisted, "but marks such as these can be hidden."

"Look closer," he said.

Nia thought for a moment that she saw something other than flesh glistening beneath that raw wound- a reddish light that moved beneath and around the area where the sign had been made. As she stared, it seemed also that the mark itself altered its shape slightly. "Sorcery," she whispered. There was nothing more to say.

The sky had darkened outside. Barrik buttoned his robe and knelt by the hearth to stoke up the remains of the fire and add more peat. "Sorcery it is," he agreed, "and it cannot be overcome. Even now there are some who think they can walk beyond the edge of the swamplands to the north of here. No one ever can."

"What happens?" Nia asked him.

"They burst into flames," Barrik said bluntly, "and they burn until they're no more than bone dust. Nothing can stop the fire until it's done, and then it dies away, and the remains of the victim blow away in the mist-wind or sink to become part of the mud. I have seen it myself."

Nia shuddered. Then, she and Barrik looked again at each other, and she knew they were thinking the exact same thing.

"I have no such mark," she breathed, and the realisation sent a sudden, soaring rush through her being. *I can escape! I can still escape!*

Then she guarded herself against hope, and glanced warily at him. "But will you let me leave?"

A long time passed before Barrik spoke. He busied himself with the fire, not that it needed any further attention, and then wandered outside into the dusk for a short while, pensive and silent. Perhaps he was looking and listening for anyone who might be nearby.

He came back in, closed and bolted the wooden door, and then he said quietly, "Yes. I will let you leave, because it is dangerous for you to be here. Eventually it would become known that you have no mark. You would be seen as an enemy, perhaps a spy for the Seven... but I ask one thing of you. Make use of your knowledge. Make use of the secrets you uncovered." He smiled mirthlessly. "Maybe one day Luudhoq will fall into its own rotten core and the spellcraft of the Seven will shatter. A mad dream, in which you come back for me, and allow me to survey the ruins for myself."

"Thank you." Nia was overwhelmed with relief and gratitude. "Thank you..."

"Wait. It's not that simple." Barrik sat down, head in hands. "First, I would need to lead you myself to the northern edge, or as close as I dare go. Second, I cannot be seen taking you there, so we must be cautious, silent, and travel in the dark of night when fewest folk are awake and about.”

“When can we go?”

“Later tonight... what is it?” he demanded, for Nia had suddenly remembered something that filled her with a great panic.

“Some of your people would have seen me naked and scarless,” she said. “They seemed not to notice at the time, but supposing they remember, supposing they...”

Barrik stared at her. “Of course,” he murmured. He lit a torch, and stepped towards the door, motioning for Nia to come with him. “We’ll go now,” he said, and they stepped out into the night.

As they walked over the rise of a grassy hill, and down towards the marsh, Nia reckoned that this night was as dark as any she had known, but as her eyes began to adjust she detected an odd, diffuse glow in the mists above them, a faint red light to her left, and a slightly brighter, whiter illumination to her right. *Archaon and Ildar,* she thought. *Even here their presence is felt, though barely.* The notion that familiar things from her own world could reach into the murk of the Bonemord, however faintly, somehow lent her determination.

They reached the water’s edge a while later, where a small rowing boat had been moored to a shrub that grew near the bank. Two oars lay inside the boat. Water lapped quietly against the sides.

Hearing noises, both Barrik and Nia glanced back. Somewhere in the distance, faint yellow lights danced. *Torches,* Nia thought. *Maybe hundreds of them.* A faint, continuous chant drifted through the mists to where they stood, sending a shiver through her.

She glanced at Barrik, whose expression she could not read. *He looks like an ogre in the torchlight,* Nia found herself thinking, and swiftly banished the observation. *An ogre who is helping you to escape this place!*

"Head directly north," he said presently, pointing into the dark, in the opposite direction to the oncoming torchbearers. "Keep going, until you..." He laughed humourlessly. "You'll eventually reach dry land. You'll know when you've left this place behind; you'll see stars above, if the night is clear." His voice grew low and soft. "I remember what stars look like. I remember that much."

"Will they harm you?" Nia asked, getting gingerly into the boat.

Barrik did not answer her question; instead, he asked one of his own. "Will you tell anyone? Of everything you've seen?"

Nia smiled at that. "Who would believe me?"

Barrik nodded as if that was exactly what he had expected her to say. Reaching down, he extended his hand and Nia shook hands with him. His hand was so much larger than hers, she felt almost like a small child. "Thank you," she said, and all of a sudden she felt tears brimming in her eyes.

Her saviour said nothing. He averted his gaze and gently pushed the boat out to get her moving, and then he turned away. After a moment Nia began to row, watching helplessly as Barrik stood statuesque next to the flickering torch. Then he began to walk back towards the oncoming torches. *To answer to his people,* Nia thought.

She rowed onwards, tears and sweat staining her cheeks as she struggled along the waterway. She willed herself to think of nothing except survival. *Do what you've always been best at,* she told herself. *Survive. Row, and keep rowing.*

Nia repeated that mantra over and over as the little boat drifted on under the cloying mists. A while passed; perhaps hours. Sometimes she stopped, utterly exhausted, her arms seizing up and her heart pounding as if it might explode. Every time she started rowing again, her arms shook more, and the time until she had to stop again would be less. *I can't do this*, she thought desperately several times, before answering herself with: *You've survived the Sanctum. Now all you have to do is row a boat. So row it, you snivelling bitch!*

At one point, something large navigating the murky water thudded against her boat, almost causing it to capsize. Nia cried out and desperately tried to regain her balance. *Not now*, she thought grimly, as the creature swam on and away from her, oblivious to the meal sitting in the boat it had struck. With the vessel steadied, she waited until she was certain that the beast had gone, and then began rowing again.

Sometime later, she saw something that anywhere else would have appeared quite ordinary, and it almost took her breath away.

Ildar's reflection danced upon the water, fragments of the bright moon rippling on the surface. Looking up, Nia saw not only its familiar face, but also well-known constellations dotting the sky.

A little further on, the waterway came to an end. Nia staggered out of the boat and stepped onto dry land. *Powers, I did it*, she thought, sinking to her knees. Elation mingled with disbelief as she stared up into the night sky again, fearing that it might suddenly disappear. *Somehow, I made it out of the Sanctum, and out of the Bonemord.*

For a moment, Nia felt a creeping, fearful sensation, as if someone or something was watching her. Swiftly she looked all around- under Ildar's light she could see well enough for a hundred paces or more across open grassland- but she saw no one. The moment of panic passed, but a nagging certainty persisted that her enemies might still know of her survival. With that certainty a dull realisation came to her.

I have to keep going, she thought. *I have to keep heading north, as swiftly and as far as I can, beyond the reaches of the Seven and the Watchers.*

And I must hope beyond hope that I never meet Kelandra and her fellow traitors.

Despite Nia's fears and her utter, trembling exhaustion, a sudden fierce elation gripped her. She curled her hands up into fists, and a cold, hard little smile played across her lips. She was not done with; she had not been defeated. Not yet.

Then, with her moon-shadow leading the way, Nia headed north across the open land.

IV – An Unfortunate Vision

The four women rode in single file through the open grassland, towards distant hills that rose gradually in the west. A bitter wind came at them from the north, bringing with it the promise of rain or sleet.

They had barely spoken for the last few days. There was much to think about but little to say. They shared the same fears. They dared to hope but not to voice those hopes. They ate, drank and rested only as much as they dared, and it seemed that every day the weather and the simple act of rising in the morning and continuing as if in determined hope became harder to bear.

Lyya spent much of the time thinking about Jaana. Where was she? Had they all managed to leave Nisstar? If so, how far were they away? Had they reached Alinnora's Haven yet, and if they had, what might the townsfolk have told them? Lyya reckoned that the bloody chaos of that morning when they escaped the *diafagh* had been etched in the minds of those people in many different ways; their memories would differ, and so would their recollections- those who relived the event in their thoughts or dreams. *They were creatures from old scare-tales come to life,* she thought, *but if the things that Fistelkarn and even Ludas said were true, then there's far worse than them to come.*

Where do you run or hide, she wondered, *when you're encumbered with children or the aged, when you have no horses, when all your neighbours who can flee have already done so? Do you make haste in some random direction, or do you hasten your own demise and that of your family?*

Lyya believed that most humans would be inclined to choose the latter.

Several times during their journey west she had almost announced her intention to turn back- it would be easy enough to follow the trail they had made- but she stopped herself from doing so, knowing full well the inevitability of one of the *diafagh*- the one meant for her, she thought darkly- finding her. It was a creature that she had no hope of killing; it was not even alive in any sense she could comprehend.

A second reason lurked not far away: Gaan, Serina's wolf.

He followed from a distance so that they rarely saw him, but Lyya felt certain that if she headed back the way they had already ridden, the creature would find a way of preventing her taking more than a few hundred paces in that forbidden direction, even on horseback.

Lyya therefore banished any hope of doubling back by herself; she was weak and hungry and often she trembled with exhaustion.

Looking ahead, she set eyes once again on Amethyst and Ileana, who rode together. *Now, if they agreed to turn back it might be a different matter,* she thought, recalling how Ileana had, for a short while at least, held the *diafagh* at bay. More recently, Amethyst had told her and Fauli how the girl had even managed to destroy others like them. *I wonder if she's like Jaana in some way,* Lyya mused. *Strong in the Old Powers.*

Just before sunset, the clouds lifted in the west and the last light of the day spread far across the windblown grass, illuminating it starkly against the thunderously dark grey clouds that massed to the north. As they reached a high point, the women saw before them a small settlement of a dozen roundstone houses huddled close on the slope. Smoke curled its way out of one of the chimneys to be carried swiftly away in the breeze. Someone knelt in a vegetable patch by the side of one of the houses, pulling up late carrots and turnips and placing them in a bucket nearby.

The women drew nearer and dismounted, leading the horses and following the narrow path as it meandered between the dwellings, and saw that the vegetable-picker was a woman of perhaps forty years. Her skirt, caked in soil, gathered more from the ground as she picked herself up with a grimace of pain and moved on along the patch; her lips moved occasionally as if she might be cursing the winter roots for their inability to pull themselves up and save her the painful effort.

"Ileana," Lyya said softly, "how far behind us do you think the *diafagh* might be?"

The girl glanced round as if they might be bearing down upon them as they spoke, then shrugged tiredly. "I can't say exactly. A day?"

Lyya turned to Fauli. "Why don't we ask this woman if we can..." But she didn't finish the sentence. The villager had got to her feet and was staring directly at them with an intensity that suggested she had somehow heard everything Lyya had said- including the mention of the *diafagh*.

Lyya took a deep breath and made her way slowly towards the villager, who stood exactly still. "Be on your way," she said quietly, as the *luyan* woman came within ten paces of her. Lyya stopped and raised a hand slowly to show that she meant no harm, but if anything the gesture had the opposite effect; the woman took two hasty steps backwards and then looked swiftly down to one side, observing her lengthening shadow on the soil as if it might move of its own accord and pull her into the soft earth.

"Please, don't be afraid," Amethyst spoke up. "We hoped that we might find shelter here tonight..."

The woman lifted up her skirts and retreated to the edge of her vegetable patch, then further still so that she stood by the wall of her dwelling, her face cast in the glow of the rapidly falling sun so that she had to shield her eyes. "I can't... can't stop you taking... whatever you need," she stammered after a moment. "I ask only that you leave me be!"

Lyya found her gaze taking in the other buildings in the hamlet. No smoke drifted from their chimneys; no sound issued from them. She could hear only the sighing of the breeze as it rippled through the grass.

"Does anyone else live here?" she asked.

"You'll take everything, no doubt," the woman told her, "for they won't be back." She laughed suddenly. "Are some of us not told at some point to follow our dreams? Well, they did. Oscar and Maeve and Jon, they left at the same time, took the twins with them, not that the twins ever had a single dream between them of the light, but what could they do, they're too young to fend for themselves, so off they've all gone. They were the last. They tried to take me too. I would have none of it."

"Into the light," Amethyst said, and shuddered. She knew what that meant, and suspected that the people from this village had headed towards Nisstar, drawn by their dreams just as Vornen had been drawn by the Gates from which that same light would pour forth.

"Into the light, yes." The village woman looked sharply at her. "But *you* people, you're headed a different way."

Fauli, who had remained silent and thoughtful throughout, spoke up. "If they're gone and they're not coming back, then we'll rest in one of these houses tonight."

"If they're lightdreamers then they'll never return here," Lyya said softly. She recalled Jaana's stories of folk who she had tried to heal- people who had been somehow touched and corrupted by the *marandaal*.

The woman had taken the opportunity to sidle around the wall to her door as they talked; she reached out to the round iron handle with a trembling hand. "Do as you wish," she said, "but leave me be. I have wards and charms against the likes of you." And so saying, she swiftly opened the door, darted inside and slammed it shut. The four companions listened to the sound of her hurriedly fastening and barring the door on the inside.

The sun slipped below the horizon, and a chill settled upon them. "Ileana," Fauli said, "if the *diafagh* came close to us, how soon would you know about it?"

"That depends how close you mean," Ileana told her. "And if I was asleep, I doubt I'd know about it any sooner than you. I expect we'd all wake up to the sound of them trying to force their way into one of these houses if you plan to stay here tonight." She stared from Fauli to Lyya and back again. "Do you truly mean to do that?"

"The light's already failing," Lyya observed reluctantly, "and we can hardly continue on through the night. I'm ready to drop. We all are." *I never thought I'd willingly spend a night enclosed by stone given a choice,* she thought, *but I'm too sore to ride any further, and I'll wager the horses are as exhausted as we are.*

They tethered and watered the horses and rested for the night in the main room of one of the houses, each taking it in turn to keep awake and as alert as possible for fear of the *diafagh* approaching.

The following day dawned bright and cool; they rode west under a clear sky. When they stopped for a quick luncheon of preserved foods taken from the house in the village, the companions looked back towards the east and were heartened to see nothing on their trail; at least, nothing they could see from this distance.

That evening they enjoyed a small piece of good fortune; the barn they came across turned out to be packed with hay and offered a passable level of comfort, and the night was warmer than of late. The following morning they rode on, and as the open land stretched ahead they saw a great forest in the distant west.

The tree line in the distance extended north to south for as far as they could see; between them and the forest stood the remains of a great stone wall. By the middle of the morning they stood at its foot. Moss and lichen grew thickly on the stones, and in some places these great building blocks had tumbled to the ground in large numbers so that on foot they might be able to scramble up and over these vast piles of rocks. Other parts of the wall stood almost intact, towering implacably above them, and in those places where the structure remained in place, archways had been tunnelled through the thickness of the wall. No way through them could be seen; choked and impregnable, they had been filled with thick knotted tendrils of bramble, vine and creepers.

They took the opportunity to dismount and stretch their legs, and soon enough their collective gaze turned to the barrier before them. "We'll never get the horses over that rubble," Lyya declared, and took a swig from her water canteen before adding, "We'll set them free, I suppose."

Ileana stepped slowly towards the shadow of the nearest archway and peered through into the cool darkness. "It could take days to hack through all that," Amethyst commented, and Ileana turned swiftly round. "No! That's the last thing we want to do. We mustn't harm it."

"Why not?" Fauli retorted, but Ileana ignored her and turned back to face the chaos of vegetation that had swarmed across the centuries to make the natural barrier. As if on a sudden impulse she reached out and grasped one of the thicker ivy vines, and the others stood in shock as a sound like a vast, subterranean groan emerged, seemingly from somewhere within the depths of the archway, as if some giant creature had been awakened.

"Ileana!" Amethyst shouted, and stepped forward, but she was too late to get anywhere near the girl; in a moment the creepers and brambles had encircled her and pulled her towards the archway entrance, easily lifting the girl off her feet and sweeping her up into the mass of greenery.

The women rushed as one towards her, longknives in their hands, but as they reached the girl, Amethyst noticed that Ileana was not even struggling; her body made no movements of its own. A cold pit opened up in Amethyst's stomach. "No," she whispered. "Ileana!"

Fauli and Lyya were both about to start hacking at the thick vegetation, and it was at that moment that Ileana suddenly spoke.

"Step back. Don't harm it." The words were uttered in a dreamlike way, almost as if she was unaware of speaking them.

Amethyst stared as thick, cruel bramble pressed against the girl's back and neck, drawing blood and tightening. *As if feasting,* she thought, and she almost cut at it there and then. Ileana could not see her, let alone tell what she was thinking, and yet she spoke up again: "Amethyst? Step back. Don't do anything to hurt it."

Amethyst watched helplessly as a thick knot of bramble slid down Ileana's cheek, and blood dripped from the cut onto the barbs, bright against the dull greenery. *It's going to kill her,* she thought. *It will crush her to death, or it will keep cutting her until she's bled dry. I can't stand by and watch this.*

But at the same time she had a strange feeling that Ileana was somehow *linked* to this monstrosity, perhaps even able to understand it at some level. The idea did not shock her; that Ileana might be able to do such things could hardly be a surprise considering what she already knew about the girl and her talents.

Finally the tendrils and thorns receded; Ileana was set back on the ground, where she sagged to her knees with a low sigh. The tangle of vegetative growth shrank back even further; the companions stared in bewilderment as it appeared to wither and eventually sink back into the wall around the archway, receding so far that it was difficult to believe a writhing monster had occupied that same space mere moments ago.

Amethyst knelt by Ileana's side and inspected her wounds; they looked shallow and should heal quickly, she judged.

"What was it?" she asked, helping the girl to her feet.

Ileana shook her head helplessly. "I don't know. But I could feel it... searching me, finding out about me. At first it thought I was..." She glanced into the ominous darkness of the archway. "We'll be safe now," she murmured. "Once we're through to the other side of the wall."

"Safe?!" Fauli exclaimed.

Ileana got unsteadily to her feet. "We'll walk through the archway and lead the horses." She stepped cautiously forward.

"As if the horses would willingly..." Lyya began, and then stopped abruptly, watching as Amethyst led hers forward and he trotted obediently alongside.

Ileana had already reached the shadow of the great arch, and passed through it as Amethyst reached the entrance. She could see the girl's slim form silhouetted against the light on the other side as she carefully led her horse on and into the gloom. For one odd moment it seemed to Amethyst that the light towards which she looked was somehow different- *greener,* she thought briefly, before putting the notion to one side. After all, the thick vegetation and light filtering down through the trees could easily combine to make it look that way.

Fauli and Lyya followed her in; a short while later they emerged into the light where Ileana waited.

"I hope we'll be welcome in Harn," Lyya spoke up as they reached a wide grassy track a short while later.

Ileana turned to look at her. "Either way," she said, "there's no going back."

Lyya looked back suddenly as if expecting their *diafagh* foes to have caught up with them. Observing the *luyan* woman's anxiety, Amethyst turned to Ileana and asked, "Might the *diafagh* also be let through?"

Ileana blinked at that and thought for a moment. "I don't know," she said finally, and Lyya glared at her before riding on, cursing to herself.

"I could have told it to only let us through, and not Lyya and Fauli," Ileana said quietly in Amethyst's ear, leaning forward a little. "But I wouldn't have felt good about doing that, and anyway I didn't think about it until now."

Amethyst nodded. She wondered if she would have let the two others through if *she* had been in Ileana's position and thought about it on the other side of the wall. She supposed she would have done- after all, no one deserved to be left to be hunted down by creatures of the Old Dark against which they had no defence. "We'll head south once we're out of this forest, and let them do what they will."

"South?" Ileana shrugged. "I suppose it's as good a direction as any except east."

"The city of Luudhoq lies in the far south," Amethyst told her, "and I fancy my chances of survival a little better within the walls of a city- even a foreign one. Let's head that way once we're out of the forest. I've had enough of fleeing through wilderness- haven't you?"

Ileana nodded tiredly.

Sometime later, the sound of an axe blade cutting through logs echoed through the forest, steady and rhythmical as if the woodcutter was a seasoned practitioner. As the women rode slowly along the track, it became obvious that they were headed towards him; a short while later they turned a corner in the track and saw ahead of them a thatched cottage set a short distance from the track. Moss grew in places on the stone walls. A thin tendril of smoke curled up into the air from the chimney. Between the trail and the cottage, a man with short, greying hair was busy cutting a pile of large logs into pieces with the aid of a vast axe. His arm muscles rippled with effort as each blow came down upon the log he was cutting.

"Good day," he said after a moment, glancing in their direction with a faint smile. Then he looked again. Amethyst reckoned he looked a little taken aback, perhaps because it was unusual to see four women travelling together. He rested on the axe, faint beads of perspiration on his brow, and regarded them each in turn. His expression was unreadable. Finally he asked, "And where are you ladies headed this morning?"

They all looked at one another. Finally Fauli spoke up. "As far west as we can." She looked as if she might be about to say more, then looked down at the ground with one of her deep scowls, perhaps wishing they had all ridden straight past rather than slowing to a halt. *And why did we stop?* Amethyst thought. For some reason she could not remember who had made the decision. Had they all somehow done so?

She tried not to let her frustration show as the woodsman glanced at each of them again. "Now there's a Hastian accent if I ever heard one. So you came through the border wall? Through one of the archways?" he enquired eventually.

"Yes," Ileana said. "There was an archway in the wall. It wasn't defended," she added, as if that might be a worthy excuse.

To their surprise, the woodsman laughed. "No," he agreed finally. "We should probably do something about that. But enough questions. You've done no harm, and I apologise if I appeared suspicious. We don't see many people pass this way, you understand. This route is not as well-used as it once was. My name is Harqan by the way. I live here with my son Jak."

"There's no need to apologise," Fauli assured him, grasping her reins a little tighter than she probably realised, "but we thank you. We ought to be on our way..."

"We have a well-kept tradition here in Fhaarluy," Harqan interrupted with an embarrassed smile. "The tradition of hospitality. I should consider it an honour if the four of you would stay for a short while. If you don't mind me saying, you all look as if you haven't eaten properly for many days. We do offer a little hospitality to travellers when we see them, in this part of the land. I venture I could also tell you the best roads to follow to get wherever you're headed."

"I really don't..." Fauli began, but Lyya said more loudly over her, "Thank you, Harqan. It's very kind of you." Throwing Fauli a cool look, she dismounted, leading her horse to be tethered to a low-hanging branch. Not knowing whether or not they were following the right course of action, Amethyst did the same, helping Ileana down. *It probably is the right decision,* she thought a moment later, as Ileana staggered and almost collapsed when her feet reached the ground.

A boy of around Ileana's age appeared at the half open doorway of the cottage as they finished tethering their horses and Harqan brought some pails of water for them. In some ways he looked like a much younger version of his father, but his hair was longer and as he wandered outside, Amethyst saw that his eyes were a clear, deep green.

"*Oh,*" she heard Ileana murmur next to her, and somehow she knew immediately the emotion conveyed in that small, quietly-uttered word. When she saw the look in the girl's eyes it served only to prove her right. *We'll be gone from here soon enough,* she thought, not without some sympathy, *and more than likely we'll never see either of them again. So it's best you don't entertain that sort of thought.*

Of course, such advice would have been pointless to offer even if she had actually made such a remark. Ileana would not pay attention to her; she might not even hear the words.

But when Harqan led them up the little path and introductions were made, she noticed that the boy's gaze lingered longest on Ileana and the look in his eyes became one almost of shock. No one else appeared to notice; certainly not Harqan, who was already cheerfully ushering Lyya and Fauli inside. *Gods, there'll be tears later,* Amethyst thought with an inward sigh. *As if she hasn't already been through enough!*

For some reason, Vornen's face swam to the surface of her thoughts, bearing the expression of a condemned man. *I hope he's at peace,* she thought as she stepped into the cottage after the others. *I hope that the end came quickly for him.*

If hospitality to passing strangers was indeed a local tradition then Harqan was undoubtedly a master practitioner. The women were plied with freshly-baked bread, roast ham and beef, cheese and even a pie of seasoned pork and winter vegetables, all washed down with watered wine and light ale. He asked very little about them, which Amethyst liked; perhaps he thought they had things to hide or perhaps not, but either way he seemed careful not to judge them accordingly. Instead, they learned more about the man and his son.

Jak's mother had died when he was only two years old, and from that point on Harqan had raised him by himself for the following twelve years. They had always lived here in the forest, but they also had a few friends in other places including one of the larger, more distant towns, a place called Mornkastle. Jak wanted to attend a Guild in Mornkastle when he was older; he had been schooled until eleven and developed a taste for learning, something about which his father was clearly proud.

Amethyst found herself feeling much more relaxed, the food and drink and the company combining to ease her worries as much as they eased her hunger. Even Fauli looked as if she was enjoying herself, to the point of sharing a joke or two with Lyya. Amethyst smiled and shook her head; in all the days she had been travelling with them, she had certainly never seen that happen before.

She sat back, uttering a quiet sigh of contentment. After all they had been through, it was about time that a little luck came their way.

Harqan closed the scullery door behind them, touched the surface gently for a moment, and then turned to his son. Every trace of good humour vanished from his face; in its place, Jak saw a hard, grim urgency.

"We will deliver them to Inerdyr," Harqan said quietly.

Jak stared open-mouthed at him and glanced at the door. Harqan shook his head. "They're under a spell, boy. They haven't even noticed that we're here and not with them. And one more thing, Jak. I've seen the eyes you've been giving that girl Ileana. She's not for you. She's a witchling, a creature of wild, dangerous magic and she..."

"I won't let any harm come to her," Jak blurted out, and bit his lip when his father's eyes widened in disbelief at that transgression. "She has something about her..." he murmured, unable to stop the words tumbling out.

"Of course there's something *about* her, you dimwit! How do you think they got through the wall without being torn to shreds or left hanging from high branches? It *let them through*, Jak. It let them through because it saw her for who she was. *What* she was. There can be no other explanation. Were you so besotted with the girl that you couldn't see the aura about her? Don't tell me you couldn't; I know you have the gift."

Jak flushed at that. "You know I saw it," he said finally. For a moment his eyes glazed over, the memory of what he had seen coming swiftly back. *I'll never forget it,* he thought. *She was like a girl fashioned from pure light.*

His father was not done yet. "We will take them to Inerdyr and that's that. If you want a girl-friend, you can find yourself one when you go to the Guild. You'll be old enough then, if you prove yourself to be a man at last."

"Don't speak to me like that," Jak hissed, and he almost cried out when Harqan seized his harm painfully. "I will speak to you as I see fit until you grow up," he told him. "You *know* there are matters of far greater importance than your own gratification. I have told you already about the *marandaal*. All the people of the Free Territories must play their part in the war to come- and there *will* be a war, sooner or later, for they will seek to destroy everything, all life. Your part in this, Jak, is to help me deliver these four women to Inerdyr, *not* to keep one of them for yourself."

His grip lessened. "This is the most important thing you have ever done, my son. Perhaps the most important thing you will ever do. For Ileana to have been allowed through the Wall, she must be a wielder of the Old Powers- the *real* Old Powers, not the minor dabblings that the likes of you and I use and shape. You already know this to be true. Now, I need your word that you will help me escort them to Inerdyr's fortress, and simply agree with anything and all things I might say to them."

"What will he do with them?" Jak wondered pensively.

"What he does is his concern, not ours. Inerdyr knows more than anyone that a great army must be raised to defend the Free Territories. He has already embarked on that task." Harqan lifted his son's chin a little. "Look at me, Jak, and give me your word."

Jak reluctantly met his gaze, and his resolve crumbled before the iron stare of his father. "I give you my word," he said quietly, and he felt as if something had broken inside him; something that could never be mended.

V – The Veins of Hatred

I

Ah, I'm still in that despicable, low place, Vornen thought as his hand emerged from his pocket with barely more than a grain of *kyush* as reward. The fragment he had found was not nearly enough; he dropped it to the floor, cursing and ground it underfoot.

I don't expect Jaana has any. I doubt she even drinks; what are the chances that she smokes the leaf of hell itself?

The guest-house was really little more than a barn, and a cold and draughty one at that. Its only other occupants were three old men who argued quietly in the opposite corner of the common-room. Their bedraggled appearance and the furtive glances they cast about marked them as refugees or escapees of some kind- but then, Vornen surmised, almost everyone would be soon if they were not already. *Soon everyone will look suspicious,* he thought, *and then I suppose no one will look suspicious anymore.* He smirked sadly at that insight.

The two of them had spent the day hurrying on from the village of Riversreach with ever greater urgency. Around mid-morning a low booming sound had come from the south-east, in the direction of Nisstar. A great tremor followed; a shiver of vast power that ran through the earth all around them. Slates had slipped from roofs; windows had shattered. Walls had cracked and buckled; dwellings built upon slopes had slipped and even crumbled away as the ground beneath them shifted.

Lastly and for a fleeting moment, the sky had grown far brighter than it ought in the vicinity of Nisstar.

"Everything we feared has come to pass," Vornen had said. He and Jaana had fled the village even as others rushed from their dwellings to gather in the main square

79

and argue about the light, the earth, the sky and the meaning of the strange things they had heard and seen.

They had encountered numerous detached and listless folk as they headed into the west; *lightdreamers,* Vornen had thought as they passed them by, and he averted his eyes, keeping one hand near his sword. But these folk were in no mood for violence. Few of them said anything at all; they were intent on a liaison with the great light of the east about which they had dreamt, and which perhaps some of them had already seen. They cared nothing for irreligious fools walking in the wrong direction; how could they when every step they took brought them closer to the Gods about whom they had dreamed?

Later, when they stopped to rest at the side of the track Vornen had wondered how the world had become so hopelessly devoid of all sense: once he had been attuned to and pulled remorselessly by Gates such as those that had now opened in Nisstar. Then he had been severed from them, for no reason he could ever hope to understand. Now he hurried away from those dark portals, and in so doing he passed by people who hurried *towards* them, their minds emptied of any notion except to head into the Great Light.

Vornen had almost laughed, but managed not to. He feared that he might not be able to stop once he started.

And so, exhausted and dirtied by the day's walk along the muddy track, they had reached Hawk's Edge, a farming and market settlement on the way to Alinnora's Haven. Vornen had a silver crown left and had used it to purchase a couple of bunks in the guesthouse for the night, but in the quiet, dark hours since then he had wondered several times if it might have been better to hire a cart and make haste as far west as possible.

I wonder what they look like, he found himself thinking. Then an altogether more troubling notion occurred to him: *How swiftly will they spread out into the land surrounding Nisstar? How many of them are there?*

Vornen felt absolutely cold suddenly; a sensation of such hopelessness washed over him that he could barely stop himself from crying out loud. The enemy could not be reasoned with; it could not be known or understood in any way. It bore no weaknesses of which anyone knew. From out of the darkness of the void, the emptiness between the stars they had emerged, and whatever the truth of their nature, it made awful sense that they might be thought of as Gods-implacable, all-conquering Gods that would crush feeble, mortal beings into dust.

Why are we even running?

He answered his own question almost at its asking, yet part of him remained unconvinced. *I'm running because I was given a second chance. I was severed from the leash I thought I'd be held in for the rest of my life. I couldn't have stayed, not then. And maybe I'll even see Amethyst again. At least, I can perhaps find out what became of her and Ileana. Gods, if I could see Amethyst again!*

On an impulse he got up and walked over to one of the windows to peer outside. The night was clear and about as bright as it could possibly be, with both moons having risen. They were fairly close together in the sky, Vornen noticed, and he wondered if they might become closer still soon, or appear to. But regardless of their movements, it was bright enough tonight for them to see the way ahead without needing lanterns, which neither of them had.

For a moment he thought that the two old men in the corner were staring directly at him, despite their continued furious muttering; yet when he turned round they had still fixed each other with baleful stares. One jabbed a finger close to the other's eyes, as if threatening to puncture them; the other bore a contemptuous snarl upon his face. Even in the dim light, Vornen observed that the man's gums were bleeding.

He had only just turned back to the window to contemplate their onward journey when the door to the common room opened and a young man dressed in travelling leathers and a robe peered in. "Coach headed towards Alinnora's Haven from here if anyone's interested? Should be bright enough even 'til dawn, says the weatherseer. No clouds to speak of."

"Yes," Vornen said on impulse, turning from the window. "We'll travel with you..."

"I've no money," Jaana added immediately. Vornen dug his hands into his pockets after finding his belt pouch empty, and found nothing of value.

The young man glanced from one of them to the other. "No need to pay," he said finally. "Have you heard the rumours coming from near Nisstar? What use will coins be soon?" When they stared at him, he shrugged and added, "Well, it's leaving in a moment or two..."

Vornen and Jaana glanced at each other and then quickly headed outside into the cool evening air, where several other people had gathered near the cart that waited at the side of the road. Packs were being checked and re-checked.

Vornen had reached the four-horse coach when he realised that Jaana had stopped more or less at the guesthouse door. Her face bore a vacant expression, so utterly detached from her surroundings that for a moment Vornen was reminded of Larien, the young man who had been utterly under the influence of the Old Dark in the form of the malign *choragh*-sword.

But that was different, he reminded himself, walking back to Jaana to see if he might rouse her from this odd, standing stupor. *This woman is much more akin to Ileana, if anything.*

"Jaana," he said quietly, aware that a few would-be travellers were already glancing their way. It would not do if these people thought she was maddened in some way. "Are you ready?"

Abruptly she looked back at him, her eyes coming back into focus. "Yes. Of course."

Vornen nodded, relieved. They boarded the coach and a short while later they were heading off along the track leading west towards Alinnora's Haven.

The night wore slowly on. Vornen decided that he did not especially like the look of the folk with whom they travelled, and so he resolved to keep himself awake. Jaana did likewise although she seemed barely aware of those around her, almost as if she had fallen asleep with her eyes open. The coach occasionally passed by small groups of people heading in the other direction; Vornen heard the driver curse and shout as a few of them wandered heedlessly into the way of the coach. By the coach's lamp light he caught a glimpse of slack expressions and dead, hopeless eyes staring momentarily at the vehicle cutting through their path; more lightdreamers, he thought, and looked away.

He noticed that one of their companions, a middle-aged woman with shoulder-length grey hair, kept glancing at Jaana; Vornen could not read her expression, but something about it made him uneasy. It seemed far too *knowing* for his liking.

Still, she's done nothing to cause alarm, he reminded himself, *and perhaps I'm reading a little too much into the way everybody looks at one another these days.*

The sky clouded over and sleet fell briefly several times during the night. They headed further into wild, partly wooded land and the track became muddy as it threaded between copses and up and down hills. Despite himself, Vornen almost nodded off; only a harsh thud as a wheel rolled over a stone that had tumbled into the road pulled him firmly back into awareness.

Abruptly the woman who had been glancing at Jaana earlier struck the roof of the carriage with her walking stick, and the vehicle rolled gradually to a halt as the coachman reined in the horses. Vornen glanced outside and saw the first light of day gradually bringing the countryside into view. *But there's nothing here,* he thought. *No village, not a single homestead, nothing. There's no need to stop here.*

"It's time," the woman said lightly, and looked around at the other passengers, who simply nodded in agreement.

"Time," Vornen found himself saying, feeling his stomach tighten as he watched them alight from the carriage one by one. "Time for what?"

But if they even heard him, they gave no indication of doing so. Then, to Vornen's bemusement, Jaana got up and followed the others out into the cool dawn air. "Jaana!" he called out, but she either ignored him or could not hear.

A cart travelling west, whose driver required no payment, Vornen thought as he too stepped out from the carriage. *Had I been less desperate to put leagues between myself and Nisstar, I would have thought it suspicious. I would have waited for the morning and then walked if I had to. Well, it's a little late for what-ifs now.*

He glanced up at the coachman, who sat slumped in his seat as if he had nodded off. His hat sat awkwardly on his head, as if it had been placed there by someone else.

"Jaana," Vornen said again, and he was about to walk over to where she stood when the woman who had called for the carriage to be stopped spoke up.

"As the lost and the witless hurry towards Nisstar, the blessed carriers of the Old Powers gather," she said quietly, "and we have one amongst us who is blessed more than most."

A murmur of assent rippled amongst the five other folk gathered shivering in the early morning light.

"It moves like a river within her," she whispered, and as those words were spoken, they all looked towards Jaana. But Jaana herself gazed elsewhere, across the distance of a field where the breeze sighed in the grass.

Vornen's hand stole to the cold pommel of his sword, but already he knew that it would be useless. *I don't know who or even what these people truly are,* he thought, *but I have some idea of their nature.*

"She will become *kin*," a young, ill-shaven man spoke up. "The next step must be taken."

Beech trees in a nearby copse sighed and groaned in the breeze, which had strengthened in a heartbeat.

"I will never be like you," Jaana said softly, and abruptly she turned to face them. Vornen saw a faint smile upon her face. "So you know me for what I am? I knew *you* for what you were as soon as I cast eyes upon you. I could sense the filth in your veins. But I travelled willingly with you. My face was turned away and yet I studied you all- low, fawning creatures that you are with nothing to call your own, no power except that which your *lords* bestow upon you. You call yourselves *kin*, but without the common enemy you would squabble and fight like scavengers."

Each one of them stared hatefully at her. The woman gripped her walking stick as if by doing so she might rein her fury in; by the poor light Vornen fancied that it turned from wood to something iron-like, and then stone. One of the men muttered something over and again under his breath, swift words that might or might not hold meaning. His hair had about it a wet, reddish sheen as if blood flowed outwards from its roots.

"We could destroy you for uttering such words," the woman said.

"They're only words," Jaana told her. "Are you frightened by them?" And her smile broadened, as if she had inadvertently stumbled upon some truth that emboldened her further.

None of them replied. The time for talk was evidently done, for now the *kin* spread out slowly to form a loose circle, their collective gaze fixed hotly and unblinkingly upon Jaana. The breeze became a wild wind, buffeting them in one direction and another, and yet the air grew inexplicably warmer. *This is their doing,* Vornen told himself, although he could not be sure if this stirring of the elements had been brought to bear by the *kin* or by Jaana, or simply by the very fact of their facing one another.

Jaana remained perfectly still as they moved slowly around her like carrion wary of their feast. To Vornen they looked cautious, pensive, waiting for an opportune moment to strike, but fearful of being wounded or even slain. *There are six of them,* he thought, *and yet they behave as if there they were one and she six.*

But then, as the wind dropped for a moment, they indeed behaved as one; they went for her in a flurry of knives and sticks and hands.

Jaana merely crouched down suddenly, brought up her hands, and bloody chaos ensued. The spokeswoman of the *kin* fell backwards; Vornen stared in astonishment as she sank into the muddy track a little way, as if it had given way under her. A snapping sound issued forth as if something within the dark earth under the road had reached out and into this woman or whatever she was, to shatter her bones. Vornen stumbled backwards as a scream of utter agony emerged from her mouth.

All of this he observed in an instant, yet other horrors were acted out at the same time, the remaining *kin* their victims. One of Jaana's foes fell forwards and somehow *shattered* on impact with the soft ground; fragments of arms and legs spread across half a dozen paces. Three of the others collapsed to the ground face down, and their skulls were crushed by an invisible weight.

Vornen watched numbly as the last surviving member of the cabal was dragged backwards, not by some unseen force but by the wires of the fence that ran alongside the track; wires that had somehow found their way loose and ensnared him. He howled in rage as they dragged him back until his spine hit a fencepost with a resounding crack. The *kin*-man's head jerked back, then forwards. Vornen thought he heard his neck snap, and yet a moment later his eyes flickered open and he spoke, still intent only on Jaana.

"So," he said, grimacing. "You saw me. You noticed me."

"Amongst your subordinates you stand out like a beacon," Jaana said. "Of course I noticed you."

"Why are we fighting each other?" he asked. "We're the same, you and I. We channel the same forces. And although you may deny it, sooner or later we answer to the same lords. These gifts are not free, Jaana."

"You know my name," she said, and Vornen felt a stab of fear through his heart; she sounded tired, resigned, even defeated, despite having slain five of the other *kin* and wrapped this one in wire that even now dug deep into his flesh. *Is it because he knows her name? Or has she simply nothing more to give?*

"We share a common enemy," the *kin*-man continued, gasping as the wire snaked across his body in a dozen different places, drawing further blood. "Our lords will reward you for your loyalty, for the way you have learned to channel your innate powers..."

"And would they reward me for slaying five of the *kin*?"

He smiled. "Call it a test of strength. They were nothing; you already know that. There will always be others like them; it's a loss of no consequence. They would never be allowed to destroy you even if they could." Suddenly he nodded to Vornen as if having remembered that he was still a witness to this swift and brutal exchange. "Now, here stands one who has stood against them before. There's still a *residue* about this man. Ah, the two of you, do you not think you would be welcome? You are natural enemies of the great destroying light, as are we..."

Somehow, Vornen found his voice. "I'm nothing of the sort. I had the bad luck of being bound to a *choragh* sword. If anything, it wielded itself. It almost destroyed me." He paused, the memory of Suli fleeing with that blade coming sharply back, as fresh and painful as if it had happened yesterday.

Neither of them appeared to have listened to him. Jaana stared at her enemy as if considering something, then spoke up suddenly. "Tell me your name. Then we will listen to what you have to say."

"No." Vornen could barely speak; the air felt thick and warm, as if it might suffocate him if he drew enough of it. "Jaana... you can't... no..."

"Be quiet," she said, and it seemed that the air became thicker still; the space between them shimmered wildly. It was as much as he could do to remain standing.

"Zaal," the *kin*-man said warily, after what felt like an eternity. "But my name in itself holds no power. Why would it?"

"I was simply curious," Jaana replied, and the wires dug deeper still, working their way slowly through flesh and tissue, tearing vital organs, compromising the man's entire body. He howled like a beast. Vornen could not look away from the methodical torture to which Jaana was subjecting him.

Finally, Vornen managed to speak. "Kill him and be done with it!" he shouted, glancing at her to see if she might heed his words.

But she would not, or perhaps could not. The wires continued on their dark and painful journey; they whipped and tore and burrowed until finally Zaal looked more or less a huddle of destroyed flesh and snapped bones, lacking definable shape, shuddering and still wide-eyed with agony, for Jaana had not yet harmed his eyes.

That moment came too, as Vornen knew it would. The last sound the trapped creature made, as his eyes burst softly and their remnants cascaded down what had been his cheeks, was a low, defeated sigh; it might even have been the wind that had started up again, or the fence of which he was now a part, sagging under the unusual weight it bore.

Vornen stared at the devastation and then looked away, his gut crawling with nausea. "Was all this necessary?" he said finally. "What sense does any long drawn-out death have?"

"They would have done the same," Jaana retorted, but she too no longer looked at the man she had slowly and systematically pulled apart. *Is she shocked?* Vornen wondered. *Has the fearful, withdrawn girl I met in Nisstar now returned?*

He could not say, and regardless of the matter Jaana suddenly sank to her knees, exhausted. Vornen swiftly walked over to catch her and hold her up as she sagged forwards.

She enjoyed it, he thought blackly as they walked on up the road, Jaana barely conscious and leaning on him as he propped her up. *Without a doubt, she took pleasure from that terrible power she wields. I saw the smile upon her face, as she took Zaal apart.*

II

Long before they reached the village of Alinnora's Haven days later, Vornen and Jaana saw further evidence that followers of the *choragh* had started to appear in greater numbers. Near one small settlement, they watched furtively from the shelter of a nearby copse as an argument between folk who planned to head towards the light and others who were convinced that the Earth Lords had appeared to them in their dreams swiftly descended into a brutal slaying. The *choragh*-worshippers prevailed- just- and the remains of the lightdreamers were burned together on a fierce pyre. The flames roared and leapt into the leaden sky and persisted even as the heavens opened and a deluge ensued; those who had slaughtered their neighbours on the basis of their new-found beliefs chanted and celebrated. One man removed his shirt and bellowed his devotion to the *choragh*, arms outstretched as he lifted his head heavenwards.

"Madness," Vornen said quietly, turning to glance at Jaana. She said nothing at all, and he could not read her expression. Finally she turned and walked quietly on, and after a moment he followed.

They avoided contact with all other travellers wherever possible, heading some way off the track if they saw anyone in the distance walking or riding towards them. Small groups of people headed south-east towards Nisstar; some of them looked as if they were families or groups of friends, and others had perhaps banded together simply for mutual protection. Watching them, Vornen wondered to himself whether or not anyone's direction of travel truly mattered anymore. Those whose minds had become twisted and corrupted by the dreams of the *marandaal* were condemned; that much was beyond doubt. But in his darker moments Vornen wondered if he and Jaana could ever escape their enemies. The *kin* would find Jaana sooner or later; that too was a certainty. Her talents made her a lodestone for them, in much the same way as Ileana.

Other consequences of the Gates opening in Nisstar became apparent. Hardly a day went by without the earth being shaken by one or more violent tremors. Walls and buildings tumbled; in a few places they saw entire settlements that had succumbed to that violence and even a couple of great schisms running through the land itself.

When eventually they reached Alinnora's Haven, the place looked untouched by any earthquakes, but Vornen needed only to take a cursory look around to see that all was not well here. A number of houses looked as if they had been abandoned in a great hurry, their doors left open and creaking in the breeze.

Jaana nodded to herself. "*Diafagh* were here," she murmured. "Stronger than most. Different, somehow."

Vornen felt his stomach tighten with fear. What had become of Amethyst and Ileana?

Blood stained the threshold of the tavern in the middle of the village. When they looked inside they saw only four men, sitting together at a table and talking in low, urgent murmurs.

"We're looking for some people who were here," Vornen spoke up as they noticed the two newcomers standing in the doorway. "Two women- well, a woman and a young girl."

"And two others," Jaana added. "A *luyan* woman, and a *du-luyan*. Were they here?"

Vornen did not like the look that passed between the four men. *They were here, without doubt,* he thought, *but something happened.*

"What occurred here?" he asked quietly.

One of the men, a stout fellow with side-whiskers and thick-set arms, looked them up and down warily; Vornen watched as his hand stole down to the dagger in his belt. "We aren't looking for trouble," he added, "and we'd be grateful if you didn't provide us with any. Turn and leave if you've any decency."

"Your friends brought trouble enough," another of the men spoke up. His eyes narrowed warily. "Yes, the four of them were here, and they fled." He pointed to the doorway. "There where you're standing, that's where Serina died. Killed by one of the... *things* that they brought back here."

Vornen understood none of this, but it seemed that Jaana had at least some inkling of events. "Lyya and Fauli were sent to Rockmire," she said by way of explanation, "to reason with Serina, to ask her to leave the Rising to its war and return here to await us."

"Us?"

"Myself, Fistelkarn and Tyrameer. Our other companions." Jaana seemed about to say something else, but stopped.

Vornen nodded. "So they arrived here, and..." He addressed the man who had spoken once again. "The two I mentioned, did they meet with those three?"

"I was here that morning," another of the men spoke up. "I saw them talking together, the five of them, out there in the yard. And a short while later..." He shook his head as if he still not quite believe what he had seen. "Those creatures appeared. One of them must have killed Serina. The four women escaped on horseback."

"Someone must have sent the *diafagh* after them," Jaana spoke up. "Perhaps someone who was angered by Serina's departure."

"Which direction did they head in?" Vornen asked.

"West. North-by-west. They took three horses. The younger girl rode with one of the women." The villager shrugged, and then fixed them both with a cold stare. "I suggest you leave as well."

Jaana and Vornen came across a food store across the street. The door stood ajar, and one of the windows had been broken; when they looked inside it became obvious that the place had been partly ransacked already. Some food remained, however, and they took some cured meats, cheeses and dried fruits that would keep for a while without spoiling.

Vornen stared around the deserted village square. A face appeared in the window of one of the cottages across the way; curtains were hastily drawn. "I'm heading after them," he said. "Are you coming?"

"Of course." Jaana smiled wanly. "What else would I do? But remember: the *kin* will come for me again."

"They will be hunting Ileana as well," Vornen said. His gaze wandered as far as the stable adjacent to the tavern. "We'll need to catch up with them, if we can. Are you able to ride?"

"I can just about stay on a horse." Jaana followed him across to the stable. A short while later they set off, the breeze at their backs.

III

Vornen and Jaana picked up their companions' trail soon enough; three sets of hoof prints visible here and there wherever the path was muddy. They found footprints as well. Jaana slowed her horse to a standstill, dismounted and knelt down near a set of these prints, then stared intently at them for a moment. To Vornen it looked as if she was breathing in some odour he could not detect rather than observing the indentations themselves. "*Diafagh*," she said finally. "But they'll never catch up with them." She paused and then added, "Maybe *we* will, though. And if we find the *diafagh*..."

"I've seen Ileana turn them to dust," Vornen told her. "They crumbled away. Can you do the same?"

"I can." Jaana smiled grimly as she struggled back onto her horse.

Yes, I don't doubt it, Vornen thought as he watched her. *She's even stronger than Ileana, I suspect- not that I can make comparisons about such matters.*

When they sheltered that evening in an outhouse set into the corner of a field, Jaana said suddenly, "There's a reason why they burned the lightdreamers, you know."

Vornen thought back to the scene they had watched unfold before their arrival in Alinnora's Haven and then glanced across at his companion, suddenly uneasy. "Everyone has an excuse for the things they do," he said finally. "Gods know I've made enough of my own."

"Those whose minds have been poisoned by the *marandaal* are as good as dead already," Jaana reasoned. "I

93

remember trying to heal some of those who had been touched by them. The *marandaal* were able to affect people in Aona long before their arrival. How is that?"

"One of the mysteries of the Existence," Vornen said with a shrug.

"I wasted my youth trying to heal people," Jaana told him. "There's another mystery."

"I'm sure you did some good, Jaana. You can't expect to win every battle. Sometimes you have to admit defeat."

"Any good I did has long been washed away now," Jaana said quietly. "Many folk have become nothing more than empty shells, their heads filled with visions of the *marandaal*. They're drawn to Nisstar or anywhere else where their *Gods* will appear. Others are stirred into defending Aona, if that's possible. And then there are those who run or hide. Running and hiding are pointless. They'll be found, or trampled underfoot soon enough."

If only I had some damned kyush, Vornen thought sourly. *I could do with leaving this world for a little while.*

"The *kin,* in their own way, seek only to defend Aona," Jaana continued. "It's true that we draw from the same well. I loathe them of course, but I understand them."

Vornen thought it best to say nothing in response. *How do you understand people who turn against their neighbours and burn them alive?* he thought as he turned away, listening to the steady rhythm of the rain for want of better distraction.

He did not recall falling asleep, but woke suddenly a while later. Sitting up, he noticed that the outhouse door had been opened and the cold night wind swirled into the building, sending hay and dirt around.

Jaana stood framed in the doorway, staring out into a night that had brightened. The light of both moons shone down. Vornen saw that she had discarded her clothing, and the memory of his meeting with Larien on the way to Ruan-Tor came hurrying back.

Does she not feel the cold? he wondered. But as he sat and stared at her, watching the soft moonlight fall on her body, Vornen found himself thinking not of Jaana at all but of Amethyst, imagining that she stood there in the doorway. *I'd be standing there with her in a moment,* he thought, *and I'd make the most of the chance I thought I'd never have.*

If she'd have me at all, that is.

Jaana squatted low on the ground and began to mutter something to herself; Vornen watched her, fearing what she might do or what might happen to her next. But after a short while she simply rose and walked back inside. He averted his eyes but could not bring himself to close them. *I can't trust her,* he reminded himself. *She's a creature of the Old Powers. She may be like Ileana in that sense, but there's a darkness to this woman.*

Jaana glanced in his direction as she dressed but said nothing to him. Then she lay down with her head resting on a bale of hay, and soon she was snoring gently.

Vornen lay awake, wondering if in time Ileana would become like Jaana- embittered, restless, nothing more than a vessel from which powers poured. Perhaps it happened to them all, however many of them there might be. Or perhaps some dealt with their situation better than others. Vornen suspected that Jaana had been unhappy for much of her life. *Maybe her powers draw on the hate she feels, and her hate draws on the powers in return,* he thought.

The idea somehow made a mad kind of sense. It kept him awake and uneasy for the rest of the night.

Three days later, they drew to a halt during the afternoon with the Border Wall before them. Vornen was surprised at its mostly ruinous state; he had heard only a little about the structure and had never been anywhere near it before, but had always heard of it as being an impregnable barrier between the two lands. In reality it looked as if nature had been allowed to reclaim it; in places the wall had become nothing more than a vast heap of rubble, and even where it remained intact, the tunnels that had been dug through it lay thick and choked with centuries of growth.

Jaana stared intently at the ruins and entangled vegetation surrounding the wall. Vornen glanced at her, could read nothing into her expression, and waited patiently for her to speak or stir. The wind sighed constantly in the trees and rippled across the long grass; shadows of clouds chased each other across the landscape.

There it is, Jaana thought.

She had sensed a presence that lurked somewhere beyond the remains of the great wall, a shadow that moved soundlessly and without trace through the depths of the forest.

Jaana could almost see it; certainly she could sense every one of its seemingly random movements- she even knew which direction it moved in each time. Yet she could discern nothing about its nature. If it was simply a shadow, then a shadow of what? If on the other hand it was some effect caused by a sentient being, then where did its allegiance lie, if it had any? She could not sense the taint of the *choragh,* but perhaps that taint had been masked somehow.

Then, inexplicably, it shifted as if turning itself inside out, and where that shade had been light now shone, powerful and bright as if many shards of sunlight poured into the same spot of ground at the same time.

Abruptly the entire scene vanished from her mind's eye. Jaana blinked and took a deep breath, unable to explain or even describe what she had just sensed. She glanced suddenly at Vornen. He wore that carefully neutral expression that he seemed to have permanently adopted. Jaana knew that the man was wary of her, although in truth he had little reason to be; unless he thought her likely to slit his throat as he slept she presented little danger to him. He was not *kin,* despite Zaal's insinuation that he had something to do with the *choragh* and their ways. Neither was he a lightdreamer; in fact he was nothing but another fugitive as far as she could tell- someone a little like her, caught between one madness and the other. That much they had in common, but that was all.

After a moment she rode slowly nearer, to the great tunnel in the wall, into which the hoof prints they had been following led. Vornen followed half a dozen paces or so behind. "How could they have come this way?" he asked her. "The trail leads into thick creepers and branches. There's no way through."

Jaana studied the faint prints for a while longer, then looked further back, where more of them could be seen, clustered together. "They waited there for a while," she said, "and then they went through. They were granted passage."

Vornen said nothing.

Jaana looked towards the thick, seemingly impenetrable vegetation that all but filled the tunnel, and in that same instant she felt a sudden ripple across her arms and down her body. *Yes,* she thought, noticing the faintest of movements somewhere deep within the morass of vines and creepers within the tunnel. *Somehow they were allowed through.*

"The wall probably lies in ruins for many dozens of leagues in both directions," she pointed out. "But something has been created in its place to defend Harn." She turned to Vornen. "Did you not say that this girl Ileana is strong in the Powers?"

"I did." Vornen frowned. "Do you think that she was somehow able to break through these defences and lead them through?"

"Not break through," Jaana said. "I'm not sure what *could* break through. But I think it *let* them through, and that she may have had something to do with it."

Vornen thought for a moment. "Can you do the same?"

Jaana shrugged. "I don't know. But we can't head back, can we? Our friends found a way through, as far as we can tell- and behind us only bloodshed, insanity, the *kin* and the *marandaal* wait." She dismounted and walked slowly to the tunnel entrance. Like knotted rope brought by an unseen hand, a single creeper slid slowly in her direction, and Jaana glanced at it. "Whatever now happens," she called back over her shoulder, "*do not* attack it."

"And if it looks like it might kill you otherwise?" he returned.

"So be it," Jaana said, and reached forth her left arm; like a snake the creeper whipped forwards and wrapped itself around the proffered limb. Jaana gritted her teeth, almost crying out at the savage pain. Finally it ebbed, but other tendrils had moved to entwine themselves around her other arm, her legs and her waist. *It could crush me in an instant,* she thought, barely daring to breathe.

The peculiar sensation of being asked questions in some unknown, ancient language came to her; she did not consciously answer them, but somehow she felt certain that this vast guardian found the answers it required regardless. And as that happened, the strands began to move back, appearing to melt or shrivel back into the surrounding rock. *It knows what I am,* she thought.

Vornen turned on a sudden impulse, drawn from the mesmerising sight of the vegetation fading, and saw immediately that the eastern horizon had changed. Figures on horseback approached, perhaps a thousand paces away still but drawing near quickly.

"The *kin* return in greater numbers," Jaana said without turning round to look, "and predictable as ever." Relinquished by the limbs that had held her, she walked back and began to lead her horse towards and through into the tunnel. "Can they follow us through?" Vornen asked, following in her wake.

"I don't think so." Jaana sounded far from certain.

They passed through the great tunnel, and behind them the vegetation gradually inched back into place, filling up the passageway once again. At the same time, the drumming of hooves and a great shouting became audible. *Perhaps they intend to cut and hack their way through,* Vornen thought at first, but then remembered the nature of their foes. *No. They'll have other means, or at least attempt them.*

By the time the vines and creepers had stopped moving back into place no creature larger than a rat could have made its way through. *But perhaps, like Jaana, the* kin *will be granted entrance,* Vornen thought. He suspected that this vast, primordial guardian of Harn's east-facing edge cared nothing for the bitterness between the *choragh*-followers and those who opposed them.

He prepared to spur his horse on along the wide track that led west from the wall's ruins, but Jaana had turned hers to face the tunnel, a look of intent on her face that he recalled seeing before. "I saw perhaps two dozen of them," he said sharply. "If they can pass through, you have no hope of destroying them all."

Jaana threw him a vaguely contemptuous smile. "You think so little of me, Vornen."

"Not at all," he said. "I have seen what you're capable of. But we all have limits."

He prepared to flee the scene, but he heard the *kin* drawing to a halt well short of the wall. Even so they had ridden near enough for one of them to shout out to Jaana, "Do you think a mere wall can stand before the might of the Powers, girl?"

Vornen opened his mouth to advise Jaana to turn and ride with him rather than engage the creature in conversation, but she spoke before he could. "Come through then," she challenged, but they either could not or would not be drawn any nearer. Vornen heard them talking quietly amongst themselves, though they remained too distant for the words to be clear.

"Brothers and sisters of ours roam the hinterlands of Harn also," someone else- a female- spoke up. "Our Lords are once again in the ascendancy. Soon enough all the Races of the world must come to us. The fate of Aona itself is at stake, Jaana. You can turn and ignore us now, but the truth will dawn on you soon enough. There are two sides, and two sides only. *Us,* and the *marandaal.* Already they have poisoned the minds of many thousands. You have seen the *lightdreamers* as they are called, possessed and stumbling towards oblivion. But all other beings of sound mind and reasoned thought know within themselves that the *marandaal* must be defeated at all costs."

Jaana said nothing. Vornen glanced across at her, dreading the possibility that she was not only listening to their words but considering the merits of their argument.

"You would be powerful amongst us," another voice chimed in. Vornen realised with shock that it had the voice of the child, and wondered if it also bore the shape of one. "Certainly you would be granted a legion of your own. Our Lords think highly of you."

"So much so that they sought to destroy me," Jaana retorted.

"You know your value," the *kin*-child continued. "Ponder the matter further, Jaana, and you will know one thing to be true- that our Lords desire only for you to join the cause. And therefore, we would not be permitted to kill you even if we wanted to. You have already passed a test we made for you."

Abruptly Jaana turned and began riding away. Vornen swiftly followed, trying to ignore the new sounds drifting over the wall to them- sounds that, inexplicably, included a wailing and weeping. That cacophony of affected despair sent a cold shiver through him; he could barely keep himself from spurring his horse onwards at a gallop along the track.

Vornen soon caught up with Jaana, who had slowed her horse to a trot. She looked troubled when he glanced across at her. "I thought about turning round and heading back through the wall," she said, keeping her gaze fixed on the way ahead.

"To confront them? How do you know you'd be strong enough to..."

"No. To join them. To observe and listen... and to try to understand them."

Vornen shook his head at that. *Another little madness from her,* he thought. Aloud he said, "I don't think they can be understood."

"And what do you know about such things?"

Ignoring the jibe, he continued, "You'd never have seen your friends again."

"That's the reason why I rode this way instead. I've made my decision, Vornen, so let's forget about it."

They continued for a long while in silence until eventually they came to a cottage set a little way from the track. Vornen saw that not only did the tracks stop here, but three horses could be seen looking out over the stall doors in a small stable adjacent to the building. Perhaps someone had arrived and left in a hurry, for the stable's outer doors hung open, creaking faintly in the breeze.

"They stopped here. Those are probably their horses," Jaana pointed out. "And look there." She pointed to another set of hoof prints accompanied by marks made in the ground by the wheels of a cart. "They continued on by cart. Or someone did, at any rate. Perhaps they're still in the cottage."

Vornen and Jaana peered through as many windows as they could and found no sign of anyone inside the dwelling. In one room they saw the remains of a meal with six places at the table, which looked as if it had been left there for a number of days. Finally they returned to where they had tethered their horses. "We'll follow the tracks as far as we can," Jaana spoke up. Vornen nodded, but at the same time he found the entire scene puzzling, even disquieting. Presumably whoever lived here had offered the women a ride to somewhere, but why would he or she have done so? Their accents would have marked them out as being from outside Harn. Surely anyone who lived this side of the Border Wall would have been immediately suspicious. And the women had horses already- why not simply offer them refreshments for their onward journey if they were truly so generous, and then allow them to continue on their way?

Vornen sighed. He couldn't decide whether he was being over-suspicious or not. Perhaps he was. After all, Amethyst was more than capable of looking after herself, and he was certain that she would have also ensured that Ileana came to no harm. Not only that but from Jaana's description of her friends they were just as resourceful. All four of them would have been watchful, careful.

Despite this, he could not help the continual sense of unease he felt, as they headed west into the afternoon.

VI – The Past Severed

I

The rain came down, relentless; with each passing moment Kian felt as if it washed away a little more of her remaining resolve.

She raised her head and looked across at Iyoth, who glared out of their makeshift shelter as if daring the weather to worsen further. She had bandaged his wounds as well as she could, using strips of healing bark as well as the rudimentary bandages he had in his pack. The gashes on his arms and the wicked slash across his chest would heal well enough in time; the *du-luyan* people healed more quickly and more completely than most other races. Some faint scars would remain, but they would be barely noticeable and a small price to pay.

He had turned away when she applied cleansing balm to the wound on his chest, grimacing. But Kian reckoned that it hadn't been the pain that caused him to look away. She suspected nothing more than simple pride; the pride and humiliation of a warrior who found himself being tended to by a barely-grown girl.

"What are you looking at?" he said roughly, without taking his eyes off the downpour.

Kian blinked; how could he have known she was even looking in his direction? "I was just checking to see none of your wounds had opened up and started bleeding again," she said after a moment.

"If they had, I would tell you and then you could tend to your helpless patient again," Iyoth retorted.

Kian said nothing, but his words took her back to the events yesterday that had led to Iyoth being wounded. As they approached the collapsed part of the Border Wall, the vegetation had moved almost as one towards them, and

Iyoth had reacted as Kian had feared he might, hacking furiously at each and every tendril and branch that came their way. Only when Kian had rushed towards the tangle of chaos and touched it- and more importantly, *willed* it away from Iyoth, had it stopped slashing and cutting into him. Kian suspected he had had only moments left to live; another few and he would have been cut to pieces.

The creepers, tendrils and branches had faded back into the surrounding greenery, and eventually the two of them had made their way through the half-broken remnants of the Wall with painful slowness, Iyoth's blood staining the ground.

Now there's another reason for him to detest me, Kian thought with a sigh. *I saved his life. That must be a complete humiliation for a man like him.*

She had grown used to Iyoth's idiosyncrasies during their journey together all the way from Knarlswood and into Harn, and for a while she had warmed to him. He in turn had softened his attitude as they made their way towards Harn following their discovery that Cai, the *du-luyan* ancestral home, had been abandoned by their people and, worse, occupied in their absence by creatures of the *choragh-kin.* For a while she thought that perhaps they had become friends; certainly she felt affinity towards him although as often as not she wondered why.

But ever since their encounter with the entity that guarded the Border Wall he had turned coldly angry, no doubt in part because he had had to rely on her. She had saved him from being cut to pieces. She had tended his wounds. She had looked after him, and he could bear none of it.

Suddenly she felt enraged by the entire situation. "You and your stupid pride," she fumed. "I seem to remember that *you* saved *my* life when we first met. That wild-cat, do you remember?"

"I remember," he said quietly.

"And so now we're even," she continued. "What do you find so unbearable about that? We were getting along fine. Now that you've had to rely on a mere woman, you can no longer live with yourself. Have you not told me several times that I need to grow up? Look at your own reflection the next time we stop for water anywhere!"

"We will never be even, Kian." If anything he uttered those words even more quietly.

"Will we not? True, you're stronger than me, you're a master bladesman, a slitter of throats in the night. I don't suppose we ever will be even, given your idea of what that word means. But you would not be sitting here now with that sullen look had I not saved you. I take no pride in that fact, Iyoth. I'm simply reminding you."

He said nothing at all in response, but simply sat with his head bowed and turned slightly away. She wondered for a while if he had fallen asleep. Perhaps he did for a while, but in any event he spoke up eventually, and his words took her aback.

"We need to go our separate ways, Kian."

She put down the knife she had been using to cut rudimentary figures from a fallen branch, and stared at him in disbelief. "Is that your way of dealing with this? Do you truly find my company that unbearable?"

He turned to look at her, but it seemed to Kian that he could not look into her eyes for more than a moment. "I don't want us to go our separate ways," she said finally. "I thought we..."

"You will," he interrupted. "You *will* want us to. Do something for me, Kian. I have something to tell you. I need you to listen without interrupting until I've finished. After that, I will leave. I should have done this a long time ago in truth. Regardless, do you agree?"

She nodded, dumbfounded. He was making little sense- *but what can I do?* she thought, feeling a sudden desperation without quite knowing why. *What can I do if he's determined to go? I don't know this land at all. What will become of me?*

Kian almost blurted these fears and questions out, but managed to remain silent. *You've no choice in the matter,* she told herself. *Whatever happens, happens. If he leaves me here, so be it. I'll find a way to survive.*

She could not bring herself to say anything. *I have to stop this madness,* she thought, but she could not.

"Twenty-two years ago, my wife and I were running from a group of people we had displeased," Iyoth began slowly. "A bitter disagreement. They intended to kill us. The problem was that we had with us a babe-in-arms. We were too young and foolish to look after an infant, but the fact remains."

Kian felt a sudden prickle of unease, but she waited for Iyoth to continue.

"We ran into the Mirk, and heedlessly on along the paths that run through the swamp," Iyoth continued. As Kian's eyes widened in shock- she had already realised where this dreadful tale was headed- he raised a hand. "You listen," he said, "until I'm done. You say nothing."

Kian could not have said anything even had she wanted to. *This is just some ridiculous tale he's made up,* she told herself desperately. *It has to be. This can't be true. It can't!*

"She fell. She drowned," he said abruptly. "I saved you, somehow. I ran on. I don't recall the detail; the entire time felt as if it could have been a dream. And then I came to Shimlock's threshold, weak and desperate, for our enemies had pursued us even into the Mirk."

Kian's eyes brimmed with tears. "You," she whispered. "You're my *father.*"

Iyoth said nothing; he did not even seem to notice that she had interrupted his story.

"You gave me away," she said then. "You gave me away so that you could make good your escape."

"He took you in," Iyoth said quietly. "But his condition was that I never return for you."

Kian was not listening. "You gave away your own daughter," she whispered.

Iyoth stood up, picked up his pack and slung it over his shoulder. Kian did not look at him but she could see the movement from the corner of her eye. "If I could take back..." he began.

"You can't," she said, and then added bitterly, "I suppose I should be glad that you at least threw me into Shimlock's arms to ease your escape, rather than the swamp."

He unbuckled one of his longknives and two of his daggers and placed them on the ground next to her. "You may have need of these," he said. "Now you at least know why we must go our separate ways. I wish everything could have been different, Kian."

"Go," she told him.

He turned and walked out from under the canopy of their shelter, into the rain. And, perhaps like his younger self twenty-two years ago, he left her in a moment, without a backward glance.

II

As dusk fell the rain eased off. Kian noticed neither the improved weather nor the gathering gloom. She hugged herself, head bowed, and swiftly descended into an agonised grief which enveloped her for the entire night. Her heart felt crushed; she drew breath after pained breath, all manner of thoughts rushing through her mind. *Why did he tell me? Why did he have to tell me? He could have kept it a secret. Instead he destroyed everything.*

As the long night drew towards dawn, Kian considered despondently that some higher power must be unravelling her life for some malevolent reason. What, after all, were the chances of her happening to meet her father again after all those years? Somehow it had happened, and now he had abandoned her twice.

Birds began their early morning chorus as the sky lightened and the stars slowly faded out. Kian sat and watched as eventually the sun rose and the forest became bathed in bright light. Exhausted by lack of sleep and the torment of her thoughts, she nevertheless forced herself to think about the practicalities of her situation. Iyoth had left her weapons, and she had food and water; she could probably forage for food in the forest, she reckoned.

And what then? she asked herself. *What will become of me? Will I remain a wanderer for the rest of my days, travelling from place to place? If I tried to settle anywhere, would I be accepted? I don't even know if any* du-luyan *people live amongst humans in Harn. I suppose we must have communities of our own somewhere; I should probably try to find them.*

She took a path that led gradually downwards, eventually leading her down the side of a valley through which a river ran far below. Moss-encrusted boulders, the remains of a stone wall built and broken perhaps centuries ago surrounded her, and sparse winter trees pressed close. As she pressed on and the path led her down as far as the river, much of the morning sunlight disappeared. The woodland had a dank smell to it here. Kian tried to recall its name: *Fhaarluy,* she thought Iyoth had called it.

As she rested by the river and refilled her water flask, Kian wondered for one mad moment if she ought to find his trail and try to follow it, and catch up with him, if that was possible. A moment later she cursed out loud, shaking her head at the stupidity of that idea; why should she go trotting after him like a lost dog, when he had willingly abandoned her not once but twice? He cared nothing for her; why should she even be thinking about him? He might even have disguised his trail deliberately to stop her from following. Kian resolved not to find out one way or the other.

"If you're going to survive, you'll have to be strong and depend on no one's skills but your own," she chastised herself. She took a swig of the icy water she had collected, grimacing as it hurt her teeth, before getting to her feet and continuing wearily on along the path as it followed the river.

During the morning, Kian thought she saw and heard a number of odd things, all of which she put down to tiredness. At one point a shaft of sunlight illuminated the river so brightly that a patch of the water looked like a swarm of insects fashioned from pure light, dancing on the water. Kian thought it seemed far brighter than it ought, and she stopped and stared at the phenomenon for a while before it abruptly faded. A little later, she thought she heard music; a lilting tune played by a handpipe or similar instrument. But when she stopped and looked around in an attempt to find the musician, the sound quickly faded away. As midday approached, she caught a glimpse of what looked like an especially bright part of the forest floor off to her left, where the sunlight that cascaded to the ground had a golden-green appearance. She imagined that it shifted from one spot to another as she stopped and gazed at it, but when she looked again a moment later, the light was neither stronger nor dimmer than it ought to have been, nor did it move any more than it ought.

You need to sleep, Kian told herself, negotiating a part of the path that had crumbled half away allowing inroads for the river water. *Find somewhere off the path, as well-hidden as you can tonight, and rest.*

And forget about your father.

She saw nothing else during the day that made her question her sanity, but she could not do as she had instructed herself; she could not forget about Iyoth. She pictured him in her mind, standing at Shimlock's misty threshold, begging the sorceror to take her off his hands while throwing backward glances into the covered gloom of the Mirk, desperate to be rid of his tiny burden.

And what about my mother? Kian wondered time and again, as the afternoon drifted on. *What was she like? Maybe I should have asked him. Was she a killer-for-hire as well, a mercenary without morals? I suppose I'll never know. And it doesn't matter now anyway.*

Eventually the river disappeared into a gorge that was too narrow and dangerous to enter; sighing, Kian made the arduous ascent up the slope of the valley to higher ground, crushing the remains of old bracken and carefully negotiating her way around thick bramble.

Something made her stop suddenly after a while.

Kian stood still, barely daring to breathe. *I'm not alone,* she thought. *Others lurk somewhere near here. They haven't seen me, but they're close.*

The late afternoon sunlight slanted across the vegetation. Everything around her appeared peaceful, except that it was *too* quiet. Kian could not make out the sounds of any animals; even the sound of the river had faded away now that she had left its route for the time being.

No birdsong, she thought. *Nothing.*

She looked up into the high reaches of the trees and saw no movement, heard no gentle rustling of the leaves.

Dead calm.

She almost took a step forward, but stopped herself, feeling certain that the sound of her continued progress would be like a cataclysm in this suffocating silence. At that moment, she heard voices from some way off, perhaps a hundred paces away, raised in anger. Kian finally dared to step through the bracken and onto a mossy path that could be negotiated more quietly. It led north and south; the voices had come from the north.

Something drew her towards those enraged sounds; nothing she could define or describe. *I know them,* she thought. *I know what they are, even if I don't know who they are.*

Kin.

That realisation very nearly stopped her in her tracks, but although she felt a cold wash of fear ripple over her, Kian could not stop walking towards them. Their sounds and their stilling effect on the surrounding forest fascinated her. Their very nature pulled her towards them.

She saw the *kin* soon enough as she came to a rise in the ground and looked down into a hollow covered in leaves and fallen branches, where two men sat cross-legged upon the ground, still engaged in their argument.

But, as Kian already knew before she squatted quietly behind an oak tree, they were no longer men, and their argument was in a language she could not understand. They sat with their sides to her, and she could see the dreadful transformations wrought by the sorcery that shaped all the *kin*. They appeared to have no skin on their faces; the exposed flesh had a leathery toughness as if it had been baked in the sun. Neither did they possess teeth as far as she could tell, although they stretched their mouths wide as if to compensate for that fact, or perhaps to intimidate each other. Both of them were naked and filthy; their feet looked more like bony, angular claws, and their bones jutted out at strange angles as if they had been hastily arranged and skin pulled taut over.

Harn is no safer than Aphenhast, Kian thought despairingly. *They are everywhere- the* kin *and their masters. They're emerging into the world again.*

An image came to her; she pictured a vast army of such abominations, marching swiftly under a dark and thunderous sky, victorious against the *marandaal,* bloated and ecstatic with power and ready to shape all Aona in their image, for all time. She had no idea if it came from her dreams of long-ago events or simply her own imagination, but it felt so real, so utterly tangible that for a moment she could barely stop herself from crying out.

I must destroy them, Kian thought, knowing in that moment that she could. These two were higher *kin,* but barely. Whatever humanity they might once have had flickered more dimly than ever. She could crush them, send them screaming into the earth perhaps. Her blood pulsed madly as if in agreement.

Somehow she stopped herself rushing heedlessly at the *kin.* To make herself known to these two would surely be madness. What if she could not quite overcome them? Or what if she killed one of them and the other escaped and alerted others of its kind to her presence? They would hunt without remorse; she would be pursued relentlessly through the forest by as many as it took to overcome her.

One of the *kin*-men rose to his feet and shambled off somewhere; he picked something up from behind a tree and hauled it back. Kian's heart leapt and she almost cried out when she saw that it was Iyoth; he had been tied securely by the ankles and wrists.

Powers, no! she thought, staring helplessly as her father was pulled along and then pushed to the ground. He had been beaten; there were cuts to his face and she could see the wetness of blood in his hair.

Now I have no choice, she thought. *I have to kill them both.*

She told herself to be calm, to be strong. Then, with a knot of fury unravelling in her heart, Kian stepped towards the *kin.*

III

For a moment, as she strode towards the two creatures and they turned to face her, Kian wondered how it was that they had neither seen her nor even sensed her presence. Had their argument distracted them so much?

112

Iyoth did not move or even speak; perhaps he could not. Kian glanced at him and then steeled herself, concentrating only on the two snapping, wide-eyed beasts that lumbered towards her. *Kill them both,* she reminded herself. *Neither of them can be allowed to escape.*

Something indescribable pulsed through her like a mad wave that coursed back and forth. Kian saw things that looked like black flames flickering at the edges of her vision, and for a moment her sight narrowed as if she was looking through a spyglass. The nearest of the *kin*-men snarled at her and suddenly ran headlong in her direction; Kian stared at him and directed the darkness that rippled through her towards his legs; they snapped backwards, and the creature fell into the mass of leaves and branches that covered the ground. The other threw a glance at its fallen comrade as it roared out its pain and writhed in the dirt before lying still, every bone in its body snapping.

Some sudden recognition flared in the beast's eyes, as if only now had its dim intellect allowed it to see her for what she was.

The Old Ways are mine, Kian thought. *They are not yours, you shambling vileness. You're only a vessel for the powers of your corrupt masters.*

For a moment longer it observed her with its red-rimmed eyes, and then it took cautious backward steps, moaning softly to itself. A breeze had developed; Kian had no idea if it had anything to do with their struggle, but it grew wilder, causing the leaves to swirl all around.

Suddenly it seemed that every fallen leaf from all around had attached itself to her, and Kian felt a sudden stab of fear; this could not be her doing. What was happening?

A fallen branch came hurtling towards her, striking her on the head. Another struck her on the back of her legs and she stumbled. She pulled a mass of leaves and mulch from her face just in time to see the remaining *kin*-man rushing towards her.

For the briefest moment, Kian fumbled for one of her belt-knives, but at the same time a voice that might or might not have been hers seemed to whisper to her: *Let it come to you. Believe in your powers. You can destroy it. Leave your knives for more ordinary foes.*

It loomed before her, snapping and fetid, and as it reached to tear her throat out, Kian suddenly struck out at it with her fist.

The *kin*-creature did not fly backwards with the force of the blow as she had imagined it might. Instead her fist smashed a hole through its chest, impaling the beast as if it her arm had been a spear. A look of utter shock leapt in its lurid, blood-tinged eyes, yet still it made futile, weakening attempts to wound her. Finally its arms fell limp at its sides, but in that moment Kian also knew with sudden horror that the ruination of this creature was not complete.

Something pulsed and trembled within the *kin*-beast's body; something that she had only a tenuous grip upon. Kian thought at first that it might be a heart, but it was not; it moved one way and then another as she tried to tighten her hold upon the mysterious entity. She was reminded suddenly of the primordial *kin* that had slowly claimed Mirkwall, in particular the blood-worms. The *peremar,* she thought, and as the name came to her she almost withdrew her arm.

No, she told herself. *They all have to die; the host and the parasites.*

Closing her eyes, she slowly strangled and crushed the life out of the *peremar* that lurked within the broken body.

Finally, with the cavity still and the grisly task complete, Kian pushed the *kin*-man backwards. Brushing away the remaining leaves that had stuck her, she sat for a moment, suddenly nauseous as she stared at her gore-stained arm.

She went over to Iyoth after a moment and helped him up. He was barely conscious, but motioned vaguely towards the bodies. "Coins," he whispered, so faintly that she could barely hear him. Kian helped him down and knelt by the bodies of the *kin,* finding a number of silver coins and a few objects which had the shape and markings of currency but which were fashioned and carved from wood.

Somehow Iyoth managed to place one foot ahead of the other, leaning on her as they left. He said nothing, and Kian was keen not to waste any of her remaining energy on talking in any case. She found a path that led roughly south-west, in the same direction as the river, and after a while she found the river itself once again.

When it became too dark to continue further, she helped him to sit down against the trunk of a tree and sat nearby, exhausted.

"There will be others," Iyoth said quietly. "We need to keep walking."

"It's too dark by now even for us, and you know it," Kian retorted, "You're in no fit state for walking in daylight, never mind at night." She walked the half dozen paces down to the river's edge and scrubbed the dried gore stains from her arm and shirt sleeve, managing to get the worst of them off before filling her water flask from a little further upstream and then making her way back up to where Iyoth sat. "I suppose you'll leave me again in the morning anyway," she remarked.

He maintained a stony silence, staring into the distance, or as much of the distance as could be seen in the gloom. "Perhaps before you leave you could wake me up and thank me for saving your wretched life *again!*" Kian snapped suddenly, and struck him hard across the cheek.

Iyoth recoiled in astonishment, his hand moving half way up to his face before he grimaced in pain and gave up. "Is that all you think I deserve?" he asked.

"Hardly." Kian uncurled her fist with an effort. "You can't even look at me. Why can't you at least do that?"

He said nothing, but eventually he did turn to look at her, reluctantly.

"I need to know what happens now," Kian said. She could barely keep herself from hitting him again. Despite her weakness she trembled with rage. "Am I going to wake tomorrow to find you gone?"

"I suggest you don't sleep tonight," he said, avoiding the question. Then, perhaps seeing further anger flaring in her eyes, he added, "I'm in no fit state, Kian, as you pointed out. I need to recover. I need to heal. May I have some water?"

Wordlessly she passed him the flask; he took a long draught from it and handed it back, wiped his lips and remarked, "For what it's worth, if I had the choice whether or not to leave, I would make it your choice."

"Because it's too difficult for you a third time?"

"Because *you* deserve to make the choice. The time when I might have made amends for the past has long gone. It's up to you, Kian." He sighed and bowed his head; perhaps the simple act of speaking had exhausted him further.

Kian lapsed into silence herself, as she rummaged in her pack for any remaining rations that they could eat. Iyoth's pack and weapons had been taken already when she happened upon him with his captors; perhaps they were still somewhere near where she had killed the *kin*-men, but going back there now- or ever- would be senseless. Kian suspected that despite everything she had done, sooner or later some minion of the *choragh* would stumble across the scene. Perhaps it would make a judgement about what had happened there, perhaps not; either way its masters would learn of it soon enough.

We'll head out of the forest in the morning, she thought, *if he can make it.*

Kian frowned, perturbed that she had somehow already made her decision. *You deserve the choice*, Iyoth had said to her. Well, she had made it without really thinking it through.

She found some dried fruit, biscuits and salt pork wrapped up in her pack and divided it up between the two of them. *Do you hate him, or do you only hate the deeds he's done?* she asked herself, handing Iyoth some of the food and looking sidelong at him. *There's a difference. I seem to remember talking with Shimlock about something like this. One of my lessons, perhaps. Might he even have been talking about this moment? Could he have somehow known that one day I would meet my father again?*

What am I supposed to do? I hate what he did, but how can I hate him? How can I willingly leave him or ask him to leave me, after all that's happened?

Iyoth glanced across at her, chewing slowly. He took a sip of water and then sat back, uttering a gasp of pain.

"Do you truly want to make up for the past?" she asked him once he had made himself as comfortable as he could.

"If it were possible."

"It *is* possible. If you stay. Did you really think you could resolve anything by running away?"

This time he looked into her eyes without any reluctance, and it was Kian who looked away first. "Promise me you'll stay," she said, blinking as tears prickled her eyes.

"I promise," he said.

Iyoth fell into a light slumber; Kian watched him for a while, and wondered to herself if she could possibly remain awake for a whole second night. Perhaps she would wake her father sometime before dawn, and sleep a little. The thought of sleep pulled strongly at her, and she banished it with an effort, concentrating instead on the sounds around her.

When she heard the first note of morning birdsong, Kian leaned across and gently woke Iyoth. "Can you stay awake for a while? Until sunrise?" she asked him. It took so much effort for her to speak.

He nodded. "Give me one of the longknives. They'll do little against more of those creatures, but anyone else..."

"Wake me if you hear anyone or anything approaching," Kian murmured, and lay back on the ground. She was asleep in moments.

Iyoth woke her as the first shards of sunlight burst across the treetops. He looked troubled, and had already begun to prepare their packs. "What do you hear?" she whispered, sitting up.

"I don't hear anything," he said, "but I saw something- something slow and dark- on the other side of the river, to the south. It might have been a forest creature, but I think not."

Kian took in the view of the tangled vegetation beyond the river gorge; although paths ran through the area, still it lay thick with bramble and briar. The lie of the land in the east was such that the sunlight had not yet reached it, and this part of the forest appeared full of deep shadows and hidden malevolence. She watched in silence for a while and finally nodded to herself. Something *did* lurk there, but it could not conceal itself from her entirely. It lay still, pressed against the ground, a concentration of darkness that otherwise she could not describe.

"I agree," she said. "We'll head north-west and hopefully be out of the forest come nightfall. Fhaarluy can't be that large, can it?"

"Mordenglen to the north is larger, I believe," Iyoth said, getting carefully to his feet. "Do you think the creatures that overcame me have spread outside the forests?"

"Only in small numbers," Kian said, slinging her pack over her shoulder as they set off. She could not be at all sure of that, but her instinct had served her well before. The *kin* clung to areas where the Old Powers were strongest, she thought, and these seemed to be the further-flung corners of the land.

Whatever entity occupied the area to the south, Kian sensed that it remained where it was; at least, certainly it did not draw closer to them. She wondered why at first, and the answer came to her when they stopped a little later for water and a brief rest: it could not cross or touch running water. Some rule of existence forbade it, or made the act impossible.

They walked on, encountering nothing in the natural quiet of the forest as morning came and went. By late afternoon's light they stopped and surveyed open land; they had reached Fhaarluy's edge. Kian reckoned that further on and further in, towards the Harn of human men and women, an entirely different set of dangers awaited them.

As they stood side by side in contemplation, Iyoth turned to face her. She was shocked to see a look of utter anguish upon his face. On a sudden impulse she hugged him fiercely. "Forgive me," he whispered in her ear as he returned the embrace.

"I forgive you," Kian told him. The words tumbled carelessly from her mouth, but a moment later she realised that she had indeed forgiven him. What else was she to do? The burden of keeping and nurturing past injustice was too great for her to bear; the distant past could not be changed.

A promise had been made, and the past forgiven. The two *du-luyan* walked on, under the darkening sky.

VII – The Dividing Waters

I

Anlerran slept. The dreams that came to her were little more than a rush of chaos, disparate parts of her life that juxtaposed themselves briefly before melting away to become other things, some of them achingly beautiful, most of them horrific.

Through all of this confusion, something followed her; a part of her own being that she had long denied and even now tried to deny, even though she had always known it existed. It was her connection to the forest, to its complex energy and its secrets, most of which she had barely glimpsed. It had remained out of reach, a faint shadow or light or movement at the periphery of her vision; only once had it truly touched her, that day in the clearing. But now it had reached to become as one with her, and she would never be the same again.

She woke suddenly, remnants of the dream still milling around in her head. *How can I be what Ruhal claims?* she asked herself, but an answering whisper came from the swiftly fading memories of her dream: *Sooner or later you would have had to face this day, and face the certainty of your heritage.*

And how am I supposed to do that? she asked herself. *I still don't know why I was taken from my real parents, if Ruhal's story holds any truth at all.*

Anlerran sat up and looked around. Ruhal sat on the ground a short distance away, moving his pebble from one hand to the other and back again, a deep frown upon his face. He glanced across at her but said nothing.

She noticed the horse quietly grazing on rich meadow grass on her other side, and blinked in astonishment. "Yes, you slept through the ride," Ruhal said quietly. "It wasn't

120

easy holding you up with one hand and keeping the reins in the other- and if I woke you up you'd fall asleep straight away..."

"I don't remember any of it," she said. "I don't even remember waking before now."

Ruhal shrugged. "We've made good time regardless." He pointed to the thick woodland in the south-east, perhaps no more than several hundred paces away. "There's Fhaarluy. We'll meet my friends there and then head on towards Anrith."

"Anrith." Anlerran thought that perhaps she had heard that name before. Had her parents once mentioned it in passing?

"Most people say it's a cursed place," Ruhal said. "But I don't believe that. People can be cursed; places cannot."

"Why are we going there?"

Ruhal sighed and put the stone back in his pocket. "You'll see soon enough."

They rode slowly along a broad grassy track between the great beeches and horse chestnuts of the forest. Shards of light, filtered from far above, came gently to earth, catching motes of dust in the air. Patches of sunlight danced upon the forest floor, and the air felt cool and still. Small animals scurried about in the undergrowth or in the trees. After a while Ruhal took another, narrower trail that led gently downwards before finally opening out near a wooden hut.

"Well, they're already here," Ruhal commented, sounding surprised. Anlerran saw a woman and two men waiting near the hut, their horses nearby; they had already seen the two of them, but she could not see their expressions or gauge their reactions yet. *Somehow I doubt they knew about me,* she thought.

Ruhal dismounted and helped her down, and they walked on. "This is Anlerran," he said to them, and introduced them in turn with a gesture: "Lura... Sarros... and Jahar."

Lura was dressed untidily in well-worn leathers, carried a battered-looking sword in her belt, and an equally battered-looking pack on her back. She was perhaps about Anlerran's height but curvaceous and strong-looking. Blonde hair streaked with some sort of red dye fell to well below her shoulders. Her green eyes surmised Anlerran; then she turned to Ruhal. "She's a little young for you, don't you think?"

Ruhal scowled. "She is *not* my lover, Lura! I'll explain in good time."

Lura stared thoughtfully at Anlerran, and shook her head. "You said nothing about bringing anyone else, Ruhal. I hope she can be trusted, or our heads will roll."

"If it's any consolation," Anlerran said, "I am not here willingly. My parents- although Ruhal says they were not my parents- were murdered. We had to flee Mordenglen..."

"Enough, Anlerran. There'll be time for that later." Ruhal's scowl deepened. "Are we all ready?"

"How is one *ever* ready to meet with Watchers?" Sarros remarked with a smile.

Anlerran glanced at him again; he looked about as unremarkable as anyone possibly could in her estimation. His hair, mousy-brown and unkempt, hung almost down to his shoulders. His bedraggled clothes looked as if they had been dragged the length of Harn and back again.

After a moment she suddenly realised what Sarros had said. "*Watchers?*"

Jahar smiled sardonically. "I suspect there's another thing Ruhal will explain in good time."

Anlerran glanced at him and looked away quickly. "Jahar is a man of few words," Sarros commented with a smile, noticing her reaction. "And little cheer."

Jahar, meanwhile, merely stared at her for a long period of time, as if surmising every strength and weakness she had and storing his findings for later use. Anlerran swallowed and looked away from him, unsettled by that steady, knowing gaze. Jahar had about him a hard, unforgiving look; his short greying hair and thin, drawn countenance somehow completed his stony, forbidding appearance. *Powers, for how long must I travel with these people?* she wondered. *And Watchers?! Why would they even think of meeting Watchers?*

She had heard her fair share of stories about such creatures; dark and fearful tales that spoke of horrific deeds carried out in the name of their eternal masters the Seven in the Black Citadel, that place which the people of the south called Luudhoq. The nature of their work was known for certain amongst everyone in the Free Territories; Anlerran was aware of this despite having lived almost her entire life within the confines of Mordenglen, wrapped up in her secluded world.

A place I thought safe, she thought bitterly, but then came a rejoining thought: *Did you? Did you really think you would always be safe from the outside world and the evil that it harbours? A part of you always knew a day such as this would eventually come. You would have to face the vileness out in the wider land as surely as you have to face your own reflection.*

As if to contradict his supposedly taciturn nature, Jahar ceased his scrutiny of Anlerran and turned to Ruhal. "You have found an interesting companion," he said, and Anlerran's stomach almost turned as he added, "She's not all that she appears to be, and yet she can be much more."

"Later," was all Ruhal said, and they made ready to ride. Anlerran maintained her worried silence, plagued by fears and by questions that demanded answers.

Around mid-afternoon, Ruhal, who was leading the way south of the forest along the overgrown track to Anrith, called a halt. As everyone drew their horses to a standstill, he turned, looking troubled. "We are being watched," he said. The breeze, which had become cold despite the brightness of the day, ruffled his hair. He stared back along the track and then towards the thicket of shrubs and small, close trees to their left. Anlerran followed his gaze, but she could neither see nor hear anything amiss. The wind sighed through the open grassland and in the nearby trees and undergrowth.

"By what?" Lura asked him eventually.

Ruhal's fingers tapped restlessly on the pommel of his greatsword. "I don't know yet."

They waited and watched. The sun fled behind a bank of cloud to the south, and in its absence the breeze felt colder than ever. Then, even before anything appeared, Anlerran felt her skin crawl as if something rippled over her, a revolting sensation that caused her to cry out. Her fingers felt almost as if they were on fire, swollen with hot blood, yet they looked no different. Something stirred inside her, like a live creature that rippled around her innards.

A figure that at first appeared human dragged itself from out of the cover to their left. Obtusely, the sun reappeared and light shone upon the dust-streaked, brown-clad man- *not a man!* a voice shrieked in Anlerran's mind as he stumbled and dragged his way towards them. Something like grass moved in his hair. A multitude of small entities writhed under the skin of his hands- somehow she could see them and *feel* their movement even from the three dozen or so paces between them. His eyes seeped a thick yellow liquid that congealed on his sallow, straw-coloured cheeks.

"*Diafagh!*" she heard Jahar exclaim.

As if in response, the man-creature dropped to all fours and scampered towards them; as it did, its mouth became larger and larger, the transformation accompanied by the snapping of jaw bones, until it occupied more than half of the dreadful face. The stench of rotting carcasses left out to bake and seep in the sun came across to them in the breeze.

Anlerran felt revulsion coursing through her body; it crept over her like a dark fog. She felt no fear, only abhorrence. Somehow she knew that this creature mocked the very earth it walked on simply by existing.

Swords will be of little use against it, she realised, not knowing how she could know such a thing.

But I can destroy it.

The thought shocked her, but the next moment it was followed by another, calmer realisation: *You knew that this would happen one day. The Old Powers are rising, for light and dark, and foulness like this will come your way. You cannot escape it; you can only ruin it.*

She dismounted swiftly, and stared at the being, aware only of the almost physical sense of horror crawling over her as if she had been bathed in some foul smelling oil. But she felt the hot blood coursing through her veins, could feel the potential surging through her body.

The creature slowed, drew to a halt and stared directly at her, mouth widening further, ruined yellow eyes blinking slowly. It reached out a hand in her direction, then swiftly withdrew it as something invisible in the air had burned it. The jaw cracked and changed shape again. Teeth snapped and others slowly took their place, rotting yellow fangs between which a fat black tongue darted as if tasting the air.

Anlerran tried to focus her revulsion and fury on the creature, fervently wishing that she could destroy this monstrosity, and that the very earth could swallow it up away from her sight and senses. Yet a part of her- that part which still scoffed at the possibility of her shaping the elements or having any power over anything- remained in shock that she had even stalled its advance.

It knows me, Anlerran thought dully, even as a

tremor commenced in her body. She could feel her blood racing, pounding. The perimeter of her vision had become mired in a dark haze. The wind in the nearby trees sounded a deep sigh of worry. The grass fluttered, making momentary, complex shapes that only she could see. The blue sky had deepened. Time itself had, to her mind, slowed almost to a halt. She breathed in, and then out; that single breath could have taken an eternity.

She glanced slowly around at her companions; their eyes were upon her. Dimly she saw the shock in their eyes, and wondered briefly what it was they saw- a forest girl foolishly standing against a nightmare out of a scare-tale, or something else entirely.

Words came to her; words that she barely understood. *You sought us out in the Rhunin, to make an end of us,* she found herself thinking. *In your dozens and in your hundreds, you came hurtling like black shards through the snow, to destroy us and turn the world into a nightmare without end. You sought me out, determined that I should not exist, that the lineage be broken for all time.*

Anlerran became dimly aware that she had not simply thought those words; she had spoken them. Voices rose in question from around her, but all she could hear were her own words- faintly, as if carried by the breeze from distant fields.

In her mind's eye she could now see the disparate fragments that held this *diafagh* together, a patchwork of filth and mad sorcery. Clasping her hands together, she squeezed them tightly, and picturing the very essence from which this being had been fashioned, she applied *pressure* to it, using her cold hatred and fury at its very existence to drive down an anvil upon her adversary.

Being born of sorcery, it immediately recognised what she attempted, and once again it lurched forward towards Anlerran and her companions. But something was wrong with the creature. The knees snapped; the head cracked open like an egg and something dark and seething poured from it. A keening cacophony issued from the creature's outsized mouth as some unseen heaviness bore down upon it.

Still it crawled nearer, dragging itself along and driven by desperation. All the time, its pit eyes remained fixed on Anlerran. It would reach her, or it would be destroyed in trying. Anlerran could see nothing now but the *diafagh,* the remainder of her vision darkened and swollen with hot blood. Nearer still it came, until a mere half-dozen paces separated them. Anlerran staggered as she attempted to crush what vile spark remained; then she dropped to her knees.

The last she saw, before a red darkness took her, was its final effort to stand. The creature shook until blurred, and finally it fell as fine black ash upon the ground. Anlerran, tasting hot salt and iron, felt all her strength depart as she lost awareness.

She woke into that deep and mysterious hour just before first light. A cool, damp cloth had been placed on her forehead. Nearby, a figure stirred and placed a water canteen against her lips. "Drink," Lura murmured.

Anlerran drank thirstily, realising soon enough by the sweet taste and the swift reawakening of her senses that this was not water but some kind of healing elixir. She sat up, groaning as her joints protested. Some yards away, the men sat around a campfire. They were talking quietly about something but she could not hear them well enough to know what it was. Lura gazed at her for a while and then said bluntly, "Questions will need to be asked."

Anlerran could not help but laugh at that. "Questions! Believe me, I have more of those than you; I'm sure of it."

Lura's look became more sympathetic. "Of course." Then she added, "Ruhal has told us about you. About who you are, and *what* you are. None of us could quite believe it at first."

"That's exactly how I feel," Anlerran said ruefully. "Maybe I just don't want to believe it."

"Maybe you don't have a choice."

A faint memory which was not her own came briefly to Anlerran's mind, like a fragment of a long-forgotten dream suddenly brought into focus. "I remember them coming for me before," she said slowly. "But I don't see how I could have remembered. I would have been an infant. They pursued us through the Rhunin." She shook her head. "A dream, perhaps."

They went and sat nearer to the fire; the men each glanced her way but kept their thoughts to themselves. Anlerran decided that she'd rather not know what they were thinking.

The five of them sat in silence and waited for first light. Once the sky had lightened and the promise of a golden dawn grew in the east, they breakfasted and rode on.

During the morning Anlerran eventually found herself talking with Jahar, though the subject of that conversation was the last thing she wanted to have to deal with.

"You held it," he remarked without any preamble. "In fact, you as good as crushed the creature."

"I don't know what I did," Anlerran retorted.

"Oh, you *do*," Jahar persisted, eyes like chips of grey ice as he stared across at her. "Given the correct training, I'm sure you could hold back a small army of them."

"Enough, Jahar," Ruhal spoke up. "Are you goading her into flying before she can jump? Or are you volunteering yourself as the girl's mentor?"

"Someone will have to teach her to control her powers," Jahar said with a shrug, "or she'll burn herself to a cinder from the inside out. And that would make you a rather poor guardian of this girl, wouldn't it?"

Anlerran shuddered at those words and said nothing.

"Jahar has a certain talent with the Old Powers," Ruhal explained, "and I'll trust no other warlock with you. If he's willing, then let him teach you what he can about controlling your talents."

"I've never quite mastered the holding back of *diafagh*," Jahar added dryly, "but"- he tapped his forehead and fixed her with another grim stare- "I know what I can take of the Powers and what I cannot take. That's how I've survived to this weather-beaten old age, Anlerran. Not through pure strength, but through knowing what to take and what to leave. Not that I could ever tap the resources that *you* seem to be able to."

"You'll find me a difficult student," Anlerran told him. "Only a few days ago I had no inkling of *any* of this. Then suddenly I was hunted, my family had been murdered, and Ruhal came to take me away from everything I knew. I don't even know why I should trust any of you. If the warden of any town in the Free Territories knew of your meeting with Watchers, there'd be armies coming for you. You'd all be arrested as traitors."

"There are greater enemies than Watchers ranged against us, Anlerran," Ruhal said roughly. "Far greater."

"The key to control is understanding your weakness, not your strength," Jahar added, continuing with his own train of thought. "Not knowing what you are capable of, but knowing what you can *never* do. What you should *never* attempt." He gave her a chilly smile. "Consider that your first lesson."

As the sun climbed to its zenith they rode into the cool expanse of a small wooded area; Anlerran wondered if they were fearful of being seen or followed, not only by creatures such as that *diafagh* but more familiar beings- those, perhaps, who worked for the lawmakers and wardens of the Free Territories. Listening to the conversation of her companions, she realised that they might indeed be anxious of discovery.

"I would not be surprised," Sarros commented, "if the Watchers had a spy somewhere, and know the extent of our progress already."

"I'd be more concerned about one of Allik's men or even a tracker in Inerdyr's employ," Lura declared quietly, but Anlerran could see that Sarros's words had unnerved her.

Ruhal simply muttered something quietly to himself.

Anlerran wisely maintained her silence, but her sense of deep unease only grew as they rode slowly on. She had absolutely no hope of escape. She had no horse of her own and this place was entirely unfamiliar to her. *And even if I had my own horse and was able to somehow put some distance between them,* she thought, *these people are vastly more skilled than me in almost every area I can think of. They would catch me quickly and punish me- and what else might they be tempted to do? If only they were* diafagh *or whatever those creatures are called!*

They're traitors, she reminded herself, staring steadfastly at Ruhal's back. *They've turned against Free Harn for some reason I can't even fathom. Why would they meet with Watchers? Have they arranged some nefarious deal?*

Anlerran had had little contact with the world outside Mordenglen, but her parents- *I will still call them my parents,* she thought fiercely- had told her the stories they knew of Watchers, the elite militia of Luudhoq, the Dark Citadel. None of them ended well, she recalled; invariably these were grim and cautionary tales of kidnappings, torture and mutilation.

She remembered something Emelle had told her one warm late summer evening years ago. Her words had been an exercise in reassurance, for Anlerran, thirteen summers at the time and a bundle of curiosity and imagination, had half-feared that the judicial shadow of the Watchers could

reach into the Free Territories. *They commit terrible deeds,
it's true,* Emelle had said, *and they're surely not human, nor
are they any other natural race. We don't know what they are,
other than creatures made from the sorcery of the Seven, the
immortals who preside over Luudhoq. But we too have great
powers, whose purpose in life is the defence of the Free
Territories against that evil. It's been this way for many
centuries; a truce between us and them. The malevolence of
Watchers and their masters can't touch us here, Anlerran.*

Instead, Anlerran reminded herself miserably,
something else just as terrifying had reached into her life
and torn it apart.

Powers, I miss you both, she thought, and angrily
closed her eyes when tears threatened to fall. *What now for
me? These mercenaries will keep me alive if I'm of use to
them, but even so I'll remain their captive unless I can think
of something.*

Overhead the canopy of leaves grew tighter as if the
trees had entwined their upper reaches around one another
to fashion a roof of green shade. Noon wore into afternoon
which faded into early evening, and the sun disappeared
entirely as it fell away to the west, hidden by leagues of
forest. Everyone dismounted as the path became narrow.
Ruhal helped Anlerran down with casual ease; when he set
her on the ground he held her for perhaps a moment longer
than Anlerran judged necessary. She looked up at the wary
eyes and hard countenance but had no time to read anything
into his expression. He turned quickly, leading their horse
along the path.

Anlerran gave an involuntary shiver as the light
dimmed and the air grew cooler. Although fewer woodland
creatures could be seen and heard out and about now, she
fancied that she saw for an instant a shape moving through
the undergrowth, dark and soundless. The very next
moment, not only had it gone but she began to doubt that
she had even seen it. *Just another woodland creature*

rushing to the heart of its home, to be away from the giants in its midst, Anlerran told herself, yet she remained uneasy.

A little later when she looked around and back along the path they had followed, her heart almost stopped as she saw a large black dog no more than ten yards away, staring at her solemnly. It made no move to attack her, and Anlerran took a deep breath, trying to ease the pounding of blood in her veins. A moment later it had darted away, making no sound, and she saw no more of the creature. She noticed faint paw prints upon the ground but even as she looked at them they faded away.

As well they might on soft grass, she reminded herself. *But so swiftly?*

She glanced around at the others; none of them had looked back when she did, so they had not seen the creature. Even if they had, Anlerran reasoned, they would have seen it for what it was rather than the apparition that she had for a moment believed it to be. The breeze sighed in the treetops, as if to say that many apparitions had passed by this day, fleeting below the boughs.

Soon afterwards they left the woods and headed across open grassland on horseback once again. The red moon Archaon rose slowly in the east and a short while later Ildar followed. Observing the moons, Anlerran judged that Ildar might eventually pass in front of its larger sibling tonight; she had occasionally seen such alignments before, when the moons would appear to touch and then slide past each other in the night sky. Her mother had called it a witch's night on the rare occasions when that happened; supposedly the element of water was stirred greatly when such alignments occurred, although Anlerran had never seen evidence for it herself.

A dark fingernail's worth of sky remained between the moons when the companions arrived at the abandoned settlement of Anrith. Looking around, Anlerran reckoned she had never seen such a scene of desolation before. Moss and lichen grew thick upon the stones of long-ruined cottages and homesteads; ivy trailed in and out of windows and doors at will. Everywhere she looked, nature had reclaimed this place with a resolute patience, a steady march of green over grey. In the centre of the small village, an ancient stone well and a tall cross-shaped monolith, both hewn from some kind of dark speckled granite, stood, cracked and lop-sided.

Next to the cross, and staring thoughtfully at it, stood what Anlerran at first took to be a human woman, tall and dark-haired.

She turned as the companions slowed to a halt, and regarded each of them in turn. Anlerran could detect no emotion or expression whatsoever on that smooth countenance. Suddenly she realised with a dread certainty that she was gazing upon the face of something that was anything but human. "She's a Watcher," she whispered, swallowing.

"Quiet. Say nothing," Ruhal murmured as he dismounted and then helped her down, looking across at the Watcher, who regarded them all in expressionless silence as the others cautiously dismounted.

"You are late," she called to them as they led their horses forwards and tied them at rusted iron poles nearby which had presumably been fashioned long ago for such a purpose.

"On the contrary," Ruhal rejoined. "You are early." He glanced around the settlement and finally returned his attention to the Watcher. Anlerran stole a glance at him. *He's afraid,* she decided, *but he's the sort of man who'd never admit it.*

From the shadows behind more distant buildings, four other Watchers slowly appeared and moved to join their comrade under the great cross. One of these was female, the other three male; each wore long black cloaks under which light chain armour glittered faintly. They moved lithely and sinuously; to Anlerran they seemed to ooze malice.

Ruhal motioned for his companions to walk a little closer and for the Watchers to do likewise; after a moment they did so, until everyone on both sides stopped, as if on some shared impulse, a half-dozen paces away.

Anlerran felt a curious prickling sensation and a need to raise her head, as if something subtle wished to draw her attention to the celestial event in the south. Archaon and Ildar touched, or appeared to. *Now I feel something of the alignment,* she thought, *as if the water in me calls to the moons. Maybe these so-called powers of mine have in turn awakened other things.*

"Give your names," Ruhal said without preamble.

The female Watcher they had seen first took a single step forward and gestured to each of her companions. "Kelandra," she said, gesturing to herself, and then: "Alturus. Kal-Myrran. Kunas. Ildoron." She stepped back, and Ruhal introduced each of Jahar, Lura, Sarros and Anlerran.

Anlerran could not keep her eyes off the five Watchers; they might as well have been carved from stone for all the emotion they showed, but she felt a strange, dark allure to them. Perhaps that was a product of the sorcery from which they had been fashioned, but whatever its source the sensation was like no other she could have imagined.

Will I now learn why this meeting has taken place? she wondered.

Lura walked abruptly away to stand in the shadows of a ruined dwelling by the edge of the track. Anlerran could not see her expression but she noted the manner of the woman's walk. Lura gave the impression that she found their new company too distasteful to bear.

"She has her reasons," Jahar said quietly from near her side, as if he had guessed her thoughts.

Anlerran was wondering what those reasons might be when she saw a movement some distance away in the deep shadows between the ruins of Anrith's smallholdings.

Something moved silently from place to place; for a brief moment she caught sight of a low, loping shape- *a dog again,* she thought, frowning. One of the Watchers- the one who had been introduced as Ildoron- frowned and followed her gaze, but it was evident that he could not see the creature. Ruhal saw him looking back at her, and glanced at Anlerran. "What?" he asked, in barely more than a whisper. "Did you see something?"

Anlerran shook her head without even thinking about it. Behind her, she heard Sarros exhale slowly. Across the track, Lura stirred and then leaned back against the wall again with a deep scowl, arms folded.

"*We* were not followed. We made certain of it," Kelandra said, staring at Ruhal. "Did you?"

"Of course," Ruhal said immediately. Anlerran thought again of the dog that had followed them here, unseen, unheard and undetected. *The same one as I saw before,* she thought, oddly certain of it, and a troubling question followed: *Should I tell them about it? Does it mean ill? It must have some reason for following.*

The possibility occurred to her that it had been sent by one of the authorities of Free Harn- some powerful warlock perhaps, given that no one other than herself had even caught sight of it yet. *If that's true, then the traitors are known about already. Will they be slain? What about me? Will I be seen as one of them, and cut down even as I scream my innocence?*

Anlerran swallowed and stared resolutely at the moonlit track before her, hoping beyond hope that neither those who had brought her here nor the unnatural fiends with which they were dealing would notice her steadily increasing panic.

"I suggest we head into Fhaarluy forest," Ruhal added. "There's high ground that I know well, within the woods, easily defended and with good sight of comings and goings. From there, we can plan out our recruitment. There are settlements further north where the people are more likely to listen to me than to the likes of Inerdyr and his lackeys."

"Good. I suspected as much." Kelandra gestured behind them. "Our horses are a hundred paces or so that way."

A short while later, ten riders set off north, towards the edge of Fhaarluy forest. The bright night became a bright morning, and they rested under the growing light before heading on and into Fhaarluy proper.

They spent the day making progress further into the heart of the forest. Anlerran looked out for the dog from time to time but did not catch so much as a glimpse of it. *If it was a sorcerous spy, perhaps it's on its way back to its masters,* she considered.

"This way takes us close to the bottomless lake—*reuuythlien* as the *luyan* folk call it," Sarros remarked a while later, as they headed along a path that sloped gently down, winding and zig-zagging down into a thickly wooded valley through which a tributary river cut. The shadows were long now, cutting across the tops of the ravine and casting the scene above in a warm orange glow whilst accentuating the forbidding shadow further down where they were headed. Anlerran could see a track winding its way up on the other side; perhaps they were now not far from the high ground of which Ruhal had spoken.

"There is no such thing as a bottomless lake," Kelandra retorted, giving him a withering stare. Sarros tipped his hat to her. "Forgive my insolence, Watchess. Regardless of its nature, we'll soon see the lake for ourselves, as it lies no more than a two thousand paces on along our way."

Sarros' words proved to be true enough, at least where the lake's location was concerned. Soon, with the last rays of the sun fast disappearing they came near to the edge of the lake itself. The waters stretched for perhaps a thousand paces or more across; a wide track wound around the shore and the almost perfectly still surface had a silvery-blue sheen.

"I do not like this place," Kal-Myrran declared, tapping a black-hilted dagger in her belt.

"You will not have to suffer it for long," Kelandra said, and looked towards Ruhal. "How much further?"

"We'll be there before nightfall," was all he said.

As the last rays of sunlight disappeared from the treetops, and a chill breeze blew across the lake, Anlerran thought for a moment that it had become suddenly darker; darker than it ought to have been even with the sinking of the sun. In a sudden panic she almost fell from the horse, convinced for no reason that something terrible was about to happen. Her heart beat furiously. Every part of her felt as if it sparked and tingled in helpless response to a multitude of forces in the air. She opened her mouth to scream, unable to help herself, but the sound died as a faint whisper in her throat.

The dog, she thought wildly. *The dog led its masters to this place, to kill these traitors.*

And then they came pouring forth from either side, trapping them on the lake shore; a man on a grey horse, grim-faced and terrible; six women dressed all in green and accompanied by huge, snarling wolves; six black-clad men, three of them pale *luyan*, on horseback, armed with scimitars and longbows.

Anlerran knew in an instant that some powerful authority had indeed learned of this alliance, and had come to deal swift revenge for that treachery. They had nothing to say; they did not gloat, nor did they list the crimes that they had come to punish. They simply came swarming towards the companions in a mass of blades, thundering hooves and snapping jaws.

In no more than a fleeting moment, Anlerran found herself drawn into the heat of battle, terrified, and unable to summon any of her raw powers against human and *luyan* adversaries. She fell from the horse as it shied away from a blade whistling through the air. Ruhal desperately sought to control the panicked beast as he drew his longsword. Anlerran rolled along the ground, fearful of being struck by hooves or blades.

The crackling of strange energies became ever more violent. The sky grew darker still, even as the lake shimmered in the quarter-light of the dying day. For a while, everything around seemed to be happening in slow motion around her. Movements appeared sluggish, sounds low and subdued. The silver and black sheen of weaponry gleamed in what remained of the light. Horses screamed. The harsh clatter of swords rose in the chill evening air. Nearby, someone fell. Anlerran could not tell who it was as she crawled away and towards the tree line, nor could she even tell if it was one of her companions or one of their enemies. She did not look back.

Now's your chance to flee! a voice desperately shrieked in her head. *This is not your battle! Let them kill each other, and run now before they cut you down!*

But fear held her captive; her legs felt tremulous and leaden, useless.

Staring wildly around, Anlerran caught a glimpse for a moment of the elusive forces that swirled across this vicious skirmish, centred around Jahar and also the grey-haired man on the horse. With the continual darkening of the sky this was almost all she could see- a phenomenon of light, colour and shadow deeper than night, as if the dreams of both men were chasing towards each other through the cool lakeside air to join in a maddened fury, a struggle that surely only she and they could see.

Elsewhere, everything was shadow and movement; blades clashed and lupine snarls cut through the air.

Finally she managed to get up and stagger towards the deep thickness of the forest, away from the fighting. Miraculously, no one saw her, or if they did then they saw her as irrelevant. *I've no part in this,* she reminded herself. *I'll head into the dark, and then I'll be free. Once I'm away from this madness my wits will return and I'll be able to run. And I'll run all night if I...*

Something grey and impossibly fast lunged at her from her right and the sound that accompanied it- a cacophonous snarl of rage- brought the world sharply back into focus, shattering the illusion.

The wolf succeeded only in biting her arm, but Anlerran's legs gave way with the shock, She rolled a few times in the dirt and then sat up to face the snarling visage of the wolf, which had come half-circle around as if prowling around its prey. It gleamed like silver; teeth, wet and sharp, stood like waiting blades in the beast's slathering mouth.

Now it bore down upon her. It pounced- and was sliced almost in half by a longsword in mid-jump. Anlerran looked dazedly up, wiping warm blood from her face, and for a moment she saw Kelandra, a blur of darkness moving swiftly away, already engaged in a struggle with a wild-looking *luyan* huntsman.

She barely remembered the rest of this nightmare, as it became darker still and impossible to tell what was going on. The combatants had somehow been split far and wide, so that individual fights continued in different places, along the shoreline- where she saw silhouettes engaged in their dance of death against the backdrop of the water- and further back amongst the surrounding forest. Anlerran staggered away, desperately hoping to put distance between herself and the bloodshed, but she could barely move more than a few steps without falling to her knees. As time went on and she peered around through the darkness, the fighting seemed more distant. It became quieter still.

Moving hesitantly forward, she tripped over a body. Peering down, she saw that it was one of the Watchers. *Kunas*, she thought after a moment. *That was his name.* His face, oddly silver, stared blankly up at her with mauve eyes that now resembled cold marbles. Anlerran shivered and moved on.

Ildar rolled out from behind a bank of cloud, and Anlerran instinctively ducked behind a bush, seeing movement up ahead where the tree line met the shoreline. Her heart sank as she saw coming into view the warlock, the grey man, with those of his comrades who had survived. Hoods covered their faces. They dragged along the figures of Ruhal, Jahar, and three of the Watchers, each of whom was bound tightly, gagged and blindfolded. The captives were dragged unceremoniously along the shoreline for some distance until the entire group left her view, taking a path south-east into the surrounding forest.

Anlerran sank to her knees, numb with disbelief. *How did I manage to avoid capture?*

The memory of Kelandra saving her from the wolf came back suddenly. The creature would surely have torn her throat out had it reached her; she owed the Watcher her life. Anlerran sighed, head bowed; she had no idea what to make of any of this.

Tired and bewildered, she felt tears well up, and she was still sobbing silently to herself when suddenly a hand touched her shoulder.

Instantly she wheeled round, crying out and scrabbling for a weapon, but her arm was grabbed and held fast. "Hold still, girl! It's me!"

"Lura?" Anlerran turned round to see the woman kneeling next to her. Drying blood marked a wound on her head.

"You and I, we must decide what to do." Lura's voice shook, as if from tiredness or anger, or grief. Anlerran watched the woman guardedly as she continued, "This was folly from the start. We should have known that Inerdyr and his followers would learn of Ruhal's scheme. We should have known."

Anlerran said nothing. *How did Lura avoid capture?* she wondered. Then, thinking back to the sight of the capture, and the companions being taken away, she realised: *Others may have done so too, if they're still alive. Sarros, and one of the Watchers. Which one? Kelandra?*

"I saw them being marched away as I hid," Lura continued. "Inerdyr's lackey Hanric will have them all executed."

"I only saw Ruhal and Jahar, of your friends," Anlerran told her, and Lura looked sharply at her. "What about the Watchers?"

"I saw three. One of the others- Kunas- lies dead not far from here."

"Then Sarros and one of the Watchers escaped... or were slain." Lura stared towards the lake, then along the shoreline in both directions. Here and there the shapes of bodies could be seen. "I don't know how they failed to see us, Anlerran," she said after a moment. "But regardless, we're fugitives now- we'll have a bounty on our heads for the remainder of our sorry lives, all for the folly of one man. Damn him! He was my friend, a true friend, but damn him nonetheless!"

Anlerran had nothing to say to that, but she suspected that Lura wept a little as she turned away.

Abruptly Lura got to her feet and began to walk along near the shoreline. Anlerran staggered to her feet and followed her. *What else should I do?* she wondered, and then: *Should I instead go my own way?*

They walked towards the path that had led them to this ill-fated place, and it was here that they saw Kelandra. She lay upon the ground, her whole body shaking, a thin trickle of blood coming from her mouth. A wolf, dead by her hand, lay with its innards ripped out nearby, its jaw still fastened upon her right arm. Anlerran looked closer, and saw that it had bitten and ripped through flesh, as far as the bone.

But that isn't bone, she thought suddenly, looking more closely.

Whatever it was, although shaped a little like bone, it looked more like intricate threads of metal, silvery and glistening in the moonlight.

"They are creatures fashioned from sorcery," Lura said quietly. "You've heard the stories. Now you see the truth for yourself."

Anlerran remained mesmerised by the sight. As she stared at the gaping wound, more detail came into focus; thin, delicate metal wires wrapped around thicker, solid pieces of the metallic substance that formed what in a natural creature would have been the bone structure. They ran through the flesh too, threading their way into the rest of her body, which still remained intact. Anlerran allowed her gaze to stray from the arm to the neck and head.

Had her arm not been wounded, she could almost pass for a human, Anlerran thought. Aloud she mused, "How could a single wound to her arm disable her so?"

"They're no ordinary wolves," was all Lura said. Anlerran glanced at her own wounded arm and saw to her surprise that not only did it no longer bleed, but it had begun to close and heal already. *Maybe I have some immunity,* she thought, *but Kelandra clearly does not.*

"I'll put her out of her misery," Lura said quietly. She unbuckled and raised her sword, and instantly Kelandra's eyes flickered open. Weakly she raised her undamaged left arm. It shook violently.

I can't allow this, Anlerran thought suddenly, not knowing how or why the thought came into her head. "Wait, Lura," she said. "We can save her."

Lura stared at her in astonishment. "Save her? What

for? This madness is done with- I'll kill this creature and then I'll head as far away from here as I possibly can. I suggest you do the same."

"She saved my life," Anlerran told her. "One of those wolves came for me, and she cut it down. It would have ripped my insides out. And if you were to band together with these Watchers, why now would you seek to destroy one of them?"

Lura stood indecisively; finally she returned the sword to her belt with a sigh.

"It's... done... now." Kelandra's words were forced, pained. Anlerran knelt by her as Lura prised the wolf's jaw away and kicked the animal's carcass to one side with a grimace. "Lura, help me take her into the undergrowth a little way where we're less likely to be seen," she said. Lura cursed to herself, but grudgingly obeyed; together they half-carried, half-dragged the injured Watcher some distance into the woodland, laying her down in a small clearing. Lura took a sip of water, and gave the canteen to Anlerran, who took a small sip and placed it against Kelandra's lips. At the same time she wondered to herself: *Should I even be doing this? Do they drink and eat in the manner of natural beings?*

Kelandra drank weakly, eyes fixed upon Anlerran the whole while. Anlerran could not read her expression, and did not want to. Lura passed her some cloth from her pack to wrap the wounded arm; Anlerran hesitantly did the best job she could, glancing occasionally at Kelandra.

"Ruhal, Jahar, and three of yours have been captured," she said after a while. "Another one- Kunas- lies dead. And Sarros..." She looked to Lura and shrugged.

"If even a Watcher can act to save your life," Lura said to her suddenly, "then how can I not at least attempt to rescue my friends?"

Kelandra smiled bitterly as she struggled to sit up using her good arm. "Irrational, like all your kind. They will be put to death. Our journey is at an end."

Silver flashed against porcelain white as Lura placed the blade of her knife against the Watcher's neck. Anlerran drew breath sharply, watching Lura's weapon press against the skin. "Without us, Kelandra, *you* are as good as dead, stranded in Fhaarluy by yourself- and you know it. Your only choice is to stay with us- and we are going to follow them and find a way to rescue them- or at least find out their fate for certain. Have I made myself clear, or would you like another wound to add to your collection?"

Kelandra said nothing, and they stared hatefully at each other. Anlerran's heart sank at the thought of being dragged along on some futile rescue mission by this impetuous, irrational woman who clearly seldom thought before she acted.

"I'll not be a fugitive," Lura added, putting the knife away. "I'd rather be slain than spend the rest of my life forever looking over my shoulder."

The small hours wore on; as the dawn light grew, Kelandra stared silently into the east, expressionless and aloof. She had not moved since her altercation with Lura.

"If by some miracle we find them and rescue them," Lura said, getting to her feet, "then we'll need to be swift about it. Swifter than Inerdyr's vengeance. Powers, that we should make such an enemy!"

Anlerran's thoughts darkened. *What will their captors do with them? Kill them, or torture them for hours, even days?* The thought of anyone being tortured chilled her, but that thought swiftly turned to another. "I never wanted any part of this," she said abruptly. "Had I known about this alliance of yours I would have ran at the earliest opportunity, or perhaps never left Mordenglen with Ruhal. I would have found a way to escape. If you want to stand against these enemies of yours then do so, but I'll have no part of it. I am leaving."

"No," Lura said grimly, stalking over to her as

Anlerran got to her feet. "No, you're not. If I find a way of
rescuing them, then I *must* have you there. Have you
forgotten so soon? Ruhal told us about you..."

Then she stopped, for Anlerran was no longer even
listening; her attention was fixed on the area just behind the
other woman, just at the edge of the clearing.

The black dog had returned.

Lura turned and stared at it, then back at Anlerran.

"I had thought it a spy or a tracker for your
enemies," Anlerran said slowly, and grabbed Lura's hand on
impulse as it strayed to her sword. "But it isn't. *He* isn't."

The dog padded unhurriedly up to them and stopped
just several yards away. Anlerran's heart beat furiously.
Whatever you truly are, show us your intentions, she silently
implored it.

"How can you know that?" Lura shook her head as if
she couldn't quite believe that she had even asked the
question. "Powers, it's a *dog,* Anlerran- what can you
possibly..."

The dog pointed its head to the south-east, appearing
agitated by something, and then stared questioningly at
Anlerran, whining softly.

"He's not an enemy. He's come back to help us,"
Anlerran murmured, staring thoughtfully at the hound.

"How, exactly, do you work that out?" Kelandra
asked from behind them.

"I don't know," said Anlerran, truthfully. "But we can
trust him. He wants to lead us somewhere..."

"To Hanric and his people," Lura muttered, and
threw the creature a forbidding look. The dog pawed the
ground restlessly as if frustrated with their inaction, and
again pointed his nose to the south-east.

"We should go wherever he leads us," Anlerran said,
and turned to her companions. "Well?"

They pressed on through the damp foliage. Mist descended,

and their guide faded at times to little more than a blur of shadow amidst the grey, although he never disappeared completely and occasionally waited for them to catch up. Soon they reached the far shore of the lake, where Anlerran inspected the ground and found that the footsteps and hoof prints that should have been visible in the soft ground had been somehow concealed. This did not entirely surprise her. *It would be a simple trick for a man such as this Hanric,* she considered.

The lack of a visible trail did not seem to affect the dog, who trotted on ahead as determinedly as ever.

Kelandra, although hampered by her wound, managed to keep up with them well enough. Anlerran detected cold fury hidden in her grim silence- perhaps at her current weakness, even reliance on her companions. *And how will she vent that anger when she is well again?* Anlerran thought darkly as she shot a glance at the Watcher. She resolved to keep an eye on her at all times- although Lura was surely doing so already.

They stopped only once, for Kelandra to pass water; she stared back when Anlerran found herself unable to help but glance at her squatting in the grass. "We drink liquids- what do you expect us to do with them?" the Watcher said scornfully. "Certain things we *have* to share with you creatures."

The day passed by wrapped in a shroud of uniform grey, which made it hard for them to tell morning from afternoon. Finally they stopped when it became too dark to continue- Anlerran called out for their guide to stop, and feared for a moment that he had simply continued on regardless, careless as to their need for rest- before a now-familiar black shape appeared from out of the gathering gloom and sat no more than a few paces away from her.

On an impulse, Anlerran almost reached across to pat the dog as he glanced back at her, but stopped at the last moment. *You do not know what this is,* she reminded herself, *and you don't even know its intentions as yet. You think it may be leading you to the others, but how do you really know?*

But there was nothing else we could have done, she tiredly reminded herself. *Things were about as bad as they could be. Lura pointed out herself that each of us would have become a fugitive, running through the shadows until eventually we'd be caught, put on trial and made an example of.*

Perhaps she looked as tired as she felt, for Lura leaned over and said quietly, "I will keep watch. Get some rest."

"You think a Watcher needs watching?" Kelandra spoke up with a bitter smile. Lura looked her up and down contemptuously. "Always," she said, and Kelandra's expression became like stone.

If they argued further then Anlerran heard no part of it; she was asleep within moments, and soon immersed in a dream in which she ran with a group of black dogs over open land she had never seen before, hurtling towards an unimaginable enemy she could not even see, under a sky of storms.

VIII – Blood and Rain

I

She was alone, and could not understand this place. But for the moment, she was *free*.

Yui sat on the grass on top of the hill and stared down into a night of untold wonders. The ground sloped away gently until eventually it reached the outskirts of a great city, glittering with lights and heavy with shadow, a mass of secrets and hopes and fears.

She was nine years old, and she had no understanding of worlds elsewhere in the Existence, yet somehow she knew without any doubt that this place would be the last to fall. *The end of the world's light,* she thought, and then visions of other worlds came suddenly to her mind; some were cold airless deserts, long devoid of life, others bore a hellish surface that heaved and moved continuously, bright with freshly-spewed lava even as their skies loomed dark and low, poisoned and choked with ash. Still other worlds defied description entirely.

They're all dead, if ever they were alive, she thought. *And this is the last world left.*

Yui struggled to understand this place into which she had been drawn. It was not the waking world, yet she knew that it was connected to it in some powerful way; by reaching out to it through her dreams she had somehow escaped the great stone fortress where she had been imprisoned and tortured, and even if she somehow returned to the world she knew, she would not allow herself to be pulled back to that place.

The world she now saw spread before her appeared to obey few rules. Luudhoq lay towards what she thought might be west, surrounded on all sides by vast open grassland, hills and forests, farms and villages for as far as she could see, but she could also see other towns of Harn, surely closer than they ought to be, as if the geography of the entire land had been folded up like a map scribbled on discarded parchment. No sun illuminated the sky, nor had she seen either moon rise even though she had sat here for what could have been days. An indistinct greenish glow emanated from the sky and sometimes even from the ground. Often it appeared subdued but occasionally it would become far brighter, as if some great secret brilliance lay in shallow seclusion under the earth and from time to time came nearer to the surface- so near that she thought it might break through the earth.

This was a place of mystery wrapped in mystery. Somehow, although she had hardly dared believe her own instinct at first, she knew that the Seven were not even aware of this place. That such terrible, all-powerful men and women could not know of this inner world was almost as much a shock to her as being here herself.

I could stay in this place, hidden from them forever, she reasoned. *I've been here for days. I haven't needed to sleep and I haven't needed to eat or drink. I don't feel any pain. I don't feel afraid any more.*

Yet tears brimmed in her eyes. The physical agony had gone but she still felt a deep, boundless rage at what had happened, and it was tempered by only one thing; fear for the safety of her father and for Alexia. By now, they would both be in the hiding place she had found for them, deep in the warrens of Luudhoq. They would have each other. Maybe they would be able to stay hidden, and the Seven and the Watchers wouldn't be able to find them.

Maybe.

The girl's thoughts turned inevitably to the woman who had tricked them into their imprisonment- *Nia,* she thought savagely. *That's your name. You don't know, but I found you again, I saw you when you were walking through the streets, I saw you with my eyes closed, from up in my own prison. And then I remembered that I saw both your faces, in the prison in Darkenhelm.*

Now I know your true face.

Yui wondered if it might be possible to find her again as she had before, and speak with her as she had managed to speak with her father and Alexia. *If I can,* she thought, *I'll hurt you so badly. I'll make you beg for me to kill you.*

The fury subsided, leaving her trembling and weak and desperately aware of how alone she was. Here there were no people- none that she had seen anyway- and even if there were, she suspected that it might not be a good idea to make her presence known to them.

But if I go back, if I can find a way back, maybe the Seven will find me again.

That thought, of being captured and tortured again, filled her with such terror that she almost screamed out loud. *I can't,* she thought, head bowed and arms crossed tightly as if to defend herself from such a fate. *I can't let that happen.*

But it was not that simple. Now she thought about it properly, she knew that her father and Alexia would eventually be caught by the Seven, or by the Watchers they sent out to hunt them down. Yet if she could return somehow then the three of them might be able to evade recapture. She had developed a sense for Watchers and other agents of the Seven, and knew when they were anywhere near her.

I have to go back to them.

Yui started to sob quietly to herself, wishing beyond everything else that they could all go back to the time before any of this, to when they lived peacefully in the palace in Darkenhelm. But the blissful past was gone forever; it was just a distant memory.

Finally she got up, wiped her eyes and gazed in each direction in turn. Everywhere she looked except at the city, she saw empty land; in one direction great mountains rose up, sharp and black against the oddly green-hued sky. *I could lose myself there,* she reminded herself. *I could wander forever, never getting tired, never needing to eat, never feeling pain.*

Yet Luudhoq or this quiet apparition of it called to her and finally Yui began to walk down towards the city.

II

Only when she drew near to the city gates could she see that they stood slightly open, and that each and every piece of them was caked in rust and dirt. *Here, Luudhoq is the least looked-after place,* she thought as she walked through. *There's something wrong about it.*

As she made her way up the wide and silent thoroughfare beyond the half-ruined gates, Yui began to feel as if she was being watched. She had no idea who or what it might be, but she knew that it could not be the Seven or their Watchers. *They don't even know about it,* she reminded herself, still in wonderment at that fact. *So who else could it be?*

Whoever or whatever it was, it remained hidden from view and soundless, and yet Yui could somehow sense that presence moving as she moved, keeping pace with her. At one point she thought she caught a glimpse of something out of one of the countless blank, darkened windows that lined the buildings on either side of the wide road, but when she turned her head nothing was there. Another time, one of the deep shadows in the road ahead appeared to move and take on a different shape, yet when she arrived at the spot where she thought it was it looked like any one of the shadows by the sides of the road.

She arrived at a point where the road opened out into a vast stone square, far larger than any in the *other* Luudhoq could possibly be. On all sides, great buildings rose high into the green-hued sky, dotted with uniformly-shaped windows beyond which neither light nor life lurked.

It wasn't always like this here, Yui thought as she stopped and contemplated the awful yet pristine desolation. *These buildings would have been a different shape. They would have had many shapes. There would have been light everywhere.*

The light of the world.

She wasn't at all sure what that meant, yet in that moment she realised the absolute, terrible importance of that thought, the *idea* behind it. This revelation in turn opened others, and they came to her so swiftly and so sharply that the child could do nothing to withstand them; she sank to the cobbles and wept openly.

Aona is fading. The Gates, the black spaces through which the marandaal *creatures are coming, were just the start. The old guardians of the world, the ones called* choragh, *have been corrupt and evil for a long time. In defending the world they would destroy it, turn it lightless, make it again in their own image. And the inner places of Aona, like this one, they too are slowly changing, becoming homes to things I can't even imagine. Like the thing I know is following me.*

Yui lifted her head after a while and gazed around. Had the buildings changed a little? She thought that perhaps they had. Some of them looked even taller now, and loomed perilously near; their windows had the appearance of spaces more than windows, more like...

More like Gates.

She looked hurriedly away from them, knowing that they could so easily drag her in if she stared at them for too long; but then something else happened.

Yui heard the sound of crying from somewhere up ahead; she got up and walked on, mystified that such a human sound- for it was undeniably human- could have manifested itself here.

She saw the girl sitting crouched by the side of the road, face turned away. She might have been about her own age. Yui stopped, noticing the girl's long, light brown hair. *The same length as mine,* she thought suddenly, and that realisation opened up a pit in her stomach.

This is impossible, she thought. *That can't be me.*

But the girl raised her head and stared wildly up at the vast, silent architecture that surrounded them, and Yui could tell straight away that it *was* her- or at least, someone who looked exactly like her.

The apparition got to her feet and walked towards a narrow, utterly dark space between two buildings. In the *other* Luudhoq, there would have been a street there; Yui thought that here it could hide anything- all manner of nightmares.

The girl disappeared into that space, and Yui took several steps towards it, her mind full of questions that could never be answered unless she somehow caught up with her. *Who is she? Is she another me?! How did she get here?*

But she stopped, reminding herself that to follow that ghost or whatever she was would be to allow herself to become nothing more than a part of this world. If that girl spoke to her, touched her, maybe even so much as *looked* at her, then...

Then I'd be trapped here forever, she told herself.

But I have to find a way back. I have to stop the Seven and the Watchers from capturing my father.

Yui took two steps back, as if the very thought of being ensnared here by her own apparition might itself be enough to make it a fact. She couldn't know for sure that it would not.

So she turned away and strode on along the empty square towards its distant end, where the gloom appeared a little less constant and the diffuse green glow somewhat stronger.

As she walked, a low and dolorous humming began behind her as if a hundred or more voices had joined in lament. This sound of grief and desperation grew into a cacophonous wail that shifted its intensity from one place to another; on and on it went, until she could bear it no longer and she broke into a run, her legs carrying her as quickly as they could across the dimly-lit cobbles towards the far end of the great square. The voices, bestial and snarling now, bellowed their misery across the shadow-city, a symphony of unrestrained rage and despair. Yui fixed her gaze upon the entrance to a street somewhere ahead of her, intent upon the shape of it, the light, the way it had somehow *forced* its way between two grey, dismal storehouses.

There isn't long! she imagined it calling to her, as if a street could have spoken. *Hurry!*

Yui reached the street knowing that a wave of darkness had already started to spread over part of the city square. She almost flung herself into the winding, narrow street- and abruptly the sound of the mad, baying voices stopped.

She sobbed in relief, and sank down to the ground, leaning against a wall of grey bricks. Eventually the pounding of her heart eased, and she looked up the street as far as she could; although it wound and twisted many times, somehow she could see around the corners and bends so that each and every dwelling, shop, storehouse, tavern or other building could be observed. She thought that perhaps she had been down this street before, or at least its other version, when she, her father and Alexia had first arrived in Luudhoq. Here of course, it had been rearranged; it led gradually uphill whereas she remembered it heading gently downwards in the Luudhoq she knew. Some of the buildings were clearly in the wrong order, although she couldn't be sure about the houses as so many of them looked alike.

Yui had an idea as to why this particular part of the shadow-Luudhoq had saved her or allowed her to save herself; she remembered that they had been happy, relieved, full of hope at that time, as Narin- *Nia,* she reminded herself- led them through the eastern streets of the city with a promise they had believed in.

Then she turned us over to her masters, the girl thought hatefully. *But I'll find her and make her pay for what she did. I don't know how, but I'll find a way.*

She set off up the street, surmising that this area represented her best chance of finding her way back to the other Luudhoq- a place she feared as much as this one, yet she had no choice but to return to it.

Not if I want to save my father and Alexia.

Not if I want to find Nia and make her wish she'd never, ever met us.

Up ahead, one of the shop signs creaked back and forth as if moved by a breeze, although the air was perfectly still. The iron bar that held the sign gleamed in the green-hued light; Yui thought for a moment that it changed shape and became more like a gnarled branch of a tree than a metal bar. As she stopped and looked more intently at it the same thing happened again, only this time the branch itself sprouted smaller branches, which themselves slowly branched out until the shop sign stood covered in and held by the complex architecture of a tree that appeared to have grown from out of the shop wall.

Yui stopped outside the shop, and noticed that the door was slightly ajar. The light within the premises had an entirely different appearance: yellow, warm and oddly comforting, and yet like the universal green glow it had no obvious source. It might have come from the ceiling, the walls, the floor or even the odd assortment of objects in the shop- books, bottles, jars, ornaments and trinkets crammed precariously onto shelves that buckled under their collective weight.

She reached out to push the door further open in order to step inside, and then willed herself to stop. *This place is full of tricks*, she reminded herself. *There are traps everywhere. They've been made to pull me further in, deeper, so I may never escape.*

But then she remembered something else.

The girl I saw, the voices, the black windows, the tall buildings around the square, all those things are happening because the world is dying. Some parts of it are worse than others, and even here in Luudhoq, the place which is dying more quickly than the rest of the world, there are parts which have already given in to the darkness and others that are still holding out against it, parts which might even help me get back.

Like this one.

She told herself to have courage and believe the truth of that idea, for she *knew* it was true. She just couldn't be entirely certain that it was safe to step through the doorway.

Be brave, she told herself, and somehow it sounded like her father's voice. It was something he had told her many times, especially when she had woken up screaming after a particularly bad nightmare. She had tried hard to be brave, but more often than not she had failed. It was difficult to find courage when she was afraid of her own dreams, frightened by what they might do to her.

I'll try, she said to him. *I'm coming back. I'm coming back to be with you.*

Yui took a deep breath, pushed the door wide open and stepped into the light.

At one end of the shop, an open doorway led through to a passage, beyond which Yui could see another room. Hesitantly she walked down this passageway and into the room, which held a bookcase, a table and chairs- and one window, through which an entirely different light shone.

Yui blinked in astonishment. *It's moonlight,* she thought, dumbfounded. *The light of Ildar.*

That means...

Slowly she walked over to the window, hardly daring to make a sound or move too quickly in case the scene might vanish from sight. It did not; she reached the window, and peered out, having to stand on tip-toes. The familiar scene of Luudhoq at night-time revealed itself; she could see and hear sounds of people passing nearby, of rowdy but recognisable nightlife. The sounds were oddly muffled, the sights blurred for some reason.

I have to break the window, she decided. *The window is the barrier between the worlds.*

Picking up one of the chairs, she struck the window with it, almost losing her balance and falling over. The glass cracked but failed to shatter, and from somewhere behind her, outside the shop into which she had walked, Yui heard that low wailing sound start up again, only this time it was no general lament or expression of rage without direction. This time it was aimed at her alone.

Shaking with fear, she somehow found the strength to lift the chair again. *I should have closed the door,* she thought, panicking as she threw a glance back towards the front of the shop, not knowing if closing the door would in fact have made any difference. The golden-hued light beyond the passageway faded slightly; Yui watched as the shadow of something unseen began to spread across the doorway.

If you don't break the window now, it will reach you. And then you'll be here forever, lost, never dying, just trapped until the world itself ends.

The sheer horror of that thought lent her sudden strength. She threw the chair against the window, and this time it shattered, a spider web of cracks spreading from the point of impact, until the weakened pane fell apart. Cold night air from another world swept into the dusty chamber, and as she gulped in sudden breaths of it, Yui heard footsteps coming towards her, stopping near the doorway where the little corridor met the fading light of the shop.

She did not need to turn around to know what stood there; it bore her shape, its flesh was identical to hers inside and out. It was a ghost of her, wretched and condemned; it hungered for others that it might ensnare and keep here for all time, and yet still it would remain utterly alone.

Please come back, it whispered, and it even bore her voice as the words echoed inside her head. *We need you. We need your help.*

Yui jumped up onto the window ledge, cutting her arm in the process, and did not take a single look back. She jumped through the shattered window and landed on wet stone, slipped and fell. Pain soared through her leg, and she cried out. As she lay there on the ground, and the agony eventually ebbed away, she took a moment to thank whatever powers had led her back, and she even smiled a little as Ildar's face dipped behind thick cloud and a little later, rain began to fall.

III

The harsh reality of the Luudhoq that everyone knew and took for granted held its own fair share of dangers of course, but these were almost routine compared with the unspeakable horrors that had followed her through the city's ghostly counterpart. Yui kept to the areas that were better-lit wherever she could, but even so she could not avoid every possible encounter. As she passed a side-alley, a fat man with a beard called out to her softly, suggesting that he could provide her with a comfortable place to stay and some silver to spend on whatever she wanted; Yui saw the predatory look in his eyes and immediately knew what sort of a man *he* was; she hurried past without a word and looked back a little later to make sure he wasn't following.

A little later, as she crossed Baker's Square, an old woman sitting slumped by the fountain peered up at her, a tremulous claw hand held out in hope. Then her eyes widened, her ruined mind having told her that she recognised the bedraggled girl heading across the open square. "Lillan!" she cried out hoarsely. "It's me! It's your mother!"

"My mother died giving birth to me," Yui said, knowing immediately that she should have not have said a word. *There's a reason why the streets are full of people like this,* she told herself.

The crone stared incredulously at her for a moment; as Yui reached Tower Road at the other side of the square she finally found her voice, and a shrieking chaos of curses, threats and spittle rose into the air; Yui shuddered at the sound of that madness and quickened her pace as she headed on up the spiralling road.

She knew where she was now, more or less, and she had a good idea where her father and Alexia were.

The rain had started to come down more heavily by the time she reached the top of the road, where a smaller side street branched off; she walked down this for fifty paces or so. It turned a corner three times before Yui made her way down a narrow alley that branched from it.

At the end of the alley stood a small outhouse which had once been used by neighbours to store grain. It no longer afforded enough protection from the elements for that purpose. *But it's good enough to keep people mostly dry,* Yui thought, and allowed herself a tired but relieved smile, knowing who she would find in there.

She looked around to ensure that she hadn't been followed- although in fact she would have known anyway- and then she opened the door and slipped inside.

When he looked up and saw her standing there, Phyqor decided at first that the last few days had indeed been a long, rambling and hopeful dream- a dream in which an officer of the Sanctum prison had taken him from his cell as far as the outer gates of that great fortress, whereupon he had been escorted by another man, equally slack of expression, through Luudhoq's warren of back streets and eventually as far as this place. *He won't remember anything from this day,* Phyqor remembered thinking as he stared into the eyes of his guide for the last time, before the man stumbled away through the cold city mist. *He'll wake not knowing what he's done, as will the guard who released me. If either of them wake at all.*

Now, as he raised his head at the sound of the door opening and Yui stepped into the dim lantern light of his hiding place, Phyqor became certain that he remained immersed in an extended, vivid dream; he must be languishing in his prison cell still, awaiting whatever fate the Watchers or their masters decided should be his to endure.

Yet he glanced at Alexia, who had also stirred at the sound and stared at Yui as if she had materialised directly in front of her.

"Yui," he whispered, and scrambled to his feet. Still he would not dare to believe. They embraced fiercely, and still belief eluded him. Only when he felt her body wracked with sobs of sheer relief, and a moment later when he knelt and wiped tears from her cheeks, did the reality of it all finally sink in.

For a time, it seemed to Alexia that time slowed; the rain outside became a procession of slow, ponderous thuds on the roof of their makeshift shelter. She could see the undiluted joy and relief in Phyqor's eyes, and an altogether more complex expression in Yui's- love tempered with something, Alexia thought. Something hard, like steel.

A moment later, she began to understand.

"Narin tricked us all," the girl said, looking at her father and then Alexia. "But there's no such person as Narin. Her name is Nia. I found her in my dreams."

"What do you mean, Yui? You're not making sense," Phyqor said gently. "Narin was a man..."

"She can change shape. She can look like a man and then change back into her real self." Yui shook her head angrily. "I even *saw* her, back in the prison in Darkenhelm, but I forgot about it, I don't know how."

Phyqor remained silent for a while; Yui's story sounded scarcely credible, but then so many extraordinary, unbelievable events had occurred in the last few days. Finally he said, "So Narin- I mean, *Nia-* instructed the authorities to have us captured?"

"She had Alexia captured first. Then she told one of the Watchers about us, and they came and arrested us. She works for the Watchers. But..." Yui frowned, puzzled. "I don't know for sure, but I don't think she's anywhere near Luudhoq now. She's running away from something. But we'll find her even if it takes a long time. I promised myself I'd make her pay for what she did. We need to find a way out of this city first though. It's too dangerous here."

"Are we safe for now?"

"Only for a little while," she said after a moment, as if she had had to calculate her answer. "Soon we'll have to find somewhere else."

They listened to the rainfall awhile longer. Yui rested her head against Phyqor's chest, one arm draped across him; he listened to her faint breathing, and thought for a while that she might have fallen asleep. *I couldn't bear being apart from you,* he thought. *That was worse than any pain I've ever felt- a deep heaviness eating away at my insides, the fear that I might never see you again, never hold you again, and never have the chance to watch you grow up.*

That was worse than anything else.

Yui stirred and glanced up at him briefly, but said nothing. Presently she settled again, uttering nothing more than a sigh, and Phyqor closed his eyes, telling himself to treasure this rare moment- a brief respite for them both.

A long while later, Alexia woke up with a start to find Yui staring through the crack in the doorway. Daylight illuminated part of her face, showing the utterly intent look she bore. Alexia felt a stab of fear as she watched the child. "Are they coming for us?" she whispered.

Yui glanced across at her and shook her head before returning her attention to the alleyway outside. "But they will," she said quietly without looking back.

"How long do we have?" Alexia asked, and Yui shrugged, again without bothering to look at her.

Alexia stifled a sigh of frustration and leaned back against a pile of old sacking, grimacing at the cramp in her legs. She was more grateful to Yui than she could ever properly tell her, but it was impossible to know whether or not they had any chance of remaining hidden from their enemies a tennight or even a day from now. They were being led by a child because of the three of them, she alone had the power to sense their approach and perhaps do something about it. *And who knows what other powers she now wields?* Alexia asked herself, recalling how Yui had somehow reached out into the mind of a man who frequented the brothel where she had been imprisoned, rendering him a slave to her will, and leading her to this place. Alexia supposed that Yui's unwitting victim had no recollection of what had happened within the brothel that day, or of this place where he had taken her. She wondered what had become of him. Might he still be stumbling mindlessly through the city streets, his mind broken? Or had he woken up somewhere missing a day of his life but otherwise no worse for wear?

And then Phyqor was brought here by similar means, she thought. *But how did Yui escape? How could she possibly have escaped from the Seven? Can she even explain how she managed it?*

"We'll leave when it gets dark," the girl spoke up as she turned away from the door. She came to sit next to Alexia. "The moons will be strong."

Alexia stared doubtfully at her. "Why do we need moonlight here in the city?"

"I'm not talking about the light. I mean that when they're in certain places in the sky, it makes it more difficult for us to be found. That's when we should be moving."

Alexia had no idea what to make of that. "Are we going to leave the city?" she asked finally.

"If we don't," Yui said, "then they'll find us sooner or later, no matter what I do and no matter how often we move around and where we hide." She looked around as Phyqor stirred and sat up, and repeated her words for his benefit. "Then how do we leave?" he asked quietly. "I doubt that we can escape as easily as we did from Darkenhelm."

"No. We can't," his daughter agreed. She looked deeply troubled. "They'll have people looking for us at all the gates leading out of Luudhoq. Not just ordinary guards but powerful people."

"A Watcher at every exit," Alexia mused, and Yui nodded. "Maybe, yes."

Phyqor smiled wearily. "If we can't leave, then there's nothing left for us. We'll be running from our enemies for the rest of our sorry lives, hurrying from one hiding place to the next until our luck runs out and they find us. And when they do..." His eyes met Yui's for a moment. "I can't let them take you again," he whispered.

"I have an idea," Yui said, but Alexia thought that she sounded oddly reluctant, as if that idea might somehow be more dreadful and laden with risk than attempting to sneak their way through the city gates.

"But I don't know if it will work," she added, "and if it does work, we'll still be in a lot of danger. Maybe even *more* danger. But we have to try. Whatever we do, we *can't* allow ourselves to be captured by the Seven or their Watchers."

"What is this plan?" Phyqor asked.

Yui took a deep breath. "There's a place," she said finally, "that the Seven don't even know about. I'm not sure anyone else in the *world* knows about it. I found myself there before. That's how I escaped the Sanctum." She sighed, clearly unable to explain her words. "It's a place like the world we know, but *different*. It's dark, mostly lonely, and it's..." Yui lapsed into silence, trying to describe this mysterious other place, and finally she spoke.

"Imagine if the world itself was a living man or woman," she said. "If it was, then this place would be a nightmare that it has over and over, forever."

IV

No one spoke for a while. Alexia struggled to understand what Yui had said. "How can that be?" she asked finally. "How can the Seven not know about it?"

Yui shrugged. "It's one of the few things I'm certain of about that place. If I can reach it again- and if I can pull you in with me- we might be able to escape Luudhoq. But I don't know what else might happen. It's a bad place. All kinds of things could happen there. But I think I've worked out how to get back there. I can do it if I concentrate on it for long enough. I'm sure I can."

Phyqor and Alexia exchanged doubtful glances. Finally Phyqor pointed out, "As Yui said, if we keep running and hiding around the city, sooner or later they'll find us." He glanced back at his daughter. "How do you do it?"

In answer she did nothing except take a deep breath and reach out a hand to both of them.

Alexia opened her eyes suddenly; she had not been aware of having even closed them. The rain had stopped abruptly along with the sighing of the wind against their makeshift shelter. The air felt somehow *more* than calm, as if all the movement and moisture had been abruptly sucked out of existence.

And yet, despite this, the door creaked open slightly.

"We should leave," Yui said. "No one may stay in one place for long. Things change."

Alexia had no idea what to make of that. Phyqor stared at the door as if he expected it to suddenly burst open and an invisible phantom to rush at them.

Yui got up and walked slowly towards the exit, beckoning them to follow. "There's one thing I need to tell you," she spoke up quietly. "You might see people who look like yourselves where we're going. Don't go near them or speak to them."

Alexia saw Phyqor looking back at his daughter, and wondered if he was thinking the same as her- that Yui, despite her obvious powers, was either mad or imagining things. Here they were, after all, in the same place as they had been before she taken their hands...

And made us fall asleep? Alexia blinked. Was that what had happened? It felt as if no time had passed, but the very next instant she had felt as if she had just been awakened.

"Stay with me, and run if I run," the child warned them. Turning away, she pulled the door fully open, and Alexia stared into a scene of abandonment, deep shadow and constant, green-hued twilight.

They stepped out of the little storehouse, and Alexia gazed wordlessly up at the starless yet dimly glowing sky whose faint illumination fell upon the utterly silent alleyway. Somehow, although it should not have been possible to tell, she knew suddenly that the entire city lay cloaked in absolute silence for a reason. *There are no other people here,* she thought in wonderment. *Gods, Yui actually pulled us into this place.*

"Now do you believe me?" Yui asked them both solemnly, and they could only nod dumbly.

They set off down the alleyway, and soon it became obvious that here- wherever *here* truly was- the layout and the architecture of the city differed somewhat. In places this difference appeared subtle; in others, violent and cataclysmic. The alleyway no longer joined a narrow street, but instead opened out gradually; it became wider and wider until they had walked out into a great cobbled square, parts of which were comprised of great gaping holes into which the dim and sickly light could make no inroads. "Don't step near those," Yui said unnecessarily as they looked in each direction.

On the left side of the square- Alexia could not tell what direction that might be- the stark remains of once-tall buildings reached like brittle fingers of stone and glass into the moonless heavens. Some disaster had ruined them, but its nature could not be determined; a few of the buildings appeared to have melted away on one side yet remained intact on the other, while the lower reaches of others had crumbled away almost entirely, inexplicably leaving heavier, larger ramparts above that had somehow failed to break and fall.

"It's never day here," Yui whispered. Suddenly, apparently perturbed by something, she set off swiftly towards their right, where at the far end of the great square a vast array of tall spires and palaces still remained intact. Alexia noticed, as she and Phyqor hurried after her, that the three of them cast no shadows. *Can this be real?* she asked herself. *Or are the three of us all mad, or dreaming?*

They reached a street on the other side of the square which wound its way uphill towards a towering palace of black stone. It was here that Alexia saw her doppelganger for the first time.

Black-eyed and hollow-cheeked, it stared at her from the window of a house overlooking the street, mournful and malevolent in equal measure. Yui and Phyqor saw it then, and Yui turned and threw Alexia a warning glance, pressing a finger to her lips.

"Always running; never safe," Alexia's image called to them. "But we're safe here. We don't need to run anymore."

Alexia's heart quickened as she stared at the apparition. Did it somehow share some of her thoughts and her memories? Might it actually be, in some way, a part of her- another version of her, and not simply some manifestation of sorcery that happened to have taken on her appearance?

She looked back to catch a glimpse of it again, but the window now stood empty, blank and dark. Alexia looked a little further back and suddenly saw it walking behind them, gaunt and barefoot, eyes fixed upon the three of them. "It's following," she whispered, and Yui pulled at her arm. "Don't *look* at it!" she hissed fiercely, and they walked on, quickening their pace a little at Yui's insistence.

Alexia kept her gaze resolutely on the way ahead, taking one step after another as they walked up the hill. But her doppelganger kept pace with them, and perhaps even gained a little ground, for its voice sounded louder and clearer than it ought when it spoke up again: "You can walk forever, but cover no distance. Where will you go, anyway?"

When Alexia failed to respond, it said suddenly, "We have something to show you."

Alexia's skin crawled at the sound of the word *we*- how many more of them might be lurking here? She almost turned and asked it what it meant then, despite Yui's warning, but instead she kept her eyes on the way ahead and the great palace that loomed at the top of the hill. It looked a lot like one she had seen before when they arrived in Luudhoq, although that had been down in the south of the city, not far from the port. *Everything has moved,* she realised, allowing her gaze to wander a little- although never

167

behind, where her image still walked at their pace. *Some places are familiar, but something has happened to them. They've moved, or they've been damaged.*

She tried to reason what this place actually might *be*. How could it actually exist? Was it simply another version of the world in which things had happened differently? If so, where had all the people gone? How had Yui managed to pull the three of them into it? Might there be a reason for the sudden blooming of her talent? Might there be other people who were able to do the same thing?

Or was this simply some kind of powerful dream? Were they actually here at all? Alexia felt a stab of panic as she pictured the three of them still sitting or lying slumped in their hiding place, not knowing whether or not the Watchers or even the Seven themselves were closing in on them.

"Yui," she murmured, "are we really here?"

"Where else would we be?" Yui responded without looking back.

"Here beyond the reach of time," Alexia's doppelganger spoke up. This time it sounded as if it was right behind her, and Alexia spun round despite being warned not to, recoiling in shock as she beheld the creature standing no more than a few paces away.

"What are you?" she demanded, knowing that she should not have spoken, yet unable to help herself. "What sort of creature are you?"

It gazed implacably back at her. Alexia heard a faint shout from somewhere, but it barely registered in her mind. She had to have her answer.

Moments passed, however, and Alexia felt a surge of fear. *I've done exactly what Yui told me not to do,* she realised, and whirled round, intent on running after Yui and Phyqor.

But when she turned again to face the direction in which they had been walking, she saw neither of her companions. They had disappeared.

Instead she saw herself; another copy, faded and translucent as if this world had drained the colour and the spirit from it. Staring into its eyes, Alexia knew a dreadful truth; this actually *was* her- a version that had remained lost here for what might have been an age, condemned to walk in twilight for all eternity, or until the world itself turned dark and formless.

IX - The Emptiness of Centuries

I

Phaedra watched Daniel sleeping, observing with faint amusement the studious frown that marked his face as he drifted through the early morning hours. She had a victory in her hands already, albeit an inconsequential one; the night that had just passed was surely the only one that any two of the Seven had spent together for centuries. And Daniel slept on, perhaps even trusting her, certainly not caring if she attempted to kill him.

Her smile faded at the thought of death, unattainable, unknowable. She stared across at the full-length mirror on the wall that faced the four-poster bed, observed the pristine youthfulness of her body, and her expression became one of cold, silent hatred as her eyes took in the smooth tautness of her skin, the firmness of her breasts, the absence of wrinkles and even blemishes anywhere on her body.

Phaedra scratched at her arm until it bled and crimson droplets marked the blankets on which she sat. She watched morbidly as her efforts faded. Then she shuddered and convulsed, rage and despair overcoming her for a moment, although she could not weep a single tear.

I last wept in the old world, she reminded herself, drawing a deep breath and glancing at Daniel's naked form, as the last evidence of her brief attack upon herself faded into memory. *I can't remember why I even cried. I was mortal then. I suppose I must have had my reasons. They would have seemed important. Life would have been urgent, and all its richer moments points of even greater urgency.*

Their coupling had been brief and detached, as they allowed their bodies to play out the functions for which they had been designed. They had looked pointedly away from each other, their attention fixed on other objects. Phaedra found the act more pleasurable if she thought distant thoughts of unrelated matters; perhaps Daniel did as well.

She remembered that in the old world, some people had said to look into someone's eyes during the act of fornication was to see, for a moment, the secrets of their soul. She had no idea if that was true or not, but she cared nothing for whatever secrets Daniel might have stowed away- she suspected he had none of any lasting consequence- and perhaps that was another reason why she had looked away. Certainly she had felt discomforted by the proximity of his oddly clear eyes, but not because she wanted to avoid whatever banal secrets he guarded. She simply wondered why he, alone amongst the Seven, appeared to hold some faint, vague hope in his heart.

And what hope is it? she asked the sleeping man, allowing her gaze to wander the length and breadth of his body. *What hope could you possibly have, that we have not already discarded? Or is it simply some remnant of your personality? It irks the others; I saw the contempt in their eyes when you spoke. They dislike the brightness of your enthusiasm. Maybe they think of you as a naive simpleton, or a man who has worn his cloak of humanity a little too long.*

She felt certain that Garret or Omir, both of them monsters bearing the shapes of men, would destroy Daniel in a moment if they could find a way. Or perhaps they would spend a decade or two rather than a moment.

Or they might kill themselves or each other first, Phaedra thought, smiling as she pictured them with knives held at each other's throats, wide-eyed and desperate for the end.

With an effort she put thoughts of her comrades and their imagined demise to one side. More interesting matters remained to be dealt with. She shared Daniel's belief that they ought to make certain of the spy-girl's death one way or another, and if that meant scanning the great western marshes and the vast effort that that involved, then so be it. Phaedra longed only for death, yet she had no yearning for the chaos that would ensue if rumours of the Watchers' origins somehow spread, and worse still, could be proved in some way. *We find a way to still rumours and keep the peace,* she thought, *and then we attend to the matter of the* marandaal. *We preserve our empire. Then we persist, until we find a way to stop persisting.*

Daniel stirred at her side and opened his eyes. "You're still here," he said, looking not at her but into the mirror.

"We have work to do," Phaedra reminded him. "I suggest we use the scanning waters to scour the surface of that miserable marshland, and look for evidence of the girl. She'll have left a trail if she survived, even if it's visible only in the effect she had as she passed through." She turned to face him, resting her head on her arm. Noting his continued state of arousal- he had just woken up after all, she reminded herself- Phaedra smiled and mused, "It's still a pleasure, don't you find, to be so unlike Garret and Issele?"

"Their hatred bores me," Daniel said. "It eats away at them daily, but something still leaves them fresh for more of the same each morning." He paused and glanced across at her. "I may as well tell you this; why should I not? Garret is a man of unusual secrets..."

"He likes to kill, rape and torture- don't we all?" Phaedra rejoined. "Such acts provide a little spark of life, of excitement, just for a moment. The city animals will breed and produce more of their own; they always do. They're easy to replace..."

"No. I don't mean that. He has other secrets. He has music that only he can conjure. It's in a room that he guards well."

"Music." Phaedra gave him a contemptuous look. "Why would you care so much about some music?"

"If you had heard it too," he told her, "then you wouldn't say that. You would be thinking of a way to access the lair where he keeps it."

"I doubt that very much."

"Tomorrow morning, I'll take you to a place where we can hear it if we listen carefully. Then you'll see. I must have it, Phaedra." He paused, and then added, "It's from the old world. It was ancient even in *our* time."

She moved her legs over the side of the bed and sat up. "Priorities, Daniel. You need to learn about them. How old were you when we arrived here?"

"Twenty-five."

"And sometimes it shows. We'll listen to your music if you wish, though I'm liable to mock you for it- what is music after all but a pattern of sounds? However, we have waters to disturb first- both here in the Sanctum and out west in that twilit hell."

II

The scanning waters had been held in their saucers, baths and fonts for centuries; they required no replenishment. One of the many mysteries dating back to the older, mostly ruined part of the Sanctum, they had originally been created for an entirely different reason now forgotten, but their use as *far-reachers* was invaluable. Somehow the water these vessels contained was linked to water elsewhere in the land, perhaps even all the water in the world. Each of the Seven had found themselves able to reach out to certain other places and discover what might be happening there by touching one or more of these never-drying pools. The process was wearying and failed to work as often as it succeeded, but sometimes the effort was worth the pain and frustration.

"Do you remember," Phaedra remarked as she and Daniel stood in the hall, "how we came to this world knowing

173

nothing of such forces? We can use them, but even as we stand here now we know nothing meaningful about them."

"Water should evaporate," Daniel agreed, "but the water here never has. Unless it condenses out of the air and somehow finds its way back to the receptacles, drawn by something hidden..."

"Oh, I prefer to call it magic. Even if you can devise a plausible theory for the replenishment of the water, you can't devise one for the *journey* that it takes us on. These are liquid windows to the world, Daniel. Fragments of the world, at least."

"I still cannot understand why we allow them to persist," Daniel said suddenly.

"I don't know what you're talking about."

"The creatures- the *failures*- that were sent into the Bonemord, and which have been allowed to reproduce and to form groups and alliances. What have we learned from them? How often do we even *observe* them these days?"

Phaedra shrugged. "I'd do away with them all in an instant myself."

They stood near one of the larger pools and reached out their hands above the water. "The Bonemord," Daniel murmured, closing his eyes. After a moment, Phaedra repeated the words and closed her eyes as well.

The water in the pool trembled, a multitude of ripples echoing outwards from various points as if a number of stones had been dropped into it at random. As they placed their hands on the surface it became yet more agitated, until they sank beneath the surface.

Phaedra had prepared herself for the savage pain that coursed through her body like a black wave, yet still she cried out. Back and forth the crushing agony ran. Perhaps its power was such that it ruined her insides as it went, and only her body's infinite capacity to heal itself saved her from collapsing dead to the ground, destroyed from within.

She forced herself through the pain. Phaedra imagined that she lay at the bottom of a vast ocean surrounded by absolute darkness, her shape defined by the immense pressure towering above her. Finally her mind glimpsed a shimmer of light up ahead, a construct not of her own mind but of the scanning waters. Slowly she moved towards it, concentrating on the halo of faint illumination that marked her exit route from the blackness between the chamber where her body stood and her destination.

After she passed through the light, Phaedra eventually saw a dim picture of a watery expanse, dotted with islands, and in the distance a much larger, taller island. In her mind's eye she moved towards it, rushing at speed over the murky waters of the marsh, until she reached a shoreline. Faintly she sensed Daniel's presence a little way behind.

Halfway up the hill on the island, a great metal spear had been driven into the ground. Two bedraggled, hideous figures stood near it, staring out over the lower marshland.

It was difficult to listen to what they were saying- the scanning waters were far better for observing than listening, much like the smaller, lesser water-mirrors that a few of the Watchers were able to use, and the creatures' vocal capabilities were in any case compromised. Nevertheless, Phaedra caught enough of their words to understand their discussion.

They'll come for us... great in number.

Barrik must answer.

No sorcery could...

She came from somewhere else.

Something- perhaps a disturbance in the atmosphere or conditions- cut her tenuous link to their muttered conversation. Phaedra tried to listen again, but could not hear anything else they said. Nevertheless, the last thing she had heard them say remained lodged in her mind. Why would a miserable creature of the Bonemord say such a thing?

Her vision of the great swampland headed onwards at her will. Daniel loomed at her side, invisible yet tangible. Time passed; they came close to other denizens of the Bonemord but found none of them worthy of investigation. Eventually they reached the far north of the marsh, where patches of drier land reached out into watery inlets. Phaedra scanned the area thoroughly, but her patience grew thin. She was about to draw back into herself and suggest trying again later when she heard Daniel's voice whisper through her thoughts.

There. Just to the left. A hundred paces or so.

And after a while, faint in the mist, she saw what he had seen; a small rowing boat and oars, abandoned.

Phaedra drifted towards the boat. She could see nothing that indicated who might have paddled it this far, to the very edge of the Bonemord, but she *did* notice faint boot prints in the muddier areas. They headed north.

Anyone who walks north to the edge of the mists dies, she recalled. *We made it so. We proved the fact time and again many decades ago, and even more recently some of the creatures themselves have proved it again for us, stumbling hopefully to their oblivion.*

So if we follow these steps, we'll find either the body of a particularly stupid Bonemord creature, or...

Or the steps will continue on and out of the Bonemord altogether.

Together they headed slowly on, the drifting vision of the great swamp growing a little darker with the passing of time. Here and there the prints faded, but sooner or later they reappeared. *Quite small,* Phaedra noted. *We can't be entirely certain, but probably made by a woman.*

The ground sloped gradually upwards, until the mists had cleared and the ground underfoot was dry. The way ahead grew indistinct in Phaedra's mind; neither of them could reach further than this. The scanning waters themselves required water, she reminded herself. They would be unable to see anything further ahead; the link would fade away to nothing.

But it doesn't matter, she thought. *We've seen what we needed to see.*

Now we leave, she said to Daniel. As soon as he agreed, she broke their connection with the marshland.

They opened their eyes in the same instant and stared at each other.

"Someone rowed to the edge of the Bonemord and then walked away north unscathed," Phaedra said. "Only someone who had wandered into that place from elsewhere could have done that. Think about what she knows- because it's undoubtedly her. She may or may not have entirely understood what she saw Omir and Stephan doing, but I'm certain she would have understood some of it. She will have fled north as far as she can go. I expect she'll keep on for a while longer."

"Beyond our reach."

"Certainly beyond the reach of the scanning." Phaedra stared at her indistinct reflection in the water for a moment. "But she may not have mentioned anything to anyone. She may be in hiding. Remember, if she heads further north than the Wall, she'll be in unfriendly territories. I suggest we send someone after her."

"Who?"

Phaedra gave a cold little smile. "Well, certainly not a Watcher. No, it has to be someone who might be able to blend in even with the savages of the north. It has to be a human. A professional, highly-trained killer who will complete the task efficiently and ask no questions. Between us all, we should find it easy to prepare a list of likely candidates and whittle that down to the best of them all. The matter should be dealt with swiftly though."

"Between us *all*, you said." Daniel frowned and shook his head. "Should we reveal what we've found to the others? I would suggest not."

Phaedra laughed despite the intense weariness she felt from the effort of the scrying. "There's a paradox of sorts in what you said, Daniel. We detest one another, we tell ourselves that the others cannot be trusted, but in truth surely we are the *only* ones we can trust. Who else has been through everything that we have experienced since we fled the old world? Oh, I mock them and I tease them and I show them the illogic of their interactions, but we are the only ones who, no matter what, can be guaranteed to remain loyal- in certain matters at least."

Daniel thought for a moment. "The High Watchers. Their loyalty cannot be questioned."

"They are machines. They do as they're told." Phaedra's tone was contemptuous. "But the problem lies with the Watchers that were created here. I suspect that unless every atom of humanity is ground out of them at the time of transformation, such issues are always likely to occur. They *question*. Oh, they obey, but they analyse a little too much. They like to look beyond the horizon of their purpose. They are remade, but there's a residue that lingers. I suppose you could call it the spark of humanity, if you were being whimsical."

"Without them, policing the city and surrounding area would be considerably harder," Daniel pointed out.

"Oh, of course. They've proved most useful. But as we've seen, some are capable of straying from the path on which they were originally set."

Daniel shook his head, ill at ease. "It's a little late for such judgements now, Phaedra. The *marandaal* gather in the east. They will come for us."

"Then if anyone or anything survives, it will know what happens when an irresistible force meets an immovable object," Phaedra said lightly.

"Do you truly feel no fear? None whatsoever?"

Phaedra leaned back against a marble pillar and regarded him with equal stoniness. To Daniel she might as well have been a statue or pillar herself for a moment- a cold figurine, pale and harsh and as brimful of humanity as a High Watcher. *I slept with her,* he reminded himself, *and for a fleeting moment it felt as if she yielded- as if a woman hid behind the monster. But it was only a glimpse. And we're all monsters now- or demons, or gods, or sorcerors, or whatever the people of the day choose to whisper.*

"I look forward to the confrontation," she said eventually. "I have no idea if they can destroy us or if we can destroy them. It's the *possibility* of it all. I've put many people to death, Daniel- some of them for trivial reasons, in my more tempestuous moments- and I've always been fascinated by that final look in their eyes. I want to defeat the *marandaal*, and maintain our empire, but I also want the possibility of dying. We all do, you included. Do not tell me you still enjoy watching the interplay of night and day, the phases and conjunctions of the moons, the changing of the seasons..."

"There's another paradox. We all want to die, but as you pointed out we also want to see our little empire last another thousand years."

"Much effort has gone into Harn. I'm sure we'll defend it to the hilt." Daniel could not tell if Phaedra was being serious or not. "We'll throw everything we have at those that would reduce our work to rubble. Truthfully though, I think we will choose to survive if we can, either by fighting or fleeing. Instinct will override the desire for an end to it all. We are still human, in a crude sense."

"Fleeing where? If they defeat us, they will eventually spread throughout Aona."

"Then we have to force-create a Gate to slip through," Phaedra retorted. "We managed it before, long ago. It can be done again."

Daniel shook his head. "There will be nowhere left to run to, Phaedra. The *marandaal* are a collective wave of destruction. For thousands of years they have spread through all space. They destroy all life they encounter. They influence and use Gates at will. They are a poison that will eventually bring an end to all life, a disease that we set in motion. Do you really think, after all this time, during which they have spread throughout the Existence, there is *anywhere* else to flee to?"

Phaedra simply stared at him.

"And so we'll fight them," Daniel continued, "because the others will realise the same if they haven't already. You know it to be true, Phaedra. You simply haven't acknowledged it."

Suddenly exhausted, he sat down, leaning against another of the hall's great pillars. Phaedra watched him and then turned to leave. "I'll request a second meeting, now that we've found what happened to the Watcher's servant," she said. "I don't expect they'll take kindly to our acting against consensus, but it's done now. I'm sure their response will be entertaining."

She hurried away without a further word, leaving Daniel alone with his thoughts of oblivion for cold company.

III

Phaedra looked forward to revealing to the other five that she and Daniel had acted contrary the agreed course of action where Nia was concerned. She had imagined their varying responses and worked out what she thought would be clever answers to each of them.

She called the second meeting without explaining its purpose, hoping that the very fact that *she* of all of them had called it might stir their curiosity sufficiently for them to attend. And attend they did, but Phaedra was left disappointed and inwardly infuriated by the lack of interest from the majority.

"Let her go," Garret said with a wave of the hand, sitting back in his high-backed chair.

"You care nothing for the rumours she may spread?" Daniel asked.

"The savages of the North feed daily on rumours and superstitions." Garret gave Daniel a look of utter derision. "All she can do is give them one more tall tale. Do you truly worry so much, Daniel?"

"Supposing she does eventually dare to speak of what she has seen and what she thinks that she knows," Issele spoke up. "Who would believe her? She would not dare to utter outlandish rumours anywhere in our territories- and if she flees into the lands of the witch-worshippers, what then? There surely cannot be any rumours about the Watchers that those creatures have not already made up over time. Information that cannot be verified and proved is useless. It's just another rumour."

"Then you intend to do nothing about her," Phaedra said. "Have you lost your appetite for pursuing your enemies, Issele?"

"Do you still think you can goad me into pointless action after all these centuries?" the older woman rejoined. "Regardless, this girl is nothing but a frightened fugitive somewhere. She'll not wish to draw attention to herself. I suspect one of two things will happen. She'll meet an unpleasant end, drawing the ire of some savage or other with an especially poor disposition towards people from civilised Harn- or she'll live out what remains of her days as anonymously as possible, perhaps as a servant or slave."

"Enough of the matter," Garret said irritably. "The girl is unworthy of discussion." He glanced at Omir. "Why have you not yet found your missing prisoner, Omir?"

"Watchers have been sent out to search for her. A High Watcher has also been placed permanently at each of the city gates until she is located and captured..."

"Interesting." Garret tapped his fingers on the table, barely able to hide his anger. "She can escape the confines of your tower and yet you think having a High Watcher positioned at each exit from Luudhoq will stop her melting through the city walls in the same way. This is your mess, Omir. I would say the least you could do would be to respond intelligently to your own mistakes..."

Dark and glowering, Omir stood up. "You do *nothing*, Garret, except sit in sullen judgement. Immortality does not sit well with you, does it? Your misery is reflected in your casual anger. It's all you have left."

Issele laughed softly to herself. Garret threw her a look of pure hatred and stood slowly, turning his attention to Omir. Phaedra noted the way his hands shook, the way his cold blue eyes shone. *Ah,* she thought, watching them both. *I know what happens now. How long has it been? Ten years perhaps? I wouldn't know; I've kept away from them.*

The two men rushed at each other in a sudden blur of fury.

Time passed, and the violence continued unabated. The other five watched in silence as Omir and Garret traded blows, gouges, even broken limbs until they both howled in pain and screamed obscenities at each other.

They're like children, Phaedra thought as she saw Garret's thumb press deep into Omir's eye socket. Even that injury would heal. *They've lived for so many long centuries, they've seen the wonders of the Existence, they've been gifted immortality for some secret reason we cannot even comprehend... but they squabble and bite like rats. They'll fight until their argument bores them; their bodies will heal but the invisible wound of their despair will grow ever deeper, ever more infected.*

Phaedra suddenly imagined a world that surely none of the Seven had contemplated before; the bleak vision swam before her eyes almost as clearly as her view of the two screaming men pointlessly maiming each other.

She saw a world where the *marandaal* had been cast out and the Gates sealed or shattered; but this was also a world where Luudhoq stood no more. The people had been decimated. The Watchers and even the High Watchers had died in the struggle against the *marandaal*. From the north, a great darkness in the form of tens of thousands of the savages marched, led by witches and warlocks who tapped some unseen, unknowable force; Mornkastle fell, and they marched on towards Luudhoq, killing and butchering whatever they could along the way.

In Phaedra's vision, the Seven awaited their enemies alone in the Sanctum, which alone of all the city's buildings still remained intact. Their empire was no more; they had no citizens to subvert or torture or play with howsoever they wished. They had tried to force-create a Gate, madly reasoning that anywhere- any world, no matter its nature- would be preferable to the empty hell that theirs had become. But their attempt had not worked. Aona was dying, the forces that it had once facilitated dying along with it. Energy seeped away to some other place, and hope drained with it.

Onwards the savages came, driven by the great darkness that had held the Seven at bay for so many centuries. Shadows slipped from out of the earth; a sickly light shone from chasms that suddenly opened.

Hell, Phaedra thought.

She almost ran from the chamber, but her exit went unnoticed even by Daniel, who remained transfixed by the sight of Omir ripping Garret's cheek apart and biting at the bright and tender flesh beneath, caught up in a frenzy that only centuries of ill will could create.

X - The Brittle Heart

I

For days after her escape from the Bonemord, Nia walked steadfastly north wherever she could- along paths, through fields and past small woodlands, up hills- where the way around would have taken far longer- sticking resolutely to her chosen direction. Occasionally she found luck on her side; she was offered a ride on a farmer's cart on two separate occasions and gratefully accepted those offers. Both journeys took her at least a further league along her way. The weather, though often chilly, at least remained dry. Most nights she found barns and outhouses in which to sleep, and curled up in piles of hay or between sacks of grain or animal feed.

Yet Nia could find no peace, awake or asleep. During the day, as she trudged wearily along she wondered how she could find or earn money to keep herself fed and alive. She remained desperately hungry; aside from late berries and fruits and some crops that she managed to take from fields and wash whenever she found a stream, she could find little to eat, and the hunger in her belly grew into a nagging, continuous pain. She asked farmers if they might have work for her, even offering to work for nothing except a couple of meals a day. On each occasion she was told that they could ill-afford an extra mouth to feed, especially with winter coming.

Aside from the troubles that each day brought, Nia had found in recent days that her sleep was plagued by dreams of being pursued by a silent, implacable presence. She had considered that this might be the work of the Seven somehow reaching out to poison her mind even as she slept, but Nia felt a nagging certainty that someone or something else was at work. Often she would lie awake with first light still some time away, shivering as she pressed herself

184

between hay bales or whatever she could find to alleviate the desperate chill, and wondering what it was that tormented her. She had long been used to nightmares- her childhood in the orphanage had seen to that- but this was something entirely different. It felt like a restlessness that settled into her each evening, an invisible sleeping partner that would not let her be.

When she eventually reached the town of Telith, Nia had resigned herself to a life of begging, at least for a short while. She had no coins; her poor diet had started to make her feel more ill even than before, and although she was desperate to keep heading north and eventually put herself beyond the reach of everything she had known, she knew that she could not continue as she had for much longer. A diet of mouldering berries and nuts and raw vegetables pulled from the mud could not sustain her. She could not bathe in streams for much longer without at last succumbing to the chill.

Nia found herself sitting at a corner between two main thoroughfares, filthy and exhausted, head bowed and hands outstretched. Several times she almost lost consciousness as she listened to the sounds of people and vehicles passing by. Aside from one or two jeers she attracted no attention.

Sometime in the afternoon, Nia felt a hand touch hers and press a coin into it; flinching in surprise, she raised her heavy head and opened her eyes. The man that squatted nearby was a little older than her, lean and lithe, his short-cut hair brown with flecks of grey.

"This could be yours if you come with me," he said quietly, and Nia looked dazedly down at the coin his finger was pressing into her palm. She was shocked to see gold glinting in the late sunlight.

A moment later she recalled what he had said. "If..." She cleared her throat and tried to speak again, but her voice had dwindled to a ragged, hoarse whisper. "If I..."

"We see few beggars on the streets of Telith, and the townsfolk prefer to keep it that way," he said. "Ah, now I see what you're thinking. But I've nothing fearful in store for you."

"What do you want with me?" Nia managed to ask, although she already had an idea.

He confirmed her suspicions with the next words he uttered, and the furtive, almost apologetic smile with which he spoke them. "The truth? I'm alone. I have needs. I'll ensure you're fed, washed and clothed. You look as if you need all three. And I see you've been less than successful in your attempts to stir the good people of Telith into pity at your plight. As I said, we see few beggars on the streets here." He withdrew the coin from her hand and held it lightly between forefinger and thumb. "What do you say?"

Nia almost burst into tears and laughter at the same time. The thought that someone should be desperate enough to approach a filth-encrusted wanderer with such an offer was ludicrous to her. He might well be a lunatic. But as he had pointed out, his was the only coin that had been offered today. In all likelihood it was the only offer she would receive if she remained sitting slumped by the street corner all day or even for a tenday.

But will he even pay me when he's done with me? she asked herself.

There's only one way I can find out.

"Thank you," she said, glancing around as she noticed that a number of people had stopped to watch their discussion. She heard some of them whispering to one another and giving the man disparaging, sidelong glances as if he was well known in the town for this sort of behaviour. If that was indeed the case, then they cared for her as much or less than they did for him; not one of them warned her or attempted to intervene, and in fact as her apparent benefactor helped her to her feet, a few people took a few hasty steps back as if she might spread whatever diseases she had on to them.

"My name is Arin," he told her when they had put some distance between themselves and the busy middle of the town. They walked along a narrow street bordered by tall, grand houses built in the old style of a century ago with thick, visible wooden beams, black iron doors and thickly whitewashed walls. "And yours?"

"Loren," Nia said after a moment. It was the first name that had come into her head; at first she was mystified as to why, but then she remembered a girl with that name whom she had known for a while at the orphanage.

I hope that isn't an ill omen, she thought to herself. Loren had suffered perhaps even more than Nia during those years. Eventually she had disappeared; amongst the other children a hopeful rumour persisted for a while that she had run away, but Nia had known Loren fairly well- well enough to know that she was not the sort to run away, at least. She suspected that the girl had simply been beaten and raped so viciously one time that she had died from the ordeal.

Arin's dwelling was one of the large houses bordering the street. He ushered her inside; Nia blinked as she took in the well-to-do, clean interior of the house. "I'll have one of the servants prepare a bath for you," he said.

Nia could only nod in response, baffled by the surreal situation. A nagging fear nestled in her stomach, and a moment later that fear multiplied; a horrifying thought had occurred suddenly to her.

What if I shift *whilst he's attending to his certain needs as he called them? It happened when that jailer forced himself on me in the Sanctum. It could easily happen again.*

She told herself to relax over and over as she was led upstairs a short while later by a silent, middle-aged woman, one of Arin's servants. *If you panic then it will surely happen,* she thought, *so keep yourself together, whatever you do.*

In the bathing room upstairs, she waited for the servant to leave, but when it quickly became apparent that the stout woman was going to sit in the room with her Nia undressed and gingerly got into the wide, wooden-brimmed porcelain bath of warm water that had been prepared. The sensation of clean water that actually soothed rather than made her yelp at its iciness almost took her breath away. She exhaled softly as she sank shoulder-deep into the bath.

Out of nervousness, Nia decided after a moment to strike up a conversation with the servant woman. "Have you been with the household long?" she inquired, rubbing days of dirt from her body and watching with a certain amount of disgust as the water began to turn murky.

The woman had lowered her head, presumably out of respect or embarrassment, but now she looked up. Nia saw a curious expression in her eyes, something akin to panic perhaps. "Are you forbidden from talking to me?" she asked softly. "You can simply nod your head if that's so."

The servant looked troubled at that invitation; neither nodding nor shaking her head, she looked instead towards the window in the side wall, through which the sky could be seen darkening. Nia had no idea what to make of that, except that the woman perhaps had permission neither to speak nor give any indication, affirmative or negative, in place of spoken words. *I expect Arin disciplines her with an iron fist,* she thought, continuing to clean herself. *Perhaps the others also, whoever and wherever they are. There must be other servants; how else is this place kept so spotless?*

It did not bode well.

Nia wondered if it might have been better had she declined Arin's offer. *I'd be sitting in the dark still, shivering with the onset of night and wondering if I'd survive it,* she thought. *I might fall asleep and never wake up, and my body would be fought over by feral dogs before the night was over.*

So what choice did I have?

But what will he do to me?

She glanced once again at the servant, but decided there was no point in embarrassing or worrying the woman with more questions. She might not even know what Arin did to women he lured or cajoled back to his house, but if she did then surely she would not be sharing such information.

With all the dirt from her body and hair finally transferred to the water a while later, Nia stepped carefully out of the bath. The servant brought her a large towel made from some soft fabric that Nia had never encountered before, and waited as Nia dried herself, before bringing a long red silk gown from a wardrobe on the other side of the room. She motioned for her to dress, and when Nia could only gape at the exquisite garment, the servant patiently helped her to do so.

The robe caressed her body so softly that Nia let out a quiet sigh, marvelling at its touch. Her heart began to thump more quickly as she wondered fearfully what any of this meant, if indeed it had any meaning. Did Arin commonly demand such facades? *I've never worn anything like this in my life,* she thought dazedly.

The servant ushered her out of the bathing room and along a high passageway that ran between a multitude of rooms. Eventually she stopped at a grand-looking oak-panelled door and knocked softly upon it.

"Enter," came Arin's voice from within. Nia was ushered firmly through and the door closed behind her.

Looking around, Nia concluded that the room was Arin's bedchamber. He sat on the edge of a great four-poster bed positioned facing her and against the back wall, dressed in a dark gown. His face was turned away at first, but then he glanced around. With the room lit by a single lantern, Nia found it difficult to read his expression properly. Perhaps he looked serious, even afraid of something, although what reason could he have for such fear in his own house?

"You look pretty," he said after a moment. "The dress suits you."

Now I know he's insane, Nia thought, and just for an instant she allowed her gaze to quickly take in the ornamentation in the bedroom. Might there be an object she could use to defend herself with, or rather attack him with if she had to? She noticed a couple of small bronze statuettes that could make useful clubs, but they had been placed on a mantelpiece some way across the room.

"Thank you," she replied, remembering what he had just said, and she tried to force a smile.

"Where were you headed?" he asked suddenly. Nia blinked, taken aback. "I saw you in the morning, long before I met you at the corner of the main street," he explained. "You looked as if you'd been travelling for a long time."

"North," Nia said, and shrugged uncomfortably. "Nowhere in particular. Just north."

"Do you have friends or family anywhere?"

Ah, he asks me that in case someone comes looking for me, Nia thought, the chill in her stomach deepening. But before she could even respond, he nodded, and the trace of a smile creased his lips. "Neither," he said softly, and Nia found herself nodding. Suddenly she felt a deep resentment stir within her, directed mostly towards herself. *No friends and no family. No one to care whether I live or die. Well, there are those who crave my death, but perhaps they won't need to concern themselves with that come the morning.*

Arin patted the bed. "Will you lie down?"

She did as bidden, and a moment later he loomed over her, urgency and a strange sadness in his eyes, and undid her robe. "You *are* pretty," he murmured, as if they were having an argument about the matter.

And you're a liar a second time, Nia silently retorted. She closed her eyes, tried desperately to swallow down the dark river of panic that stirred inside her and willed herself to be brave; above all else, to be brave enough not to lose control and *shift.* If she allowed that to happen then surely a fate far worse than death awaited her. She would be handed to the local authorities- once Arin had had enough of her of course, which could be either sooner or later depending on his preferences- and eventually she would be returned to Luudhoq to face the inquisition of the Seven and the High Watchers and spend every moment of her remaining days screaming for them to end her miserable life.

She kept her eyes tightly closed as he discarded his robe and pushed himself into her; the penetration hurt, but then it had never been anything better than uncomfortable. Nia was surprised only that on this occasion it hurt relatively little. After a while, she found the sensation not entirely unpleasant. And then, Arin confounded her further. He whispered in her ear, "I'm sorry."

"Please make it quick," she mumbled, and he did, though not entirely in the way she had imagined. He shuddered, held her tightly for a moment, and withdrew. *What now?* Nia wondered, still seeing nothing but the darkness behind her eyes. *What will you do to me now?*

Arin did nothing to her. She heard him wander across the room and sit at a table. When eventually Nia opened her eyes, she saw him sitting forward, head in hands, weeping silently.

This chain of events was so different to the one she had expected that Nia had no idea what to do. She watched Arin's apparent distress for a while longer, but eventually her fatigue, exacerbated by the bath, lulled her to sleep.

II

Nia woke with natural light falling into the room. The curtains on one side of the room had hidden a set of vast windows which, now revealed, showed her a panorama of Telith's eastern half and part of the land beyond.

She sat up, noticing immediately that her robe had been tied again. A chair had been placed by the side of the bed; her clothes lay neatly upon it. Inexplicably, they had been washed and pressed.

Someone knocked upon the door, making her jump. After a moment, the handle turned and another servant, a cheerful, blonde-haired woman perhaps a little older than Nia, peered in. "Ah, you're awake," she noted.

Nia stared helplessly at her.

"Please, once you're dressed, come downstairs to the morning room. Breakfast is served," the servant continued.

"Wait," Nia said suddenly as the servant turned her head and prepared to close the door. "Why are you speaking to me? The other woman... she wouldn't say a word..."

"There's a good reason for that. Martha's quite dumb, and a little shy with it. My name is Elina, by the way. It's good to meet you, Loren, however briefly."

Once Elina had left, Nia undid her robe and put her clothes on, marvelling at how soft they felt. She caught sight of herself in the mirror on the other side of the bed, and stood transfixed for a while, barely able to recognise the woman she saw staring back at her. *Still not pretty,* she thought, *but even I look a lot better after a bath followed by a night in an actual bed.*

If anything the confusion she felt now was stronger than ever. Why had Arin brought her back here, and provided her with a hot bath and a bed for the night, when he could simply have done what he needed to do and thrown her away, if that was all he wanted? And now, apparently, she was to be served breakfast.

What more does he want? There has to be something, but I can't even begin to guess what it might be.

She made her way downstairs, and found the morning room soon enough, for the door to it had been left open. Airy and spacious, it had a long, ornate table set at its centre on which a mouth-watering array of food had been placed. Arin sat at the head of the table, but he appeared to have eaten nothing. In fact, he looked lost in his own thoughts.

Finally he glanced up and gave Nia a faint smile. "Did you sleep well, Loren?"

"I... I did," she replied, and then added uncertainly, "Thank you."

"Have something to eat," he said, gesturing to the freshly-baked bread, sliced ham, cheese and fruit that awaited her. He then began his own breakfast, as if he had been waiting for her before eating anything. Watching him, Nia judged that the food was surely safe enough to eat; she sat at the table and began her breakfast, which turned out to be every bit as delicious as its aroma. She tried to keep herself from cramming it all down in a hurry, mindful of the danger of doing so after eating so little for so many days; nevertheless, by the time she finished and sat back, she felt replete almost to the point of bursting.

Arin glanced across at her. "I'll give you your gold before you leave," he said, "or would you prefer a dozen silver stars? If you happen to drop one of those without noticing, well it wouldn't be the end of the world."

Nia gaped at him.

"Ah. You didn't entirely expect payment, did you?" He pushed his plate to one side, took a draught of water, and smiled to himself. "Tell me, what *did* you expect?"

"I don't know," Nia said after thinking for a moment. *Is this some kind of trick?* she asked herself. "I'm not sure I cared what happened. I was exhausted and hungry. I couldn't have walked further, so I was at the mercy of anyone who happened along."

"I have a reputation in this town," Arin remarked. "One which is not entirely pleasant. Since my wife's death, I have sought the comfort of other women."

Nia nodded, not knowing what to say, although she wondered why the folk of Telith would be so ill-disposed to him simply for that reason. Surely that was what any man would have done? If he thought of his reputation as *not entirely pleasant,* what in the world might he have made of some of the men *she* had known during her life?

"They stay awhile- some for a few days, if they wish- and then they leave," Arin continued, as if he needed to explain himself. "I pay them, of course. Most are from other places, like you. Telith is not the largest of towns, and word spread some time ago of my activities. The local women steer clear of me for the most part, although of course there are always a few who value gold more than moral code. But whoever they are and wherever they're from, I tell myself every time that this will be the last time. Yet it never is. I have disgraced the memory of my wife so many times now that a part of me urges the other part of me to continue my behaviour. I loathe myself."

Nia nodded, thinking briefly back to his distress the previous night.

"It's a fleeting comfort." He looked her up and down. "That said, it's a comfort nonetheless."

"Thank you," Nia said uncertainly.

"For the shelter and the food? Or for turning you into a whore for the night?"

"I've suffered far worse." Nia paused and then added, "I've also done worse things myself."

"And would you have cared to stay a while longer, if I paid you? If you were not so intent on hurrying north?"

When she nodded, he smiled to himself; to Nia it looked like the saddest, most defeated expression she had ever seen. "I have gold," he said. "In fact, that's all I have. I'm still astonished by the things people will do for gold. But you have some mission that no amount of wealth can force you to put aside- am I right?"

Nia nodded. "I have to leave this morning." The thought came to her suddenly of agents of the Seven arriving in Telith with her description and being readily told that she was at Arin's house, or had been. What might they do to him, if she was indeed still being hunted? For a moment she considered telling him, warning him, but with an effort she stopped herself. It would do no good. He might even have her held as a fugitive and an enemy of Harn if he knew who she was running from. He didn't seem like a man with any special affiliations, but she could not take the risk.

No, she told herself, looking down at the floor. *I can't tell him. I can't tell anyone. I can just keep running in the hope that my luck will change for the better. If he lets me go, and with a bag of silver for my troubles, then it might well be changing already.*

"I won't ask what sends you," he remarked, "but I see so much pain and fear when I look at you. I hope you find peace, one way or another."

He left the room, and returned a short while later with a small pouch which he opened, showing her the twelve silver stars glittering faintly inside. "I hope they'll accept these beyond the Never-Built Wall, if you're headed that far," he remarked.

As far as that and much further, Nia thought.

A short while later, as she stood on the threshold and glanced back at him, he said to her, "Good luck to you, Loren."

Nia struggled for words. "And to you," she said finally, and walked swiftly away; she could no longer bear that look of immeasurable grief in his eyes.

III

For days afterwards, Nia's tentative hope that her luck might be turning appeared to bear fruit; she purchased foodstuffs at small villages and farmsteads, rested in a guesthouse each night if one was available, and felt a measure of her energy return. The worst pains she suffered were those caused by blisters and cuts, and they paled in comparison to the hunger and exhaustion that had plagued her before her arrival in Telith. She paid for further rides on carts or coaches heading north, until eventually she realised- by attending to a conversation between two people nearby in a village market one afternoon and listening to their accents- that she had travelled beyond the Never-Built Wall.

Yet as the days went by Nia's mood inexplicably soured; the unease that had gripped her in the days before her luck had improved returned with a vengeance. Whenever she dared to glance back she saw nothing to cause alarm, but that did nothing to ease her worry.

She grew to dread the nights even more than the days, not because she feared that one of her enemies would steal up and slit her throat, but because of the vivid, frightening dreams that now came as she slept.

These nightmares had one constant: Yui.

Sometimes the girl would pursue her, following at an oddly relaxed pace as if it hardly mattered how fast Nia ran or whatever attempts she might make to evade capture. She would slowly gain on her as Nia hurtled over open land or through some unknown forest or town, before suddenly appearing in front of her. During the first few such episodes Nia recalled her speaking, although she could not hear any of the words the child uttered. As the nights went on however, she began to hear them, faint and yet laced with a cold menace. They conveyed a grim promise: *I'm coming for you, Nia.*

Several times Yui found a way to twist her dreams so that she was incarcerated in the Sanctum once again, or in the Bonemord, or even- inexplicably- back in the orphanage as a child, which to Nia was every bit as bad as being held in the Sanctum.

Each morning she would wake suddenly, screaming or weeping, even scratching madly at herself as if the malignant presence of the child she had helped incarcerate had somehow embedded itself in her flesh and could be removed by physical means. The bright urgency of the nightmare would diminish a little as she sat up, took deep breaths and told herself that a dream was a dream and nothing more; yet some semblance of it would remain throughout the day that followed. She could neither forget it nor even put it to the back of her mind. The core of the nightmare, the image of the moment when a smiling and triumphant Yui caught her, remained etched sharply in her mind, a bright and terrible picture that refused to fade as the day wore on.

Whenever she stopped to rest during the day, Nia would attempt to reason that these dreams were the inevitable result of an illness of the mind. The idea was plausible enough; she had met a number of people who had developed such afflictions, and knew that often they happened because of terrible events in their lives. *I've had my share of those*, she told herself, *so maybe that is what's happening to me. I'm starting to unravel.*

That notion was frightening enough, but the fact that she could probably do nothing at all about it was even worse. Nia tried to tell herself to have courage, but the days of weariness and solitude allowed too much time for dark thoughts to eat away at what mental fortitude she had left; then of course she had the nights to look forward to.

One evening, as she bedded down in a guest-house on the edge of a small town, she heard the screams of a distressed child through the walls of her room. For one chilling moment Nia fancied that those cries sounded exactly like those Yui had sometimes uttered during their journey to Luudhoq. With a trembling hand she reached down for the bottle of cheap root spirit that she had brought up with her in the hope that it would calm her nerves as well as help her sleep. Grimacing as she swallowed the foul liquid, Nia sat up on her bed and waited for the wailing to cease.

She heard a woman- probably the child's mother- comforting the girl and singing a lullaby until finally she stopped sobbing. Nia smiled sourly to herself in the gloom, took another swig of her drink and wondered briefly if lullabies had some subtle magical quality that eased horrors of the mind. *If only I could learn to sing one to myself,* she thought.

IV

Nia woke up screaming, doubled over in front of the mirror- and *male.*

I'm losing control, she thought fearfully when she lifted her head and stared back at her wide, tear-stained eyes. *I'm losing control because of my dreams, and there's nothing I can to do to stop it.*

She considered that these night-time episodes, in which Yui always appeared sooner or later without fail, were not exactly dreams: they were *invasions* of her dreams. She could be anywhere, doing anything, but no matter where she was and no matter what events took place, the girl would eventually appear, sloe-eyed and malevolent, and more powerful than Nia could have believed.

And always she says the same thing, Nia reminded herself, *when I can understand her at all.*

Everything bad that's happened to me and my father and Alexia is because of you. I'm going to make you suffer for the rest of your life.

Nia took a deep, trembling breath and tried to calm herself. Once her pulse had slowed and the panic had dissipated a little, she *shifted* to her natural form and returned to her bed, where she sat staring at the floor.

There are two possibilities, she thought. *Either I'm losing my mind...*

...or Yui is losing it for me.

The notion of being rendered insane terrified her, but even that could not compare with the horror of Yui's actual presence in her dreams, engineering the devastation of her mind.

198

"Can you hear me?" Nia whispered. "Can you know what I'm saying or thinking, even now? What will it take for you to leave me alone?"

No answer came. Nia jumped as a shadow passed behind her in the mirror- perhaps a bird flying past the bedroom window, but her heart leapt as if one of the Seven had materialised in the glass.

Could I reason with her? she wondered. *What if I pleaded for forgiveness? Would she then leave me be?*

Nia had no idea. If Yui truly lurked in her dreams, turning them into shrieking nightmares, then there was no saying what she might do. The actions of a nine-year-old hell-bent on revenge could not be predicted.

Mid-morning had arrived by the time she roused herself from these thoughts and dressed. She made her way downstairs and out of the guest house, into the little courtyard. Soft rain fell; the flagstones gleamed almost silvery blue in the gradually strengthening light as the sun struggled to burn through the clouds. Nia breathed in the damp air, and glanced through the archway and into the street. Only a few people were out and about.

Who might be able to help me? she wondered desperately. *A physician or healer of some sort? Could there be someone here or anywhere else who might understand or even believe what's happening to me? Who would I dare tell about something like this?*

Sighing, she turned and sat on the high steps leading up to the side door of the guest house and tried to figure out what to do.

She considered approaching people to ask if they might know of someone who could help with illnesses of the mind. Consideration was as far as she got; she wandered up and down the street, not daring to speak to anyone, fearful of their reaction. Occasionally villagers would stare at her, some with curiosity and others with outright suspicion. Nia averted her eyes and kept walking until she had reached the other end of the settlement. Tiredly she wiped strands of hair away from her face and sat on an old tree stump by the side of the track, at a loss.

The morning wore on; eventually the rain eased off. Nia's thoughts turned for the time being to other matters, the most pressing of which was her need to find some more coins for food. She had only a few copper stars and one of the silver ones that Arin had given her. It was either that, she reminded herself, or she would be forced to steal, and her punishment if caught would no doubt be especially harsh- she could pass herself off as a girl from Mornkastle, but in a remote place such as this even a citizen of Mornkastle was probably viewed with suspicion.

I could offer to work for food, she thought. *I may have to at this rate. But would I find work even then?*

"Troubled?" enquired a voice from behind her. Nia jumped and whirled round, to find a woman of late middle age standing a few paces away, leaning on a sturdy polished wooden stick. "I saw you arrive yesterday," she said. "You're far from home, yes?"

The woman's accent was so strong that for a moment Nian struggled to make out some of her words. "I am," she said finally, and added, "I don't suppose you know of anyone who needs any work done? Any sort will do. I'll work just for food and a bed if I have to..."

"No, no." The woman raised a hand as if Nia's pleading had already become too much for her. "But in any case, you'll not be able to do a decent day's work in your state."

"What do you mean?"

She shuffled a little closer. "I said I saw you arrive yesterday. You didn't see me, I expect, but I paid close attention to *you*. Oh yes."

"Why would you do that?" Nia asked uneasily.

"I could see plainly that something ailed you even as I watched you walking along the road. Some people walk in darkness. I see them as easily as others see the colour of hair or eyes." The woman shuffled a little nearer. "Some illness plagues you. Maybe you think you cannot talk about it, certainly not to strangers in a strange place. Am I right? I believe I am. And you'd be right to keep it to yourself. Darkness of the mind frightens folk. They have no idea what it might do to *them*. As if it's catching!"" She grinned at her own observation, and then nodded as Nia gaped at her. "Yes, I have a gift for knowing such things. My name is Xunaal..."

"I'm... mine is Nia. Do you... I mean, are you..."

"I'm a healer of difficult afflictions. That doesn't mean I can heal *you* by the way, even if I can see a little of what it is that eats away at you. But I can try. You fascinate me." Xunaal tapped the stick thoughtfully on the grass at the edge of the track; the breeze moved her white-tinged hair across her face as she stood in silent contemplation. Nia wondered what she might be thinking.

Then with a sinking feeling she remembered something. "I have only a silver star and two copper stars for my food and lodging, no more," she said, then added as an afterthought: "Maybe I could do some work for you, if you could..."

"There's no need. If I need work done I do it myself." Xunaal stared at her. "And if I choose to help you, it's because I'm curious about you and what desperation drove you here. Keep your coins. I request other, fairer payments."

"And do you?" Nia asked quietly. "Do you choose to help me?"

Xunaal pointed to a stone cottage set away from the street a little way. "I live there," she said. "I will try to help you. I'll give you the opportunity to be helped, at the very least. Will you come with me?"

Wordlessly Nia got up and followed Xunaal as she shuffled across the road. The sun emerged at last as they reached the threshold of the woman's house.

Xunaal took her down a flight of creaking wooden stairs and into a basement. As they arrived in a cool chamber lined with stone walls and shelves, her attention was grabbed by the grisly assortment of body parts in jars that stood upon the shelves. Nia stared, transfixed but wishing she could look away.

"Is this the payment you spoke of?" she asked faintly at last. "You take something from each man and woman you help?" As she walked along she caught sight of a man's penis, sickly white and bloated in its jar of vinegar of whatever other preserving fluid had been used, and she almost retched. Briefly the memory of the jailer in the Sanctum came back to her.

"I take nothing that has not already been agreed." Xunaal frowned and shook her head in admonishment. "Payment is only due if I can heal whoever comes to me. And he or she may decide which part to give as payment."

Nia glanced back at the severed member floating in its glassy prison. What crazed man would willingly give *that*?

She was at a loss for words. What reason could Xunaal have for keeping body parts? Why not simply accept payment in silver stars or whatever else they used as currency in these territories? Did she simply find gratification in coaxing such severe, such *final* payment from those desperate enough to come to her?

Am I one of those who are desperate enough? she wondered then.

"Perhaps you are wondering to yourself why I would do this." Xunaal had shuffled some distance across the room and stood mostly in shadow; Nian could see very little of her expression except for the predatory glint of her eyes.

"It had crossed my mind," Nia said lightly, hoping that this madwoman could not tell just how fearful she was. She glanced briefly towards the staircase and tried to calculate how quickly she could reach it and sprint up the steps.

"I don't think you would understand if I told you." Xunaal walked a little nearer and looked Nian up and down as if selecting some part of her for herself. "But I'll tell you anyway- why should I not? Everyone who makes the payment is willing to sacrifice a part of himself or herself; the part that he or she chooses is sometimes a statement in itself. Now, when I saw you pass by yesterday, I saw the weight upon you, I even thought for a moment I could see *into* your misery and catch a glimpse of its cause."

Nia said nothing, but glanced at the exit again. Xunaal smiled. "Cease your worrying! I'll not keep you here against your will. Leave if you want to leave- or if you truly wish to be helped, tell me the nature of your affliction."

"I'm being destroyed slowly through my dreams," Nia told her. "Every night I sleep, I feel that I lose a little more of myself. Every scream with which I wake loosens my hold on the waking world. I fear I'll wake one morning and I'll be no more, nothing left but my own wreckage, and her revenge will be complete..."

Xunaal licked her lips as if anticipating the imminent promise of a body part. "What will it be? What will you give me, should I rid you of this curse? Let me guess. You're a stranger here, far from home, and I'd say you still have travelling to do, so you'd be a fool to offer me a foot. Maybe a hand? Perhaps. Or an eye?" She stared thoughtfully at Nia. "No one has ever offered me an eye."

"I won't be the first." Nian took a deep breath and forced a smile. "In fact, although I thank you for your kind offer of help, I've changed your mind. I don't wish to be healed. I'd rather be dead and done with, and I'm sure I will be soon, so I'll leave now."

Xunaal shrugged. "As you wish. But you're only fooling yourself, girl. Everyone who comes to me wishes to be healed, and it sounds to me as if this dreamreader or whatever she is will want to keep you alive and torture you for a while longer. Who knows, perhaps she has the ability to torment you just enough for you to keep your sanity and remain aware of each and every act of retribution she carries out against you..."

Nia closed her eyes, unable to bear that thought.

"Turn and head up those steps if you want," Xunaal said with a wave of the hand, "but I make no second offers."

Nia glanced up the stairs. One part of her screamed out the need to be away from this mad, cruel witch-woman. The other calmly reminded her that if she turned and left now, Yui would continue to torment her until finally her sanity caved in entirely. Nia tried to will away the thought of that terrifying possibility. *I escaped the Sanctum,* she reminded herself, *and then I escaped the Bonemord. Somehow I've eluded all my other enemies so far. I'm a fugitive, but I'm alive. I will not let a vindictive, vengeful child destroy me.*

"I decide which part you take?" she said, looking back at Xunaal, who smiled as if she knew she had only to wait and Nia would volunteer her fee. "I keep every promise I make, girl."

"Very well. If you can remove the girl from my dreams, from my mind, you may take my left hand."

Xunaal nodded, looking a little disappointed; perhaps she had expected a more unusual offering. "The tissue will be healed after the amputation. You'll not lose much blood, nor will you be infected. I take good care of my patients."

Nia was ushered into the middle of the room, where a single lantern hung ominously from a frayed rope attached to a hook in the ceiling. "Now the deal is made; your words and mine are binding," Xunaal told her with evident satisfaction. Nia panicked at the finality of that statement. She bit her lip and said nothing, but the sallow-eyed sorceress read the expression in her eyes and shook her head imperiously. *Too late,* that gesture said.

"Be still now." Xunaal held her by the shoulders, long fingers pressing against flesh and bone, and stared directly into her eyes. Nia could not help but gaze back, transfixed by the terrible, remorseless intelligence that commanded her. Finally, Xunaal nodded, and the pressure of her hold lessened. Finally she removed her hand. "It's there," she said. "Someone is connected to you." She frowned. "Someone of considerable power."

"Can you get her out of my head?" Nia whispered, fearful that Yui might be listening somehow.

"Oh, yes." Xunaal gave a crafty smile. "But were I you, I'd ensure that I never find myself in her physical vicinity. I can't destroy her; I can't even harm her. But I can shield you from her, and that shield will last until you encounter her again."

Nian smiled weakly. "I don't intend to ever again go anywhere in the South."

"Better that you don't. Now, close your eyes. You will feel my hand on your head again. Whatever you do, until I release you *do not open your eyes.*"

"I understand." Nia closed her eyes.

Xunaal's left hand grasped her head, fingers pressing almost painfully into her scalp. Almost immediately, Nia felt the response of a dim and distant presence, like a black little ball of horror, leaping up to protect its link to her. In Nia's mind's eye she could see Yui for a moment suddenly waking from her slumber, confused at first and then enraged as she realised what was happening.

Nia saw the girl staring hatefully at her, eyes like black little stones. *Powers, what has she become?* Nia thought fearfully.

I'll kill you, Nia. Yui's words etched themselves in her mind. *One day I'll find you again, and I'll kill you.*

Nia felt Xunaal's hand shaking on her head, fingers pressing ever harder. At the same time, she saw Yui smile and close her eyes.

Then she heard Xunaal cry out, and for a moment, even though Nia kept her eyes tightly shut, she could somehow see a concentration of light around her, as if the solitary lantern that lit Xunaal's grisly chamber had flared up to an impossible brilliance.

Xunaal's grip grew so tight that Nia thought her fingers might fracture her skull by sheer force. Then, the witch-woman let out a terrifying shriek of agony that utterly chilled her. It rose to a crescendo and then something even worse happened. Xunaal lost her grip on Nia's head and collapsed to the floor, and *two* voices rose up as one fearsome scream of pain and fury. Nia's eyes flickered open and she stumbled backwards, transfixed and horrified by the sight of Xunaal kneeling upon the floor, staring up into the light of the lantern, which had indeed become far brighter than it ought. The witch's mouth stretched wide open, continuous screams emanating from her as if no force in all Aona might stop them.

Nia backed away as far as one of the shelves and accidentally knocked over a jar containing half-disintegrated body parts. She barely noticed as the receptacle shattered on the stone floor, sending the cloying stench of preserving fluid into the air.

Abruptly Xunaal's mouth snapped shut and she stared directly at Nia, who gazed helplessly back, no longer knowing who or even what looked out from behind those dim and malevolent eyes.

Xunaal whispered something; Nia could not tell what it might have been and would never know; the woman's neck snapped back in one violent movement and then to the side. Nia heard her bones breaking.

For a while she remained where she was, staring at Xunaal's dead and broken body. Somehow, Yui had been able to reach out and destroy Xunaal even as the witch was shielding her from the child's destructive intent. How had she done that? How could she have become so powerful?

Nia took a few steps towards the stairway, jumping as broken glass crunched under her boots. A few more strides and she reached the stairs, and then made her way up into Xunaal's front room. Inexplicably, it appeared to be morning; had the witch's battle with Yui lasted the entire night? Nia shook her head wearily; she could no longer be sure what to believe whether she saw it or not.

She left the house and made her way swiftly away from the village. She would be hunted now, if anyone had seen her with Xunaal the previous day. But no one followed her for the moment, at least no one she could see or hear. Dusk found her bedding down in a barn for the night and wondering if Yui's link to her really had been severed.

When Nia woke the following morning, cold and shivering, she wept with sheer relief; whatever dreams she had had, she could remember none of them- and the hateful figure of Yui no longer lurked in her mind. Her distant enemy, terrible and vengeful but surely still a prisoner of the Seven, incarcerated within their fortress and raging against its vast walls.

V

For three days after she fled the dreadful scene of Xunaal's violent end, Nia felt elated. The link that Yui had somehow created had snapped apart, and although she still shuddered whenever she recalled Yui's enraged scream as she realised what had happened, Nia told herself over and over that she had been luckier- over a period of many tennights now- than she could possibly have hoped to have been. *Arin's unnecessary kindness for a start,* she thought, *and now the breaking of Yui's link to me. All I need now is some work and to be paid for it.*

As she sat in the common-room of a guesthouse in another village, eating a meal that would have constituted a tennight's rations not so long ago, Nia pondered the nature of luck, glancing occasionally through the window at the pouring rain as it turned the earthy road to thick mud.

I have so many enemies, she thought, wiping the last few scraps from her plate with a hunk of freshly-baked bread. *So many enemies. But so far I've evaded them all. I've had a lifetime of luck recently. How did that happen? Was I simply due such luck? Until Kelandra employed me, I had precious little good fortune. But to look at it another way, perhaps something else would have happened to me, if she had chosen someone else as her eyes-and-ears. Maybe my luck would have changed regardless. And then perhaps I would never have encountered Yui, would never have known of Kelandra's treachery, would never have been jailed.*

I would never then have known the things I know now.

Nia smiled to herself. Knowledge was power, the Watchers said, but that certainly did not apply to her. She would silently carry with her the truth about the Watchers until the day she died. Theirs was a tale that could have been spun from the air, impossible to prove. At best it would be added to all the other rumours about Watchers that the people of the Free Territories passed around, and Nia knew there were already hundreds of those.

Over the last few days she had occasionally thought about Xunaal and the witch's horrific demise- but Nia had successfully reasoned each time that the witch would have surely known the risks she was taking, or at least something about them. Eventually she had put the matter to one side, considering that it was good for the world at large that a witch who collected body parts as payment was dead and gone, her body and mind crushed from the inside.

Nia found herself truly in the north now, far beyond the Never-Built Wall, beyond Yui's reach and surely beyond the reach of all the enemies she had made. *Now I need only fear those I make in the future,* she thought, and her instincts forced her to look surreptitiously around to see if she had caught anyone's attention, however fleeting. It appeared not; the few other people who were here looked to be wrapped up in their own thoughts and worries to find any fascination in their fellow-travellers. She idly listened to a conversation between two men who were discussing something about war in distant Aphenhast, and something else that they referred to as the "Great Enemy". *That will be the war that Kelandra and those who followed her sought to unify all Harn against,* Nia recalled, and she wondered what had happened to them. Had they eventually been captured and brought back to Luudhoq to face trial? Or had they fallen foul of other forces such as the warlocks and sorcerors who held sway in the North?

If by some remote chance I ever see Kelandra again, Nia thought, *I'll beg for one last wish before she kills me- and if she grants it, I'll tell her my great secret. I'd like to see the look in her eyes. Watchers always know the truth when it's spoken, after all. I would love to see her world fall apart.*

The village where she had rested lay with the barren mountains of the Wistledge no more than a day's walk to the west, and Nia had already pondered the option of heading that way. Only the unfriendly reputation of the western nomads had stopped her from doing so.

Nia took a sip of water and found herself reflecting suddenly not on what she would say to Kelandra- who she would surely never meet again- but instead on the fate of those who had helped her on her way so that her story could still be told, not that she intended to ever speak of it.

Barrik had led her to the edge of the Bonemord when he could simply have killed her; he had more than likely paid for that kindness with his own life. Why had he chosen such a path? Nia suspected that it had a lot to do with her telling what she had seen and heard in the depths of the Sanctum. He had believed her; was that why he had let her go? Had he really thought she might spread that story wherever she went in the north, even when she had told him no one would believe her? Or had he foreseen the miserable life she would have endured in the Bonemord- an outsider in the midst of perhaps thousands of people who were trapped here? Or perhaps the Seven would have located her eventually, and he knew that.

I'm not sure why he believed me, Nia mused, *but I doubt many others would. Oh, a few superstitious or imaginative types might hang on every word, but what good could that rumour do even if it was spread by them? It would serve only to draw attention to me, and attention is the last thing I need.*

Arin was attentive in his own way, she thought suddenly, and frowned, confused as to why she should have suddenly thought of him.

Nia did not know what to make of her encounter with Arin. He had effectively made a whore of her for the night, although she had lain with him willingly. Instead of showing himself to be a predatory monster he had demonstrated a quiet, resigned desperation and a deep sadness and shame for his actions. Nia wondered if that was what usually happened to people who fell in love and then lost the object of their adoration; did they while away their days hunting shallow companionship whilst knowing that the devotion for one who had passed away continued to eat away at them?

I might have stayed, she thought suddenly, *if he had wanted me to, and if I hadn't needed to keep running.*

Nia looked up as a newcomer entered the common room. Tall and upright, he walked with a purposeful gait; although his hair was greying and his face worn and wrinkled, he looked like a man who knew how to look after himself.

The man looked around, and then, much to Nia's unease he strolled over to her table, taking a chair from another nearby and seating himself. Nia stared down at her luncheon plate, willing herself to be calm, and took a sip of water for good measure. "Do I know you?" she asked politely, looking up and meeting his eyes with a tentative smile.

"No, no. My name is Ghoreth. I am the Warden of a town far to the north of here. I doubt you'd even know the name of the place." He smiled back, and Nia felt her stomach lurch as he added, "I know who *you* are, however."

Nia glanced outside. With a sinking feeling she noticed three brown-cloaked men, members of a local militia no doubt, all of them watching her attentively.

"Yes, the Warden of Westheath- that's the village you passed through three days ago, by the way- kindly lent me some assistance," Ghoreth continued. His friendly smile had not waned at all. "Just in case you decided to cause trouble, you understand. But you're a clever girl; I can see that for myself now. You'll be no trouble at all, will you?"

"I'm not sure I understand," Nia said, feigning bemusement.

"Then let me enlighten you. Xunaal- who was my elder sister, by the way, although I won't let that affect my judgement of you- lived in Westheath, yet she was of a clan much further north in Darkbrook, therefore you fall under the jurisdiction of that district. I am the Warden of Darkbrook."

"I didn't kill her," Nia whispered, vaguely aware of heads having turned to look in their direction and listen to the conversation. "Upon my life..."

"Please." Ghoreth held up his hand, an expression of distaste upon his face. "I'll hear no sworn oaths or promises from a southerner; such words mean nothing to me. Maybe you did, and maybe you did not. That's to be decided in Darkbrook."

He stood up. "Shall we go?"

Matters moved swiftly from thereon. Nia's wrists were bound by one of the militiamen; half a dozen others wearing different, darker uniforms then arrived. Judging by their deference towards Ghoreth and the similarity of their accents to his, these were his own men from Darkbrook. Nia was bundled into a coach, along with two of the men; two others prepared to ride on horseback behind, and three others in front including Ghoreth.

Two of the men from Westheath then brought something into the coach with Nia and her guards; Nia saw that it was a makeshift coffin. As she stared at it, one of her guards leaned forward and asked her with a mocking smile: "Would you care to guess what's in there?"

"No," she said faintly, looking away as she saw a dark gap between the side and the lid of the wooden box. "I would not."

The coach moved forward along the track as the driver urged the two horses onwards. Soon they had left the village far behind. Nia closed her eyes in despair, her luck and all hope gone from her life.

XI – Light From Stone

I

Ilumor bent closer, attentively, as the once-woman opened her mouth. She could not speak. She could not utter even the faintest whisper, and yet *something* still emerged: the faint memory-thread of a life before. Ilumor waited with mute fascination as images, swift and fragmented, came to him and were lost in the next instant. He saw a vivid scene (through her eyes, he guessed) of someone running across an empty field, towards what appeared to be an odd shimmering in the air. The next moment, an argument with a man, though it was impossible to tell the reason for the altercation. Then, utter darkness and indescribable pain, nothing more or less than that.

Ilumor drew back, reaching out a hand to close her mouth. A trickle of thick, dark blood, suffused with the resonance of the *choragh,* oozed from one side of her mouth and swiftly coagulated.

He was drawn to that first image. What might that shimmering in the air have been, and why might she have been so drawn in its direction, running towards that phenomenon so heedlessly?

He couldn't know what it might mean; he couldn't know the purpose or reason for any of these fragments. But he knew what the look in her eyes, swimming with a deep redness, meant. It conveyed a message, summoned with the all the strength that the old, perhaps even human, part of her could bring to bear.

Destroy me.

Ilumor would do no such thing. His was a restless mind, ever eager to explore new possibilities and experiences, and even as he looked upon her calamitous state, her innards burned and consumed so that her body must be nothing more than a

213

smouldering cavern except where her preserved blood festered, he entertained the notion that she could somehow be remade, almost as he himself had been remade twice before. Thrice before, if one counted Serina's desperate and miscalculated summoning.

Of course, she would remain subservient, he thought, reaching out and pinching the skin that covered the knuckles of the once-woman's left hand. Dead and useless, it came apart with ease, revealing white and gleaming bones that jutted pebble-like from the ruins of her flesh. Ilumor whispered a word, replaced the skin and pressed his hand to hers. When he removed it, the skin looked more or less as before, as if it had never been removed.

I would like to have her remade, he considered, then reminded himself: *But subservient to me. Always.*

He left her then, pushing all such fancies to one side as he made his way down the dank, cool passageway. At the edges of his vision faint shapes and shadows leapt, swirled and occasionally lingered, attracted in some primordial way to *kin* as powerful as himself- for they too were *kin*, these ancient entities that had occupied Mirkwall along with Shimlock. They had in fact occupied the place for far longer than that persistent warlock; Ilumor suspected that they had weaved their way into the fabric of this place no later than a few centuries after those of the Younger Races who called themselves the First- how contemptuous and laughable that name was, he thought- had created Mirkwall and infested it with a perversion of the Old Powers that had taken a long time to break through entirely.

Ilumor could not have detested them any more if they had been starspawn.

The starspawn. The marandaal.

He frowned, thinking back to the measured retreat his forces had made at the orders of their Lords, as far as Mirkwall's forlorn walls and then further in. How quickly might the enemy press on? Their advance had by all accounts slowed to a crawl as they came within a dozen leagues of Mirkwall, but sooner or later they would arrive at the outermost reaches of the Mirk, especially if more Gates opened and if more of their number emerged into Aona. They might slow, but they would not retreat; for *marandaal* to retreat was impossible.

The elusive primordial *kin* rippled and changed in ever stranger ways, responding to Ilumor's train of thought. They could not *read* his thoughts of course, but they could certainly sense their nature and they reacted accordingly; a pensive stirring went amongst them.

Our allies lie scattered, Ilumor noted as he reached a hall from which as many as two dozen archways led. *Arrko and the others of the higher* kin *face the threat in the far north, and Inerdyr...*

Ilumor's lip curled in distaste. Inerdyr was not *kin* of any kind; he was simply an old, human man who believed he could retain that so-precious trait while still serving their Lords. Inerdyr walked an unnecessarily dangerous path, Ilumor thought, but then again the man was quite mad. The fact that his ardent human followers had no inkling of that lunacy was something Ilumor found quite amusing.

All we can do, he reasoned, *is to withstand them for long enough. Long enough for our Lords to gain further strength, reach out fully into the world and beat them back and out of Aona. And then, if we can, we will destroy the very possibility of more Gates forming.*

He smiled, surprised at that ambitious thought. Might it be achieved? If it could be, and if *he* could find a way of doing it, then surely his reward would be great.

Ilumor chose an archway that led into a stepped passageway. The way before him turned sharply three times before it emerged onto a small balcony overlooking the closeness of the Mirk. Carried by endless random breezes, clouds of thick grey fog moved, joined and dispersed. The nature of the Mirk itself remained a mystery to the higher *kin* and perhaps even to the *choragh* themselves; it had been brought into being early in the history of Mirkwall, although from what Ilumor knew there had been less of it then. Somehow it had grown.

Mirkwall had natural defences against the *marandaal,* but that in itself was a matter of interest because its creation had been for a very different purpose: to commemorate and preserve in stone the perverse defiance of the Younger Races, and their leaders the First, in their victory against the *choragh,* using the very powers that they had seized.

And how did that ever come to be? he wondered, idly tracing a finger over the cold, damp stonework that edged the balcony. Had some unfathomable aberration been created by Aona itself? He supposed that might be possible. Certainly transient Gates that appeared, occasionally wreaked havoc and then vanished out of the Existence were aberrations- how they could not be? Those holes in the Existence were after all the mechanism by which the *marandaal* had gained a foothold in the world.

Why, Ilumor wondered, *would the world be so self-destructive occasionally? Almost intentionally self-destructive?*

His attention was drawn suddenly to an odd area of brightness down below near the waters of the Mirk; it looked as if a light shone from out of the depths, partly illuminating the ever-restless mist. Ilumor frowned and stood still, watching to see if the light changed or moved. Eventually it faded from sight, and as the mist swirled around he could no longer be precisely certain as to which spot it had occupied.

What was it?

He knew only what it was *not*; certainly it could not be a construct of *marandaal* sorcery. Conceivably it could be some residue left over from the defence of this place by the First, a wild fragment of sorcery that happened to manifest itself in the form of light under the water.

Is it important? he asked himself. *Is it a threat to us here?*

Ilumor had always been certain that Mirkwall would be a safe place in which to regroup and gather together those of the *kin* who were wandering in smaller groups around the land. It belonged to them all now; it was their fortress, the lower *kin* having slowly recovered it from the clutches of Shimlock and his predecessors over numerous centuries.

And here we await the next move, he mused, wondering what form that would take. Would the *marandaal* attempt to surround Mirkwall and place it under some sort of siege? He suspected not. Their singular purpose was the destruction of all life, presumably by the swiftest means possible. They would in all likelihood not even understand the concept of sieges, and in any case he and the *kin* were quite capable of surviving on the structure and shape of Mirkwall itself; he had not been a humble, mortal man for a very long time, and he could wait decades, centuries even, if he had to. The *marandaal,* on the other hand, were driven to destroy.

It makes them predictable, he silently noted. *Therein lies one possible advantage.*

Ilumor headed away from the battlements to the chamber he had made his own, deep within Mirkwall. It had been Shimlock's until recently; he had sought it out upon his arrival and spent a while gazing at the scene of quiet desolation. A few bones, including part of the sorceror's skull; a damp and rotting bed; a thousand or more holes in the walls and the ceiling, the impressive results of insistent burrowing by the *peremar.* They had reached the old man eventually, although Ilumor suspected that he had already died by then. The residue of another being had lingered about the place when he arrived; he could still almost taste it with his mind as he recalled discovering that taint when he first observed the mouldering deathbed.

His apprentice, he had thought, but then, as he stood still and breathed in the ghostly remains of that presence, it revealed itself a little more. *His adopted daughter, a little* du-luyan *bitch. But there's more than that; she's of the First, she carries their taint, their stolen powers.*

The peremar *and the others who lurked here, waited until she left.*

Ilumor hated that idea; the notion that even humble *kin* such as the *peremar,* little more than flesh-eating worms, should be repelled simply by the presence of a mortal girl who in all likelihood had no inkling of the taint carried in her veins.

But she's gone now, fled like so many others, he reminded himself, as he closed the door behind him and lay upon the cold stone floor. *She will either perish or come back to her true masters, but either way she's of little consequence.*

He closed his eyes and waited. Gradually his breathing slowed; his pulse became faint. The temperature of his body dipped. He looked as if he might be in a deep sleep, and in a sense he was; but he was also *elsewhere,* and presently his body even looked as if it had somehow faded into the background of the stone, as if it might be little more than a man-shaped rise in the floor, lacking in discernible colour and substance.

In an entirely different place, Ilumor sat up, opening his eyes to a scene that was impossibly alien, and yet as natural to him as any place could be.

He appeared to be sitting on a beach of dark sand. To his left and to his right, the shore extended into a distance that could not be determined, for it *had* no distance in any physical meaning of the word. Before him a fathomless ocean loomed, black and impenetrable. Small waves lapped at the shore; they too were artefacts or features, part of this bubble or inner world that Aona had created for itself.

It was a place to which his masters had gained access, and they in turn had gifted him with the same.

Ilumor marvelled at this place, the minute detail of which still shocked him. He could count individual grains of sand, had he the time; he could touch or even drink the water and it would feel and taste like the water of an ocean. He could cast a pebble into the inky depths and it would make ripples that resonated outwards exactly as they ought.

Thinking on that exact action, he wondered for a moment what then happened to that pebble. Did it continue to fall towards the sea bed, coming to rest as it should? Did it wink out of existence entirely? Was the observation of what he *expected* to happen simply that and nothing more?

He felt suddenly uneasy. Not afraid, but perhaps diminished in a small way; certainly his blood felt colder here, his pulse more laboured and less even- although in part that could have been a reflection of his physical form laid out like a partly-hidden corpse of stone within the vastness of Mirkwall. The Endless Shore, as both he and others of the higher *kin* who could reach this place had named it, represented a poorly-known and far-flung corner of Aona's secret inner world, and perhaps it was natural for him to feel that way about it.

The constellations in the sky- not that it was truly a sky of course- also bewildered him. This, his fourth visit to the Shore, had been accompanied by a circle of bright stars almost directly above, and another dimmer pattern far ahead near where he supposed the ocean surface met the equally black sky, but on previous occasions he had seen other, more elaborate constellations, and some stars that were so bright that they would have competed with Ildar itself had that moon ever appeared. Ilumor knew enough ancient lore to know that such bright light marked the end of a star's life, a cataclysm of violence on an unimaginable scale. Why was he presented with such varied sights on each visit, as he woke into the gloom of the Shore and gazed up into these false heavens? Might there be a reason to any of it? Might Aona itself be attempting to show him something of importance?

His thoughts were interrupted; from the corner of his vision he saw a movement, and turned to see the figure of another man, sitting up on the sand.

As if on a joint impulse they got to their feet and walked slowly towards each other. Ilumor already knew who it was.

"Arrko," he said quietly.

The *kin*-lord of Aphenhast's far north merely nodded in response. They stood together and waited, listening to the rhythm of the waves and watching the shimmering of stars that were not stars. Soon there came a movement and a stirring somewhere to their left and a little behind them, and a moment or two later they were joined by a third companion.

Inerdyr looked ill at ease; of the three, he was least used to such journeys as these, but- as Inerdyr liked to remind himself- he was not *kin*, and it required more effort for him to reach the Shore. *Little wonder that he looks grey and drained,* Ilumor thought contemptuously. *How do our lords allow him to continue in the form he has clung to for so long, human inside and out? There will be a reason, of course. Perhaps his humanity suits them for the moment; after all, Inerdyr has many followers and considerable influence amongst the human fodder of Harn's middle north.*

"There is a witch-taint to the Silver Road," he said as the old man reached them and stared out at the sea. "It's no place for us to discuss matters of importance. This is why we meet here. Of course, it's an easier journey for true *kin*."

Inerdyr turned his head and stared at him, and Ilumor laughed at the icy, forbidding look. "We are immersed in the flows of the Old Powers here, and they help shape us. Given time, and a little concentration of the mind, we should be able to change our forms if we so wished."

"Why would you wish to do such a thing?" Inerdyr retorted.

"Why would you wish to commit the... *interesting* deeds that you do?" Arrko spoke up, and smiled when Inerdyr turned and glanced at him. "Do not feed us tales of our lords providing you with such urges. They do not *urge;* they command, and you obey. Still, you're only human, and we must suppose you do these things for some *human* reason- perhaps to feel alive? Often that's the excuse given for their actions by men such as you."

"Arrko, what news do you have?" Ilumor asked. He enjoyed baiting the old man, and ordinarily he would have been interested to see how far Inerdyr could be goaded, but the three of them had met here for a far more important reason.

"We hold the north. Ruan-Tor and the surrounding areas remain ours. No more disturbances have been reported in Ethanalin Tur-morn, not even the faintest hint of an opening. It's to be expected, Ilumor; many of the people of northern Aphenhast have held firmly to a belief in the true powers of the world. Many of them have given sacrifices willingly, offering up others to be rendered into char and gristle; some have even given themselves, their entire selves, and become true *kin.*"

Ilumor smiled at that; he felt certain that Arrko's words contained a barb pointed directly at Inerdyr.

"There are more *kin* waiting in the foothills of the Pinnacles," Arrko continued, "for the starspawn to come again to our lands. We expect more Gates to appear sooner rather than later. What of the situation in Nisstar?"

"The *marandaal* are welcome to Nisstar," Ilumor said dismissively. "Its destruction is of no consequence. We were told to fall back and gather together in Mirkwall."

"Mirkwall is ours at last." Arrko nodded in satisfaction.

"An indignity dealt with," Ilumor agreed. For a moment he considered mentioning the strange illumination he had seen in the waters of the Mirk, but thought better of it. Whatever it might be, he decided that it certainly was *not* a residue of the stolen powers stored and used at will for centuries in the stony fastness.

A little later, their talk finished with, they turned their backs to one another and began walking. Had anyone been able to witness their departure, they would have seen the three of them gradually fading into the dark backdrop that extended to each side, stretching into the indeterminate distance.

II

Over the next three nights Ilumor's dreams were haunted continuously by the light he had seen within the waters of the great marsh. At first he ignored the interference, but gradually an idea took root in his mind that some great secret of the Mirk eluded him. That notion nagged so persistently that at last he left the castle and walked along the grassy path near to the spot where he had seen the phenomenon unfold.

Ilumor squatted on the damp path and gazed intently at the dull, muddy surface of the water. It bore resemblance neither to the light-infused pool he had seen nor to the subsequent incarnations from his dreams. Impenetrable and thick, it lay choked with slime and other marsh-dwelling flora. It did not look as if it could have transformed momentarily into the clear and brightly-lit expanse he had glimpsed.

He wondered for a moment if it had been an unexplained feature of the Mirk itself, or some entity within it yet independent of it. *A being fashioned from light, but of this world,* he thought. *Whatever it was, it had nothing to do with the* marandaal. *All of us here would have sensed the proximity of starspawn. Did this creature purposefully reveal itself to me, or is it only some simple manifestation, a glimpse into Aona's inner workings perhaps?*

Ilumor became aware of something watching him from up in the ramparts of the great castle. He looked up to see the mute and desolate once-woman staring down and wondered if she might throw herself from the wall; after all, she was something more than *diafagh*. Some faint pulse from her former life persisted within her slowly rotting brain. Looking at her he recalled the taste of her fading memories: glimpses or whispers of a past that could no longer be pieced together. He recalled again her faint imploration for him to put an end to the little of her that remained.

But you're mine until I'm done with you, he thought, watching as she leaned slightly over the parapet to wordlessly view the drifting of the eternal mists. *If you fall, I'll retrieve you. You'll be mine until you're no more substantial than the Mirkfog itself.*

A subtle movement beneath him caused Ilumor to attend more closely to his surroundings. To his shock, he no longer stood on the path but instead almost knee-deep in the shallows of the Mirk. *That could not have happened,* he thought, yet somehow it had- through a weave of sorcery he could tell nothing about, which had caressed him from one place to another.

Then, as if the sun itself had bloomed from out of Mirkwall's waters, the light appeared. It grew from a hint of illumination until almost a hundred square paces or more of marsh on all sides glowed furiously, shot through with savage rays of the purest white light. Ilumor stared in wonderment at the miracle; he yearned to know the nature of what he beheld, to know whether or not it represented a threat to their holdfast of Mirkwall or if it had even appeared in order to help them.

Briefly he glanced up towards the castle walls. The once-woman could no longer be seen, and Ilumor wondered for a moment if she had fallen into the glittering waters, perhaps entranced by their sudden and beguiling transformation, or if she had simply turned and trudged back into the castle. He suspected that he would not have noticed if she had fallen into the marsh, such had been his initial shock.

Something attached itself to both his legs, and in an instant he was pulled down under the water and into the brilliance of the Mirk, a place now consumed with a beautiful, alien presence. Fear swelled suddenly and uncontrollably within him, and he struggled vainly against the force that pulled him ever deeper. Then he opened his eyes- or perhaps something forced him to open them- and that panic deserted him immediately.

The apparitions that surrounded him had the appearance of recognisable beings: human, *luyan*, *crommari* and others swirled around him, impossibly beautiful, ephemeral, their expressions and even their shapes changing from one moment to the next as if defined by the currents of the clear, bright water. They gazed not at the stranger in their midst, but into him, all-knowing yet dispassionate. One of them touched his lips with hers, and his need to breathe vanished. His heart slowed as he drifted ever downwards to the heart of the great light, no longer borne by whichever of these beings had torn him from the world he knew, but perhaps by whatever lay hidden within the light.

As he descended further, Ilumor noticed something that he would have thought impossible. Somehow the illumination had begun to *replace* the water, as if he was leaving the Mirk itself far behind and being pulled into pure light, his body pulled across the interface between the two realms into a formless and incomprehensible expanse.

Ilumor became certain that this place into which he had been helplessly pulled was somewhere that even his masters could not reach. That certainty confused him; surely it could not be possible. The dominion of the *choragh* was the world itself, all parts of it; therefore what could this place be if not some hidden and deeply magical part of Aona?

The light is a Gate and the beings that brought me here are its guardians, he decided, but an answering thought came to him immediately. *That can't be.*

A voice spoke up, inside him but around him simultaneously. It had neither gender nor accent; it was impossible to even imagine the appearance of its owner.

Still he understood it. *You have lived many lives in many places,* it told him.

Ilumor found himself forced to reflect on those lives, each one but the first bestowed upon him by his lords except for the curious exile placed upon him decades ago by Serina as punishment for a transgression against her now-scattered coven, the Circle.

This life will be your last, Ilumor. My light pours into you. You will serve me, even as you appear to serve those who call themselves the Earth Lords.

Ilumor cried out, but he could make no sound; he struggled but could not escape the invisible grip in which he had been caught. He closed his eyes but the light burned behind his eyelids regardless. Finally he uttered a silent, desperate plea to his masters, but they could not hear him; this place existed outside their realm.

Now he felt savage, unbearable agony, as bright and as fierce as the light that now bore into every part of him, coursing through the channels of his body. His mouth opened in a silent scream; his body shook violently as the light fought with the natural defences that all the higher *kin* had.

Finally Ilumor's awareness faded; the last of his senses to persist was his hearing. Even after the light had faded he could hear the sound of white brilliance crushing the writhing shadows of the *choragh* essence within him;

each fragment an instrument playing the sound of his destruction and remaking.

Cold mud and mist greeted his opening eyes. Ilumor lay still upon the path, watching in silence as the Mirkfog drifted. Finally he lifted his head. A memory came to him of sinking into the Mirk and then into light, but as he stared around at the grim and dark swampland it swiftly faded.

He got to his feet and made his way slowly back to the castle. For the briefest moment a faint light glowed within his hands, illuminating his flesh from within; Ilumor did not notice it. He had no recollection of anything after having found himself knee-deep in the Mirk.

Later, when he reached his chambers within the castle, he found the once-woman standing in the passageway outside. Ilumor breathed in the odour of her corrupted flesh, and considered laying with her again. Perhaps he would do so in complete darkness this time.

But instead, he stood and watched her for a while, undecided. *You should return her to the earth,* he thought, but that notion itself almost made him jump. Where had such an idea come from?

Yet it took root and became persuasive. What use was she, in truth? Were there not others like her? And even if there were not, could he not fashion some with no more than a little effort?

Ilumor watched as his hand reached out; idly it caressed the remains of her face. His hand moved up then, to her skull. Patches of bare bone gleamed in the last light of the day. From somewhere distant within Mirkwall, Ilumor heard shouts and laughter, and a few sounds that even he could not describe; the noise of *kin* as they whiled away the waiting hours until the starspawn came for them.

His hand pressed harder upon her skull. Perhaps that last remaining spark of what she had once been realised the nature and purpose of his action, for her eyes widened and Ilumor thought for a moment that something as complex as *relief* stirred within them.

"I release you," he murmured.

She became dust in a moment. As flesh shrivelled away and limbs crumbled, their remnants tumbling to the floor, something dark flickered and disappeared, vanishing into the surrounding stone. The dust drifted away, borne by a sudden breeze that swept along the corridor, until no evidence remained that the once-woman had lingered here at all.

Everything must end, Ilumor thought, and without a backward glance he turned and headed into his quarters to sleep alone.

XII – The One River

I

Rocan could not look away; the sight of the woman transfixed him utterly.

It was neither her nakedness that drew his gaze nor the odd, sudden movements she made as she squatted low upon the floor of the abandoned infirmary.

Rocan stared helplessly at her because she was, to every intent and purpose, just like him. Her eyes swam with the dark lure of the *choragh*; she was *kin,* his father had explained when he brought him to this place, and he had made her so.

"Why?" Rocan had asked him. "Why would you spare her, or condemn her, when so many others in Ruan-Tor have been sacrificed?"

"Spare or condemn?" Arrko had replied, a smile upon his lips as the snow swirled endlessly outside, venturing through the open doorway. "Which do *you* think I did, my son?"

"It doesn't matter now. Why her?"

"Why *not* her? She's a beauty, wouldn't you say?"

Rocan had agreed without saying anything, and his father had interrupted his expression of longing, turning his face towards him as he said quietly, "She's my gift to you, Rocan. *Kin* such as us still retain our human urges; our lords do not ask us to entirely abandon our shapes and our desires. You may do with each other as you please, in the small dark hours when we rest between the burning and the burying."

The burning and the burying. Those words had made Rocan's vision swim and his stomach crawl; Arrko had forced him to stand and watch as others of the *kin-* some of them human-shaped and others with the semblances of hell-

228

creatures he had seen drawn in religious books- burned and buried those few people of Ruan-Tor still left alive who had been hiding in their homes and hoping for the end of winter. "Could you not at least kill them first?" he had pleaded; Arrko had shook his head and continued looking on with evident satisfaction.

"This is senseless!" Rocan had shouted. He would have said much more, but caught sight of Ulan, the Chief Guardsman, being dragged to a pyre by a slathering, long-tongued creature with hot red eyes and a vast mouth of needle teeth. He had had no idea whether to rejoice or despair at Ulan's demise; the man had had a hand in welcoming the *choragh* and their minions into Ruan-Tor, but might they have found their way in eventually regardless?

"Railing against the inevitable is senseless, Rocan," his father had pointed out. "Closing your eyes to universal truths is senseless. You and I, every one of the *kin*, the highest and the very lowest, serve the single greatest cause in the Existence." As if on an impulse, he had grasped Rocan's shoulder so fiercely that Rocan felt his nails digging into his skin even through his shirt. "We are *alone*, Rocan. All of us here, all of us who defend Aona- we are alone."

"I don't understand," Rocan had said. His shoulder had started to bleed; the wound felt like fire above and beyond the unnatural warmth he had felt ever since leaving the Council fortress many days previously.

"As high *kin*, I have been granted certain knowledge," Arrko told him. "In the very distant past- much longer ago than we can properly imagine- humankind lived on one world only. It was a commonly held belief that other worlds held other beings, and the day would come when a meeting between these worlds would be possible. Indeed, this happened. It happened over and over. The Existence became like a succession of pathways trodden by more races, more beings than you could dream of. But the *marandaal* also spilled forth; and over time, they have turned each world dark. They have crushed everything under their path. Aona is the last of all worlds, Rocan. The *marandaal* found it before, eons ago, but we forced them back into the void. Now they reach forth again..."

"Why Aona?" Rocan had asked. "How has it persisted for so long when other worlds have fallen?"

"Aona," Arrko had told him, "is the only world that has our lords to defend it. It *must* persist, Rocan. It must."

Why must it? Rocan had thought numbly, staring around at the glowing ashes of old pyres and the bright heat of new ones, the cacophonous baying of a hundred or more *kin* and the fresh mounds of soil under each of which a dozen or more screaming men, women and children had been thrown. The snow had already turned the grisly disruptions more white than dark, as if it hurried to hide the atrocity. *If this is the price to pay, why must Aona itself continue regardless and day still turn to night and night to day?*

His focus came sharply back to the present, for the woman's gaze had shifted. He had been watching her for a long while, but her sudden intent look indicated that for some reason she had only now noticed the man standing by the doorway.

"Are you not cold?" he asked her, pointedly trying to ignore the intense blackness of her eyes and thin trickle of blood from her nose. *Cold is the least of your worries,* he thought.

"No colder than you," she said, and walked slowly over to him. "My name is Ellyn. I know you. You were a knight-commander once, a church man. Brave, noble Rocan."

"I'm none of those things now." Rocan flinched as she reached out a thin, long-nailed hand. The flesh looked frozen but it almost burned him with its feverish heat. He closed his eyes, shivering as she traced a route down his cheek and neck. "You have doubts," she told him, "but this is no time for them. You've seen the end of the old world we knew. We have been saved..."

"My father saved *you* for *me*," Rocan said. Her arms encircled him and he could feel her hot breath upon his face, but he kept his eyes tightly shut, fearing what he might see if he opened them, or even what he might see reflected in her eyes.

"Then I must thank him," she said, and Rocan felt a sudden stab of fear as he heard her voice change for a moment; it became something more akin to a low growl. His eyes flickered open, yet he saw nothing more or less than Ellyn looming before him, cold-hued and hot, an expression upon her face of lean hunger and silent invitation.

They fornicated more or less where they stood, violently and in desperation as if the end of both their worlds had already eaten its way to this snowbound, half-ruined infirmary. They drew blood. They wounded each other but even the pain of those wounds dulled swiftly. Rocan finally disentangled himself from her near-limp form, and stared at the ragged mess he had caused between her legs as she slid slowly down the wall to sit leaning against the cool stone. A red tinge lurked around her eyes now, and blood-tears escaped from them as she blinked slowly, a smile upon her lips.

I've become a beast, primal and savage and inhuman, Rocan thought, but even as the notion sickened him, it excited him. He turned his head slowly, surprised to see that night had fallen; Archaon's dim light illuminated the snow outside. How much time had passed? It no longer mattered. He licked his lips and tasted the sourness of blood.

For a moment the image lingered in his overheated mind of the great pyres and hasty, shallow graves, a vast and hellish spectacle amidst the ruins of Ruan-Tor. But it faded from his mind along with the guilt, the grief and the horror, as Ellyn read the still-unfulfilled desire in his eyes.

She opened her legs and held out her arms, and he went to her. Where else could he go? Spared or condemned, either way they were empty now, creatures of the new world, once human but now *kin*, and they had only savagery, desire and the mechanics of flesh to share with each other.

Arrko watched them for a while from out in the snow, dimly fascinated. Finally he turned away and went out to the great fortress in whose courtyard he liked to sit in contemplation. Perhaps he was attracted to the peculiar resonance of this place, where he had brought Rocan in from out of the cold, from ignorance and fear into the world of their lords. Oh, his son had protested, he had begged, and even now a part of him still railed dimly against what he had become, but in time that too would pass.

He'll see the truth of things. He'll know that occasional moment of which I spoke, that instant when the secrets of the Existence open, when the paths and numbers and natures of all things show themselves.

In the corner of the courtyard, a shadow appeared. Arrko watched it gain in substance and develop a shape that might have been human. He recognised its nature, and immediately he bowed low, his head touching the freshly-fallen snow.

Look up and listen to me, the *choragh* commanded him. Arrko did so immediately, forcing himself to look at the blur of chaos where in mortal beings a face might have been.

Three Gates will open, two nights from now, two thousand paces to the east of here.

"Three?" Arrko swallowed, willing himself to fight the unease he felt.

The starspawn will pour forth. You must ready the kin *for a great battle. Bring those who still remain the mountains and have them prepare.*

"As you command." Arrko bowed low again.

The imminence of the Gates has strengthened us further. Some of us will join you in the battle. When the starspawn are vanquished, then we will shatter the Gates.

"Your presence honours us." Arrko pressed himself into the snow. When finally he judged it appropriate to raise his head again, the *choragh* had vanished.

II

The mass of creatures that descended on Ruan-Tor the next day defied proper description. Some of these beings scuttled like vast, bloated insects; others lumbered awkwardly forward ogre-like, rippling with knotted, glistening musculature. There were those that looked truly fearsome, armed with long claws, spiked tails and razor teeth that snapped irritably at the cold air or at some perceived slight by another creature nearby. Others had no obvious means of attack or defence that Rocan could see; white-hued maggoty hulks that pulled their way ponderously along, or small and spindly creatures whose appearance he thought more akin to wintry, withered branches than living beings.

Large or small, fearsome or pathetic, aggressive or submissive- they arrived in their many hundreds. Some were human, but the extent to which they were still human varied widely. Rocan saw men, women and children who still walked upright, wore clothes and spoke a recognisable dialect, but he saw others who, like most of the *kin,* were naked. Some of these walked on all fours and communicated only in bestial growls. A few urinated or defecated as they walked, in the manner of thoughtless herd animals.

They all obeyed the same lords. They existed for one cause only. But this was nevertheless a restless and savage army. Rocan saw numerous mutilations, rapes and even a few killings as he watched the arrival of the *kin* from a window high in the Council Fortress. The humans squabbled and fought on a less bloody scale, content mostly to gather in small groups and argue, fight or fornicate as the mood took them. *Diafagh* walked amongst them too, listless and dead-

233

eyed. Rocan could not see how such creatures would be of any use against the starspawn.

His father had told him about the forthcoming battle, and he had seemed satisfied- perhaps even pleased- when Rocan had shown enthusiasm for it. "If I perish," Rocan had added as an afterthought, "will you promise me one thing?"

"If I have the power to grant it," Arrko had told him.

"Burn my body, so I may never return as *diafagh*," had been Rocan's request. To his surprise, Arrko had readily agreed. "You're my son, and made for better things," he had said. "But you'll not perish."

Rocan's enthusiasm had however stemmed from that precise possibility. He could not disobey his father, nor could he disobey the *choragh*, but all the desire to live had leaked out of him days ago. The blood in his veins had darkened; a mad urge would frequently take him and he would seek out Ellyn- she was never far away- to commit unspeakable, depraved acts. Somehow, every wound they caused each other healed sooner or later. The principles by which he had lived his former life were a memory that grew more distant by the day. *I would like to still retain some faint recollection of life before all of this,* he thought, *when these Gates open and the* marandaal *spill forth to shine the light of death into me.*

With full darkness came the *choragh*- five shapes bearing the likenesses of men, little more substantial than shadows except for the flashes of colour that made temporary eyes or mouths, perhaps to communicate more readily with their minions. Rocan feared them utterly; he watched with Ellyn at his side as their arrival caused a howling, reverential stir amongst the thick mass of *kin*. A dozen or more of the creatures not only knelt submissively before their lords but also eagerly mutilated themselves; the snow swiftly became littered with their numerous offerings. A jabbering, leathery beast that might once have been human gouged out its eyes; another sliced open its own belly and howled as its innards tumbled glistening onto the ground.

The *choragh* observed dispassionately, content to watch and listen to the baying cacophony of adulation that rose into the chilly sky.

Rocan did not sleep that night, but he had no need for sleep. He lay down with Ellyn at his side, listening to her coarse breathing and occasional shouts of nonsense that she uttered in her sleep, and to the continued and varied sounds made by the *kin* camped outside the fortress as they waited impatiently for dawn and for battle.

At sunrise there came a powerful tremor from the earth; Rocan watched in alarm as walls shook and even cracked in places. The two of them hastened outside where Arrko and others of the higher *kin* gathered. Arrko glanced in Rocan's direction; he nodded but said nothing to him.

A light came out of the east that outshone the sun. Rocan saw three dark objects like tall slabs of stone in the distance. *Gates,* he thought, as a howl of rage and hunger went up amongst the *kin*. *Now the* marandaal *will step forth...*

"Are you afraid?" Ellyn shouted in his ear above the tumult of fury.

"Not anymore," he said to her. *Not if I die today,* he thought.

A command came from one of the *choragh,* or perhaps from all five: *Forward.* The *kin* required no further invitation; they surged forward, a snapping, screaming mass of flesh, and Rocan found himself carried along, the corrupted blood in his veins pounding so fiercely with the thrill that it almost sang.

They covered the distance swiftly, hurtling towards the Gates. Rocan felt a deep rage stir within him, more powerful than he could have imagined, and directed at the light that poured from the Gates. *The starspawn shall die at our hands,* he thought over and over. *We shall crush the light into darkness. Aona is ours; never theirs. We shall destroy them; at all costs and by any means.*

So many times did these same thoughts whisper through his mind that eventually he could not be at all certain they were his; they could have been a chant uttered by the *choragh,* to stir their minions into an unstoppable fury.

Shimmering with silvery light, the *marandaal* appeared from out of the Gates. A wind blew behind the *kin,* pulling them ever more quickly towards the enemy. More tremors rippled through the earth; Rocan heard the sound of Ruan-Tor's buildings tumbling far behind them. The sun disappeared behind a roiling mass of black clouds that had formed in moments. His skin twitched and rippled as if live creatures underneath it fought to be free.

The *kin* and the *marandaal* met; day turned to night.

Rocan found himself on the ground, blood pouring from a gash to his head. He could not tell who or what had caused the wound; it could have been one of the *kin* rushing past. All around him chaos reigned; nearby a writhing mass of creatures surrounded what was surely one of the *marandaal.* Rocan stared at it, utterly transfixed. One moment, the *marandaal* looked as if was fashioned from pure light; the next, it could have been silvery metal, or stone. It changed shape and perhaps even the material from which it was made, at will. Parts of the *kin* became trapped and consumed by these continuous transformations, but for every creature that was snapped apart or simply pulled from existence, another would join the desperate struggle to destroy what appeared indestructible.

This is it, Rocan thought numbly. *This is the entity that desires nothing more than to turn the entire Existence lifeless, and crush Aona to a cinder, a dead and silent world.*

The power it brought to bear was immense; Rocan watched as a shard of light extended in a moment from the creature's mass, coiled around one of the larger *kin* beasts, and sliced it into half a dozen parts. As the creature's segments fell to the already blood-soaked ground, the *marandaal* shifted into white stone, and pounded another of the *kin* so powerfully that it crushed the beast into the ground itself, sending great clods of half-frozen earth through the air.

Rocan turned and looked around. All he could see in the darkness were points of brilliance surrounded by shrieking, roaring *kin*. The struggle extended into the dim distance. To the east, he felt the relentless pull of the Gates, and after a moment he realised that he could see *into* them. *Doorways with stars behind them,* he thought, and wondered madly what it might be like to step through one of those portals.

He might even have taken that final journey, but he could not walk in that direction. Instead he found himself rooted to the spot, swaying as blood trickled down his cheek and hardened.

Something crashed into him, breaking his arm in several places; as he fell to the ground, crying out at the savage pain, Rocan saw a dark-skinned, many-legged creature that snarled in his direction and then gesticulated to the battlefield as if furious at his unwillingness or inability to fight. Rocan could not have stood even if he had wanted to obey this abomination; all his strength had departed. For a moment he wondered if he might be able to crawl towards one of the *marandaal,* not to fight but for it to crush the life from him; no longer could he hear the whispered mantra of the *choragh* in his head.

The hope passed; perhaps the *kin*-beast saw the thought reflected in his eyes, for it kicked out at him, sending him flying across the snow and gore. Rocan felt a great blackness rise through his vision; he had no time even to wonder if he had caught his last glimpse of the world.

Morning came, and brought with it a scene of carnage that stretched as far as the eye could see.

The Gates were Gates no more, but great standing stones, cracked and split. The air hung cold and still, and silent. The bodies of *kin* lay strewn upon the battlefield in their many hundreds.

Rocan rolled over, gasped in pain and spat dark blood. After a while spent struggling, he sat up and observed the scene in silence without comprehending its meaning. Finally, he stood up and wandered slowly and painfully without purpose, back and forth. *Kin* that had survived-perhaps there were a hundred in all- breakfasted on the flesh of their fallen comrades. Rocan saw one creature that looked like a huge, malformed *orkar* pulling the still-warm intestines from a human man and chewing on them. It growled and snapped at him as he passed by; Rocan hurried away from the slathering beast.

A while later, he found his father.

Arrko lay in the snow, a leg and an arm missing-neither limb lay anywhere nearby that Rocan could see. A gaping wound had opened up his stomach. Rocan stared at the blood-drenched snow that surrounded him. "Father," he said quietly, kneeling on the ground.

Arrko looked up at him. Rocan thought he saw a faint smile for a moment. *Why would he smile?* he wondered, and the thought suddenly occurred to him that his father too had secretly wished for death. The idea that a fervently loyal servant of the Blood Lords could desire such a thing did not seem possible, but Rocan could not let go of the idea. He opened his mouth to ask the question, but his father spoke suddenly, his voice shaking with the pain and effort.

"It's done. A victory. We're all sacrifices in the end, even our masters," he said. "Do you understand now?"

Rocan stared at him, and Arrko repeated the question; he nodded, not understanding anything.

"Go to Mirkwall," his father whispered. "*Mirkwall.*"

"Father, I don't know where that is..."

"South. A long way. But you'll be faster once you heal. You'll be... safe there." A spasm of pain gripped him, and blood dripped from his mouth.

Yet Arrko had one more demand to make. His remaining arm shook violently as he reached out and grabbed Rocan's hand. "Burn me," he whispered, and fell back.

Rocan's inability to reply was of no consequence. He could see that his father would not have been listening; he had passed away as his head hit the ground.

Rocan sat for a while longer in silent contemplation. Little of what his father had said made any sense to him. He did not feel any grief, but neither had he expected to. He had never truly known him, and the man who had eventually returned to Ruan-Tor was no man at all but a warrior and a servant of the *choragh*. That he had also fathered a child was incidental.

Burn me.

With an effort he dragged Arrko's corpse across the snow using his good arm, towards the ruins of Ruan-Tor. *Kin* that lingered nearby feasting or squabbling cast malevolent looks in his direction, but none moved so much as a step towards him. *My father was higher* kin, Rocan reminded himself, *and perhaps I am now.* A few of the great sacrificial pyres still burned, and when eventually he reached the remains of the town, he staggered as far as the nearest of these and summoned up the effort to cast the body into the embers.

Rocan stood and watched as flames leapt eagerly up to consume the flesh of his father; after a moment he opened his hands to the warmth and waited until Arrko's body had been turned to ash.

The pain in his broken arm had dulled; when he moved and tentatively explored it a little more, he realised that it had already begun to heal. He could move it up and down, back and forth. Some bruising remained, but Rocan felt certain that it too would fade swiftly. His hand moved to where the gash had been opened in his head; he could no longer find it.

You'll be faster once you heal.

Go to Mirkwall.

He had no need to obey his father now; the man had gone forever. But Rocan wondered to himself where he might go if not Mirkwall. The name meant something to him, though he had no idea why.

Where would I go? he asked himself. *Ruan-Tor is gone. I am* kin *now, changed forever. The* choragh *bend me to their will if and when they choose.*

Mirkwall is safe from the marandaal, he thought suddenly, *or as safe as any place in this world can be.*

He turned to face south, where distant mountains separated the Plains from lower Aphenhast, a place that might as well be a different land altogether. After a moment he began walking, pausing only when he reached the Council Fortress to gather provisions and equipment for his journey. *I once came here out of concern for the people of Ruan-Tor,* he recalled. *I suspected and sought out the darkness at the heart of this place. And I found it, or the darkness found me.*

Rocan strode away past the ruins of houses, past the burned and broken shell of the church, the skeleton of which stood starkly against the snow and sky, a reminder to him of the futility of faith and all the things he had once believed in and held dear.

He reached the fallen southern gates, and walked on across the snow, eventually breaking into an almost effortless run. A smile appeared on his lips, as with every stride the bitterness and resentment at the supersession of his old life faded further. Soon enough, those feelings became lost entirely.

XIII – In Open Hiding

I

Fhaarluy still lay under a blanket of cold, damp mist a day after they had set off as Anlerran, Lura and Kelandra arrived at a round stone tower that rose higher than the surrounding trees. Moss encrusted almost every grey stone, as if it had stood here for centuries. As they walked around the structure part of the way it became quickly apparent that this was no ordinary tower- for no way in or out of it existed as far as any of them could see. Anlerran looked warily for the slightest hint that this structure was guarded in any way, but she could find none.

Lura and Anlerran exchanged glances and shrugged. They were about to continue when the dog suddenly barked and trotted up to the wall of the tower.

"Lead us on," Lura said, but instead he barked again and pressed his nose against the tower wall. A chill descended on Anlerran. *This tower has the appearance of a tomb,* she thought suddenly. *I can see no way in and no way out. Is this what happened to our companions? Were they incarcerated here? And if that did happen, are they dead or still alive? Not that it matters either way if they're shut away inside this place.*

Powers, I'm thinking of these people as my comrades as much as Lura's and Kelandra's, she silently remarked.

She stared at the moss upon the walls. *Maybe this did not grow here naturally. Might this ancient appearance have been created deliberately and recently?*

She raised her head and looked up at the top of the tower, some hundred hands or more above them. *Perhaps there is a way in at the top,* Anlerran thought suddenly. "There'll be no climbing that," Lura commented as if reading

241

the younger woman's thoughts. "There are no handholds or footholds deep or wide enough for a start, the stones are wet regardless and..."

Lura stopped as the dog barked again, more insistently, and again pressed his nose to the wall of the tower. Anlerran wandered over and looked at the stones near where the hound stood. As far as she could tell, they looked the same as they did in the other parts of the tower. Cautiously she pressed one of them. It gave slightly at her touch, but something else happened; as she touched the rock, a strange, hot sensation surged at her fingertips, and for a moment she thought she could see what appeared to be tiny black veins spreading through the stone and disappearing into the tight cracks connecting it with those around it. Instinctively she withdrew her hand and glanced at Lura and Kelandra to see if they had noticed. It seemed they had not.

The dog barked again several times, even more urgently. Anlerran pushed the stone further and it dropped into some sort of dark cavity dug into the earth. She tried again with another, as Lura and Kelandra looked closer. The same happened, and she continued until eight stones had been pushed forwards into darkness; she could move no more of them. *But perhaps I can reach in and move more of them,* she thought.

"If they're in there," Lura said, "if Hanric has killed them and then had them buried within the stone..." She shook her head and stood up, looking away. "If that's what happened then it ends here."

"Watchers cannot kill themselves," Kelandra spoke up, her odd words arresting their attention.

Lura stared at her. "Are you asking me to kill you before I put an end to myself?"

Kelandra smiled coldly. "Well, if I did ask you, I suspect you would refuse despite your earlier promise."

"I owe you no favours, and I'll grant you none," Lura

retorted. "Your code of honour- if creatures such as yourself can understand such a thing- is your own concern, not mine. Hanric's fighters- or indeed anyone else who Inerdyr sends- will make an end of you regardless."

"Wait," Anlerran called to them, alarmed at the direction in which the conversation was swiftly turning. "We don't know that this is where they were buried. We don't even know that this is anything but what it appears to be- a mass of stones."

"Then how did you manage to move some of those stones?" Lura stared at the narrow tunnel that Anlerran had revealed at the base of the tower and scowled. "If they *are* buried here, then this is surely a trap. Perhaps Hanric knew that we would find a way to track them down, and left a way for us to worm our way in and bury ourselves in the same place. I'm sure that would please him..."

"If he knew that we still hid out in the forest, surely he would have done everything possible to hunt us down," Anlerran reasoned. "Perhaps he thought that all of us had been captured. Or it could be that he was satisfied with Ruhal's capture."

"They shrouded the tracks they left," Kelandra reminded her, "so why would they expect us to reach this place? I don't even see any paths leading to or from this tower, unless they too have been somehow concealed."

The dog pawed frantically at the wall and whined softly. Anlerran glanced at him and took a deep breath. "I can fit through the passageway. I'm slim enough. I can push more of the stones aside, perhaps. I can find out if this really is the tomb of your friends. If not, then I suppose we continue to look for them, if our friend here can help. But if this *is* their tomb, then promise me that you'll let me go. Kill yourself if you want, but I had no part in your plans, and I'll take my chances. Agreed?"

Lura glanced doubtfully at the tunnel into the tower. "If you lie about anything you find, I'll know about it," she warned.

"I've nothing to gain from such deceit," Anlerran said with a shrug, although the thought of doing so suddenly occurred to her. She very much doubted that Lura had any special truth-finding abilities, and felt that if the prize was her own freedom then perhaps she could lie convincingly enough. *Would I though?* she wondered, not certain.

"I don't like it," Lura continued pensively, shaking her head as Anlerran lay down and began to push herself into the aperture. "I still say it could be a trap..."

I don't think so, Anlerran silently replied as she felt her way ahead, nothing before her but utter darkness. *We would not have been led here if it was a trap left by Hanric. The dog was sent to help us- I'm certain of it. Maybe one day we'll find out who sent him. And what about the part of the wall that I could push to one side, making the stones sink into the ground?*

I think only I could have done that, though I have no idea how.

Anlerran continued to inch herself forward, feeling her way along cold, dank stone and earth. All sounds subsided almost immediately except those she made while scraping her way along. All the while, her hands felt as if they were burning, and although she could not see anything up ahead, she felt oddly certain that somehow she was creating this low, cramped passageway as she crawled along, moving earth and stone aside even though she neither see nor hear it being moved. She tried to tell herself that that made no sense whatsoever- *How can I make stone melt away or sink into itself simply by being near it or touching it?* she wondered- but that did nothing to dispel the disquieting notion that somehow she was able to force her way through these layers of stones that would remain an implacable barrier to anyone else.

The passage ended at a blank rock face. Anlerran pushed at it, but it would not give. Frustrated, she pushed harder, and eventually the stone wall fell forwards with a dull groan. Light issued from a central torch positioned in the middle of a circular chamber, painfully bright at first.

Shackled with chains at iron posts around the circumference of this dank chamber were their companions, heads bowed. *Dead and hanging,* Anlerran thought, observing the scene with a shudder.

Then Ruhal- who had been fastened to the wall directly across from her- slowly raised his head. The sudden gleam of light in his eyes was almost too much to behold. Anlerran pulled herself out of the low passage and staggered over to him. He whispered her name faintly.

Anlerran glanced around at the others. They all lived; indeed none of them looked worse for wear than might be expected after the battle. *I expect Hanric left them here with a torch lit so they might see and hear one another die slowly,* she thought with a shudder.

How can I release them from the manacles? she wondered, but in an instant she knew the answer. Barely thinking about what she was doing, she touched the stone into which the manacles holding Ruhal had been embedded; after a moment it shrank back, almost as if it dissolved at her touch. *I still don't believe it,* she thought in wonderment, as the metal chain fell from the wall. By the look on his haggard face as he sagged to the earthy ground, Ruhal could not believe it either.

She made her way along the wall of the chamber, pulling the manacles free with ease. "Stronger than I thought," Jahar murmured with a faint smile, and Anlerran glanced towards the tunnel she had somehow created in order to reach the centre of the tower. Could she perhaps crawl her way back through it, and widen it further so that the others might be able to follow her?

"Follow me," Anlerran said to them all, not knowing if they could, not knowing if she was able to make the passage wide enough. She stared at the opening, and an intense prickle soared through her hands. *I can,* she thought, and she went over to where she had emerged into the round chamber. *It's no ordinary stone,* she realised. *That's why I can shape it. I can undo a small part of the sorcery that was used to create this tower to begin with. I cannot take it apart, but I can unravel a thread here and there.*

As she pressed her hands against the stone, something that felt like a wave rushed through her, starting from her hands and coursing through her arms, down through her torso and into her legs. Anlerran cried out, fearing that some hitherto unseen spellcraft embedded into this place had been stirred into action; but then she *felt* that same ripple leave her and travel along the tunnel she had crawled through to find the captives. She heard nothing, and could see nothing in the absolute blackness of that space, but she could sense the rock being pushed back further still, widening the tunnel.

Soon it was done, and she made her way slowly through to the cool open air.

When she emerged, the sky had already started to darken, a process made swifter still by the ever-present mist. Lura sat cross-legged nearby, and Kelandra some distance away. They looked up as she emerged, followed after a moment or two by the others; Lura and Kelandra stared in disbelief as they struggled from the tunnel one by one, then went over to help them to their feet. Lura gave Ruhal a hug so fierce that he groaned in pain; she laughed, perhaps oblivious to it in her joy. Jahar, meanwhile, raised a hand to ward her away in case she was thinking of subjecting him to the same treatment.

"Wait," Lura said, frowning as she looked around. "Where is Sarros?"

II

They listened in silence as Ruhal recounted how Sarros had left with Hanric's fighters, unharmed and unchained. Lura's expression grew cold and grim with every moment of the retelling until finally, when Ruhal stopped- to take a deep draught of water as much as anything else- she said quietly, "We should hunt him down and make him pay for his treachery."

"Which is what Hanric decided to do to us," Ruhal reminded her. "He's Hanric's man, Lura- or perhaps he follows Inerdyr directly. Maybe he has for a while. I don't know, and in truth it no longer matters." He sighed and glanced at Anlerran. "I don't know how you did what you did. We thank you for our lives. But there are many more problems now facing us. Our weapons, food and horses were all taken. We are fugitives now."

"We were resigned to becoming fugitives even before our capture," Jahar pointed out.

"As soon as we are seen by the wrong man or woman, then we will be hunted down again," Ruhal continued, "and next time I'm certain our fates will be decided far more quickly."

"*We* became fugitives the moment we left Luudhoq," Alturus pointed out, gesturing to the other Watchers. "We cannot go back."

"There can be no going back for any of us," Ruhal agreed. "I can't say if Inerdyr will order Hanric to return and dismantle the tower, and find us gone. I suspect he might come by in time, if only to gloat over our skeletal remains- but we will be seen and reported long before then."

"How did they incarcerate you?" Kelandra asked thoughtfully, staring up at the imposing silhouette of the tower.

"They put enough stones in place to chain us each," Jahar said quietly, "and the others... grew from the earth.

Our prison formed around us. The power they must have used..." He shook his head.

"Our rescue may have created an alert of some sort," Ruhal added, looking around at the rapidly darkening forest and taking a swig of water from the flask that Lura had passed him. "We should be away from here- and indeed away from Fhaarluy- as soon as we can, even if it means travelling through the night."

"And then what?" It was Kal-Myrran who spoke up. She stared contemptuously at Ruhal. "We continue running? We continue hiding, scuttling from place to place until the *marandaal* come from over the Daymorn Peaks to destroy Harn? Did we forsake everything we had, for *this*?"

"We always knew we'd make an enemy in Inerdyr and his people," Ruhal said to her. "We were undone by the snake in our midst."

"Yet that was enough," Ildoron told him coldly. "I can assure you that *we* dedicated ourselves to this cause- what of your companions?" His icy gaze took in Lura, Jahar and finally Anlerran.

"It's done," Jahar said, "and the facts remain. If Lura or I thought to plot against Ruhal, we would have been with Hanric and Sarros now, don't you think?"

Ildoron said nothing.
Jahar turned to Ruhal. "I suggest we head north, through and beyond Mordenglen to the places where folk are better disposed towards you, Ruhal. I'd be surprised if even Inerdyr sends an army after us if we're lucky enough to reach the far north. He has other enemies to consider. He's not raising an army to crush the likes of us."

Ruhal nodded, though he did not seem convinced. "The sooner the better. The further the better."

"Provisions and equipment will need to be found from somewhere," Jahar pointed out. "We will be on foot, and few of us will be armed. That situation needs to be remedied as soon as possible."

On a sudden impulse Anlerran looked around, remembering their guide who had brought them here and without whom they surely would never have found their companions. The dog was nowhere to be seen, and although she did not look for long, she knew that it had left no tracks for them to follow.

Anlerran exchanged glances with Lura, who shrugged and turned to Ruhal again. "This will sound like a strange story, Ruhal, but we would never have found you at all had it not been for... well, a *dog* appeared and led us here. Powers only know who or what sent the creature. It's gone now."

"That makes no sense," Ruhal said after a moment. "We have no allies; none of which I'm aware, at any rate." He smiled. "Certainly no *dogs* can be numbered amongst our followers."

"There's our answer then," Jahar commented dryly. "It was sent by an ally of whom we're yet to be made aware."

Ruhal frowned uncomfortably and glanced around again into the dampness and the gathering dusk. "Let's be gone from here whilst we can."

Without further ado they headed directly north-east, in order to be through and beyond Fhaarluy as soon as possible. Anlerran felt ill at ease; she found the forest oppressive, full of eyes and scurrying movements. She told herself that most if not all of what she heard was harmless, yet the reminder did nothing to calm her nerves.

The companions reached the outskirts of Fhaarluy at dawn the following morning, by which time Anlerran felt ready to fall asleep standing up. They continued on over open ground for a short while until they reached the upper grasslands that lay between the two great forests, before resting behind an ancient stone wall that meandered through the grassland, just as the sun rose over the Daymorn peaks in the distant east.

By dusk they reached a village in the middle of the grasslands; the same earthy track led out that led in. At this point, Jahar muttered something quietly to Ruhal, who frowned at first and then nodded as if something had been agreed between the two of them. Jahar walked ahead a little way, and knocked upon the door of a large house with adjoining stables. After a while Anlerran heard bars being removed and bolts drawn back from the other side of the door which then opened, and Anlerran saw the warlock talking to a gaunt, aged man in the warm yellow light of the porch. She watched him place his hand- as if to comfort- upon the man's shoulder, and it was at this point that Anlerran felt an odd tingle all around her as if lightning was about to strike, although surely that was impossible in the cool air, under a cloudless sky. *He's doing something to him,* she thought suddenly, and turned to Lura at her side, wondering if she could also sense that prickling in the air. It had something to do with Jahar; she was certain of it.

Lura glanced at her and perhaps read her expression correctly, for she pressed a finger to her lips in warning.

A moment later, Jahar turned slowly and waved them all forward. As they walked into the light, the old man peered at them and then smiled and nodded in greeting, waved them all inside and ushered them through to a comfortable hall as a servant closed the door. "My name is Udal and my house is yours," their host murmured. "I'll ensure you're well fed and watered for the night, and bedded down comfortably…"

Ruhal spoke up, glancing at Jahar. "We thank you for your kindness."

Udal gave a short bow, and set about ordering his servants to make good his promise of hospitality. "Coercion," Kelandra said quietly to Jahar. "We're well used to such measures. We have something in common, it seems."

"Perhaps." Jahar's eyes fixed on the Watcher's; the shadows cast by the flickering wall-lanterns danced across his face in macabre fashion. He did not appear entirely comfortable with that idea. Lura, who had heard those words, paled as if the possibility itself made her ill.

And why are they together at all? Anlerran asked herself. *If I'm to be kept with these people I should have them explain their mission to me, if they will.*

She walked over to Ruhal. "Will you tell me why you banded together with Watchers?" she asked him quietly. "You intend to keep me with you- although you don't seem to know what to do with me, I've noticed- so I deserve to know what madness you're involved in."

"Madness. In hindsight that seems a good choice of word." Ruhal smiled grimly.

"If you'd told me you intended to consort with the guardians of the Black Citadel when we first met," Anlerran continued, lowering her voice still further, "then I'd never have come with you."

"I'd have brought you regardless," Ruhal said roughly; then his expression changed abruptly and he looked away. "I wish matters had happened differently, Anlerran. I had no idea that your guardians... your *parents*- had such little time left. I had explanations in mind; I'd gone over them often enough. I care about what happened. I care about *you* and what happens to you."

Anlerran blinked, taken aback. She hadn't expected such a raw, remorseful response. She was not even sure that she had expected any response at all except a curt dismissal.

"And you're right," he added quietly. "I don't know what to do with you. I've lived with the promise of this task for many years, Anlerran, but I was never told *how* it would happen. I don't know what happens next. I wish I could give you some certainty, but I cannot. But I won't leave you."

She nodded, still nonplussed, and glanced up at him for a moment. The conflict of emotions she saw shocked her; here stood a man who appeared to be making an excuse and perhaps an apology at the same time, when she had expected neither; here also stood a man who had willingly made himself and his companions fugitives in the name of some cause or other. *He's a leader and a brave one,* she thought, *but he makes mistakes, and his heart rules his head more often than not.*

"So, perhaps at least you can explain to me why we stand here with Watchers as companions," she said, more lightly than she felt but still unable to help the tremble in her voice.

"We sought to show that unity is possible between north and south, to put it simply. There are forces stirring far in the east, in Aphenhast- the *marandaal.* Unless ancient enmities are put aside they will crush Harn, or the *choragh* will subvert and enslave all the Races in destroying the *marandaal.*" Ruhal smiled at her expression. "Is that plain enough for you?"

Anlerran nodded. Their plan seemed like an insane one to her, but of course there was nothing to be gained from pointing that out now.

Ruhal glanced around to make certain that the Watchers were not nearby before continuing, "The Watchers- *these,* at least- recognised that same fact. They are far from their southern citadel, far from the certainty of their former lives- their ingrained ideals of logic, of a magic regimented and drilled into their very beings, even the places they haunt. They've given everything they can except their lives. They may yet pay with those. All of us may. But the alternative? There is no alternative. Our aim is to say as much to those who might listen. We stand as one, or we fall."

He laughed suddenly. "Powers know what atrocities our southern companions have committed in the name of their overlords. Yet we're no better, Anlerran. We all carry a darkness inside. You're a beacon of light set next to us and our ill-marked histories. But then, some might say that we're all well-matched."

And then he walked away before Anlerran could utter a word in response.

The evening passed; they ate and drank the offerings of Udal's household, which were straightforward but delicious. *So much has happened,* Anlerran reflected later, as the mood of the gathering became a little more relaxed and she sat back in her chair. *It feels as if a lifetime has come and gone in the space of a tenday.*

She felt an abrupt pang of grief at the murder of her guardians, without whom she could never have even survived to this day, never realised her innate powers. Her sight blurred with the painful memory. Taking a deep breath, she drank from her replenished cup of wine and resolved to make the best she could of her situation.

Whatever spell Jahar had put the master of the house under, it appeared to be potent. After plying them with food and drink that must have cost half its own weight in silver, Udal further insisted that they each sleep in a chamber made up especially for them. Anlerran felt less than comfortable with this; she was unused to luxury of any sort, and these offerings had effectively been tricked out of the man- but she appeared to be alone in her views. The Watchers would, she suspected, take whatever they could and care nothing for the right or wrong of the act, and Ruhal, Jahar and Lura- well, they were desperate fugitives and no doubt this was only one of many desperate deeds they would readily commit.

Soon enough she found herself lying on top of her bed in the cool darkness, far from easy in the immaculate chamber and unable to sleep. Stars shimmered through the arched window across the room; she gazed at them for a while and decided to count them in case it helped her to sleep, but then gave up on the idea.

I'm lost, alone in the company of strangers, and now I'm a part of the web they've weaved, Anlerran thought. She cried then, for the things she had lost and for the life that had been taken from her, and for the frightened helplessness she felt at being taken north into Powers knew what nightmares.

Sighing and wiping tears from her cheeks, she got up and walked over to the window to stare out over the dark land. On the wall of one of the outbuildings next to the house, a lantern had been lit, and although it was sputtering it still gave out enough light to show part of the nearby courtyard.

As she stared at the faint light, not thinking any particular thoughts, the dog appeared again, padding silently out from the shadows between the outbuilding and a larger structure that probably served as a barn or storehouse. Anlerran stared at him, and as she did so he looked up and stared directly back at her, impassive and solemn.

"Why did you help us?" she whispered. And then, on an impulse: "What do you want with us?"

Silently she followed those questions with *What are you?*- for she could not be certain that the creature was what he appeared to be.

The dog gazed up at the girl framed in the bedroom window for a short while longer, and then, perhaps tiring of the effort, he turned and headed unhurriedly out beyond the range of the lantern light.

The following morning they left Udal's home not only with full stomachs but also equipped with new daggers and longknives and equipment for those who needed them- Jahar had politely requested these after breakfast and Udal had been ready to provide the requested weapons and provisions. Anlerran had thought this would prove to mark the limit of the man's hospitality, but Jahar quietly pleaded with him for the use of horses from his stable which stood behind the house. Udal had appeared taken aback at the idea, but Jahar had laid a hand upon the man's shoulder again, looked into his eyes and repeated the question. "We must travel as quickly as possible," he added, and eventually Udal had reluctantly agreed. Anlerran could barely look at the bewildered servants as they led horses from the stables at their master's insistence, and she looked pointedly away when their suspicious stares fixed upon the companions. *How often does Jahar employ such coercion?* she wondered uncomfortably.

Soon they headed north again, towards the eastern edge of Mordenglen where it met the foothills of the Daymorn. As they set off, Anlerran wondered how long the fog of compliance would rest over Udal, and what his reaction might be when finally Jahar's sorcerous weaving dissipated. *They seem to be experts at making enemies,* she mused silently, casting a quick glance back to see Udal still waving as he stood on the threshold of his home.

Later, as they rested with the sun high in the sky, Anlerran decided to speak up about her sighting the previous night. "It was as if he sensed me watching him," she added. "Whoever sent him, he seems intent on following us."

"I don't like any of this," Kal-Myrran said quietly, her cold little face full of misgiving. "I say if we can't interrogate it in some way..."

"Had it not been for this creature, you would still be chained inside that tower," Lura said quietly. "Personally I'd shed no tears over your fate, but you should consider yourself lucky. It must have had some reason for appearing when it did, and it must have a reason for following us this far."

"I would rather that we know its origins," Ruhal admitted, "but we certainly are not about to harm it." He stared meaningfully at Kal-Myrran, who shook her head and looked away as if disgusted with the decision.

They each owe the creature their lives, Anlerran reminded herself. *After all if it had not been for the animal, would they not now be dying of thirst in the tower or dead already? Perhaps then they would have remained incarcerated for centuries, their quest forgotten. Can Kal-Myrran not see that?*

"It's almost as if it *chose* you," Kelandra spoke up thoughtfully. "You saw it first; it seemed to address you if I remember correctly. And now *you* happen to have noticed it again. Why would it have chosen you?"

"I honestly do not know, Kelandra. I just happened to look out of the window when I did." Anlerran forced herself to look the Watcher defiantly in the eyes, although her heart began to beat more quickly.

"Chance, or luck. Who knows?" Lura scowled at the Watcher.

Kelandra continued to stare at Anlerran, ignoring Lura. "There is something about you that sets you apart from your companions. You are not the same as them."

Anlerran felt as if her stomach had caved in on itself. "I... I don't know what you mean," she began, but Kelandra shook her head dismissively. "You're speaking with law-keepers of Luudhoq, girl. We know about lies and concealment better than anyone; we have been experts at rooting out those who would hide matters from us for many centuries. I thought there was something different about you when I first saw you. As did my companions."

Ildoron and Alturus nodded grimly; Kal-Myrran looked at her with a predatory smile.

Ruhal stood up and packed away his water canteen as if he meant for them to collectively prepare to move on. "Anlerran's origins have no bearing on the task ahead of us," he said abruptly.

The Watchers stared at him as one; none of them rose from where they sat. "We could not exactly fathom *what* she is," Kelandra said quietly after what seemed an age. "Something flows in her veins that has nothing to do with... *humanity,* if you would call it that. It isn't the blood of *luyan*

or *du-luyan*, or even *crommar*. It's something else; something
that we have not encountered before."

"She's of no danger to you..."

"Then you can readily explain her to us, Ruhal. And
you can do it here and now; we're a league from any
settlement or homestead. What is she?"

Kal-Myrran grunted in what might have been
agreement. Eventually Ildoron spoke up quietly. "If you
think Kelandra's demand unreasonable then think on this.
How many of you would consider journeying with us to the
heart of our citadel? To the Sanctum itself? Would you do
that, for the same reasons that brought us here?"

"That is not the point," Ruhal said, "as nothing exists
to aid us there- only your people, who have forsaken you and
hunt you as ours hunt us..."

"I think it *is* the point," Jahar interrupted. "They
have risked much by coming this far. To travel to the far
north, past Mordenglen- that's something unheard of
amongst their kind. Tell them what they need to know,
Ruhal, and be done with it. We've still a way to go today."

Ruhal threw his pack down in frustration and
eventually seated himself again. "As you wish," he said.
"You're correct in your observation. Anlerran's ancestry is
not entirely human. She is part-*illeagh*. A quarter, if you
wish to be precise."

He shook his head when they failed to react. "Do you
even know the word? Presumably you have at least heard of
the *choragh*?"

That word at least created a response. Anlerran
almost cringed as the Watchers stared at her, and she could
feel Lura bristling with readiness at her side.

"A demon," Kal-Myrran said. "A creature of the
untamed forces and the chaos that we banished from the
south. We should have known."

"That is the word the Seven would have used,
certainly," Kelandra agreed.

"The *illeagh* are not the *choragh*," Ruhal continued. Anlerran thought his patience might snap at any moment. "They are distant brethren, you might say, but they are not the same. Before your time, when the *choragh* sought to enslave the younger Races, they departed the known world, choosing exile over brutality."

"She has power over creatures made by the *choragh* or their *kin*," Jahar added. "We've witnessed it ourselves. We *will* need her, if we survive the attentions of our more mortal enemies. Perhaps that itself has something to do with why Ruhal was tasked with bringing her with him. It seems timely." He shrugged. "We can only second-guess the possibilities. But it *is* fortunate that Anlerran is with us. In time, you'll see the truth of this for yourselves."

"Enough has been said on the matter," Ruhal declared. "Time to move on."

Around dusk they rested at the head of a valley where a river ran; Ruhal headed off to hunt game; Lura sat with Jahar, smoking pipeweed and watching the last light of the day disappear on the grassy slope of the valley. The Watchers, meanwhile, talked amongst themselves, but not so quietly that they could not be heard. They did not discuss Anlerran, much to the girl's relief; occasionally she caught one of them glancing her way, but the look harboured no greater suspicion or hostility than before Ruhal had revealed her nature to the Watchers. *Our circle is no weaker than before, and I no longer have a secret to keep from my comrades,* Anlerran thought, and then frowned at that same thought. She had thought of them as her comrades without even realising. *I suppose they are now,* she decided. *Who else do I have in the world? I certainly wouldn't choose them, but I don't have the luxury of choice in the matter.*

Despite that thought, suddenly she felt as if a great weight had been lifted from her shoulders.

In the morning they swiftly rode north-west, and Anlerran found herself looking across towards distant Mordenglen. For her entire life that forest had been her home, and yet somehow the sight of it- deep, dark, close and silent, a dense carpet of secrets- filled her with dread. *I'll not return there,* she thought, certain of it without knowing why. *That place is forever closed to me now.*

Not one of the companions looked behind them as they pressed on, fearing the pursuit of a silent, obsessed enemy.

III

As they rested around noon Anlerran took the opportunity to speak with Kelandra. The fact that the Watcher had saved her life had weighed on her mind for a reason she did not entirely comprehend. She still could not help but be a little afraid of Kelandra and the other Watchers, and reckoned that she cared little for her, but regardless of that she said quietly, "It may not matter to you, but you saved my life in that battle with the Hanric's men and creatures. I have not forgotten the debt, nor shall I. That wolf would have torn me to shreds."

"Be cautious with whom you claim to owe a debt," Kelandra said. "There are many who might call upon a favour accordingly. I would count myself amongst them. I suspect you failed to consider that before speaking."

"I would willingly do any such reasonable favour," Anlerran told her earnestly, and Kelandra gave her a strange look. "Humans are indeed strange, and those from the north are odder still. The tales Luudhoqians tell of the wild folk from the twilit lands have some foundation. Of course, we encourage them wherever the stories encourage caution. To an extent, we believe them."

"And our parents conjure terrible stories of the Black Citadel to instil obedience," Anlerran murmured, recalling

259

several that her parents had told her. "It's the unknown that people fear the most."

"Is it true that you saved Anlerran?" Ruhal spoke up from the other side of their fire.

Kelandra shrugged. "I happened to. It was luck, fate, chance- whatever you wish to call it. There was no time to think. I did not set out to save her. Luck placed me there."

"Thank you," Ruhal said. He glanced at Anlerran, who smiled hesitantly; she had no idea how else to react. Kelandra merely shrugged as if she had already grown bored with the matter.

Anlerran gazed at Ruhal a while longer, even after he had returned his attention to something unseen- or perhaps nothing at all- out in the surrounding darkness. *This strong, brittle man has no idea what to do with me,* she reminded herself. *He is keeping an old promise he made, but he has no idea how to eventually fulfil it.*

Strong; brittle.

Handsome; damaged.

Anlerran blinked at that sudden thought that had found its way into her head. Yes, he was handsome enough in a rough way. But damaged? She could not know that and yet somehow she was certain of it. He had made grave errors; he was driven to do whatever he felt was the right thing, he was a man of conviction and instinct; yet his judgement and character were flawed.

By all the Powers I don't know how I can fathom such things, she thought.

Talk turned inevitably to the journey ahead. Sooner or later, they agreed, Inerdyr and his followers would realise that they had somehow escaped, and would be in pursuit. Even Jahar admitted that perhaps he had been optimistic when suggesting that Inerdyr would let them roam free even in the distant north and east, distracted by his task of raising his great army. Perhaps Hanric and his cohorts would be sent after them again to make amends for letting them slip the leash before. "But I fear also that as we head towards Steepleford and beyond," Jahar warned, "we may find that the *choragh* have awakened in no small number."

Anlerran could feel the unease of the Watchers as they listened to those words. Fear was perhaps too strong a word, but nevertheless disquiet hung about them like a shroud.

Three days later, after heading north-west through the lower land, they reached the outskirts of Steepleford. Sleet had begun to fall, and the afternoon gave way to an early dusk under the cloud. "This is where I shall be tested, if I still have friends here," Ruhal said with a grim smile. "The Warden of Steepleford and his people are no friends of Inerdyr and those who follow him."

"I doubt that means they will easily become allies of Watchers," Ildoron remarked, his gaze fixed upon the nearest dwellings of the town.

"We will ask less difficult things of them first." Ruhal urged his horse onwards and the others followed.

As they rode down the wide track the sleet began to come down harder. A cold breeze lashed at them from out of the north. Anlerran shivered and pulled her cloak more tightly about herself, and wondered just what Ruhal had planned. She feared that he had simply left matters to sort themselves out and that he had nothing to say beyond a reiteration of his message about unity between the long-divided north and south. *What would I do if I was one of these townspeople?* she asked herself, casting glances to her left and right at the few folk whose business required them to be out in this weather. *What would I do if Ruhal arrived suddenly in my town accompanied by four of the creatures known to everyone here as the torturers and enforcers of the Black Citadel?*

I expect I'd take it less than well.

Anlerran did not voice these fears of course; nothing could be gained from doing so. Judging by the looks of foreboding on the faces of Lura and Jahar they knew the sort of reaction to expect. The Watchers meanwhile remained stony and expressionless. She wondered what they were thinking.

A large inn stood just off the square in the middle of the town, and it was here that they halted. A small crowd began to gather as Lura scraped together some coins for their keep. Anlerran did her best not to look around and stare at anyone, but she heard their whispers plainly enough. Most of these people sounded frightened, and perhaps confused that a man most of them seemed to recognise had brought Watchers into their town. *Black Citadel,* she heard. *Watchers! Torturers! The eyes of the Seven!* Some of those who gathered quickly decided that they had seen enough, and hurried away either to warn their friends and neighbours or to barricade themselves into their homes.

No one dared walk within two dozen paces of them of course, but as the terrified bartender whose ill luck it had been to be on duty this afternoon appeared at the doorway, the sound of galloping hooves came from one of the roads leading into the square. Six men on horseback, five of them clearly guardians of the sixth, drew to a halt no nearer to their group than the citizens of Steepleford who were brave, curious or stupid enough to remain. The sixth man, middle-aged but well-built and upright, had a grim look to him which darkened further as he threw a glance towards the Watchers and then to Ruhal, pulling his dark grey robe more tightly about himself.

"Well?" he said. "I trust you have some reason for this? Are they prisoners of yours? Have you drawn out their sorcerous powers?"

"I assure you..." Anlerran heard Kal-Myrran begin to speak up, but Kelandra laid a hand upon her shoulder and whispered something in her ear. To her relief, the other Watcher said nothing more.

"Warden Kerith," Ruhal said quietly, giving a short bow in the Warden's direction. Kerith scowled at him. "Enough of your formalities, Ruhal. You use them only when you've nothing better to say or do. You have spread fear already, merely by bringing these... *creatures* here. What madness are you involved in?"

"They are allies of ours," Ruhal responded, wiping sleet-dampened hair from in front of his eyes. He repeated his words a little more loudly for those folk who had remained within earshot and then added, "You already know of the dangers that Harn faces: dangers that will come from the east. The land must be united. All those who love Harn must face the enemy as one. That is why I- that is why *we* are here." He glanced around at those people who stood listening. "I will speak tomorrow evening, here at this spot. Tell everyone you know; your friends, your families, anyone who will listen. I ask only that you *do* listen to what we have to say. Old enmities must be put aside, for the sake of Harn itself."

The Warden followed Ruhal's gaze. He seemed about to say something, but instead he remained silent, contemplating. "Do as Ruhal says," he spoke up finally. "He deserves to be heard."

As those who remained began to drift away, discussing what they had seen and heard, Anlerran wondered how many might return the following evening, and how many others would join them. *And what will Ruhal say?* she asked herself. *I still can't tell if he's a man of great speeches. I expect he will need to be. And will Kelandra or one of the other Watchers speak as well? How will the people of Steepleford react to that? What will we do if a crowd of perhaps many hundreds becomes hostile?*

"What will you do," Kerith asked quietly, turning to Ruhal, "if the people decide that your idea is nothing but the madness it appears to be?"

"We move on. We take our message to places where it will be heard and perhaps accepted." Ruhal shrugged wearily. "What else are we to do? The North needs the South, and the South the North. If we cannot help people to accept that simple fact then we may as well lay down our weapons and await our end."

The Warden said nothing to that. He turned his horse and slowly left, accompanied by his guardsmen.

Only half a dozen people sat in the tavern, but Anlerran felt a palpable sense of fear amongst them as she and her companions walked in. Within moments, all the patrons of the place had departed, leaving tankards and games of threedice and stones all unfinished.

The innkeeper cringed visibly at the sight of the Watchers, and flinched as Ruhal walked to the bar. "We need to stay for two nights," he said. "We'll share rooms if we have to. How many do you have?"

"Four." The innkeeper stared over Ruhal's shoulder at the Watchers.

"Never mind my companions," Ruhal told him. "Pretend they're not here, if that helps. None of us have harm on our minds- not to the people of Steepleford at any rate." He dug in his pocket for some of the silver that Lura had given him earlier and passed two coins over. "Is that enough?"

The man nodded a little reluctantly and set about providing drinks for everyone as they sat at the largest table in the tap-room. Anlerran listened to the discussion regarding Ruhal's speech, but her attention was arrested a short while later as the door opened and two newcomers walked in.

Well, she thought, surprised. Du-luyan. *I'm sure they don't set foot in human settlements any more often than they need to. What might these two be doing here?*

Anlerran could not help but stare, fascinated by them. She had met members of this race only on a few occasions previously, wandering through Mordenglen on their way to some other place. They had been polite enough, but wary and distant. These two looked much as she expected- dark skin, yellow, almost feral eyes that were tilted slightly, and a lean, muscular physique. One was female, and a good deal younger than her companion, who looked fearsome despite his obvious fatigue. Their clothes were dark grey and dark brown, and each held in their belts an array of knives, darts and a curved longknife. *Ready for whatever may come their way*, Anlerran thought warily to herself. *As if trouble was not already likely tonight or tomorrow.*

But then something happened that made her forget all about the threat of unrest in the tavern or out in the town.

The young *du-luyan* girl turned slowly while her companion was talking to the innkeeper, frowning as her eyes scanned each and every part of the tap-room and each and every occupant. Finally her eyes rested on Anlerran, and suddenly widened as if in shock.

As if she somehow recognised me, Anlerran thought, her heart beating more swiftly. *But I don't recognise her. Why would I?*

For a moment her hand stole instinctively towards the pommel of her longknife, but then she stopped, uncertain. *I feel as if I know her somehow*, she thought, *but that's impossible. I'm sure I've never seen her before. But there is something about her; something familiar...*

Her companions had seen the pair but had barely glanced at them, still busy with what was becoming a heated discussion about what should be said tomorrow evening and by whom.

Anlerran suddenly felt as if she should go over and say something to the girl, though she had no idea what, but she remained seated and indecisive, and a moment later it was too late in any case; the *du-luyan* man, whose conversation with the innkeeper had become increasingly angry, muttered something in their own language and then turned and stalked out. As the girl trotted after him she threw one last glance at Anlerran, who could not read her expression exactly. It was perhaps a look of wonder or confusion, or recognition, or even all three.

As they strode along the poorly-lit road with the sleet still spitting, Iyoth turned to his daughter. "There'll be another tavern somewhere in this place; it's big enough. Powers damn our luck that we should have to seek shelter in a human settlement. Be on your guard, Kian; these people will slip a knife between our ribs given half a chance."

"Something happened when we were back there," Kian spoke up.

Iyoth stopped and stared at her from under the hood of his robe. "Can it wait? I'd sooner hear whatever it is if we can find somewhere dry and warm to stay."

"It can wait," she said reluctantly, desperate to tell him what she had discovered.

Their luck was not entirely damned; they found a smaller, far more modest guest-house where a silver piece allowed them not only a room for the night but a meal and flagon of ale each. Iyoth looked ill at the thought of eating food prepared by humans, but their meals turned out to be more than edible. They sat and ate in an alcove near the back of the main guest room, near enough to the hearth to feel the warmth of the log fire crackling below. After a short while, Iyoth glanced around and then, seeing no one within earshot, said quietly, "Did you listen to what some people were saying as we came here? What do you make of it?"

"I heard some mention of the folk who were in the tavern on the other side of the town," Kian ventured, "and an alliance with the Black Citadel. In fact, I wanted to talk to you about one of..."

"The Black Citadel is a name they use throughout the north of Harn for Luudhoq, the capital city of the south," Iyoth told her. "Those people seem to be the only subjects of conversation this evening. I think I know why. From what I heard, some of them are *Watchers*."

"Watchers. I think I've heard of them," Kian frowned.

"Good. You learned a few things about the world in Mirkwall, then." Abruptly he looked down, tight-lipped; they had agreed not to talk about Mirkwall or Shimlock, or indeed the past in general. They had both forgotten to keep to that agreement several times, which had caused some embarrassment on both sides during their journey to Steepleford. "I apologise, Kian."

"What about them, anyway?" Kian asked, eager to continue with the conversation rather than dwell on her upbringing.

"For folk of the north to be companions, allies of such creatures is... unknown," Iyoth said, finishing off his meal and taking a swig of ale before continuing. "But no doubt they're aware of what has happened in Aphenhast and what may happen here. Strange times make strange allies." He looked at her suddenly. "You said something happened when we were there, only a few paces from them. What do you mean?"

"There was a girl amongst them, even younger than me I should think," Kian said, recalling the incident perfectly. "I can't really describe what happened, but I became suddenly certain that she was... she was like *me*."

Iyoth tapped his fingernails pensively on the table. "You mean..." He lowered his voice further, although they were still the only folk in this part of the guest-room. "You mean she has the same *abilities* as you? She draws the..." He said no more; even though they were alone, he could not bring himself to utter *Old Powers* here.

"Yes. I'm certain of it. And I'm not sure, but I think she suspected it too, or at least she felt *something*. It happened when I looked into her eyes. I knew for sure then."

Iyoth contemplated silently for a while. Finally he said, "From what I have heard, these people seek others who would join their cause. Do you think they know of this girl's gift?"

"I don't know," Kian said, "but probably."

"What future lies ahead for us," he continued, "except wandering this land, unless we find companions and a common cause?"

"Are you saying we should ask to join them?" Kian smiled at that. "I find that hard to believe- my father choosing to fall in with a band of humans. Humans *and* Watchers."

Iyoth did not return the smile. If anything he looked grimmer than ever. "Most of our own people seem to have disappeared, Kian. I've looked for signs but even the signs are missing. Make of that what you will, but one thing is certain; we'll find it harder to survive whatever comes, by ourselves. With them, perhaps we stand a better chance. Of course there's the risk that we put ourselves in greater danger. No doubt they have plenty of enemies. But I think our best chance lies in falling in with them, as you put it."

"If they allow us to," Kian mused.

"They will. They are desperate for allies and they're a long way from raising even a small army. We can travel with them awhile, as long as we remain on our guard. When you sleep, I'll remain awake, and when I sleep, you watch. If matters take a turn for the worse, we'll leave them to their fate."

Kian frowned at that, but her father leaned forward and lifted her chin so that she looked reluctantly into his eyes. "Survival," he said quietly. "Survival at whatever cost. I will never abandon you again, Kian. Together, until the world itself takes us. Agreed?"

His daughter nodded and murmured her agreement, but the face of another kindred spirit swam into view in her mind- the countenance of the young human girl, another wielder of powers she could not understand or perhaps even control.

IV

Afternoon came and went the following day, and with dusk came the brave and the curious, those people of Steepleford who had decided to hear for themselves what Ruhal and his strange comrades had to say for themselves. Men, women and children gathered in the open area where several streets met, less than a stone's throw from the inn, some of them in family groups and others by themselves or with friends. Anlerran watched from one of the windows downstairs as a couple of wooden pallets were being arranged near to the front of the inn for Ruhal to stand on when speaking, so that more of Steepleford's folk might see him.

She remained full of misgivings, and felt oddly helpless as she watched the preparations. *I feel as if I'm watching my own life galloping away like a runaway horse,* she thought, tracing a hand along the windowsill and watching the crowd grow thicker. A low, continuous murmur rose into the air and she wondered what most of these people might be thinking and expecting. Ruhal was known and liked by many in this town, or at least he *had* been liked. Anlerran suspected that these folk demanded at least an explanation, and wondered if it would satisfy any of them.

More lanterns than were probably normal had been lit near the building and out in the square, although as she

269

walked outside to join the others a little later, Anlerran felt a shiver of unease through her body; looking at the mass of people waiting, she could see only a few of them clearly. Most stood in deep shadow with the crowd now many rows thick. She wondered if archers or daggersmen stood amongst them. Might they be moved to anger by Ruhal's speech? Or had the sight of Watchers in their territory already been enough to move such people to plan cold-blooded violence? *I hope fear and common sense keep them from such ideas,* Anlerran thought, but for a moment she pictured this evening ending in uncontrolled bloodshed.

At Ruhal's asking the Watchers stood together and further back, yet still visible. Anlerran reckoned this was a good idea. Having them stand in shadow would only accentuate the suspicion that doubtless already circulated wildly about their intent, namely that it was ill. Lura and Jahar stood to either side of the wooden pallets, pensive and silent as Ruhal stepped up and faced the crowd.

Those who had gathered to listen hushed at first, then became restive as Ruhal paused, surveying them all. Anlerran could see very little of his face from the side as she moved to the doorway to listen, but her heart sank. She felt oddly certain that he had no idea how to begin, despite his speech having been worked on and reworked throughout the day.

I wish I could help him, she thought desperately, but in that moment Ruhal suddenly found his voice.

"Many of you might say I've lost my mind, to ride into Steepleford in the company of Watchers," he began. "You know them as the servants of the Seven, the lawmakers and enforcers of Luudhoq, the Black Citadel..."

"We know them as the *enemy*," called a man's voice from somewhere in the crowd.

Even as the inevitable murmur of agreement rose into the chilly evening air Ruhal pressed on, "No longer are they such servants; not these four. They turned their backs on their masters and risked everything for our common cause- a land united. Worse enemies slowly gather in the distant east; you will already have heard the rumours from out of Aphenhast. But my companions and I have already been marked by some as traitors, either to the south or to the north. Most of us were incarcerated by followers of Inerdyr, and left to rot within the walls of a tower made for that purpose."

"You have indeed lost your mind, if you choose the mad sorceror as an enemy," someone else called out.

"He chose *us!*" Ruhal shouted back. "Inerdyr believes that preserving the division that has cast a shadow over Harn for so many centuries is of greater importance than the defence of our land. Through his militias, run by the likes of Hanric and Ayvin- most of us here know those names- he rules much of the middle lands with little more than fear. Fear of the same beings you see standing by us now. You know this to be true. The rift must be mended, and this is the start."

Anlerran had fully expected the responses from the crowd to grow uglier, but to her surprise they sounded more like people who were discussing rather than dismissing Ruhal's words. *He's well-known to them and they've respected him in the past by all accounts,* she reminded herself.

"What would you have us do?" one man shouted after a while. "We're not warriors, most of us. You can't expect an entire town to take up arms."

"In the times to come, those who don't will be dead," Ruhal told him. "That's the harsh truth of the matter. And if Harn remains divided then divided it shall fall. We- my companions and I- intend to say as much to all who will listen. If too few listen, then too many will die. That day will come, for a certainty."

An older man leaning on a walking stick stepped forward from the mass of people and fixed Ruhal with a solemn stare. "I've seen conflict enough in my lifetime," he said. "Sometimes I feel as if life has been one long conflict. I know your history, Ruhal, as do many gathered here."

"Which account do you subscribe to?" Ruhal answered with a mirthless smile.

"None of them. There's confusion enough concerning your military exploits or escapades, whichever way one looks at it. I know you've dedicated much of your life to the guardianship of Mordenglen in recent times, and that you've done well as Protector. But my concern is simply that your ambition in this matter far outstrips your capability."

A ripple of laughter spread around the square. "Explain," Ruhal demanded. Anlerran watched his hand curl into a tight fist, and her heart sank again.

"In the eyes of the most powerful sorceror of the North, you're a traitor," the old man said, and the crowd fell entirely silent as he continued, "You admitted so yourself. Inerdyr will soon learn of your continued existence if he has not already. You know him well enough to know he will come for you and crush you. You say you've thwarted him or his militia already, although I must say I'm mystified as to how. Regardless, he'll not give you a second opportunity. If you intend to raise an army against him, you will be pitting your own people against each other. You'll be asking many of these people here to walk to their deaths in the name of your united land. Inerdyr has many followers. Many *powerful* followers."

"I intend to bring people to their senses," Ruhal answered.

"But intent is not enough. Supposing that by some inexplicable good fortune the greater number of our people flock to you. Sooner or later you will have to face *him*. Blood will be shed. Thousands will die, even before the threat from the east brings darkness to Harn."

"He must be made to understand..."

"But you have as good as told us that he cannot be made to understand. And regardless of what happens between you and he, how do you then stand against the God-rulers of the South, the Seven? They certainly will stand against you. Could you take the Black Citadel, weakened by conflict already? And if not, where then is your united land? The land will seep with the blood of its people, long before the Great Enemy reach out to turn the world dark."

When Ruhal did not reply, the old man simply turned and melted back into the crowd. Anlerran saw him for a moment, shuffling in the light, and then he walked into shadow and she lost sight of him entirely.

Ruhal remained standing where he was, even as it became evident that he had nothing more to say. The crowd, seeing that the speech was done with, began to slowly disperse. As if to accentuate the finality of the moment the heavens opened and cold rain began to fall, stirring up the mud and hissing on the roofs. The Watchers gathered to one side under the wide eave of the tavern to shelter, grim-faced. Lura and Jahar exchanged glances and walked back into the tavern.

Anlerran watched some of the townsfolk glance towards her as they left; she imagined that a few of them stared directly at her, inquisitive, perhaps even *knowing* something, and for a moment or two her heart almost skipped a beat. It was far from inconceivable that allies of the *choragh* mingled with the people here, sowing seeds of suspicion and resentment wherever they went. Might the old man who had stilled Ruhal's speech have been one such creature?

Finally, Ruhal turned and stepped off his makeshift platform. He glanced at her and walked over. "Is it over, Anlerran?" he mused, the rain dripping from his hair. "Is it over already?"

"You'll carry on regardless," she said, somehow certain of it. "You'll carry on because there is nothing else for you to do. I don't think you're a man to die on his knees."

Ruhal's smile was oddly gentle. "I don't know what kind of man I am half the time. But I have one other task at least; I must keep you by my side. There's a reason why I was taken to you at this time; I'm sure of it. There's a reason why you're here with us now."

To her surprise he brushed a stray lock of hair from in front of her face, stroked her cheek and then said quietly, "If only I knew what to do with you."

"What would you like to do?" Anlerran found herself saying, and raised a hand to her mouth, horrified at the way that had sounded.

"I have to protect you at all costs," he said abruptly and perhaps in a harsher tone than he meant to. Swiftly he strode through the doorway as if desperate to be away from her, leaving Anlerran blinking in bemusement and wondering why she had said what she had.

The evening wore on; Anlerran retired to her chamber eventually. It was small, and she had to share the space with Lura, although she didn't mind. Exhausted by everything that had happened during the day, she fell asleep quickly, lulled by the steady rhythm of the rain against the window.

Anlerran opened her eyes sometime later, not knowing what had caused her to wake. The rain had stopped. Darkness did not paint the room entirely; the dim light of Archaon passed through the window. She sat up and glanced across at Lura, who snored faintly in her sleep on the mattress across from her.

Something woke me, she thought, and she knew in that moment what it was- or *who* it was.

It therefore came as no surprise at all when she got up and padded silently over to the window, that the great black hound waited for her down in the yard below, solemn and pensive and pacing slowly up and down over the moonlit slabs, pausing every few paces to stare up at her.

What do you want from me? Anlerran asked, but she knew that she would not have that answer until she went outside and stood with the creature...

...and let him lead me to wherever he wishes, she thought, and immediately she glanced back at Lura. The woman was still fast asleep.

I must go and find out what he wants, Anlerran thought. As quietly as possible she put her boots, trousers and shirt on, ensured that she had a couple of daggers in her belt- who knew what enemies might be wandering around in the dark at this time?- and slid back the latch on the door, stealing a quick look back at Lura. In truth she had not expected her to stir; Lura and Ruhal had both knocked back a large amount of wine during the evening and both probably slumbered a little more deeply than usual.

Anlerran made her way downstairs and undid the latch and bar at the door leading out into the street. Once outside she made her way around to the side of the building where she had seen the dog waiting. He sat on his haunches and fixed her with an almost anxious expression as she approached and cautiously knelt in front of him so that they stared into each other's eyes.

"What is it?" she whispered. "What do you want with me? I don't understand. Why are you still following us?"

On an impulse she reached out slowly to pat the dog's head, half-expecting him to shy away or even growl in warning. But instead he simply remained completely still. "Thank you for saving us," Anlerran said softly, remembering the creature's invaluable role in the rescue of her companions. Then she suddenly thought to herself: *I need a name for you. I have no idea what your true name is, but I must name you.*

Soon enough a name came to mind, not without a twinge of sadness; it was the name of her parents' old dog. He had died when she was no more than four summers old, and Anlerran remembered only a little about him, but for some reason his name felt right. This dog looked not unlike him from what she recalled.

"Culos," she said quietly. "I will name you Culos. If you keep coming back to me, you deserve a name at the very least."

Abruptly the dog got up and began walking slowly towards one of the side streets, looking back after a short while. Hesitantly she walked after him. He continued to pad along at an even pace; occasionally glancing back to make certain that she still followed. Soon they left the remaining lights of the town behind; Culos headed on along a narrow path that led between two recently-dug fields. At times Anlerran could barely pick him out in the faint moonlight, but he never left her sight completely.

Sometime later she glanced back, and when she saw nothing but the faintest glow where Steepleford stood, Anlerran felt a stab of fear. "How much further?" she called out as loudly as she dared, and the notion came to her that Culos could simply continue on his way through the night, and morning would find them in entirely unfamiliar territory.

Anlerran was about to call for him to stop- though she suspected that the plea would be ignored- but at that moment she saw what looked like a light moving slowly in the distance up ahead. Indistinct and elusive, it faded whenever she looked directly at it.

Then she saw that Culos had indeed stopped, and was sitting on his haunches to watch the same phenomenon.

The light stopped moving; now it hovered somewhere directly ahead. She could not tell its distance from them, or even its precise shape. At that moment, Anlerran heard a rustling in the fields to either side, although the night was utterly still. Turning her head, she saw that the grass rippled as if caught in a strong breeze. From some distance away she also heard the groaning of tree branches as if they too had succumbed to this unfelt wind.

Culos remained unperturbed by all of this, even when the light became brighter and nearer. *I should be afraid,* Anlerran thought as the sound grew in intensity. But she was not. Instead, she felt as calm as her companion looked.

Without knowing why, she knelt in the mud and gazed into the light, which hovered so near now that she could perhaps have reached her arm out and into it. There came a rumbling in the earth, and she feared for a moment that the ground itself might suddenly split and she would tumble into an abyss.

Out of the light came a voice; it was not human. It had no gender that she could detect. The words that issued forth were urgent, fractured, distant, even pained.

Listen to me. We have very little time.

Open-mouthed and speechless, Anlerran knelt, stared into the light and listened.

You must come to us in the Rhunin, as swiftly as you are able.

The Rhunin, Anlerran thought dazedly. *The great mountain range in the far north, beyond which there's nothing but icy wastes that may as well stretch forever into the distance.*

The place that Ruhal says that he took me from as an infant.

She tried to open her mouth to speak, but could not. Some unseen force had rendered her entirely numb and helpless.

We can do nothing until the request is made.

I don't know who you are, Anlerran thought desperately, *and I can't head into the mountains. My companions intend to keep me close, and they have their own agenda. They intend to...*

The voice cut through her thoughts; whatever this entity was, it had read them. *We know what they intend, and as matters stand they are doomed to failure.*

Anlerran felt hollow and defeated at that harsh statement, but in truth she had known the same thing since the old man had stepped out of the crowd and challenged Ruhal. Perhaps he had been an agent of the *choragh*, perhaps not- Anlerran suspected now that she would have known if his nature was such- but he had pointed out the futility of what they were attempting, and the crowd had listened.

But as she had said when the damage had been done and the people of Steepleford wandered back through the dark towards their dwellings, Ruhal would continue regardless, and he in turn had as good as promised to take her with him.

Unless I escaped, she thought, but she no longer wanted to escape from him or the others. She had no other companions; she had no friends. There was no one to whom she could have turned even if she had wanted to.

Why would I want to remain at his side? she asked herself, *when his cause is hopeless and his direction uncertain?*

But she wanted to remain regardless.

You must convince them to go with you, came the voice again. *There is no other way.*

Somehow, Anlerran found her voice. "I can't convince them! I'm not their leader! And even if I could, what then? What if we find you?"

No response came.

"I don't even know what you are!" she shouted.

Ask yourself instead: what are you?

Abruptly the light vanished. Anlerran blinked, shocked at its sudden disappearance. *Something happened that wasn't supposed to,* she thought. *It was as if whoever or whatever reached out to me was pulled back or interrupted by something, its link severed.*

Something moved to her left; she jumped, startled, and then relaxed; Culos had rejoined her and sat patiently at her side. She hadn't even seen him walk back towards where she knelt in the dirt.

Powers, Anlerran thought suddenly. *Might the voice and the light have been... the* illeagh?

It seemed impossible. Had they not faded from the world? Yet Ruhal himself had said that her natural father was half-*illeagh*? How could that be?

Even if it is true, Anlerran thought, *how could I possibly convince Ruhal and his companions to abandon the task they have set themselves and choose this instead?*

Unless this is the only way for them to unify Harn.

She was exhausted, and could barely put her thoughts together. Somehow she struggled to her feet and began the long walk towards Steepleford, Culos trotting quietly along by her side.

When she finally reached the vicinity of the inn, Anlerran looked down at her mud-stained clothing. *Nothing to be done about it now,* she thought, and glanced around, suddenly aware that Culos had once again wandered away somewhere.

The door into the downstairs bar-room remained unlocked, and made little noise as she opened it. Anlerran stole quietly upstairs and opened her bedchamber door, closed it behind her and walked over to her mattress. *Lura will have questions about all this mud in the morning,* she thought, glancing warily across at the still-sleeping woman.

Anlerran was too tired to think about how she might explain herself. She sank down onto her mattress with a faint sigh, and within moments she was asleep.

The events of the night had beggared belief; yet it was only when sunlight fell on her slumbering form and she opened her eyes to the morning that Anlerran truly began to doubt her own sanity.

V

"A good morning to you," Lura said, turning round as she heard Anlerran stir on the mattress behind her. She had already mostly dressed and was busy lacing up her boots.

Anlerran immediately recalled the events of the previous night, and sat up swiftly, staring down at herself. Her confusion only grew when she saw that she was wearing only her undergarments and shirt; her trousers and boots awaited her adjacent to her mattress. When she looked at them she saw that they were clean, or at least they did not appear to have been worn while she walked along a muddy path into dark wilderness during the night.

Bewildered, Anlerran looked for any trace of mud, and could find none. If she had indeed knelt in the dirt, no trace of that dirt now remained.

Lura stared at her. "Are you looking for something?"

"No..." Anlerran shook her head and managed a wan smile. "Nothing."

Lura returned her attention to lacing up her boots. "We're as good as damned," she said over her shoulder. "I had misgivings about this whole idea. Maybe if it hadn't involved *Watchers,* well..." She shrugged. "It's done now. If we can't rally the people of Steepleford to our cause then the cause is already lost. It's Ruhal's home away from home, or as good as. He's always been well thought of here. I think that much of that goodwill has been lost now though. It's time for us to part from the Watchers, I think; perhaps then some of us will survive Inerdyr's wrath." Lura laughed suddenly. "Am I trying to convince myself? Perhaps."

She turned and looked at Anlerran. "He's a true friend, Anlerran, and a good man. In some ways, even a *great* man. But this idea stank of desperation from the start."

"Yet you went along with it," Anlerran found herself saying. "He'll continue anyway. And I'll stay at his side."

280

When Lura's expression changed, becoming something close to sardonic amusement, Anlerran blushed. "I mean, I have nowhere else to go. I have neither friends nor family. What else would I do?"

"He'll keep his promise," Lura said quietly after a moment. A shadow seemed to pass over her, as if she had foreseen something grim and unpalatable. "Whatever happens, he'll stay by your side. He'll find a way of continuing along both paths at the same time if he can, with or without the rest of us. It'll bring him to his knees, and more than likely he'll lose his head and you yours."

Fragments of the events from last night swirled through Anlerran's mind suddenly.

You must convince them to go with you. There is no other way.

She blinked, the room coming sharply back into focus. "Are you abandoning him?" she asked the other woman.

Lura glared at her. "I didn't before, when I could have. Why would I do so now? I'll be hunted down regardless. I'd sooner be hunted down amongst friends. We'll take as many of Inerdyr's lackeys down with us as we can."

"You said it was done." Anlerran swung her legs from the mattress and got up, staring down at her trousers as she pulled them on. *This makes no sense,* she thought dully. *Was it only a dream? Does that make it any less important?*

"That may well be true," Lura said, "but whether we give up or not, our days are numbered. Inerdyr will send his militiamen again. Maybe he'll come for us himself, if he doesn't trust Hanric or Ayvin or any of his other close allies to do the job. He forgives no one, Anlerran, lest you forget that. Cross him once and you cross him for all time."

Not even Inerdyr would chase them through the Rhunin Heights, Anlerran thought suddenly, tracing a finger over the mud-free upper of her boots. Aloud she asked, "Will there be a discussion this morning?"

"As no one seems to know what's to happen now, I'm certain of it," Lura said, getting to her feet. "I long for this morning to be done with, one way or another."

"Do you fear death?" Anlerran asked her suddenly, wondering what the answer might be.

For a moment Lura looked as if she might not even favour her with a reply. Finally she shrugged. "A little. Don't we all? But to be truthful, Anlerran, I don't have a great deal to live for. No family and no friends except those here with us. I had another life once, but it may as well have been lived by someone else. If death is going to come for me, then it may as well come swiftly."

Anlerran could think of nothing to say to those bleak words. She finished dressing and then ventured, "I think I might have sleepwalked last night."

"Well, you wouldn't have sleepwalked very far. I would have known about it. I might have sunk more wine than befits a lady- not that I'm much of a lady- but I sleep lightly and always have done. I would have heard as soon as you got up and started stumbling around."

"I suppose it must have been a dream," Anlerran admitted. She was struggling to comprehend what had happened or not happened. No evidence could be found that she had gone anywhere at all last night, and yet she felt certain that she *had*. It did not feel like a dream; it was *not* a dream, she silently asserted.

Lura shrugged disinterestedly. Anlerran followed her downstairs where they waited for the others to make an appearance. The Watchers already sat at the back of the room, silent and grim. Anlerran suspected that they had already had a meeting of their own and perhaps reached their own decision.

Once everyone had gathered together, Ruhal spoke up quietly. "I intend to continue, through the other settlements north and west of here. I need to know who is with me still- and who intends to turn and leave."

"Do you intend to raise an army?" Kelandra asked. "Do you think you can? An army to stand against Inerdyr and his followers?"

"A war between two factions within your Free Territories does not seem to me to be a logical choice of action," Ildoron remarked.

"Well, it isn't a choice," Jahar said, looking up from the table. "Here is a fact for you. As long as he lives, Inerdyr will make no pact with the South. To him, Watchers are nothing but agents of the Seven and always will be. It follows therefore that the path to unity requires that Inerdyr is either killed or somehow captured, rendered impotent."

"Likewise, the Seven will make no pact with the North," Ildoron countered. "We would need to take Luudhoq by force. Perhaps some within the city will side with us if they feel we have a chance. But the Seven and the High Watchers, and perhaps most of our own kind- they will fight to the bitter end."

"The Seven are immortal," Alturus added.

Jahar smiled at that. "Are they? Or do they simply age and change so slowly that even over centuries they appear not to have altered at all?"

The Watchers glanced at each other as if the idea had never dawned on them. Anlerran suspected it had not. Certainly she had never considered the idea that immortality might simply be relative.

"Do you truly believe you can raise an army great enough to challenge Inerdyr and keep him at arm's length, or even make him surrender, Ruhal?" Lura asked. "Remember, if he doesn't already know of our rescue then he is bound to soon. He will send his lackeys again. We may not have time to raise such a force. It may not be possible in any case, even if the people of other settlements are better disposed towards us. In truth, we need to consider if military might is the way. I don't wish to be party to thousands being herded and sent to their deaths on the battlefield in a losing cause- do you? Would they fight for us anyway? Would you ask that of them?"

Ruhal said nothing. The look that Anlerran saw on his face pained her; it was one of abject desperation. He was a man who now could see only the obstacles in their way and not the way around or over them.

I have to speak now, she decided suddenly. *This is my only opportunity. After this gathering, the group will either fragment or they will continue headlong over a path that will destroy them.*

She had no idea what she was going to say, and the words tumbled from her mouth before she could even think about them. "I had a dream last night," she blurted out.

The Watchers merely stared at her. Jahar and Lura smiled in faint amusement. Ruhal did not even appear to have listened at first, but finally he turned his head and looked at her. "You had a dream," he said flatly.

"Except that it was not a dream," Anlerran continued hurriedly, feeling heat rise in her cheeks. "It was more than that. I was *there*. Out in the fields beyond Steepleford. Culos led me there..."

"Culos?" Ruhal frowned.

"The dog. The black dog. He came back. I named him." Anlerran cringed, blushing furiously as she felt the collective gaze of everyone around the table bear down upon her. She felt as if she was speaking to them like a little girl, and that only served to deepen her embarrassment. "I followed him out into the fields. I saw a bright light before me, and a voice. I..." She paused, a strange, cold feeling sweeping over her. It was a sensation of absolute certainty, and she almost passed out with the shock of it.

"It was the voice of the *illeagh*," she said eventually. "They told me to take you all to them."

The stunned silence that followed was broken eventually by the sound of the outside door opening. Two figures wandered in, silhouetted for a moment by the low morning sun that poured through the dusty windows until they came nearer to the companions' table. Anlerran recognised them as she shielded her eyes; they were the two *du-luyan* people she had seen the other evening. In an instant she recalled the odd feeling that she somehow knew the girl.

The man stepped a little closer. "My name is Iyoth. This is my daughter, Kian. If you will have us, we wish to join your cause."

Kian then spoke up, gesturing to Anlerran. "She is strong in the Old Powers. So am I. My father is a weaponsmaster. We can be more than useful to you."

Although it was not her place to do so, Anlerran found herself nodding in agreement. "You are both welcome," she said, barely aware of both Ruhal and Kelandra frowning at her presumptuousness. It was perhaps just as well that she did not even look at them, when she continued, "We're headed into the Rhunin Heights, where we will find the allies we need. Make yourselves ready. We head north this morning."

XIV – Words Left Unspoken

I

Ileana yawned and sat up, rubbing sleep from her eyes and wondering how she had managed to sleep so heavily. A hesitant knock sounded at her door, and she wondered if it had been a previous one that had disturbed her. "Who is it?" she called out.

"It's Jak." His voice sounded muffled from behind the door. "I brought you some breakfast. Are you dressed?"

"Wait!" For a moment she panicked, thinking he might come in anyway, and then relaxed, remembering that she had barred the door.

Ileana dressed quickly and opened the curtains to look out over the village. She had a good view from up here on the top floor of the coaching house. They had arrived yesterday having made good progress; Harqan had reckoned that they would be in Mornkastle in under a tenday unless the weather worsened.

Remembering that Jak still waited outside her room- and wondering why he had gone to the trouble of bringing breakfast to her- Ileana unbarred and opened the door.

He walked in holding a tray of delicious food and set it down on the table at her bedside as Ileana closed the door behind him. "You didn't have to do this," she told him, and hastily added, "But thank you" when he looked worriedly at her.

"I wanted to," he said uncomfortably. "I brought enough for both of us. And I wanted to speak to you without the others listening. But let's eat first."

Ileana wondered what it was that he might want to say. She was about to ask him, but the aroma of the food was too tempting; the two of them ate swiftly, pausing only to agree about how good the breakfast was.

286

"He's a kind man," Ileana remarked as she took a gulp of fresh milk to wash down the feast. "Your father," she added when Jak looked quizzically at her. "He didn't have to take us all this way. I'm sure most folk wouldn't even have invited us in when we happened to pass by."

Jak smiled faintly, perhaps embarrassed.

"What did you want to say to me?" she continued, remembering what he had said before they had eaten.

Jak looked lost for words. Not for the first time, Ileana wondered if he was one of those people who were occasionally simple and lost their ability to remember what they had said and to whom they had said it. She remembered that Ethanalin Tur-morn had been brimful of people who behaved like that, long before the events that had driven even the remaining sane to suicide and consumed the populace of that town.

Still, he's better-looking than any of them, she mused, staring into his eyes.

"Why are you smiling?" he asked her, flustered. Ileana abruptly adopted a neutral expression and apologised.

"Now I can't remember what I wanted to say," Jak mumbled, although Ileana looked at him and felt sure he could remember perfectly well. *In fact, I think I know what he wanted to say,* she thought. *I like him too. But I'm not sure now is the right time to say it. We don't even know how much longer we'll have to spend together after we reach Mornkastle.*

She did mention it a little later though, not to Jak but to Amethyst as the two of them sat by the fountain in the village square waiting for some minor repairs to be carried out on Harqan's cart. Jak stood and watched with Harqan on the other side of the square; Harqan seemed to be explaining something to his son judging by the way he occasionally put a hand on his shoulder and stooped a little to say something to him. Ileana wondered what they might be discussing;

every now and then Jak turned and glanced around at them, although Harqan did not.

"I expect they'll be headed back home soon after we arrive in Mornkastle," Amethyst told her, giving her a sideways glance.

"Do you think so?" Ileana felt a sudden unpleasant lurch in her stomach at the thought. She had grown used to Jak's company almost as much as she had become accustomed to Amethyst's. "But it's a long way for such a short visit. Surely they might spend some time in the town. Several days, maybe even a tennight. Don't you think?"

Amethyst smiled at the girl's hopeful look. "Be prepared for separation, Ileana. Always be prepared for separation." Her smile faded, and Ileana reached across and squeezed her hand. "I think maybe if you'd told Vornen you loved him it might have broken the spell of the Gates..."

"That's storybook nonsense, Ileana." Amethyst shook her head ruefully. "Regardless, I didn't know for certain until it was too late and he'd gone forever. Often we realise what it is that people mean to us after they're dead and gone. That's just the way it is. It dawned on me at the last sight of him, not first."

Ileana had no idea what to say to that. Even now, a long while after they had parted company with Vornen, Amethyst would sometimes descend into a quiet melancholia. Ileana knew what she was thinking, more or less; that she could retrace their steps, step back in time and attempt to somehow break the man's invisible, intangible curse. Of course, she seldom mentioned anything to do with it; Ileana reckoned Amethyst was a tough woman, or at least she tried to be.

But Amethyst was not the only one whose thoughts were with those who were elsewhere. Ileana had noticed for a long while that Lyya often talked about the possibility of heading back and seeking out her friend Jaana. On several occasions even since their departure from Fhaarluy she had announced her intention of doing so. Fauli had eventually shrugged and suggested that she do just that if she thought she would ever find her. "Aphenhast will likely be in turmoil now," she said. "If you think you can survive it, *and* find her, good luck to you. But I doubt that even *you* are as bull-headed as to fancy your chances on the other side of the Border Wall."

Fauli and Lyya were sitting some distance away from them, silent and thoughtful as usual. At least they were not arguing at the moment. Perhaps they were too tired, or they finally had nothing left to argue about.

Finally, with the repairs to the cart completed they were on their way again. Ileana sat next to Jak at the back of the cart, and at one point she took the opportunity to whisper in his ear, "What was it you wanted to say to me before?"

Jak cast a worried look towards his father- perhaps even a fearful look, Ileana thought- and mouthed to her: *Later*.

She eventually found out four days later, or at least she found out *something* that he had wanted to say to her. "I've never met anyone like you," he said suddenly in a low voice one morning as they breakfasted together in her bedchamber- something that had quickly become a habit despite Harqan's silent but fuming disapproval.

Ileana smiled at that, relieved that he had finally plucked up the courage to say those words. In truth she had been expecting him to say something similar for days. "Are you saying you like me?" she inquired.

"Like you? Well, yes. Of course I do. I mean..." He put the breakfast tray to one side. "When I first saw you, I... I just knew."

Ileana's smile widened; she recalled how she had felt when she first set eyes upon him. Then a pang of fear struck her, though she had no idea why. "Knew what?" she asked him sharply, and he stammered, "I knew... I just knew you were for me, that's all..."

Jak looked about to work his way up into a state of panic. On a sudden impulse she leaned forward and kissed him upon the lips. "I wish you could stay in Mornkastle for a while when we get there," she said, and added hopefully, "Perhaps you can ask your father? Didn't you want to study in one of the Guilds? You could make your enquiries about your studies while you're here."

He gave her an unfathomable look. She watched his fingers brush against his lips as if he could scarcely believe that she had just kissed him. *I'm not sure I believe it myself,* she thought, feeling oddly light-headed.

"I'll ask him," Jak said eventually, and then he left in a hurry. Ileana sat in her room for a while, finally coming to the conclusion that Jak had only told her a part of what he wanted or needed to say. Much more remained unsaid; of that she was certain.

But she had no idea what it might be.

They rode south through the morning, soon leaving the village far behind. As the cart rolled along the wide track, Ileana found herself thinking more and more about Mornkastle- the second-largest city in Harn, and according to Harqan the place where the north held back the south. She wasn't entirely sure what that meant, but the thought of seeing the place filled her with excitement and made her stomach churn at the same time. Still, she was more than able to eat her lunch when Harqan called a halt late in the morning, and they sat under a lone tree set away from the track a little way, looking out over the rolling meadows.

Two more days passed, and the good weather held. Each day they rode from first light to last, and Harqan seemed satisfied with their progress; his sober mood lightened to the point that he even encouraged Jak to cheer up. *I'd rather know the reason for his melancholia,* Ileana thought, wondering if it had anything to do with not being able to stay with them in Mornkastle. *Why doesn't he just ask his father if they can stay awhile?* she wondered. *Especially now while he seems to be in such good spirits. If he doesn't then I've a good mind to ask him myself.*

Around mid-morning the following day, they finally arrived at the crest of a wide, gently sloping hill, to find before them a view of Mornkastle in all its ancient splendour.

Ileana gaped openly at the beauty of the city. A grandiose but eclectic order suffused the place- something that had been altogether missing in every other settlement they had passed through during their journey. Great spires and fortresses reached into the azure sky, stone points that rose like finely-crafted needles, all fashioned from the faintly blue and green stone for which Mornkastle's architecture was apparently famous. The streets, some of them wide and others so narrow that no vehicles could be drawn through them, wound comfortably around each other. Here and there, market squares and guild courtyards could be seen. Even from their still-distant position she could tell that the place bustled with activity and trade. In the morning light, it looked a wonderful place, alive with untold possibilities.

A short while later they waited outside the northern gate leading into the city as Harqan spoke with the guardsmen. Ileana saw them look at a scrap of paper he produced before handing it back; coins were also handed over to them. It suddenly struck her as odd that Harqan, a man who lived deep in a remote forest, should have so much money. How had he become so wealthy?

Nevertheless, Ileana allowed her thoughts to wander as the gates were opened, the cart trundled through and she had her first opportunity to properly take in the sights, sounds and smells of Mornkastle. A livestock and produce market was in full swing as they made their way through a sun baked square of many-coloured cobbles, towards the spires and turrets that marked a great fortified castle. All manner of people milled about the place, buying or selling, bartering or arguing, or simply perusing. *I suppose I could live here,* Ileana thought, wondering how difficult she might find life in this city. *Would I be able to find myself a profession and be useful in some way? Could I at least make enough money to eat well and perhaps even have somewhere comfortable to live?*

II

Ayvin sat back in his leather chair, barely able to hide his contempt. The woodcutter clearly thought of himself as a servant of considerable talent, all the more so after having- apparently- brought these Hastians all the way from Fhaarluy. Even more irritating was the fact that Inerdyr of all people appeared to have a soft spot for him. Ayvin could not see why; the man had some minor talents as a trickster but was otherwise unskilled in the Old Powers. His son, so he had heard, was a different matter, but that too remained to be seen.

He turned slightly to favour Harqan with a considering look. "You're probably right about this girl Ileana," he admitted, "although it does not take great powers of deduction to realise that she must be special if she forced a path through the Wall. Still, if your son saw her for what she was, then that indicates how she made her way through." He smiled. "You'll be well-rewarded, Harqan. I'm sure Inerdyr will see to it even if I somehow forget."

Harqan bobbed his head in gratitude, quite ignorant of the jibe. "I thank you, Lord Ayvin. What should be done with them all?"

"They can be sent to Inerdyr's fortress where they'll be kept, for now. We need to ensure that this girl becomes a potent weapon, and that means that we keep them all fed and watered and treated well. I will send a message by carrier bird to Inerdyr today. You say the others have nothing of the Powers?"

Harqan shook his head. "I asked Jak also, and he thought the same. Still, they'd make good tough fighters for the cause. They can all take care of themselves, these women."

"Ground troops. Yes." Ayvin could not bring himself to sound interested in that matter. *If we could find and train every descendant of the First, we'd have no need for a vast army and the problems that such an unwieldy host brings*, he thought briefly. *Where are they all? Ileana may well be one, but there must be others- and they will know something of their powers and their heritage by now, awakened by events in the distant east. In all likelihood, they'll accidentally spread rumours of themselves as their talents come to the fore. And with a little luck, we'll hear about those rumours and locate these greatest of weapons.*

"It will be a relief to hand them over to Lord Inerdyr's keeping," Harqan remarked. "The girl has already bewitched Jak. I've seen the looks they give each other. And I think it may have gone beyond *looking*." The woodcutter's eyes narrowed, his anger apparent. "They think I don't know, but I do. She's softening the boy. Separating them will save him."

Ayvin pondered the matter. "I disagree," he said finally, his mind made up. Harqan opened his mouth, an incredulous look on his face. Perhaps for a moment he thought about arguing the matter, but wisely decided against it.

"Allow me to explain," Ayvin continued. "Ileana will be of great use to us, if she is handled properly. If she and your son have fallen for one another then so be it. He can stay with her. That will keep them both happy while she is being trained and honed for the struggle that lies ahead. A happy student is more easily trained, I feel. You cannot dispute the logic of that."

"I would not presume to." Harqan continued to look unhappy. "What should *I* do, meanwhile?"

"Ask Inerdyr. He can decide if you're of any use within his household, or if you're to return to your shack in the woods. Be gone, Harqan. I will send my message out now, and you may take them to the castle tomorrow. I will arrange for guardsmen to accompany you, to ensure your safe journey and arrival."

After Harqan had departed, Ayvin thought for a while longer about the possibility of other descendants of the First- assuming that Ileana genuinely was one of them, and there was no reason to suspect she was not- coming to light. In all likelihood, they would struggle to control and contain their newly-awakened powers. Inerdyr would demand, quite rightly, that any who became known should be brought to him and trained swiftly in time for their talents to be used against the Great Enemy, the *marandaal*.

Of course, Harqan's son Jak would also be of use to them. Apparently gifted with the ability to discern those who were strong in the Old Powers, he too could be of significant help in the search for descendants of the First, as could Ileana herself.

For a moment, he clenched his fists, frustrated at what had been said by Sarros when that miserable little ferret of a man had been summoned the other day. There had, Sarros assured him, been a girl who might well have been a descendant of the First. "And much more besides," Sarros had added, but Ayvin had cut him short with a punch that had knocked the man to his knees. "You thought to tell me now, when they are all dead inside the tower?"

"But she wasn't with them," Sarros had persisted, spitting blood upon the floor.

"And you did not see fit to point this out?"

"I didn't look around me to count my companions," Sarros had said. "I bowed my head and did as I was told. I only realised afterwards, when we watched the building of the tower. By then, I thought she would be long gone."

"You had both eyes on your reward," Ayvin had told him, and then he had the man horsewhipped and thrown into one of the castle cells.

He informed Inerdyr as soon as possible. Spies and trackers were sent swiftly out, north and east; the information with which they returned was sobering. Ruhal and his companions still lived; rumour had it that they had reached Steepleford.

Ayvin walked to the window of his study and looked out over the castle grounds. Sleet had started to fall again, and he had heard from the resident weather-seer that snow was on the way. Certainly this was the worst possible season to be preparing for war, but they had no choice but to prepare; from what few reports he had been given, the *marandaal* had started to spread throughout Aphenhast, and they would eventually reach the Border Wall. Of course, that would take some time to breach, either north or south, but eventually it *would* fall, and then the fight for Harn- and the entire world- would begin in earnest. The Great Enemy did not care for seasons any more than they cared for the spark of life itself.

III

The following morning, Harqan and the companions set out north to Inerdyr's fortress under a clear and sunlit sky. Ileana noticed that Harqan appeared subdued, his mood even black on occasion. The reason became apparent when he finally explained that Jak would be staying with them. "I'll more than likely be heading back alone," he added, and looking to Jak he added bitterly, "Looks as if you're going to have to become a man sooner than you wished, eh?"

Jak did not know what to say to that, but despite the surprise he flashed a smile towards Ileana a little later when his father was busy looking to the road ahead. Ileana smiled back, but she could not help but wonder who had instructed that Jak stay with them and for what reason. *Perhaps I'm being too questioning,* she thought to herself as she sat back and watched the countryside roll past. But she couldn't help but wonder why they were now accompanied by eight heavily-armed warriors, picked from the retinue of men within the castle where Harqan had gone the previous day. Four rode behind and four in front, grim-faced and watchful at all times. Ileana supposed that they ought to be grateful for the protection but for some reason she felt uneasy, particularly as Harqan had provided no adequate explanation for it. *It feels strange that they should go to so much trouble simply for four women from another land,* she mused on more than one occasion.

By the failing of the light they reached the outer gates of Inerdyr's grand and fortified residence. The shadows cast by the stonework were long and dark, making the castle and its grounds cold and forbidding. After the guardsmen in the watchtower had come down to open the gates and they rolled through into the outer courtyard, Ileana saw Inerdyr himself- somehow she felt certain that the old but upright man waiting in the courtyard was the master of the castle.

"Welcome to you all." Inerdyr did not give the impression of being a man used to smiling, Ileana thought as they dismounted from the cart. The sorceror had about him a grim, austere look; clearly he suffered no fools.

"I have heard the news from Aphenhast," Inerdyr continued. "You did well to flee when you did. The *marandaal* have destroyed Nisstar, and already spread to other places. But I can assure you that we in Harn are prepared for the enemy." He turned to two immaculately-clad servants who hovered nearby. "Please, take Lyya, Fauli, Amethyst and Jak to their chambers and make them welcome. Pay Harqan for his trouble- the agreed amount- and let him be on his way. And whatever our guests may have need of, provide it for them. I'm sure they are hungry and tired after their journey. Ileana- there is a matter I must discuss with you before you rejoin your friends. Will you come with me?"

Ileana threw an uncertain glance towards Amethyst and then Jak, who looked dismayed. "I require her only for a short while," Inerdyr assured her companions, placing a hand that felt like cold iron on her shoulder. Ileana looked up at him and managed a polite smile. But as they walked away towards an archway in the inner walls of the fortress, she could not help the sense of dread that had entered her heart. *What does he want with me?* she wondered. *Does he somehow know about my abilities? Did he know as soon as we arrived and he looked at me?*

Inerdyr took Ileana through great long corridors whose ceilings gaped high overhead, across hallways with floors of chequered stone, and up two flights of grand, wide stairs carved from polished stone. The entire castle felt opulent and unwelcoming at the same time. *And as cold as Inerdyr himself,* Ileana thought.

Finally he ushered her into a large study-chamber, the walls of which were all lined with bookshelves. A fire roared in the hearth on the far side of the room; the servant whose duty it had been to tend it bowed and scurried away at their approach.

Inerdyr offered Ileana one of the two large armchairs in the room. He sat in the other one and they faced each other seated on either side of the fire. To Ileana the chair felt *too* large; as she sank back into it and tried in vain to sit up properly she felt like a small child. *What does he want with me?* she asked herself again as Inerdyr placed his hands together and frowned in contemplation.

"It must have been difficult, growing up knowing that you were different to other people," he said finally.

Ileana blinked, taken aback. *Well, it seems I was right,* she thought uneasily. *He could simply tell as soon as he saw me for the first time. That must be why I was separated from the others and brought here.*

"I'm not sure what you mean," she began despite herself, but when Inerdyr looked up she could tell that there was no point whatsoever in pleading innocence.

"You always suspected, of course," the sorceror continued. "Deep within yourself, you must have known for some years. You would have remained apart from those around you, never thinking of yourself as one of them. A recluse, perhaps. An outcast in some ways, without quite knowing why. I am guessing, of course. But until recently, I doubt that you realised what it was that you were *meant* to be. Even now, your powers confuse you. You find them difficult to control. When you draw on them they weaken you."

"How do you know about them? Did you simply look at me?" she asked weakly. "Is it that easy?"

Inerdyr shook his head. "Sadly that talent is not one I possess. No, Ileana. *Jak* looked at you, when you met him and Harqan. Harqan knows his son well enough to know when he has seen a descendant of the First."

Ileana could think of nothing to say. She swallowed and blinked back tears. *I've been a fool,* she thought. *I should have realised that they would not normally have been so hospitable to strangers from beyond their Wall. Why would they? And so they decided to bring us here. That escort of warriors from the fortress in Mornkastle now makes sense. It should have done before now. I've been so stupid!*

"It has fallen to me to raise an army to defend the Free Territories from the onslaught of the *marandaal,*" Inerdyr added, apparently oblivious to her distress. "Your powers will be of great value, as will those of any other descendants of the First we find. They are, perhaps, the key to our survival."

"I can barely control what I do," Ileana said, wiping away a tear that had started to fall down her cheek. "I don't think I can be of any use. I almost fainted and collapsed when I held back the *diafagh*..."

"In time, with training, you will learn to control these powers. They exist- the Old Powers as they are known- for one reason above all others. They are intended to defend Aona against the *marandaal*."

Ileana thought for a moment. "Are *diafagh* and their masters not also part of the Old Powers?"

He looked at her as if he had been expecting the question and was somehow amused by it. "They are a lesser concern," he said finally. "In time, the Old Powers will align and be wielded as they were meant to be- against the *marandaal*. That is their singular purpose."

Ileana nodded and forced a smile. "You must think me a fool," she said. "I barely know what I'm doing here. I fled my homeland still knowing nothing about myself..."

"A fool? Hardly. Tell me, Ileana- did you ever know your natural parents? I suspect not, somehow, but I'm keen to know."

She shook her head. "Was this another thing that Jak mentioned? I told him when we were travelling." She bit her lip, trying to remember exactly how much she had told Jak.

"No, no. I refer to a peculiarity amongst the descendants of the First, which seems predominant in times when Aona has a great need of them. Most of those whose powers will later awaken are adopted."

"Why would that be?" Ileana asked.

Inerdyr shrugged. "I have no idea. I can guess, but nothing more. But we've talked enough for now. I'll have someone escort you to your chamber, and you can meet with your friends. If there is anything you need, ask a servant and they will inform whoever needs to make it so."

As Ileana walked through another part of the castle accompanied by a silent and uniformed servant, she felt an odd chill settle over her, and could not fathom how and why. She did not feel as if danger lurked here in Inerdyr's fortress, and yet she had an almost desperate urge to leave the place.

It's because he knows about me, she thought, *and I didn't want anyone to know about me, except those who already know. But I suppose the truth would come out eventually one way or another. I don't think anyone would be able to keep secrets from Inerdyr for very long.*

But I don't want any part in this war. I don't want to learn how to control my powers, or use them, or do anything with them.

If I could, I would lose them in an instant. They're nothing but a hateful curse.

Ileana felt a deep rage stir within her. *This is all Jak's fault,* she told herself. *He told his father, and Harqan decided to ensnare me by bringing me here. And he was paid for his trouble, from what I heard earlier. Paid very well, I expect.*

"Take me to see Jak," she said quietly, glancing across at the servant, who merely nodded. She was escorted as far as the door on a landing. "And your room is just across the corridor, my lady," the servant murmured, and Ileana did not know what to say or do when he gave a little bow and then loitered as if expecting her to say something or make a request. "You may go," she said finally.

Once he had departed, Ileana rapped upon Jak's door. When he finally opened it, her fury had dissipated somewhat, but enough cold anger remained for her to push the door open further and slap him hard across the cheek. "We're prisoners here because of *you,*" she hissed. "You *knew* about me! You told your father..."

"I... I had to," he mumbled, one hand pressed against his cheek and shaking wildly at the shock of her assault. "He already knew, or he had guessed. I couldn't keep anything from him, Ileana- even if I tried. Please..."

She shook her head in disgust and turned to leave, but he grabbed her arm. Furiously she turned to strike him again, this time with her fist, but he said quickly, "*Please, Ileana. Let me speak. In here?"*

Ileana reluctantly allowed him to pull her into his chamber. So emotional did she feel that she barely noticed the grand comfort of the room which was far bigger than it needed to be and equipped with full-length mirrors in two of the walls.

Jak closed the door behind them, and after they were seated he tried to explain what he had seen when he first caught sight of her. To Ileana it sounded like nonsense at first, but reluctantly she acknowledged to herself that if she was able do the things that *she* could do, then surely it was reasonable to suppose that other people had their own special abilities. Why would they not?

But the feeling of unease inside her only grew, even as her remaining anger at Jak subsided. "We can't stay here," she murmured, glancing around the walls as if expecting something terrible to emerge from them.

He stared at her. "We have to, Ileana. What choice do we have?"

She dropped her voice to a whisper. "There is something *wrong* here, Jak. Something to do with Inerdyr. I will not be a part of his war. These... these *powers* of mine are a curse and nothing more. I want nothing to do with them. I will find a way to escape. Will you come with me?"

When he blinked, unable to say anything at all, she ground her teeth in frustration. "Let me put it another way," she continued after a moment. "Would you let me hide and run through this foreign land, alone and unprotected?"

"Of course not," he whispered. "Of course I'd come with you. But it's not going to happen. Do you really think Inerdyr hasn't already thought about that? He won't *let* you escape."

"I will find a way," she said, surprised at the certainty in her voice, and in the same moment she realised something. She *would* find a way, or she would die trying; whatever happened, she would not allow herself to become part of the sorceror's plan.

IV

Inerdyr leaned back against the wall, a smile upon his face. Had anyone been in the room to observe him, they might have fled or shrieked in terror at the sight of the sorcery that had almost engulfed his body. Great tendrils of moving stone had emerged from the wall and held his arms and legs and even his neck in a vice-like grip; smaller threads of material from the interior of the wall worked their way even into his limbs, somehow drawing no blood. Inerdyr had become a temporary construct of his fortress home; it held his physical form in rigorous place.

The man and the stonework shared a primordial understanding. The architecture of the great building had over many years become suffused with a power that was partly of Inerdyr's making and partly a construct of the *choragh*. More recently, the *choragh* had perhaps had a little more influence. Inerdyr, observing the increased power that it afforded him, thought of that strengthening as a gift for his loyalty.

This link between Inerdyr and his fortress home allowed him to watch and to listen unimpeded throughout. Having noted Ileana's reaction to him, he had listened to her conversation with Jak and laughed to himself at the futility of her plans for escape. Jak was right about one thing: Ileana would not be allowed to leave the confines of the castle. She could think about it as much as she wanted; Inerdyr decided he would allow her that little luxury and let it go unpunished. If it sharpened her mind then so much the better.

302

She'll be one to watch regardless, he thought, idly wondering to himself when Jak would bed her, now that his father had been sent back to the forest. *I'll look forward to watching them fumbling in their desperate young lust.*

They had both left now though, presumably to find their other companions, so that would have to be a pleasure for another time.

He scanned the remainder of the castle methodically, looking as ever for signs of treachery, deceit or displeasure. He found nothing of particular interest beyond a few complaining servants. After a while, he saw Hanric being escorted up to his chambers; in moments, the wall behind Inerdyr became smooth and still. The sorceror moved to his study and waited for his militia captain.

When Hanric was admitted in and seated in the same chair that Ileana had occupied only a short while earlier- his bony frame did not fit it much better than the girl's had done- Inerdyr quickly came to the point. "I need Ruhal and all but one of his fellow traitors dead," he said. "No holding towers this time. It was a worthy idea, but it seems that amongst those who miraculously escaped your clutches was a descendant of the First. I suspect that she was instrumental in their escape from the tower."

"When did we learn of this?" Hanric asked in surprise.

"Our rat amongst the rats saw fit to tell Ayvin *afterwards,* upon his arrival in Mornkastle." Inerdyr's lip curled in distaste. "Ayvin should perhaps have chosen someone a little more reliable for the task. Still, we know of their whereabouts, and they seem intent on spreading their words of dissent even now."

"What will happen to Sarros?"

"Do you care?"

"If he had opened his idiot mouth a little sooner, I could have scoured the forest and brought the girl back to you before now," Hanric said roughly. "I care that whatever happens to him is painful." He shook his head. "How could I not have noticed her myself?"

"Ayvin has him in the cells in Mornkastle." Inerdyr leaned back and gave his underling a thoughtful look. "If you bring me back the heads of Ruhal and his comrades-in-madness, *and* the descendant whole and *unharmed*, you can have Sarros to yourself. Ayvin has no imagination; I believe he just had him beaten and locked up. Whereas you..." He smiled. "You could do so much more. I might like to look in on his treatment myself."

"I'll skin him," Hanric said. "Slowly. And then..." Inerdyr saw that Hanric was trembling, but that was not unusual. Whenever the man had an opportunity to explore the possibilities of pain, he became caught in an urgent flight of fantasy. He suspected that the militia commander would need to find someone tonight- a substitute for Sarros, to satisfy his needs until he returned with the spoils of victory to claim his reward.

"You can have him for as long as you can keep him alive," Inerdyr said, "on these conditions. The heads of each traitor, brought to me. Including the Watchers. The girl, the descendant- she is to remain unharmed. Tie her, but not unkindly. Do not rape her or hurt her in any other way, and keep the filthy hands of your men away from her. Feed her well. Ensure that she knows that *she* will be treated as befits one with her talents. She is a weapon, Hanric. You know about looking after weapons, don't you?"

Hanric nodded. Already he had about him that familiar restless look, like a savage dog desperate to head off along the trail. "When should we leave?"

"Go now. Take the main road towards Steepleford. They may be long gone when you get there, but you'll find their trail easily enough. You'll only need to ask the people in any settlement you reach."

Inerdyr sat back and allowed his thoughts to wander, once Hanric had been sent away. Finally he grew restless, and he returned to the room from where he could reach into each and every corner of his great castle, reaching out a hand to touch the wall and stepping back to watch it slowly ripple and move in reaction. Perhaps he would visit Jak and Ileana again and be pleasantly surprised or perhaps, as was usually the case, he would have to watch in amused curiosity as servants fornicated roughly in their quarters, thinking their brief moments of pleasure a secret from their master.

V

Ileana found that her determination to escape subsided as the days went on. She spent time walking around the castle- at least, as much of it as she could explore without one or other of the servants politely but insistently explaining to her that a certain area was out of bounds- and she walked around the gardens and courtyards, observing the high, spiked walls and the heavily armed guards positioned at each of the gates and archways. If Inerdyr's fortress had a poorly-guarded spot she certainly could not find it. Eventually she tired of plotting how she might run away. Jak was right, she reluctantly told herself. She could not escape, and if she so much as tried, perhaps all pretence of goodwill would vanish in an instant and she would be punished in some terrible way.

And I mustn't let that happen, she thought as she sat on the edge of a stone fountain in one of the smaller gardens, listening to the bubbling of the water and watching birds flitting amongst the branches of the cherry trees across from her. A servant hovered near one of the archways, nervously trying to be as unobtrusive as he could. *If I'm punished,* Ileana told herself, *then I'll be pulled away from Amethyst and from Jak...*

She had wondered several times if it was normal to fall in love with the only boy her age she had ever been friends with or even known properly. Finally she decided that it didn't matter, and when she had finally confided in Amethyst about the matter, Amethyst had agreed.

She hurried back to her chamber a little later as dusk fell, and a short while after that she heard Jak knocking on her door. Ileana smiled, knowing it was him purely from the hesitancy in the sound.

"When do you think Inerdyr will start your training?" he asked quietly as they sat together on her bed.

"I don't know." She shuddered. "I don't want to talk about that."

"I'm sorry." Abruptly he brought a bottle from out of his inside jacket pocket. Ileana stared at it. "What's that?"

"One of the servants gave it to me. He said it was a gift from Inerdyr, and it was for us to share." Jak peered at the orange-hued liquid in the bottle. "It's an expensive spirit of some sort, I think..."

Ileana stared at him in alarm. "Who knows what it might do? What if it harms..."

"Ileana, stop!" he exclaimed. "Why would he wish to harm you? He knows how important you are. You're the *last* person he would wish to harm! I'm sure it's safe." Walking across the room, he returned with two glasses taken from the table at the far end, uncorked the bottle and poured them both a generous measure. Ileana took a sip, grimaced and took another sip, then shrugged. "Maybe it gets better after a while."

They sat and drank in silence for a while. Jak poured them both more when Ileana had finished. She glanced across at him, feeling curiously light-headed. *Maybe I'll only have a little more,* she thought, taking another sip and putting the glass down on the bedside table. "I'm glad you stayed," she said suddenly. "I wouldn't want to be apart from you. Ever."

Jak smiled shyly, which in turn made her smile. As he sat next to her again and placed his arm around her, Ileana took a deep breath and asked him something she had been working up the courage to say for days, knowing that he wouldn't dare ask her himself.

She kissed him on the lips and then said, "Will you stay with me tonight?"

His eyes widened and he blinked nervously. *Please don't run away,* Ileana thought, squeezing his hand. "You mean...?" he managed to say eventually.

"You know what I mean," she said softly.

"What if we're found out?"

"We won't be. And if we are- well, we haven't been told any rules about it. It's only your father who wanted to keep us apart. No one else does."

He reached out and stroked her hair. "Of course I'll stay with you," he whispered. "I'll stay with you forever."

It won't hurt, Ileana told herself a while later as Jak loomed above her, urgent and trembling. *This will be different. I love him. It will be different.*

But it did hurt when- with some help and after three attempts- he eventually found his way inside her. It hurt enough to make her glad that the only light left in the room came from the glowing embers in the fireplace, so he could not properly see the grimace on her face. She reached up to touch his hair as it cascaded down, and when only moments later he collapsed on her, spent and shaking, she put her arms around him, feeling the tautness of his shoulders and the fresh beads of sweat prickling his body.

Ileana kissed Jak on the forehead as he rolled over to one side, and then stared up at the ceiling. *We made love in the dark as if it was shameful,* she thought, *or because we were nervous. Maybe we didn't want to see into each other's eyes. But I'm glad he didn't see me hurting. Maybe it will be better next time.*

She exhaled slowly, frowning at the unexpected complexity of the thoughts running through her head. *I wanted to pretend it was my first time,* she mused. *I wish it had been. Even if it hurt and even if it felt clumsy and embarrassing.*

Jak stirred at her side; presently he draped an arm over her. "I won't let anything bad happen to you," he murmured.

She smiled into the dark, loving the sentiment but knowing the futility of it. Jak wanted desperately to be her protector; that was one of the things boys and men wanted to think of themselves as, she guessed- those few who were not simply predators. He was wrapped up in that warm glow she had heard about, that people were supposed to experience after lovemaking. Ileana suspected that in this moment he would have readily promised her anything at all and meant every word.

But Jak couldn't determine her fate, and he certainly couldn't stand in the way of the future that she feared would come to pass.

He fell asleep quickly, and Ileana was wondering how long it might take her to do the same when a sudden, urgent sensation washed over her- something she had never experienced before and could not hope to describe. Without knowing why, she slipped out of bed and wandered over to the window where she stared out over the castle's buildings and walls into the east. A presence that she knew on an instinctive level drew her gaze into the distance.

"There's someone else nearby," she whispered. "Someone like me..."

Ileana had no idea how she could know such a thing, but the more she stared out into the night the more certain she became that somewhere not far from the castle grounds someone else strong in the Old Powers lurked. For a moment she almost saw a vision of the woman- it was definitely a woman- but it melted away.

Abruptly she felt a pang of deep unease. Fear stirred within her, and she stepped away from the window as if whoever this sorceress was, she might see her.

Ileana could not tell how, but she knew that something had changed this night.

Inerdyr's eyes flickered open. With an effort he slowed the beating of his ancient heart, and waited as the material of the chamber wall rippled, moved and eventually set him free.

He stood in silence for a moment, a smile upon his face. This truly was a fortunate night. He had watched and enjoyed the laughable yet oddly satisfying spectacle of Jak and Ileana's coupling, full of the clumsiness and uncertainty of youth. That in itself would have sent him to his own bed fulfilled for the night, and he had been about to do so- but Ileana's words as she gazed out of the window meant only one thing.

There's another, he thought. *Another Descendent. She must be found and brought back here.*

He dressed swiftly and summoned Serimand, the captain-at-arms of the castle. "Ride east with a dozen men. No, twenty," he said. "Anyone you find camping out in the wilderness, bring them back here. Search any outhouses and barns. Do not return empty-handed. *Someone* will be out there. And whatever you do, treat them well. No violence. Tie them only if you have to. Do you understand?"

If Serimand had thought his master insane then he hid his thoughts well. "As you wish, Lord Inerdyr," he murmured, and left quickly to do as bidden.

Inerdyr did not sleep; he paced his chambers and waited. Dawn was fast approaching when the captain-at-arms was admitted again. "Well?" Inerdyr demanded.

"We found a man and a woman sleeping in a barn, m'Lord. Only them. We brought them back. They came willingly enough. They're being guarded in the main hall. Their names are Vornen and Jaana. And here's the odd thing- they're Hastian. Don't see many of them roaming Harn."

Hastians, Inerdyr thought. *Well, well.* "Take me to them," he said abruptly, and turned to one of the servants guarding the door. "Bring the Hastian girl Ileana to the main hall. Wake her if you have to."

He headed swiftly down to the hall, and found the two of them sitting at one of the smaller tables, with guardsmen standing around them but at a respectful distance. They both looked quite ordinary, he thought, and worse for wear after their travels. But perhaps one of them was anything but ordinary.

"I apologise for having you brought here," he said, forcing a smile, "but I will explain everything in due course. You will be treated well, I can assure you. May I ask where you were headed?"

The man glanced across at his companion and then ventured, "We were following our companions' trail and hoped to catch up with them."

Inerdyr considered that they too must have been allowed through the Border Wall by virtue of their powers. *Am I close to finding more Descendants?* he wondered. *So close, so soon?*

His thoughts were interrupted by a door opening on the far side of the hall. The servant walked in accompanied by Ileana. "Did you sleep well, Ileana?" Inerdyr inquired as the girl was brought to the table.

But Ileana gave no impression of having even heard the question. She stared directly at the two people seated at the table, oblivious to everything else. And curiously, not only did the woman stare back at her equally transfixed, but the man also did.

Now we shall see, Inerdyr thought to himself.

"Ileana!" the man exclaimed finally.

Ileana shook her head as if the entire scene was too much for her. "Vornen! But how... how can you..."

He smiled wearily. "It's a long story. Is Amethyst here also?"

"She is..." Ileana laughed, utterly bemused. "She won't believe her eyes when she sees you. How did you..." She stopped suddenly, glancing quickly across at Inerdyr, who favoured her with a benevolent smile. *I'll have all your stories soon enough,* he thought. *They seem interesting. And clearly this meeting was meant to happen, engineered by our Lords no doubt. Some might call it fate; I wouldn't.*

"Are the two others who arrived here with you?" the woman spoke up suddenly. "Two women- one *luyan* and one *du-luyan.*"

"They are here, and being well looked after," Inerdyr told her before Ileana could reply. "Are they friends of yours?"

She nodded. "May I see them?"

"Of course. I expect you are both exhausted after your travels, however. The servants will find suitable rooms for you and ensure that your every need is taken care of. And tomorrow evening, we will all dine together."

He left them then, and retired to his private quarters to mull over this turn of events, a smile upon his face as he pictured distant fragments of a puzzle coming swiftly together.

Amethyst, Lyya and Fauli were all dumbfounded to see their lost companions, but Amethyst could not bring herself to believe that Vornen stood in front of her at first. Even when they embraced, and she hugged him so fiercely that he laughed and joked that she might snap his bones, she still suspected that she was dreaming and would shortly wake into another day like this one only without him.

"I still don't quite believe it," she commented with a smile, a long while later as they sat in her room.

"Neither could I," he admitted. "I waited for the end in Nisstar. The end came, but I was no longer there. I was freed, and I have no idea why or how that could have happened." He paused and glanced soberly at her. "So this man- this *sorceror* Inerdyr- intends to train Ileana and prepare her for the war?"

Amethyst's good humour vanished. "Yes. But she isn't happy with it, and to be truthful neither am I. There is something unpleasant about him, Vornen. A side he keeps hidden, but I can see it nonetheless. As can Ileana."

Vornen shrugged. "I couldn't say one way or the other. But in any case, what can either of you do?"

"I don't know. But I feel certain that he means to corrupt her somehow. I cannot let that happen."

Vornen smiled at that. "What do you find so amusing?" Amethyst demanded.

"It's odd how matters work out," he said. "It's as if you're her elder sister."

Amethyst smiled faintly. "Someone needs to look after her, especially here."

On the other side of the great castle, Inerdyr watched as Jaana sat in the chair on the other side of the fireplace in his study. *Oh, she's very different to Ileana,* he thought as she gazed warily back at him. *There's a hardness to this woman. She's brittle and indecisive. She doesn't know which way to turn. But I can help her with that. I think she'll be a little less... difficult than Ileana.*

"Your journey through Aphenhast must have been an interesting one," he commented.

"My escape from Nisstar was interesting enough. All my other companions perished. I had to tell Fauli and Lyya about that. Fauli was especially close to them, I think. Certainly it upset her, finding out about their deaths."

"You're a brave woman," Inerdyr told her. "But the things you must have seen..."

"Most people we saw as we headed west had already started to turn on one another," Jaana said. "We watched lightdreamers being burned on a pyre. We saw beheadings and mutilations." She shrugged. "And the *kin* came for me more than once…" She stopped suddenly and glanced uneasily at him.

"I know your nature," Inerdyr told her. "You've nothing to fear from me, Jaana. In all honesty, I sent out my men to bring you and Vornen back here because I sensed you. I became suddenly aware that someone strong in the Old Powers was nearby. I took it upon myself to have you brought back here to safety."

"Thank you." Jaana gave an audible sigh of relief.

"Have you ever wondered why they cannot harm you?" Inerdyr asked suddenly.

"Because of my ancestry," Jaana said. "Because I'm descended from one of the First."

Inerdyr smiled. He had expected her to say almost those exact words. "You need to look beyond that, Jaana."

"I don't understand."

"Essentially, the old ways flow through some and not others. Through me, but not the vile Seven in their Black Citadel. Through you, but not through your friends Lyya and Fauli. You can sense the powers in others, can't you? You could sense them in Ileana when you first saw her."

"She's strong. Maybe as strong as me," Jaana commented.

"Well, that remains to be seen. But these same forces shape the various beings of the Old Powers- the *choragh,* their *kin,* and many others. We may all look very different, but in many ways we are the same."

Jaana frowned. "That can't be so."

"Of course it's so. The Old Powers have a primary purpose, which is to defend Aona against the *marandaal.* That is our objective, Jaana, yours and mine. It's why we are here. Defeat of the *marandaal* at all costs is imperative." He leaned back, watching her think his words over. "Two thousand years ago the *choragh,* aided by the *kin* and by all the races of Aona, joined as one to defeat the *marandaal* and send those that survived crawling back into the abyss whence they came. At the head of that mighty force, not only *choragh* but human, *luyan*, *du-luyan*, *crommari*, *ko xhoth* and many others, channelling that same power."

"But I thought…"

"I can guess what you thought. That the First freed all the races of the world from the cruel yoke of the *choragh*. I'm afraid that's an example of history being rewritten, Jaana. The truth and what you believed to be the truth are two very different things. And unfortunately there are those in Harn who persist in maintaining and spreading their own version of what happened all those many centuries ago. These rebels seek to divide the Free Territories for their own selfish reasons. If they succeed in doing so then the *marandaal* could well overrun Harn. That cannot be allowed to happen. Even if it does not, such division would still weaken us. We could destroy the *marandaal*, only for the Seven to overrun the free North. Have you heard much about them?"

Jaana shook her head.

"They are the overlords of Luudhoq, the Black Citadel. They are immortal; at least, they appear to be. Their evil knows no boundaries. I'm sure you'll learn more about them in time. But enough of the Seven. I am more concerned about those within the Free Territories who seek to divide us."

"What about the *kin*? How can they be on the same side as us?"

"The *kin* have their ways, which are different. But I'll expect they uttered some truths."

Jaana shivered. "One of them said we were the same. He said that sooner or later we would answer to the same lords. But I'm not a subordinate of the *choragh*, nor will I ever be."

"The *choragh* are the guardians of Aona," Inerdyr told her. "In that sense, they are also the guardians of the entire world's people. One could think of them as lords. We cannot understand them, and perhaps we cannot understand the *kin*. But they are not our enemies."

He looked thoughtfully at her. "Did you kill them?"

"Yes." Jaana's expression grew wary.

Inerdyr nodded. "Be at ease. I have no intention of judging you. Did you enjoy killing them?"

Jaana stared at him, clearly not knowing what to say. Inerdyr smiled and said quietly to her, "Whatever you say here will not be uttered anywhere else. Anything you say to me, I will keep to myself. I ask only that you maintain an honest tongue. The fact is, Jaana, I am attempting to bring together as many warriors as I can. Those who wield the Old Powers. Those who are willing to fight for the sake of Harn and for all Aona. Your powers mark you out as special. I ask for your loyalty, and in return you have mine. We will fight together, against the *marandaal*. There is no greater honour, no greater responsibility."

He paused and sat back in his chair. "Did you enjoy killing them?" he asked her again after a short while.

"Yes. I enjoyed it." He could hear her voice trembling. "I thought about it many times afterwards. I relived it over and over. I even thought about how I could have done the deeds differently, and hurt them even more before I killed them. I told myself that I'd killed all but the last of them too quickly." Jaana's eyes brimmed with tears. "I felt so full of hatred. I thought perhaps that torturing and destroying the *kin* might relieve me of those feelings, of all the rage. But it didn't. I feel it even more now. Maybe I shouldn't have killed them. But I did, and I enjoy thinking about what I've done. Does that shock you?"

Inerdyr shook his head. "At my age, very little has the capacity to shock anymore."

"I was once a healer," Jaana said bitterly. "But I couldn't heal lightdreamers."

"No one can," Inerdyr pointed out. "The fact doesn't shame you. Better that their throats are slit than they persist as slaves of the *marandaal.*"

"And now I'm nothing," she continued. "Why should I have such powers as these, when I don't even know what to do with them?"

"Your life needs direction," Inerdyr said softly. "I want you to be at the vanguard of my army, Jaana. An army of all those who are willing to defend Harn against the *marandaal,* and against the traitors in our midst. What better purpose can there be? I will teach you to hone and develop your powers."

Jaana nodded gratefully.

"And nothing you said here will be mentioned to anyone else." Inerdyr paused, considering. "It might also be for the best if you didn't mention our talk about the *choragh* and the First to your friends. Particularly to Ileana." He shook his head sadly. "I think she has a stubborn streak to her, and she appears to distrust me for some reason. Perhaps in time she will see for herself the truth about her powers. Until then, she will have to be guided in more subtle ways. Befriend her, if you can. You are the only one here who can understand what it's like to bear such powers. Use that fact to your advantage."

After Jaana had left, Inerdyr smiled and nodded to himself. Not only would she make a useful weapon in the war to come, but she might also make a useful, pliable lieutenant. *She needs direction,* he reminded himself. *I can provide her with that. And certainly she likes to kill.*

I can help her fulfil that desire.

XV – The Slow Withering

I

Alexia could no longer feel the passage of time. That moment when she realised she had become separated from Yui and Phyqor might have been just a moment ago, or days or tennights could have passed.

She stood on the roof balcony of a tall house, watching slow changes happening to the architecture of the shadow-city. Perhaps the place where she stood and observed would also fall or mutate, crushing her between walls of stone, but Alexia had no fear of death now. She wished only that it would hurry on its way.

The faint green glow in the starless sky remained constant, but the amount of light around the city varied continuously. She caught glimpses of an altogether different illumination to that which suffused the heavens; a warm and bright glow that appeared for brief moments, sometimes from a distant window or a crack in the cobbles of a street or square, or a doorway left ajar. But in other areas the darkness was absolute- an absence of all light, a pool into which nothing could shine.

Alexia watched the interplay of light and dark, and fancied that it represented some sort of eternal struggle, a reflection perhaps of events in the world she had left behind. When the bright white or yellow light disappeared, it filled her with a strange sadness that made her yearn to see it again in the same place, as if some sort of welcome might await her somewhere within it. When her eyes took in a widening chasm of blackness she looked swiftly away, fearful of being drawn in regardless of how far away from it she might be.

Distance, she reminded herself, had as much meaning here as time.

If that's so, I could reach Yui and Phyqor in an instant and a single step, she reasoned, *if only I knew how.*

She knew that was a fanciful notion. They might have even left this place altogether now. In all likelihood they had already considered her doomed, and had pressed on.

And still a small part of me clings to the idea that I'm asleep and dreaming, Alexia thought, *and that I'll wake up in the world I know to be real.*

Alexia wondered, as she leaned over the balcony wall, how long it would take her to reach the ground if she let herself fall. Would this place of endless trickery slow her down, or would the ground open up gratefully to swallow her? Or would she simply hit the ground and remain there in a bloodied heap, maybe still alive and in agony?

"You are here for a reason," a voice spoke up from behind her- *her* voice. Alexia did not need to turn round to know that its owner not only sounded just like her but would look more or less the same as she did. Perhaps a little thinner, a little more translucent, as if its life force slowly seeped into the stone and glass and metal that made up this world.

"The child was too strong. Her will could not be broken. In another time, keeping her here would have been easy. But I grow weak."

Alexia still refused to turn round and face the creature, but the words struck her as odd. *I grow weak.*

"How many of you are there?" she asked finally. Conversing with the ghostly denizens of this place could surely do her no further harm. It would pass the time, if time passed at all here.

"I speak through this vessel. I speak through others. But vessels are all they are. I am *one*. In this Existence, I am Aona."

Alexia turned slowly round, no longer knowing what she expected to see. The creature that bore her image still stood there, slack-jawed and dead-eyed. It gave no indication that it even knew it had spoken.

The sudden realisation came to Alexia that this place- this *world*- was an inner version of the physical world she knew, something that was deeper, and...

"This is the heart of Aona," she murmured. "The secret inner world."

And it's a place that's dying, she added, gazing around at the desolate, ever-changing cityscape. *Perhaps Luudhoq is where the corruption is greatest, and that's where the darkness shows through the most, but soon it will seep everywhere. What is causing it?*

Perhaps her doppelganger heard those questioning thoughts somehow, for it spoke again. "You will see through the window for yourself."

The creature turned and headed slowly back into the gloom of the building. After a moment, Alexia followed. *What else am I to do?* she asked herself as the two of them headed down the spiral staircase that led to the lower ramparts of the building, and from there out into the streets.

The shadow-Alexia set off along a narrow street that had not been there when she entered the building, however long ago that might have been. That fact did not surprise her; if anything her environment had changed with ever greater frequency the more she observed the phenomenon.

The street became narrower and more twisted; soon it began to spiral downwards, and the surface was no longer smooth; steps had been cut into the cobbles, and Alexia carefully made her way down these, seeing little in front of her except her doppelganger heading down into ever deeper darkness. Presently she saw what looked like a glimmer of light in front of them, flickering in the indeterminate distance, and at the same time she became oddly certain that some creature she had not sensed before had begun to follow them. She turned but could neither see nor hear whatever curious being it might be that walked in their wake.

Ever steeper and tighter the spiral went, until it seemed that this stone staircase and the building walls looming on either side of it made up the entire world. In places the steps gleamed with moisture, the source of which could not be determined; Alexia reached out a hand to the wall of the building on her left in order to steady herself and almost stumbled in shock as her hand sank into the wall a little way. She recoiled and stared at the brickwork, although it looked intact and unyielding.

From further down the ever-narrowing path of steps, the shadow-creature that bore her image turned and gazed expressionlessly at her. *Does every downward step bring me closer to my own oblivion?* Alexia asked herself as she continued cautiously on. *But then, why does it matter? I'm condemned regardless.*

The green glow had grown gradually dimmer, so that soon she could see nothing around her except the faint illumination that always stayed somewhere ahead in the depths towards which she struggled. It did nothing to light her way, and Alexia stumbled three times, very nearly tumbling down into darkness. She wondered if her doppelganger would die with her if they collided and fell together to end up as a mass of flesh and broken bones, and then she wondered if it cared, if it even felt any kind of pain, or if it was simply as it appeared- a version of her that had lingered here possibly for a longer time than she could imagine, all its humanity stripped away.

The world had truly become a stairwell now; the spiral tightened no further and simply continued downwards. Exhaustion overcame her at one point and she sank down on a damp step, sobbing with sheer misery as she leaned against the cold brick wall, no longer caring if it became less than solid and pulled her into some unimaginable interior. A pale visage she knew from so many mirrors stared up at her; the creature did not speak, showed

no emotion and waited for her to recover her wits sufficiently
to carry on.

"Let me die," Alexia whispered, fancying for a
moment that the world might heed her despair and open up
a chasm beneath her in pity.

It did not. Trying not to contemplate the loneliness of
eternity, Alexia struggled to her feet and continued her
descent.

The stairwell ended finally at a door that looked as if
it had been created from wood, metal and glass in roughly
equal parts, the textures swirling seamlessly and merging
together. In the world she knew, such craftsmanship could
not have been possible, but Alexia had become used to
miracles such as this.

She blinked, suddenly aware that her doppelganger
had disappeared, perhaps through the door or through the
wall. Alexia considered that that disappearance itself might
signal something- her arrival at some sort of destination
perhaps.

She pushed tentatively against the door. The
sensation against her hand was unlike anything she knew; it
bore no resemblance to wood, metal, stone, glass or any other
material. The door swung silently open and she stepped
through into a vast, perfectly round room whose wall was
one continuous window. Fashioned from clear glass, it
afforded glimpses into other places- other parts of Harn and
even other lands, Alexia guessed. The scenes changed all the
time, as if she was looking from the eyes of many different
birds soaring above the skies around the world. Alexia stood
mesmerised by the multitude of sights and dumbfounded by
the clarity with which she was able to see them. After the
endless murky twilight of the shadow-city above, this was
almost too much for her to bear. Without thinking about
what she was doing, she touched the glass, yearning to be on
the other side of it even if that meant hurtling through the

air to her death. She had never longed so much for the sun, the wind, even the rain.

Alexia looked behind her; she did not expect to see the door still in place, and it was not.

A voice filled her mind. So powerful was the torrent of words that issued forth that she collapsed to her knees, eyes and mouth wide with shock. She thought that her head might burst, and the strangest vision came to her, of light pouring forth from cracks and fissures that opened up in her head. *The light of the world,* she thought numbly. *The last light of life in all the Existence.*

At first she could make no sense of the words that spilled forth inside her head, but eventually she could understand them, despite having no idea what language they were spoken in.

The child will be in great danger until you take her to the others who share her gifts.

Alexia stared through the glass as the scenery changed dramatically. She saw a group of people heading through some hilly part of the world. As she watched, she was drawn nearer to one of them, a young, dark-haired and pretty girl. Then she was drawn towards another young woman, a *du-luyan* who walked alongside a man of the same race.

"I don't understand," she murmured, but the scene changed completely. The travellers and the hilly country through which they walked melted away, replaced by an opulent bedroom. A girl stared out of the window, lost in thought. Alexia reckoned she was even younger than the other two she had seen- little more than a child.

Remember them, the voice warned. It sounded tired, faint, as if some great energy had been used in order for these sights to be shown to her. *The child must link with them. There is no other way.*

Then, it said something truly chilling. *If they perish, there can be no hope. I am the light, but the light will die.*

Alexia shook her head in bemusement. "How do I find them? How do I even find Yui to begin with? I'm lost! I can't even find my way out..."

Abruptly the glass around her cracked and finally shattered to reveal nothing but darkness before and behind her, as if the voice's grim prophecy was already being fulfilled. The glass floor disappeared from underneath her, and she fell screaming through the void.

II

Alexia's eyes flickered open, and she stared up into a sky festooned with stars.

I'm no longer in the city, she realised numbly, sitting up and staring around. *Where am I?*

Then she saw Phyqor and Yui sitting nearby; they turned as she stirred, and she cried out, "What happened? I became separated from you... how did you find me?"

"I told you not to talk to them," Yui said solemnly. "They're dangerous. You fell to the ground, and we had to carry you. We couldn't wake you."

"What? That's impossible. I was separated from you. I spent a long time lost; it could have been days, tendays even..."

"Yui speaks the truth, Alexia," Phyqor said gently, draping around her shoulders the blanket on which she had been lying.

Alexia did not know what to say, but the relief she felt almost overwhelmed her. She exhaled softly, looked around the field in which they were sitting and asked, "Where are we?"

"Outside Luudhoq," Yui told her. She spoke slowly and as if each word required a vast amount of effort. "I'm not sure how far away we are from the city. I think we're still in the south of Harn. We have to head..."

"North," Alexia interrupted. The memory of everything she had seen and heard in her dream- *If it was a dream,* she thought- had begun to flood swiftly back in detail.

"Beyond the reach of the Seven," Phyqor agreed, and was about to say something else but Alexia continued, the words tumbling from her mouth, "There are others we have to find. We have to take Yui to them..."

"What do you mean? What others?" Phyqor frowned.

"I was taken somewhere." Alexia shook her head, unable to adequately describe everything she had seen. "I was shown the faces of other people- others who have powers a little like Yui's..."

Yui stared wide-eyed at her. "You must have been dreaming," Phyqor said, glancing across at his daughter. "You were with us the entire time. You were not taken anywhere."

"We have to find them." Alexia felt desperation well up inside her. She was no longer sure that she could remember the faces of the three women she had seen, but at the same time she felt more certain than ever of their importance.

The sky had lightened a little, heralding the new day. "We'll be on the move once the light is good enough," Phyqor said. "Are you well enough to walk?"

"We have to find them," Alexia repeated, barely listening to him, but the details of her dream were slipping away rapidly. She tried her best to hold on to them, commit them to memory, but she couldn't.

Morning came, and Alexia stumbled along with her companions, wrapped up in her cloak and feeling nothing but a numb emptiness inside her. She had been given something important to do, but that was all she could recall from her dream; she had forgotten the detail. She could remember nothing of the faces she had been shown, the people that were important. She had even forgotten *why* they were important.

It was a dream, she told herself, *and that's why I woke up from it. That place through which we travelled was real enough, but perhaps everything else is as Phyqor and Yui say it is- I lost consciousness, I had to be carried, and eventually they found their way out of the shadow-Luudhoq and out of that twilit world altogether, bearing me along with them.*

Alexia shivered, a chill settling into her that had little to do with the cold eastern breeze slanting across at them as they hurried through fields and along country paths. She felt entirely adrift, as if she had left a part of herself in the dream- a part with which she could not be reunited unless she recalled the things she had already forgotten.

XVI – A Forgotten Fastness

I

The air became bitterly cold as the companions rode north from Steepleford over the great open grasslands and on towards the moors that marked the first hint of the Rhunin Heights. These crags, the highest and most inhospitable range of mountains in the known world, already loomed before them in the distance, their icy heights stretching into the heavens. Just glancing at them made Anlerran feel colder still.

Ruhal had been the first of the companions to voice his agreement with Anlerran's intent to head into the Rhunin. As soon as those words had spilled from her mouth- childish and impetuous, she had thought in horror at the time- she expected nothing but derision, even retribution. But Ruhal had remained silent, thought for a short while- she noticed that he had his etched pebble in his hands as he did so- and then said abruptly, "So be it. We head into the Rhunin."

That decision had caused fierce argument to flare, not only with the Watchers but also with Lura, who had called it a "fool's errand". Only Jahar and the two *du-luyan* had remained silent on the issue. By some miracle however, agreement had been reached.

Where else would we all have gone anyway? Anlerran had thought afterwards as they rode out of Steepleford, watched by hundreds of suspicious eyes. *If we wandered from settlement to settlement, west or south, Inerdyr and his people would reach us quickly- and what then? We all recognised that fact, and that's why there was agreement eventually. There would be no escape a second time. Will his followers pursue us into the depths of the mountains?*

A chill had settled in her stomach at that thought. *No, of course they won't. Only the mad and deluded head this way, with the depths of winter soon to arrive. Our enemies would expect us to die in the mountains, and perhaps we should be prepared for death too.*

Throughout the day, her thoughts lurched one way and then the other. They were all quite insane to be riding north on the basis of what might or might not have been a dream. But they had no other choice other than conflict and annihilation.

During the afternoon a familiar dark shape appeared from wherever he had been lurking and ran alongside them. Anlerran glanced at Culos and felt immense relief; after all, the dog had in part been responsible for the decision she had made, and the fact that he had appeared again now to journey with them somehow gave credibility to that choice.

Sometime after sundown with Archaon already rising over the jagged skyline in the distant east, they espied lanterns and torches ahead swaying in the gloom. Ruhal softly called a halt, and they watched as the lights then stayed exactly where they were. Iyoth whispered after a moment, "I see them well enough. Perhaps a hundred paces."

"They look like *orkar*," Ruhal murmured.

"They are," Kian spoke up. "Should we expect trouble?"

Anlerran immediately heard a stir of consternation amongst the Watchers, even before Ruhal replied. Clearly the enforcers of Luudhoq knew the name. The *orkar* had a mixed reputation even in the North; she could only hazard a guess as to what anyone from the Black Citadel might think of them and what tales they might have heard.

"Be still. Show them we mean no harm," Ruhal said quietly. "No weapons. Keep your hands where they can see them. A pact exists between all the Races in this part of the land. We'll honour it and ask the same of them."

Ildoron said something about *savages* and Kal-Myrran uttered words that Anlerran could not make out, but a furious glare from Ruhal was enough for them to hold their tongues as the party of *orkar* folk drew nearer.

The oncoming group drew to a halt after a short while, and then a single rider moved slowly forward. The imposing creature sitting on the horse- which itself was a fearsome-looking beast at least four hands taller than any of their own mounts- wore a plain metal helm and ragged-looking chain and patched leather armour. Anlerran shivered as she saw the *orkar* man bare his array of sharp teeth until she realised that the expression was in fact no more than a smile.

Ruhal rode a few steps forward, showing an open hand; the *orkar* man nodded and then shook his great head in bemusement. "Ah- it's taken me a moment, but I know you."

"You do?" Ruhal peered uncertainly at him, and then added quietly, perhaps even reluctantly, "You may indeed. Wistport?"

"Wistport!" The commander of the *orkar* nodded with evident satisfaction. "Many pirates were hanged that day!"

"Many innocents lost their lives as the Anvarian pirates retreated," Ruhal added. "We did what we could, but matters seldom run smoothly in battle. I recall also that lies were spread about the *orkar* involvement, which saddens and shames me."

"I remember your name. Ruhal. I am Garrok." As they shook hands, Garrok half-turned in his saddle to bellow something in his own language to those of his people who lurked behind. A murmur rose amongst the front ranks, and Anlerran could just about hear it being passed like a whisper on the wind, back towards those who still waited behind in the gathering gloom. She thought it might be a murmur of appreciation, although it was impossible to be sure.

"The people of the far west remain in your debt," Garrok said. "Yes, many lives were lost- but many more were saved that day."

Ruhal nodded, tight-lipped. "I thank you, Garrok, but that's not how everyone remembers that day. If you don't mind my asking, what takes you so far from your homelands?"

"Disturbances and darkness. A time of ritual seems to be upon us again in the outer territories." Garrok clenched a fist. "The Faceless Ones, who once enslaved us all, work their way back into the world, and their hold was always greatest in our land. Many of the outer settlements have been abandoned. Now we seek help from others. From anyone who can help keep order and sanity and hold back the... *return.*"

He looked towards the others and observed, "You're headed towards the Rhunin. With deep winter no more than a whole moon away. In the company of..." He glanced around at everyone again, his sharp eyes missing nothing. "*Duluyan,* and..." He paused as his gaze fell upon the Watchers, and for a moment he looked deeply troubled. "Creatures of the South," he said finally. "Times are changing quickly, Ruhal. We've seen many odd things only in the last tennight. I'm sure you have a good reason for the strange path you follow."

"I do. We all do," Ruhal said grimly.

"And if we should meet your enemies?"

Ruhal held his hands open and sighed. "You must say and do whatever is best for your people, Garrok. Keep them safe; keep the peace, if you can."

Garrok nodded as if considering that, then with a savage-looking grin said, "I think I shall deny ever meeting you and your friends, Ruhal. May the Powers and all luck be with you!"

"And to you, and your people," Ruhal responded with a short bow.

Garrok bowed briefly in return, then barked a command for his people to continue forward, waving his arm. As a mark of respect- not to mention common sense- Ruhal urged everyone from the path, and they watched as the garrison of *orkar* thundered past in a stream of vast black horses, swaying lanterns and threadbare armour. Perhaps a hundred or even two hundred passed by. Even long after they had gone and their lights and noise had faded into the backcloth of darkness, Anlerran could hear the sounds of their passing ring in her ears.

They camped with the onset of full darkness shortly afterwards. As they gathered around a fire, Iyoth spoke up. "It would seem that you're held in some esteem amongst the *orkar* people, Ruhal."

Even by the reddish light, Anlerran noticed Ruhal's embarrassment and hid her smile behind her hand. "Make your point, Iyoth," Ruhal said curtly, taking the cork from his water canteen and raising the vessel to his lips.

"I intend to." The *du-luyan* glanced around at everyone before continuing, "I have no particular knowledge of these events- I certainly know next to nothing about Anvarian pirates, although I've seen enough pirates on the Southern Ocean. I don't speak the *orkar* language, but we all heard the response from the nearest of his people when Garrok spoke to them. I expect he was telling them who you were."

"He was," Ruhal said reluctantly, "although there was no need for it."

"Ruhal prefers not to speak of the events at Wistport," Lura frowned.

"Does he not?" Iyoth favoured her with a cool stare. "Well, regardless of what happened there and whose account we choose to pay heed to, he wishes to unite Harn and the Races, bringing together all factions and ending the rivalry and hatred that no doubt runs through this land like a poisoned vein."

Iyoth turned to Ruhal. "To do that, you must have followers- many thousands of followers. You must have an army, even if you're reluctant to use force against your people. If the *illeagh* can be found and will offer their help then so be it, but such beings will not drag the Races out of their internal struggles. They would surely seek only to ensure the *choragh* cannot bring chaos to your land, and to ensure that the *marandaal* never set foot inside Harn. Beyond that, they surely have no wish to make firm footsteps within this harsh physical world. Why would they? Our problems are for *us* to resolve. And for that to happen, you need the will of the people. All people apart from those who are too corrupt to care. Those who have already given themselves over to the *choragh*."

He turned then to the Watchers and told them, "You speak of returning to Luudhoq either in victory or death. From what little I know of them, the Seven care more for the power they hold in their citadel than for Watchers or the human populace. If ever you knock upon the gates of Luudhoq it must be with irresistible force behind you. Power that cannot be withstood. Only then can you break down that last barrier within Harn before you then turn east to face the *marandaal*."

He smiled and returned his attention to the flames, adding, "You know this already, of course. And I may be wrong on some points."

Deep silence followed. Everyone considered what Iyoth had said. Kian glanced across at her father and Anlerran noticed how much pride there was in the *du-luyan* girl's expression. Just for a moment she thought of her own guardians, and felt an immeasurable weight of grief- still there, deep inside her. *There's something that can never heal,* she thought, and looked down, blinking back tears.

"He's right, Ruhal," Lura said eventually. "Mend this proud land, and perhaps it can face down any foe- even the *marandaal*."

Ruhal laughed, shaking his head. "So easy to say, Lura! Have you counted our enemies recently?"

"All great deeds start with a thought," Jahar spoke up, "and you're far from alone. Somehow you have bound all of us together for a common cause. There is little that lies beyond you, with our help."

"I must admit," Iyoth added, "that Kian and I had little beyond survival on our minds- and perhaps finding our people who fled the settlement of Cai in Aphenhast- when we came to Harn. Only a short while ago, never would I have considered joining this venture into the Rhunin."

"What changed your mind?" Jahar asked him.

"She did," Iyoth said simply, looking to Anlerran, who smiled uncertainly and looked down at the ground.

Conversation turned to the minions of the *choragh*, which as Ruhal pointed out might become a greater threat as they headed further north.

"I first saw the *kin* when I lived in Mirkwall," Kian spoke up. "At first, when Shimlock was still alive they were uncertain, afraid even... but as he weakened somehow they gained in strength." She shuddered. "I remember when he died- I remember seeing them there for a moment, gathering in the gloom. Then I fled."

Iyoth shook his head and scowled. "Aphenhast was a condemned place with or without the coming of the *marandaal* and the rise of the *choragh*. The bitter war between the Rising and the city of Nisstar would quickly have spread. The fields and the cities would have run with blood regardless."

"The *kin* travel through the forests without fear," Kian said, glancing at her father. "Perhaps in ever greater numbers with each passing day. We encountered two of them even in Fhaarluy."

Jahar scowled, shaking his head. "One crossed our path- well, not *kin* as you would know them- *diafagh*. But I suspect we'll find more as we press on into the mountains."

"They're drawn to me," Kian said quietly, then glanced almost apologetically in Anlerran's direction. "To her also."

Jahar stared at the *du-luyan* girl. "You destroyed the *kin*-beasts you found in Fhaarluy?"

"She destroyed them, and in so doing she saved my life," Iyoth spoke up before Kian could respond. Then he blinked as if surprised at himself for admitting such a thing.

"I don't know about Kian," Anlerran put in, "but I am barely in control of myself when I encounter such creatures- if the *diafagh* that stumbled across us is anything to go by. I honestly cannot say if I'll be of use or not."

Kian nodded. "It's much the same for me."

Jahar smiled sardonically. "I have two students then. Not that I have your talent, but I know a little about controlling other talents. It's about time I work out whether or not I can put such knowledge to use and help the two of you. Better that I at least try, for all our sakes."

The following morning they packed and rode on as tendrils of morning mist were slowly burned away by the sunlight. By midday they had reached the foothills of the Rhunin; ahead of them, the mountains rose to a snow-capped blue haze, sharp, impossibly high, impossibly vast.

II

For three more days they continued steadily northwards. Snow fell, but not enough to build up on the ground. The wind remained bitterly cold, more so as they pressed on towards the Rhunin proper and the great mountains loomed closer. Whenever they stopped to rest, Jahar took Anlerran and Kian to one side and spent time with them, talking about ways of controlling their powers and concentrating their minds to ensure that they could avoid being overwhelmed by them. Mostly these sessions, which also touched on meditation and visualisation, frustrated more than they taught, all three of them finishing without having felt as if they had gained any insight into themselves. *It's so difficult to even imagine, when I can't even invoke these powers,* she thought more than once, and she even said as much to Kian as soon as Jahar was out of earshot. The *duluyan* girl nodded soberly. "I would say it's difficult for him too," she remarked. "He's a sorceror of some power himself but he isn't like us. I think he tries to imagine what it's like when we come up against the Old Dark- but it's something I can't even describe."

Despite their slow progress however, Jahar's teachings on meditation and concentration eventually gave the two women a certain confidence and calmness that they had not had before, and they agreed that they at least no longer felt utterly helpless.

On the afternoon of the third day, with low grey cloud pressing in- surely it would snow soon, Anlerran thought to herself as she shivered in her cloak- Ruhal pointed into the distance where several hundred low huts and other buildings could be seen huddling in a wide flat area within a shallow valley. "There lies Kaalin," he said. "The most northerly human settlement before the Rhunin. We'll buy or barter supplies there if we can. Thick fur robes will be the first amongst them."

Anlerran stared away into the distance, firstly at the settlement and then into the west where the last of the sunlight was fast disappearing, making orange streaks amidst the snow-clouds that scurried on the cold winds. "It must be a hard place in which to live," she commented.

"Perhaps a little less so if it's the only place you've known," Jahar spoke up. He turned to Ruhal. "As you said, thick winter cloaks and hats for everyone. Food to last us tennights. We also need good care for our horses- if we emerge from out of the Rhunin to tell the tale, we shall need them in good condition. They won't be able to ride much further; they will need to be left and taken care of somewhere. If this is the frontier then they should be left here."

Everyone fell silent in the wake of those words; none of them had thought about what might happen if and when they did return, and whether or not it would be with new allies. After a moment Ruhal glanced down at Culos, who solemnly returned his stare. "With any luck, your hound will lead us part of the remaining distance when we leave this place, Anlerran."

"Any coins we have left are of little use here," Jahar pointed out. "I only hope we can pay for whatever supplies we need in some other way."

"If they can even spare anything at all," Iyoth added darkly.

Lura spoke up. "I think we've already been seen. Some of the villagers are heading this way. I can't see how many exactly..."

"I can," Kian said suddenly, then looked abashed as all eyes turned to her. "There are twelve," she said, then narrowed her eyes, staring into the distance. Anlerran wondered how she could see so well from this far away. "They carry bows and longknives."

The companions waited as the group continued to approach, all dressed in thick robes and furs. They stopped about a dozen paces from the companions- nine men and three women- and one of the younger men stepped forward. He nodded brusquely, dark eyes looking at each of them suspiciously, although Anlerran noticed that he did not look any more suspicious when his gaze took in the Watchers. *Perhaps in this remote place they have no idea what they look like,* she thought. *After all, I had no idea what to expect and I was shut away from the wider world most of the time.*

"I am Larn Mharock, chief huntsman of Kaalin," he said finally. "What brings you into our territories?"

"We are headed into the Rhunin," Ruhal spoke up, "but we request your hospitality before we venture further.

We can perhaps return the favour if you find a use for us, or..."

"You're intent on heading into the Rhunin, with winter arriving fast and hard?" Larn stared at him. "Why would you do such a thing?"

"It was not a matter of choice," Ruhal replied. "Time is short. I can explain further if we may rest in Kaalin awhile- we'll ask no more than a day or two. We bring no harm. We'll pay by any means we can that will be of use to you, whatever skills we have that you require."

We may bring all sorts of harm, Anlerran thought, looking down and watching snowflakes begin to spiral gently to the ground. *This Inerdyr sounds as if he would send his men this far at least.*

One of the women, a striking lady with long black hair spoke up. "You may indeed be of use. A meeting is about to take place..."

"Hailissa, outsiders are not welcome at such meetings," Larn said, turning to her, but Hailissa stared calmly back at him. "Why not? These folk are clearly able to take care of themselves. Let them attend and listen. If they can help, then there's the payment for our hospitality and whatever else they might need."

"Attend the meeting of our people," Hailissa continued, addressing Ruhal. "Listen to what is said there. Then say truthfully if you can help us. If you cannot, then you may continue on your way into the Rhunin."

Ruhal frowned. "Without the opportunity to pay for provisions and equipment?"

"If you cannot help us, we have no incentive to help you," Hailissa reasoned.

Ruhal nodded reluctantly. "As you wish."

They headed down towards Kaalin in silence. With the sun having disappeared a while ago, gloom gathered swiftly and the darkness was almost total by the time they reached the settlement.

The companions were led along the single broad street that snaked along the valley floor near a partly-frozen river to a large, long barn-like house, fashioned from hard and flinty black stone. The snow now swirled thickly about them. "This is the meeting house of the People's Council," Hailissa said briefly by way of explanation. After their horses were led to the stables they made their way into the light and warmth of the meeting house. An interested murmur rose amongst those who had gathered; Anlerran saw suspicious looks aplenty from the corner of her eye, even after Larn and Hailissa had gone some way towards explaining their presence in the hall.

The place was perhaps half-full when the companions arrived, and packed by the time an elderly man rose from his place at a table to declare the meeting in session. Anlerran was glad that attention had turned from her companions, for the moment at least.

"We gather to hear reports of unusual activity and sightings to the north and east, in the Khyrin Valley," the speaker told them all. "Larn, perhaps you can begin?"

Larn stepped forward so that he stood encircled by most of the townspeople gathered in the hall. Lamplight danced upon the walls and the meeting house fell silent as Larn considered his words. "Fellan carries tales back from the mountains that we should well listen to," he said.

"And where is Fellan?" a man from the assembly called out.

"He is being well tended to by the healers. He returned from the hunt yesterday, after dark. He is still not well enough to attend. Unfortunately, Fellan could say little about what had happened."

"And what are these tales, Larn?" The speaker's mild and reasoned tones fell softly in the hall.

"Fellan and Artur- who as we know, is still missing- lost each other in the gathering blizzard at the same time as something attacked them, up at the height of the Khyrin

Valley, beyond the reach of the furthest trees. Almost at the base of Rhunin Toran itself." Larn took a deep breath. "Fellan told me it was one of the Earth Lords."

Immediately the hall descended into a quiet chaos of uncertain laughter from those who seemed to know what the word meant, and bewilderment from those who did not. Anlerran glanced across at Ruhal, who stared stonily around the hall.

Looking at the mingled confusion and unease that accompanied Larn's words, Anlerran felt an almost desperate pity well up within her. *He spoke of beings so ancient that barely the names themselves remain. But still a name is power, even if the meaning has been twisted and become blurred down the centuries.* She glanced around the hall and watched fear and confusion flit from face to face by the lamplight. The shadows of the folk gathered about the place danced upon the walls, writhing as if in response.

"We will hear from Fellan when he is well enough to speak before the Council," the speaker intoned loudly, pausing for the gathering to become quieter before continuing, "In the meantime, enough of such myth. Artur is in need of help, and we should go to him. And whilst we are doing that, we need more people to go out and bring kindling, and check the remaining traps that are still set. Who will volunteer for this task?"

Hailissa stepped forward. "You will all have seen the travellers in our midst this night. They come to us requiring our help. In return, they agree to be of whatever use they can- indeed, they have agreed to *pay by whatever means they can.* Look to these people, I tell you. They are headed into the Rhunin, for reasons that perhaps we are better off not knowing about. These are warriors and sorcerors of repute, mark my words and let them not protest otherwise. Look at them- especially at those cold-looking creatures in their grey cloaks. Where might they be from?"

A murmur of unease spread through the hall, but Hailissa continued, "Let's put their origins to one side. I say we use whatever skills, whatever powers, they can bring to bear- and if possible use them to bring Artur back to us."

With that, she stepped back, but not before flashing a triumphant glance at Larn, who nodded approvingly.

Anlerran quickly glanced at the others, fighting an awful feeling that they were damned if they did and damned if they did not.

She glanced around the hall. *One of the ancient terrors of the world*, she mused, *assailing two hunters in the dark and cold. How could Fellan have escaped such a creature?* With a sinking feeling doubts began to creep through her mind. Could the *choragh* even have allies in this room? Might this be a trap?

She glanced down to the great hound by her side; he stared glumly back at her as if he might be thinking the same thing.

Disturbed by this, Anlerran took a deep breath and murmured to Ruhal, "We have no choice. We need the aid of these folk. But surely all in justice they can ask of us is that we try and rescue this lost hunter of theirs or account for his fate."

Ruhal gave a barely perceptible nod. A moment later he spoke up. "We will of course be glad to help you find Artur, in return for whatever provisions and equipment you can spare us."

A murmur went up amongst those gathered in the meeting hall; Anlerran did not know what to make of it. Something here was not right, and yet she could not tell precisely what was wrong.

"We would ask Hailissa or one of the others to show us where the hunter was last seen," Ruhal added. "Do you agree?"

"Hailissa and Larn will go with you." The speaker looked across at him. "Before that, however, we would all wish to know why you are headed north into the depths of the mountains. These are our territories, you must understand. We must know the business of those who pass through them."

"We cannot tell you," Ruhal frowned. His words sounded perhaps harsher than he meant them to; murmurs and whispers passed around the meeting hall once again.

The speaker stared expressionlessly at him for a moment. "As you wish," he said finally. "You'll receive places to sleep for the night, and you'll set off in the morning. We ask only that you do your best for us. In return, what supplies we have to spare, we will provide you with. We cannot promise much; we have little to give."

Something about the hard, knowing look in the man's eyes made Anlerran uneasy. On an impulse she glanced across at Kian, and the *du-luyan* girl met her eyes; a moment later she gave a barely perceptible nod. Anlerran knew immediately what that meant; she could see it plainly in the other woman's eyes.

This place had indeed been infiltrated by agents of the *choragh;* it had the work of the *kin* running through it, even though they had made efforts to hide themselves. *How could I not have seen this for myself?* she thought.

"Ruhal," Anlerran said quietly, hoping that her voice would not start to shake, "may I utter a few words in private?"

He glanced at her and nodded. She reached up and whispered in his ear, "This place is ruled by the Old Dark. There are *kin* here. They hide in plain view. Kian knows it. *I* should have known as soon as we entered this place."

Ruhal said nothing; he retained his look of almost eerie calm. Anlerran saw him look towards Lura and Jahar; she heard what she thought was a faint whisper from Jahar, although his lips did not move. Lura's hands rested on her hips, near the pommels of her sword and longknife; she appeared to have not moved so much as a muscle, but

Anlerran could almost feel the sudden, coiled readiness of the woman.

The Watchers, meanwhile, had no need to be warned; they were never anything less than completely alert.

"Forgive us," Ruhal said after a moment, "but we have less time than we suspected. We cannot aid you, unfortunately, and naturally we would not expect charity of any sort from you. We will leave now, and we beg forgiveness for having wasted your time."

The ripple of disquiet that echoed around the walls now had about it a taint, something malicious. Those amongst these people who weaved the *choragh*'s web knew that their work had been discovered, Anlerran thought. This sound was of them stirring, preparing themselves. Her stomach tightened in fear; she could feel the blood pounding in her ears.

"Ah! So you don't need your supplies as much as you thought," the speaker said, addressing Ruhal. "Why the sudden change of heart?"

"We must leave," Ruhal said stonily. "I cannot tell you more than that."

Anlerran looked one way and then the other; she caught glimpses of people walking amongst and behind the mass of other folk who had gathered. She could barely see their faces, and as the light of the torches around the walls seemed to dim, the shadows in which these figures walked became deeper, so that soon all she could see were flickers of movement, and all she could hear was the faintness of their footsteps.

"We see you." It was Kian who spoke, her clear voice ringing around the hall. "If you seek to stop us, stand aside from those you have corrupted and show yourselves!"

Presently, someone did step forward; she appeared to be a drab woman of early middle age, dressed in a shawl; she could have been one of any of the settlers. But she was not; Anlerran had only to glance at her to know that. This woman had given herself over to the *choragh,* heart and spirit and mind, and she was their vessel and their voice.

Calmly addressing the people of Kaalin, this creature said, "These people you see before you, my friends- look at them. See the ones who stand aside a little way, clad in their grey cloaks. Hailissa touched on an evil truth moments ago. I ask you to look closely at these beings. Do you think they are human men and women? No; you suspected as much already. I will tell you what they are; I'll reveal to you the nature of these creatures. They are servants of the distant Black Citadel; they are the inquisitors, torturers and punishers of that fell place."

The noise in the hall rose almost to a crescendo, yet the *kin*-woman's voice could be heard above it all, a subtle weave of sorcery rendering it clear and strident without her needing to shout. "Now you know the truth, and they cannot deny it. But there is more you need to know. Those of the North you see with them, these mercenaries- they have forsaken their heritage, the ancient allegiance of their people to the Powers. Did you hear how we were told that we had been corrupted- *corrupted!*- by the age-old beliefs we hold. These people come to Kaalin and accuse us of some unspecified evil, and yet they walk with servants of the Black Citadel!"

Shouts of rage rose now, but she quieted them with nothing more than a raised hand and a grim smile. Then another voice spoke up, one whose owner could not be seen. It came from a thickness of shadows in a distant corner that the torchlight had abandoned entirely. It sounded like the voice of a child, yet as it spoke Anlerran knew for a certainty that it was not; not a human child at any rate. It asked a simple, plaintive question, simultaneously ridiculous and horrifying: "Can we burn them?"

The woman in turn addressed the Speaker of the Council; the question had simply been her prompt. "We can all see the truth of the matter here. These strangers are an affront to our beliefs; they are miscreants, traitors, renegades. Is it a crime to put an end to their miserable lives? Let us not burn them, however, but make meat. We have little enough food this harsh winter."

"Are there not dangers to eating such creatures?" the Speaker remarked.

"Dead and cooked, they are meat and nothing more," she said. "The sorcery that runs in their veins will flee as smoke into the night. Our Lords will chase it away from their roasted remains. No, they will be rendered entirely edible. The humans, at least. The servants of the Black Citadel must be crushed into ash."

At the sound of the word *edible*, which she stressed and slowed, all eyes had turned to the companions, hungry and intent, as if they saw through the companions' thick layers of clothing to the skin beneath. Anlerran saw looks of almost painful longing, and a need to consume, to tear the flesh from their bones.

"Are matters so desperate that *choragh*-worshippers feast on any travellers unfortunate enough to pass by?" Ruhal asked the leering congregation. "I thought you sacrificed your own children first in times of hardship, or picked those in your community perceived to be less subservient to your masters. You are all condemned already- your *lords* will bleed you dry over time and crush you when you become useless- but if you wish to continue living your pitiful lives under their yoke, then stand aside and allow us to leave."

Kelandra then spoke up, as icy as the wind outside: "If you do not, we will cut down every one of you. You'll find all your tales about the guardians of the Black Citadel to be true."

"We will turn the *kin* amongst you inside out," Kian whispered, but Anlerran heard her voice shaking.

The Speaker looked them all up and down. Finally he turned to the *kin*-woman and nodded. "Seize them and tie them. Have them slaughtered."

Anlerran and Kian both knew that the *kin* would send the other folk before them, and on they rushed, an eager mass of men and women and even children, armed with knives and cudgels and whatever other crude weapons they could bring to bear.

They rushed to their own deaths.

Ruhal and Lura were quick, but the Watchers were swifter still. Little more than a collective blur of movement and shimmering blades, they spun a dance of destruction amongst the people of Kaalin, engaged in one near-silent execution after another. The villagers stumbled and fell, clutching at the gaping wounds opened in their throats or chests. Those few who got close enough to wound, were dealt with brutally. Ruhal hacked an arm clean off one man, and Lura shattered both knees of another with a swift downward sweep of her sword.

Even before the *kin* moved forward, many of Kaalin's denizens had decided to abandon the fight and flee for their lives. They poured through the great wooden entrance doors, fighting amongst each other in their desperation to flee the bloodbath that their meeting hall had become.

Six figures remained; six *kin*. Anlerran suddenly noticed that Kian was standing next to her. "Send them back into the earth to be crushed," she heard the *du-luyan* girl murmur.

The simmering rage that had been swirling around in her head exploded into white intensity. For a moment, she could see nothing but bright light, and the vague forms of her would-be assailants, dark dents in the brightness of her vision.

The *kin* rushed at them as one, faster than either of them had expected, but Culos was quicker still.

In an instant he had leaped forward and fastened his great jaws around one of the creatures' neck, and a sickening snapping sound ensued as the head was severed from the body. With a vast-sounding growl that sent a chill through everyone still left in the hall, Culos ripped one arm from the body, then the other. The body itself twitched briefly, a dark red blood the colour of rancid wine seeping, then it was still.

Two others of the *kin* fell; Kian clenched her fists so hard that they shook, and the creatures howled in anguish as their limbs came loose from their sockets and their skulls snapped, crushed under an invisible weight.

A fourth, the *kin*-woman who had spoken earlier, tried to reach Kian; Anlerran used every ounce of her strength to keep it at bay. Finally it stepped back, blood-tears dripping from its black pit eyes, and looked to the three others. As if on a collective impulse they stepped back towards the entrance. *We'll come for you again,* one of them silently mouthed, and then they were gone, out into the snow and the darkness.

Perhaps a dozen or so people still remained in the hall; they covered their faces, shivered and sobbed. They expected to be slain, and perhaps they would have been had Ruhal not stepped in front of Kelandra. "Leave them," he said. "They are no threat. They're damned in any case."

"They all would have had a hand in killing us given half a chance," the Watcher said coldly. "Step aside, Ruhal. What are they to you?"

"The wretched," Ruhal said simply. "They are ruled over by a vast and ancient cruelty; their lives are not their own."

"Then it would be a mercy..."

"Since when is mercy a characteristic of Watchers?" Ruhal stared implacably at her. "I suspect you know of it only from observing the human people who *you* once ruled over. I say again; leave them."

Anlerran heard audible sighs of relief as Kelandra stalked away to rejoin the other Watchers. One or two of those who remained dared to scuttle outside and away, presumably to their dwellings. A moment or two later, seeing that their fellows had been allowed to leave unscathed the others did likewise, and in only a short while the meeting hall was occupied only by the companions and those people of Kaalin- and *kin-* who had been slain by them.

When the companions gathered outside the hall the blizzard had stopped and stars mapped out the sky, with Ildar high and bright. The wind had lessened to a faint but chilling breeze.

Ruhal stared around the settlement. Its people had either gathered in their dwellings, fearful of being seen outside, or they had fled the place entirely. "Anlerran; Kian; do you sense any others of the *kin* here?"

Both women shook their heads. Anlerran had no idea where the three surviving *kin* had fled; if they had left footsteps, they were gone now, already hidden by fresh snow. But she was certain of one thing; they had put considerable distance between the companions and themselves, despite their promise to return.

"Every step we take away from this place will be a good one," Jahar said, "but we need to obtain extra clothing and blankets and food before we leave."

Ildoron called to them softly from near where he stood by the stables. "They have slain the horses. Their necks have been slashed and their stomachs opened. Parts of their insides are missing."

Everyone stared at one another, dumbfounded. They walked a little nearer to the building, although Anlerran stopped as soon as she caught the harsh, salt odour of blood on the wind. She had no desire to see whatever the *kin* or their minions had done to the horses.

Lura shook her head. "Sooner or later we would have had to continue on foot- and is this not the final settlement before the Rhunin? We would have had to abandon them. But no creature deserves this."

"I had thought to keep them here, with a little bargaining," Ruhal said, looking away from the scene within the darkness of the stables in disgust. "It was not to be."

"Those who survived will be hiding in their hovels," Kal-Myrran spoke up. "We can still kill them."

"No more butchery," Ruhal glared at her. "Are you ever sated?"

At that moment Culos brushed past Anlerran and trotted twenty yards or so ahead of them, before turning back and fixing her with an impatient stare. Anlerran did not need to read the dog's thoughts to know what was on his mind. "The sooner we find the *illeagh,* the better chance we have of survival," she murmured, as the great hound gave a short, urgent bark. *Time is already running out,* he seemed to be saying, as the sound echoed towards the still-distant mountain slopes.

III

Once they had taken thick winter clothing and provisions from a storehouse used by the huntsmen in the village, the companions trudged onwards through the intensifying winter. Culos stayed more or less the same distance ahead, a lithe black form trotting across the snow and pausing only every now and then to turn and stare back at them. To Anlerran's mind, the hound appeared to grow more impatient than ever and bore a frantic look whenever he turned.

They passed between vast mountains for a further three days, following long ravines that ran like deep scars through the wilderness of the Rhunin. They made progress deep into the range, although they slowed their pace as the going became tougher and they were forced to take rests more frequently. The sky remained bright and clear, a

347

serene, almost crystalline blue which turned deeper as the sun slipped behind the western peaks and the shadows lengthened, moving up towards the last stretches of sunlit, snowy crags that marked the high points of the Rhunin.

Light was failing fast on the fourth day after their departure from Kaalin when they reached a wide windswept plateau where the ruins of an ancient city stood before them. Odd stony structures loomed from the frozen ground and glittered faintly in what little remained of the day. As one the companions walked up as far as where Culos awaited them, and for a long while they stood in mute wonder.

Looking around at her comrades, Anlerran thought, *I feel sure that none of them has even heard of this place. I certainly haven't. And there cannot be much history that Ruhal, Jahar and the Watchers for that matter know nothing of.*

A thought that was best described as *emptiness* came back to her. The notion that this place could exist for so long, unknown, chilled her as much as the night breeze that had already stirred. Judging by the peculiarity of the stone shapes that remained, most of its buildings had been of timber, and these had long since become weed-shrouded mounds of earth forever locked under the frozen ground or blown away in snowstorms or the dry winter wind. Anlerran fancied that strong gales often howled through this flat wasteland high up in the mountains, and if they were to be caught at such a time, surely they would all perish, no matter how well wrapped up they might be.

It seemed that an age had already passed when Ruhal finally spoke. "Jahar," he said softly, "I recall nothing about this place. Do you?"

"No." Jahar glanced at the Watchers; Kelandra shook her head, looking oddly troubled.

"This place feels... more than centuries old," Jahar added after a while. "*Ages* old."

"Is it possible that the *illeagh* built it?" Anlerran ventured, shivering as she drew her cloak more tightly about herself.

Ruhal shrugged. "Perhaps, although I've never heard of them building such settlements. It could even be that another race dwelt here in the distant past. Even before the First Age as we know it."

"Some of these buildings still afford some protection," Alturus noted. "The nights will surely be colder than ever here especially if the wind increases tonight."

The companions fell silent as they reached one of the better-preserved stone buildings, roofless but with its walls mostly intact. By now they were too tired to talk much further even of this vast mystery, and sat in silence within the building. Kelandra used what looked like the last of the firepowder that she had, and they gathered around the flames, eating only as much as they dared allow themselves.

A long time passed before Lura finally asked the question that had been lurking at the edges of Anlerran's mind throughout the evening. "What then, do we do," she spoke up quietly, "if we cannot find the *illeagh*? I know you believe that Culos is leading us to them, Anlerran," she added swiftly, "but what if he cannot find them? What if these beings simply cannot be found by such as us?"

"A valid question, Lura, though a little late in the asking," Jahar commented dryly before Anlerran could answer. "We're here now. What exists for us even if we do go back?" He glanced around at everyone, a humourless smile upon his face. "I expect we are the most wanted felons in all of Harn by now, and I would not put it past our enemies to pursue us *this* far, and even further."

"No one wants to head back," Ruhal added, "but we must prepare ourselves for failure even as we press on. If we cannot find the *illeagh*, or if they don't find us perhaps, then we perish. We knew this."

"I for one can think of better ways to reach my end," Kal-Myrran muttered.

"I would rather Aona herself take me than die in a prison, my mind doubtless already fled or torn apart even before my body gives up the struggle," Lura said, fixing the Watcher with a glare. "Be that one of Inerdyr's infamous stone circle courts, or the Sanctum in Luudhoq- where I believe torture is thought of as a form of artistic endeavour."

"Enough." Ruhal's voice was quiet, but contained enough anger for the bickering to cease immediately. "We'll follow Culos for as long as we remain able; that's why we are here. That's what we agreed, and it remains our agreement."

Anlerran had started to doze off when a short, urgent bark roused her suddenly. Culos stood in the doorway of the ancient building, a black silhouette against the moonlit night sky. As he barked again, everyone who had begun to slumber woke swiftly. Anlerran heard two words in her head, powerful and strong, clear as the night air itself.

Follow. Now.

Why now? she asked blearily. *Why can we not rest? We can't continue...*

A reply came swiftly, with a hint of anger. *Follow!*

"Wake up," she muttered, staggering to her feet. Cramp and fatigue caused her to grimace in pain for a moment. "We need to go. Quickly!"

As they struggled to ready themselves and head off into the darkness, Culos paced back and forth almost as if caged, occasionally howling quietly to himself. *How near are they?* Anlerran asked, but he either could not hear her thoughts or chose not to respond. Once they were ready he trotted onwards, uttering a low bark once again.

The companions stumbled on over the ghostlike tundra, bleary-eyed and shivering. Eventually they reached the far end of the great plateau where a dark ravine loomed between two vast mountains; Anlerran noticed then that the darkness was not absolute. Three small points of light shimmered near the entrance to that ravine. They shifted in luminosity and colour, hovering at the entrance to that pitch-black valley of ice and snow and rock as if they might be waiting for her.

Anlerran stared, transfixed, only dimly aware that her companions had stopped further back. She could not help but continue onwards towards the lights, with Culos a silent presence at her side.

The night breeze played with her hair as she walked ever nearer, her eyes fixed upon the swaying lights. She did not look back to see if the others had started to follow her again. Culos remained evidently unconcerned by her side, lending her some confidence and comfort. Whatever these were, they were not *choragh* or their allies. *But I know that,* she thought. *I have seen lights like this before. We both have, near Steepleford.*

Then the three points moved closer together until they merged. Anlerran watched in astonishment as they gradually took on an almost human-like form. Together, Anlerran and Culos walked on until they were no more than a dozen yards or so from the shimmering apparition.

Delicate and with a certain fragile beauty, it stared into her, the eyes a deep, sapphire blue, the lips thin and tight like a scar across the too-perfect features of the face.

At last she appears. The voice was rich and mellow, neither feminine nor masculine. *Here to divide us as foretold.*

Anlerran's physical exhaustion suddenly manifested itself; she sagged to her knees, barely hearing the anger in the voice. "My companions... and I need shelter. We cannot survive for much longer." Every word she uttered took vast effort. She felt utterly exhausted. After a little while she tried to lift up her head and rise from her kneeling position on the hard ground, but she could not. She might as well have been frozen to the spot, and for a moment she thought that she had indeed become frozen, rendered as hard and cold as the ice and rocks that festooned this savage landscape.

Slowly she felt herself being lifted up. It was then, as she was borne away by something unseen, that she lost consciousness.

Anlerran woke suddenly and found herself surrounded by water. Instinctively she lashed out until pain and fatigue made her cease her movements, and the moment she did so the ache throughout her body subsided, then faded away entirely.

No, she realised. *This is not water.*

She could not tell what the liquid might be or where she had been placed, except that she was in some kind of pool surrounded by almost complete darkness. She could see faint light somewhere ahead but every time she tried to focus on it the illumination faded away. The substance in which she was immersed up to her shoulders was a little thicker than water, and it had no scent whatsoever. She could not tell if it had any colour; the depth of gloom made it impossible to know.

As her eyes eventually adjusted to the darkness, Anlerran realised that the stone pool lay in a hall from which archways led out at various points. Other shapes that looked a little like perhaps statues or sculptures loomed vaguely from out of distant walls, but she could make out no detail of them. Whatever their nature they remained silent and unmoving.

Anlerran dragged herself out of the pool with an effort and wearily got to her feet, suddenly aware that she was completely naked. *Powers, did my companions remove my clothing!?* she wondered, aghast. *Or did the* illeagh *do it? What was that creature I saw at the entrance to the ravine? One of the* illeagh*? Where are the others? Where is this place?*

Her legs wobbled at first as she stepped cautiously forward. With an effort she staggered towards and then through one of the archways. The air felt oddly warm and still. As she made her way slowly down the passageway beyond the exit the ground underfoot became smoother and the air slightly warmer. A moment later she tripped; she tried to get to her feet but a hand or something that performed the same function reached suddenly out of the dark and hauled her up by the neck. Anlerran cried out but the sound died in her throat, and she could no longer speak as she was now borne along the tunnel at a swift pace by something that made no sound and which she could not see.

She was carried into an arena where a central fire blazed, green-hued flames rising almost as high as the vast, oddly-patterned ceiling.

Realising that she had been released, Anlerran turned to look at whatever it was that had hauled her into this place and left her so perilously close to the fire. But she could see no indication that anyone or anything had ever walked this place. No footprints marked the dust.

From the upper reaches of the great arena came the sounds of someone or something stirring, but for a while still she saw nothing moving up there. Finally light gathered and moved towards her. It came to a halt no more than four paces from where Anlerran stood, becoming human-shaped as she stared at it.

With difficulty, Anlerran managed to speak. "Where are..."

They are well, and have received attention.
Anlerran looked for a trace of compassion or curiosity, but knew within herself that to do so was pointless; this creature was a shimmer of light and shadow. Perhaps, like the creature out on the bleak mountain plain it had formed itself into a human-like shape so that she might be better able to speak with it, but it made no other concession. *Should I have expected anything more?* she asked herself.

Yet the words that Anlerran now heard shocked her.

You are able to conceive. The line continues, beyond all expectation and reason. Aona herself has intervened, for a third time. There can be no other explanation.

Anlerran stared at the *illeagh*, speechless.

The being made its way towards an archway on the far side of the hall, and not knowing what else to do, Anlerran followed. Many thoughts flashed through her mind. *What shall I say, if I'm permitted to speak? How can I convince them to help us? How can they help us? And what was that substance they placed me in? Some kind of healing fluid?*

She paused, wondering if her companions were somewhere nearby. "It's the custom of my folk to wear garments when in the company of others," she murmured hesitantly. "May I have my clothes?"

You have no need of clothing here. The temperature is regulated at all times. You will feel neither too cold, nor too hot.

Anlerran opened her mouth to speak, but the *illeagh* interrupted her. *This is the optimum temperature for the existence of your race in its various environments. Your three-quarter race.*

She blinked at that. "I don't know what you mean..." she began, but her companion appeared to have lost interest already and moved through the archway and down the softly-lit corridor beyond. Anlerran followed, padding almost silently after her consort and trying to cover herself as best she could.

As she followed her guide many thoughts rushed through her mind, circling endlessly. *Surely it was the* illeagh *who had called me and my companions to them. They wanted something from us. But at the entrance to the ravine, I was told that I'd come to divide them.*

What could the illeagh *want from us? What price will they demand?*

She was led down a number of passageways before eventually the way ahead opened out into a vast hall where tiers of stone seats rose in semicircles into silent darkness. Seated apparently at random around on these seats were- she could only assume- other *illeagh*, all bearing at least some resemblance to her guide, though in some ways they were even odder. Most bore shapes that were vaguely humanoid, but these shapes were fashioned from light or shadow or even a physical material that might have been stone. Some appeared to be constantly in flux. Anlerran counted herself lucky that these particular oddities sat just out of full range of the low, green-hued lighting.

So transfixed was she that her guide touched her on the arm- an almost fluid sensation that ran up to her shoulder- and when Anlerran flinched, it pointed to one of the larger *illeagh*.

Address the Lord of the Speaking Hall, it intoned. *The name to use is Kughyr in your language.*

There were many things she wanted to ask, but at first she could not. She glanced around, hoping suddenly and unreasonably to see Culos, but she saw no sign of the great hound.

"Did... did you send the dog to me? To help my companions?" She paused, uncomfortable in the deep silence that followed. It almost felt as if she was speaking to nothing but the dust and the gloom, despite the unearthly beings gathered around her on all sides. A ripple of something- perhaps a response to the words she had uttered- rose for a moment. And something more- almost as if some of the *illeagh* knew what she was talking about and others amongst them still had no idea.

"He has been our saviour," she added, silently hoping that the *illeagh* hound might eventually accompany her out of the Rhunin, if she ever left. *But I cannot ask for that yet,* she reminded herself. *Give as required, and ask for nothing until they're satisfied.*

The Lord of the Speaking Hall had nothing to say to her about Culos. *You stand before us, a creature that all logic states should not exist. But then, your father should never have existed. Still, despite what we thought, Aona made his existence possible; then she intervened again, making you possible.*

Another voice spoke up, fainter and further back in the shadows: *Dilution will end us all.* The voice was mellow, deep and yet somehow as cold as ice. Anlerran shuddered visibly at its sound. *I must know whether my blood parents are still alive,* she thought suddenly. *I must!*

If dilution is the will of Aona, then it will happen, the guide who had led her here said. Although it was impossible to tell, Anlerran felt sure that animosity loomed between the two.

Kughyr stood then, and Anlerran gaped at the vast, luminous form of the *illeagh* lord, a mass of tangled light and stone whose smooth countenance looked ageless, expressionless. She saw what she supposed could be eyes, where the lights dimmed in two places to create pools of shadow. Had it not been for those features, she would have found it impossible to concentrate on any one part of this alien splendour.

At first Anlerran could not help but quail before the impassive, cold stare of this being. She had not known what to expect when she set foot in their lands, but she had the impression that they had all agreed to take on these human-yet-not-human forms, some making more effort than others judging by the shapes that loomed and fluttered in the darker echelons of the arena. Either these transformations were for her benefit or they made a deliberate mockery of the human condition itself. The thought made her shudder, and it was swiftly followed by a fearful notion: *Are they able to read my thoughts?*

It was possible, she supposed, but for the moment there loomed before the more pressing issue of standing naked before this creature that cared nothing for her or her race- her three-quarter race as it had already been called.

With an effort she raised her head as Kughyr's words echoed around the chamber and inside her head at the same time. *So, you come to us, the child of a child of a strange union, one that was thought impossible. What is it that you seek?*

Anlerran blinked at that. Could he truly not know why she was here? Might this be some further trickery?

"Harn, and inevitably all of Aona is under threat from both the *marandaal* and the *choragh* as they vie for control of the lands," she said eventually, choosing her words carefully. "Surely you must know already that the *choragh* power is strengthening again?"

Not one of the *illeagh* responded or made any sound.

"They mean to crush all races under their darkness as they did once before. And if *they* cannot withstand the *marandaal* then we face annihilation regardless. We seek your help, your intervention."

Anlerran felt the urge to say more, but stilled her voice. *Perhaps you've already said too much,* she thought fearfully. Her heart hammered like a caged bird in the silence that followed as the *illeagh* lord's makeshift eyes stared firstly at her, and then turned to the *illeagh* nearest to it.

Once, the *illeagh* intoned finally, *we were as one with the beings you now know as the* choragh. *In a sense, they are our brethren, carved of the same elements that pre-existed all the Younger Races. Thus you ask us to turn against our brethren- what you might call our flesh and blood, though such things have little meaning to our kind.*

Against her better judgement, Anlerran spoke up again. She suddenly recalled Ruhal's words from what could have been an Age ago, when he had first attempted to explain her heritage and the history of the elder Races. "It was because of the treatment- the *use*- of the younger Races by some of your kind that you retreated from the places where the younger Races existed. Unlike those who were to become the *choragh*, you bore no ill will against humankind or against any others of the younger Races."

And we bear you no ill will now, countered the *illeagh, but that does not mean we walk to war with you. We are not Gods. There are no Gods as far as any of us are aware.* It smiled, as if either some great secret of the Existence had been uncovered with those words or the statement had been engineered to deliberately mislead her. The expression bore no resemblance to any smile she had seen before; it looked like a wound opening.

Anlerran could think of nothing more to say. She stared at the floor, mute and helpless. But Kughyr was not done; the *illeagh* leaned forward intently and spoke again.

You talk of the younger Races, yet some of the creatures you brought with you to this place are not of any Race that we understand. The creatures that call themselves Watchers, from the city of Luudhoq- they are the products of some sorcery we cannot comprehend.

Sorcery they cannot comprehend, Anlerran silently echoed. *Of course. They have spent more than an entire Age shunning the world and its machinations. Despite their power there must be much they struggle to understand. I myself stand here as evidence of a world that has moved on, as would the Watchers if they stood at my side.*

Kughyr remarked suddenly, *It seems that a small group of us took it upon themselves to entice you here, for the same reason that you seek our help. The matter will be discussed. I for one do not believe the* marandaal *will come here. I believe the* choragh *will vanquish them. They pour back into Aona from the far places where they slept; their power grows. They are now the guardians of the wider world.*

Anlerran stared fearfully. What did this mean? Argument or even open war between the *illeagh? Powers that be,* she thought miserably. *It's happening again. Just as*

Ruhal and his friends defied Inerdyr, just as Kelandra and the other Watchers defied their Seven, now it seems that some illeagh *may need to defy their own people? Is that what will happen? Are we destined to be traitors, all of us, an uneasy gathering with enemies wherever we look, and yet the only united force to stand against those who would take us back into the darkness?*

"Do you care nothing for Aona?" she asked eventually.

Aona's destiny is her own, came the inevitable reply.

Anlerran shivered; a bleak despair began to chill her soul. She had set so much store on this meeting, had invested so much hope. *For what?* she asked herself bitterly. *To find yet another race blind to the threat that seems likely to engulf the world as it has before? And surely that is the greatest enemy of all- the blind foolishness of those who could unite to drive back the* marandaal. *How can it be that the lessons of past centuries and past millennia are always forgotten before they're needed once again?*

"I am no prophet," she said eventually, "but I don't need to have the gift of foresight to know what will happen, if events continue as they have." She lifted her face and looked with an effort of will at the face of the Speaker of the Hall. That inexplicable visage moved and shimmered before her as if its near-human appearance had either become harder to maintain or the creature cared less about maintaining it.

"The *marandaal* will triumph and make a wasteland of Harn as they have made of Aphenhast," Anlerran continued, the bitterness in her soul pouring forth with her words as they echoed harshly around the great stone theatre. "They will spread throughout Aona. The entire world- this refuge of yours included- will wither and die along with everywhere else. If any are left alive, they will count the dead fortunate."

Anlerran paused, and gazed around at the implacable *illeagh* gathered before her in their timeless hall. "Once the *choragh* drove the *marandaal* from these lands. Now they send hundreds of *diafagh* and *kin* against our people. They would enslave us. A world claimed by the *marandaal* would be truly dead, but a world where the *choragh* have triumphed would be one of eternal darkness of a different kind. We would be the living dead."

An indeterminate shifting commenced in the upper echelons of the hall. Perhaps the mention of *diafagh* or *kin* had caused it. But at the same moment, something else in the theatre- a primal energy coursing through the stone and structure of this place- had gradually become more obvious to her, as if the entire hall was a vast body whose nerves and vessels she could gradually see coming into view from beneath the hard and ancient skin. She could even feel something akin to it rushing through her own body, perhaps even in tune with it.

Anlerran remained silent and still for a moment longer, picking up the staccato beat of the heart- the heart of this underworld- immediately. Suddenly she became certain that the entire fortress was alive in some barely comprehensible way. *To a small part of me, this is home,* she thought. *It knows me. Might I have been born here?*

Anlerran looked to the *illeagh* lord, hoping for a sign that her words had made some impression but seeing nothing that gave her hope. She ploughed on regardless: "As for the *marandaal?* We know only that they would come against the *choragh* sooner or later, to turn the world to ruins. Aona *cannot* save herself. Her destiny is *not* her own."

The rustling and the subtle shape-shifting became more animated. In the upper tiers, Anlerran espied beings that no longer had any appearance she could describe. Colour, light and form chased and fought, casting shadow and illumination in turn upon the higher, more distant parts of the great hall. "We *need* you," she whispered.

Anlerran had nothing more to say. She bowed her head and closed her eyes, dreading their response. But the *illeagh* fell silent as one, and when a while later she dared to look up, she stood alone in the great hall; her desperate plea to her audience might only have been a dream.

XVII – Vessels of Light and Dark

After a tennight spent running across the plains, through the deep valleys between the great Crescent mountains, across the pastures and woods of the middle lands and finally through the eternal misty twilight of the Mirk, Rocan reached Mirkwall itself.

He stood and contemplated the great castle, his blood almost singing as it pulsed through his body. *I belong here,* he thought. *This is a sanctuary where the power of my Lords holds sway.*

During his long journey Rocan had slowly changed. As he bowed to the inevitable, he became less man and more *kin.* He grew stronger, faster and more resilient; his wits sharpened. He could see further and in great detail. The bitterness of the season did not affect him. One night as he camped out on the snow he glanced up at Archaon's ruined face and recalled words spoken by his father: *Rising in the sky, each mountain and valley of the great red desert moon.* Arrko had claimed to know the geography of that unreachable world; now his son nodded to himself, realising that in all likelihood he had spoken the truth. Certainly he could feel the secrets of the Existence being slowly revealed to him with each passing day.

His eyes, darker now, took in every detail of the place. Here he would find the *kin*-man called Ilumor, whose name had come to him days ago. Here he would also find purpose. The *kin* gathered in this place would eventually expel the *marandaal* from Aona and send them into the void between all worlds.

A short while later he stood in one of the entrance halls. The doors had opened for him; he had known they would.

I belong here, he reminded himself.

His entrance had not gone unnoticed. *Kin* of numerous shapes and sizes appeared furtively at archways; none of them approached him. They would not dare, he told himself. He was higher *kin* as his father had been. He stared at any that lingered for more than a moment, and they melted away in haste, scuttling or slithering.

Rocan made his way up several flights of stone steps and then along several corridors until finally he came out onto a balcony and stood for a while watching the mist and glimpses of the marshland far below.

"Who sent you?" someone said from behind him. Even before Rocan turned, he knew that this was Ilumor.

When he first looked the leader of Mirkwall's *kin* in the eyes, Rocan felt a sudden stab of unease, as if something was *wrong* with the man- something that he could not define or understand. But the moment passed swiftly, and he thought no more about it.

Ilumor looked more youthful than Rocan had expected but otherwise unremarkable. That he was powerful *kin* was evident in the fluid ease with which he carried himself, and the darkness of his eyes was accentuated further by the paleness of his skin. But in other ways, he could at a casual glance have passed for a normal man.

"My father sent me to you," he said.

Ilumor frowned. "Your father?"

Rocan nodded, and told him briefly of the battle at Ruan-Tor and its aftermath. Ilumor listened in silence, and then wandered across to look down into the mist. Rocan followed his gaze but could see nothing of note. Finally the leader of the *kin* turned to look at him. "No death is in vain, in the struggle against the starspawn." He paused and then added, "Do you mourn him?"

Rocan shrugged. "I hardly knew him. He came to Ruan-Tor with the intent of giving it over to our Lords. He did that. I should have thanked him instead of resisting- I was a man of no consequence before he arrived. Now I have purpose. My eyes are opening to view the secrets of the world for the first time."

"Yes. The secrets of the world." Ilumor looked at him strangely. "What of Ruan-Tor? Do you mourn the place itself?"

Why is he asking me such things? Rocan wondered. Aloud he replied, "Had I remained a man without the gifts and the knowledge of the *kin,* then perhaps I would." For a moment, bright and violent images came to him of the slayings and sacrifices after Arrko's followers had arrived in the town, but they no longer shocked him. Even his recollection of the screams of pleading mothers and the sounds of children's bones being crushed failed to move him. He could almost smell the piles of flesh roasting, the flames of the vast pyres roaring as they devoured the fat from the bones of the dead.

It meant nothing. "Settlements can be rebuilt if needed," he reasoned, "and the people will always breed. When the war is done with and the starspawn shut out of the world, sooner or later they will return to what they know best; fornication, and the spitting out of mewling infants into the world."

Ilumor smiled at that. "Yes. It's a matter of perspective."

Rocan stared into the mist for a short while, restless. "What am I to do here? My father said I would be safe here, but I didn't come to Mirkwall in order to be safe. I realised as much during my journey. The *marandaal* will enter the Mirk sooner or later..."

"They will," Ilumor agreed. "They are close to the edges of our territory. You ask what you are to do, but you needn't worry. The *kin* gathered here need only a little instruction; instinct will guide them the rest of the way. And I think you can trust your own instincts absolutely. You will know what to do when the time comes."

Rocan nodded. They stared at each other in silence for a moment. Distant shrieks and something that might have been laughter floated across to them in the mist from some far-flung corner of the great castle. The *kin* had settled into every part of Mirkwall now, ready and waiting to defend the fortress that had taken them so many centuries to capture.

"I have something for you," Ilumor said eventually. "In honesty, Rocan, I would have given it to another of the higher *kin* if I had to- for I don't need it any more- but I think you will make a worthy bearer."

He slowly took out the sword from the scabbard at his side, and Rocan watched as a sliver of pure blackness came into view like a tear appearing in the daylight. Ilumor held it out to him with the blade flat across his hands. Rocan stared at the weapon in mute shock; he had not seen it before, but somehow he *knew* it.

"Take this," Ilumor said.

As soon as held the pommel of the sword, Rocan gasped; its history was revealed to him in one blinding moment. In that instant, he knew who had carried it and when, from the day that a mad-eyed, emaciated youth had pleaded entrance to Ruan-Tor, through the passing of the blade to Vornen Starbrook of all people in Ethanalin Tur-morn, and later, its theft by Suli Garranson of all people. She had given it to one of the *choragh*, but in turn the Earth Lord had commanded her to take it to Ilumor.

But the sword did not only feed him with its own history; it revealed much more. It had forced Suli to take it. Already mad and half-dead, she had passed it on to one of their Lords, and she herself had been somehow remade. And when she arrived at Rockmire where Ilumor and some of the *kin* camped amongst the ill-fated Rising...

As if he had been there with them night after night, Rocan saw in his mind's eye images of Ilumor laying with her, abusing her flesh in every conceivable way, refusing to let her completely die. The pictures of them naked and red-hued under Archaon's light burned savagely into his memory- Ilumor smiling and engorged in his lust, Suli a picture of blank misery.

A rage began to smoulder inside him. He trembled, feeling the dark song of his Lords echoing through his being. The urge to give that power the freedom it craved became unbearable. The desire to reach out and burn Ilumor from the inside out almost overwhelmed him. But then a cold, harsh voice- the voice of the sword, he thought- spoke two simple words.

Not now.

Slowly the fury ebbed away to a small, residual core. He accepted the scabbard that Ilumor passed to him and a moment later the sword was hidden from view, but its words echoed in his mind. They somehow conveyed a promise. *Not now*, he told himself, *but later.*

Ilumor said nothing more. He nodded, turned and walked away. Rocan watched him, and gradually he became certain that the sword knew something about Ilumor; something that perhaps not even their Lords knew.

The leader of the kin *is not what he appears to be,* Rocan thought as his hand caressed the cold hilt of his new companion. *He hides something. Something important.*

He knew he ought to care nothing for Suli and her fate, but somehow he could not dismiss the images of her slow demise, now he knew what Ilumor had done to her.

It shouldn't matter, he told himself, pressing his head against the cool stonework as if the act might somehow dampen his simmering rage. *I am* kin *now. Past alliances and past needs are nothing to me.*

But he could not let go of the images in his head, nor could he erase the memories that were not his.

Rocan wandered the corridors of Mirkwall as darkness fell outside. He barely noticed the *kin* that shrank back at his approach or, seeing him come towards them from a distance, found themselves another route that avoided the concentration of malevolence heading their way.

The idea that Ilumor kept some important secret would not let go of him. *I will find whatever it is he hides,* Rocan silently swore, *and I'll reveal him before our Lords. I will do our cause a great service and have my revenge in the same instant.*

He smiled, and continued his wanderings through the unlit castle, imagining himself as the lord of Mirkwall less than a day after seeing it for the first time.

Ilumor had stepped out into the night. He also walked restlessly, along the many twisting paths that ran back and forth through the marshland. Giving up the sword had been a relief; he could not fathom the reason for the disquiet he had felt in recent days, whenever he happened to touch it or even look at it, but in any case it made sense to him that it should be given over to one of the higher *kin.* If he was to defend Mirkwall against the starspawn, then he could do so without that device. It would react in whatever way was best, whenever the *marandaal* came for them, and surely any of the higher *kin* could wield it. Of course, it might no longer appear to be a sword by that point, but the form it decided to take was unimportant. The device would do what it had always done and take whatever shape it desired.

Why has Arrko's son come here?

Ilumor felt ill at ease. It made sense that Rocan had been sent here by Arrko in his dying moments after the battle in the far north. It made sense that he was *kin,* that Arrko had made him so. It even made sense for him to be given the sword.

Then why do I feel that something else is happening here? Something I don't know about?

A faint movement of light under the water caught his attention for a moment, and he stopped, the memory of his dream coming swiftly back. Ilumor sank down in the mud, and bowed his head; something tipped him forward, and a voice whispered in his ear: *This is where you belong. You are mine.*

Ilumor could barely breathe as he was pressed against the cold dampness of the muddy path. *When Rocan's usefulness is at an end,* the voice whispered to him, *then kill him.*

As he made his way back into the castle later without a single look back, Ilumor gave himself reasons for the unexplainable things that had happened to him recently. *My Lords have found new ways of speaking to me,* he thought. *They masquerade as things they are not, in order to test my loyalty.*

He knew however that these ideas were lies. His Lords knew nothing of the things that he had remembered over the last tennight: the light under the water, the entity that had somehow poured something of itself into him, the invisible creature or creatures that almost crushed his body and whispered to him in the night, reminding him to remain obedient. The *choragh,* all-knowing and all-sensing, had no inkling of any of these things.

That was impossible of course, but somehow it could not stop it also being true.

In the small silent hours before dawn Ilumor lay awake, pale and naked in his lightless bedchamber, grim notions his only companions. For the first time he could recall, he craved nothing but death. *The light will give me peace,* he found himself thinking over and over, but he could not quite believe it. Beneath the hope he felt the dread certainty that he would be made to live another life, and another, and so on until the end of time and the Existence itself, whichever masters he served.

If you enjoyed *The Endless Shore*, the next book in the Aona series, *The Spiral Heart*, is available on Amazon.

Please also take a few moments of your time to review this book on Amazon and Goodreads and any other book review websites- even if it's just a few lines!

For a FREE fantasy novel, exclusive stories, articles and other goodies, subscribe to the author's newsletter: https://www.simonwilliamsauthor.com/freebies.php